THE REPO

THE REPO

A JACK MERCHANT AND
SARAH BALLARD NOVEL

BILL EIDSON

KATE'S MYSTERY BOOKS
JUSTIN, CHARLES & CO. PUBLISHERS
BOSTON

First edition 2003

This is work of fiction. All characters and events portrayed
in this work are either fictitious or are used fictitiously.

Library of Congress Cataloging-in-Publication Data is available.

Published in the United States by Kate's Mystery Books,
an imprint of Justin, Charles & Co., Publishers,
20 Park Plaza, Boston, Massachusetts 02116
www.justincharles.com

Distributed by National Book Network, Lanham, Maryland
www.nbnbooks.com

10 9 8 7 6 5 4 3 2 1

Printed in the United States of America

In memory of Mary and Bill Eidson

I would like to thank Richard Parks, Frank Robinson, Kate Mattes, Stephen Hull, Carmen Mitchell, Catherine Sinkys, Krisztina Holly, Jim McNeil, Amy Jacky, Nancy Childs, Sibylle Barrasso, and Richard Rabinowitz for their help with my career and this book.

Special thanks to Brad Ferguson for sharing stories and details of the marine repossession business.

And, as always, thanks to Donna and Nick.

THE REPO

PROLOGUE

HE HAD BEEN SAILING in New England waters all his life. But he had spent relatively little time off the coast of Connecticut, and had never sailed into Prescient Cove before.

To add to it, the wind was howling, and he was being pelted with sporadic raindrops that promised a great deal more any minute. The barometer had been dropping steadily all night. Storm warnings over the radio.

It was just past 3:00 A.M.

Under sail, the boat sluiced along at better than seven knots.

The chart said the water was good all the way in. Better still, the GPS was glowing on a bracket attached to the binnacle. The GPS was programmed for this cove right down to each channel marker.

The monitor blinked and a small tone sounded. He was reaching a way point, and there should have been a can to his port side. He picked up the flashlight and played the beam across the port bow. Sure enough, the light picked up a reflective band across the top of a buoy not fifty yards away.

"Jesus," he said, under his breath. He wished there were other devices along the way to help get them out of this mess.

He started the engine and swung the bow into the wind. For the next few minutes, he worked at securing the sails. But he was a good sailor, and his boat was set up well for single-handing, with lazy jacks for the main and a good roller furling system for the genoa. He went back to the helm and began motoring along the new course. He looked for visuals. It was so damn dark that he could pick out only the expected lights as outlined in the harbor guide. He flicked on his flashlight and reread the approach instructions:

> When making a landfall at nighttime, look for the lit steeple of the First Methodist Church to line up with and then eclipse the clock tower of a factory approximately one mile back. Once the tower is eclipsed, proceed directly toward the steeple. Take care to maintain course within the channel as Langley Point to your port is shallow at low tide to as little as three feet, with a rocky bottom. Once past the point, and inside Prescient Cove, the Chalmer's Marina should be visible directly off your port beam.

Both the GPS and the visual cues agreed — something for which he was blessedly thankful. The entire thing could fall apart right here if he ran the boat aground. And there was too much at stake for that: a thought that had been in his head for the past two days now. Too much at stake.

To his port, he passed a mass of darkness that blotted out the lights of the town entirely. He supposed that was Langley Point, hoped it was. And then, minutes later, he was past.

The glow of a single fluorescent light over the gas dock at Chalmer's Marina was like a welcome beacon. He put the wheel over slowly and brought the boat around to an open space on the gas dock. He backed her down, crabbing the hull up to the dock gently.

Immediately out of the shadows, a shape appeared.

He started. Even though this was what he had been expecting.

It was her.

She held on to the rail as he jumped off onto the dock and quickly tied the boat down. When he was finished, he put his arms around her. She was wearing a rain slicker too, and both of them were wet on the outside, insulated from one another.

"Thank God," he said.

He leaned over her, their hoods meeting and hiding their faces for a moment. He kissed her, and he could feel the rain on her face and lips, and by the set of her mouth he knew she was scared or angry. Most likely both.

But she kissed him back, and then she pressed her head against his chest. "Thank God is right," she said. "I've been here for an hour, and have a few things to say to you for being late."

"I'll tell you about it once we're under way. Everything go all right?"

"No."

"Why? What happened?"

She turned away from him and walked back into the shadows. When she returned, she was dragging the big plastic container. "I tried," she said. "It just didn't work. There was someone there. He saw me, and he asked questions. It wouldn't have worked. I just left."

"Ah, Christ. Now what?"

"Just what did you want me to do?"

He sighed. His wife was no baby. In truth, she was harder inside than he was, by a long shot. If she said it wouldn't work, it wouldn't work. It was just that they had been trying like crazy to throw this together, and neither knew what they were doing. Slapping this thing together, hour by hour. All with too little experience.

I wouldn't invest in this company, he thought suddenly. Paul and Julie, Inc. He would have — did — every day of their previous life. The two of them had been a great bet. The thought made him smile. Not a happy smile, but a smile nonetheless.

"What?" she said.

"We don't have a choice. And that simplifies things. So get onboard with me, and get into some dry clothes."

She paused, silent. Thinking, thinking. And coming to the same conclusion he did. She smiled at him suddenly, still his girl inside this frightened woman. God, he wanted to take her where she could lose that scared look.

He heaved the plastic case into the cockpit, and then, on an impulse, he swept Julie up in his arms as if he were walking her across the threshold to their new home. As if they were just married, instead of eight years in.

She laughed, and that made him feel strong, in spite of being wet, cold, and scared himself. She said, "Are we going to be all right?"

"Sure," he lied. "Everything's going to be just fine. Let's go pick up a mooring and spend the night."

"I don't want to stay here. I don't think I was followed, but we can't stay in case I was."

He told her about the storm.

"We can't stay," she said. "We can't." The edge of panic in her voice.

He hesitated. "All right, then. We'll go." He placed her on the broad cockpit coaming, and he kissed her once more, gently on the lips. He felt her smile, and relax into the kiss, and in that moment, he really felt they could make everything work out.

He untied the boat and shoved her away from the dock. He climbed onto the stern, and already his wife was at the wheel, slipping the idling engine into gear.

They motored off into the gathering storm.

1

JACK MERCHANT was drifting.

At the moment, he didn't care.

The outboard to his inflatable raft was silent, but nothing else was. Around and above him, machinery roared. He was drifting just inside the Charles River Dam, in what he thought of as sort of an industrial lagoon underneath the construction of the Big Dig.

Around him, everyone was working hard at the fantastically expensive construction under way. Beneath the girders of the overpass, a half dozen bright yellow boxcar-size containers were stacked like building blocks. A battered aluminum powerboat — presumably used by the work crew — looked like a kid's toy underneath all the serious construction. Billions of dollars were being poured into an enormous hole in the ground, the most expensive public works project in history. Or so Merchant thought he'd read.

It was early morning, and already the smell of diesel was in the air, the whine of car tires on the bridge. A construction worker was poised on the edge of a beam. He lifted both arms wide when signaling to the crane operator. For a moment, his body almost mirrored the shape of the new cable stay bridge behind him. Merchant raised his Nikon, got it. It was a digital camera, so he took a moment to look at the LCD on the back, cupping his hand around it so he could see the picture without the glare. "Yah," he whispered.

It was a decent shot, the man being aped by the glittering tower of concrete and cable steel. His arms were a bit low, however.

Merchant had played the role of a photographer, so he knew the details mattered.

But Merchant wasn't a photographer. Not a real one. Or not yet, anyhow.

If he had been a sniper, he would've had a hell of a shot, too.

But Merchant wasn't a sniper, either. He'd known plenty during his time in the Drug Enforcement Administration, but that was over now.

His raft started to drift around in the wrong direction.

He let it. Didn't matter really, not if drifting was your goal. He thought awhile about whether "drifting" and "goal" together constituted an oxymoron.

He decided not.

He put a wider lens on his camera and began to take some shots of the locks and pumping station. Two huge brick buildings connected by a glassed-in walkway over the three locks. The pumping station on the left, the State Police on the right. The three locks were closed now, the retractable pedestrian walkway continuing over each of the three massive gates.

He often walked to Boston from his marina over the locks. He'd go through the Paul Revere Park, over the pedestrian bridges into Boston. It wasn't even a ten-minute walk — assuming the warning lights didn't start swirling and one of the little bridges retract to let a boat into the lock. If it did, well, these days, Merchant was usually content to check out the boat or read the Plexiglas-encased facts posted along the walkway. By now, he pretty much had them memorized:

Six pump engines that can each displace 630,000 gallons of water per minute . . . alewife and blueback herring are attracted to the fish ladder by the flow of fresh water and make their way up the Charles to lay their eggs . . . the main purpose of the locks is to keep the Charles River at eight feet above low tide, and a haven for recreational boaters . . .

Merchant took another few shots, trying to ignore the fact that his inflatable raft was leaking again.

He looked down and swore softly. Pushing at the sides, feeling that they were soft. His boat was soft and his butt was wet. "Damn," he said. "Damn, damn."

He'd patched the inflatable with a bicycle tire repair kit, and he could see from the bubbles along the inside floorboard that the patch was worth about as much as the nickel or so he'd paid for it.

He looked over his shoulder and saw that the construction worker had moved. Merchant raised the camera again.

This time, the composition was even better. The construction worker's arms were out completely now, waving to the crane operator, who was bringing in another I beam.

Merchant released the shutter, took several quick shots.

He stared at the LCD again, and scrolled through the pictures he'd taken that morning. None of the shots of the dam did it justice. He erased them. Of the construction worker shots, two were just OK, but two were pro quality.

He studied them both and decided one was perfect.

Merchant deleted all but the best shot. Figured someday he'd get around to printing it. But not now.

He had some skill, some talent. But not enough money to waste on a high-quality print that no one wanted to buy.

Definitely not a pro yet.

He knelt in the stern and started the outboard. It was awkward to do with the camera bag strap around his neck, trying to keep the bag balanced on his back. With all the water in the boat, he couldn't just set it down.

He pulled the rope, and the small motor growled to life. He sounded his air horn, two long blasts and two short, and waited while the lock operator up in the glassed-in walkway opened the gate of the smallest lock. Smallest, maybe, but able to handle a yacht. Several of them, in fact.

Merchant twisted the throttle and his eight-foot dinghy entered. Water was bubbling up around his legs now, and he squirmed a bit, and put the camera bag on his lap.

The high cement walls rose on each side. He puttered slowly toward the second set of gates. Once the water level matched the harbor, the gates would open and he could head out into the harbor.

Big production for such a small craft. He felt a bit silly, sitting in a small waterlogged boat plinking pictures that no one wanted. But the lock operator up there presumably had nothing else to do. The way Merchant saw it, they were giving each other some reason for being.

At last, the gates swung open.

Merchant twisted the throttle and headed to his marina. Not a long journey, it was all of about two hundred yards away. He saw the yard owner out near the sliding doors of his office. Merchant kept looking straight ahead, hoping they could leave it like that.

But the owner came onto the deck outside the office, his hands on his hips. He had a face like a hawk, with a nose to match. Just staring.

Merchant had paid his dock fees every month on time, but the owner seemed to be reading how close it was all getting.

Merchant kept the outboard puttering along, trying to look like a guy who could pay his bills. Shouldn't have been hard: he'd paid his way all his life without a problem.

But with the water sloshing around the boat bottom, the outboard overdue for a tune-up and coughing up a small cloud of blue smoke, he didn't look the part. He nodded to the owner, and the owner nodded back and went into the office.

Merchant brought the inflatable up to the dinghy dock and killed the engine. He put the camera bag on the dock and tied the boat off. He was relieved that the marina owner didn't come out to talk with him, and that pissed him off.

The lawyer had pretty much wiped out his savings. Even so, Merchant had thought he'd be all right when he came back to Boston. He had taken on some boatyard work just to pay the bills. Mindless stuff, scraping hulls and docks and painting. But it was summer now, and the regular crews had everything under control. And Merchant hadn't yet figured out a new career. Not even close.

He slung his camera bag over his shoulder and started for his boat, the *Lila*. She was a forty-foot sloop, bought during his very different life, which had pretty much ended about three months ago. He loved having her, but she consumed money, digested bales of it. Just last month, a minor engine repair had turned out to be a major overhaul. Nevertheless, Merchant wanted to keep her. He wanted that very much.

He thought quite a bit these days about how the boat was a gift from his past. A gift from a different person, almost. He wondered if maybe everyone's life was like that, full of pieces and tools that could be taken and reshaped for something new.

The photography maybe. There might be something there. He had the equipment, and it seemed like he might actually have some talent for it. Maybe a pro photographer with an emphasis on marine life? Highly competitive field. Every yahoo with a nice camera thought he could do it. And that was all he was at the moment, a yahoo with a nice camera.

He wondered what gift he'd find in Boston.

Charlestown, actually. The marina was a stone's throw from Boston proper and yet so insulated and clannish it might as well have been a thousand miles away. A place where a lot of very dangerous people had good reason to hate him.

Early in his career with the DEA, Merchant had spent a year undercover in Charlestown chasing down a major cocaine and PCP distribution ring. People were being killed, and yet no one dared speak. With his black hair and weather-burned skin, Merchant could pass for Black Irish. He had thrown himself entirely into his role, making trafficking-weight buys and sells to small-timers until he could bust them and turn them out. That done, he'd send them in wired. On a few occasions he got in himself. He was able to bring down a half dozen men, who each found time during their defense to meet his eyes across the courtroom, to let him know that he had made an enemy for life.

Back then, he didn't care. It was worth a promotion and a new assignment in the Virgin Islands.

Now it gave him reason to look over his shoulder.

He couldn't even explain to himself why he'd decided this would be his new home; maybe it was a perverse sense of entitlement that, even if he had been drummed out of the DEA, at least he could go wherever the hell he wanted to go.

A perverse sense of entitlement.

He liked the sound of that.

He was busy with the steady mental debate about what he should do with himself now that he was flat out of a career when he saw through one of *Lila*'s cabin portholes something move.

There was someone on his boat.

His overwhelming feeling at the moment was sadness. Even as he started back to get behind another boat on a finger dock. Sadness. Even as he was checking to see if there was other movement, if he was already surrounded.

Sadness that some aspects of the life would never change, no matter how much he wanted them to.

Automatically, he reached into his camera bag for his handgun. It was always there, a nine-millimeter SIG-Sauer.

He came up empty.

This was a change, another gift from his recent past — he no longer carried a gun.

It almost made him laugh.

Almost.

2

MERCHANT WAITED and listened.

He heard a thin, whistling tune from whoever was onboard. The tune sounded familiar, but he couldn't place it. And a few moments after that, he smelled bacon frying.

Merchant boarded his boat, picking up a winch handle as he stepped into the cockpit.

Sarah Ballard was standing in the galley, the fry pan filled with bacon. The galley was a mess of flour and open cupboards. Sarah looked up and saw Merchant standing there, the heavy chrome metal glinting in his hand. She said, "You want bunny ears on your pancakes, or plain?"

"Sarah girl," he said, letting out his breath. He slipped the handle back into the winch and said, "Bunny ears."

He stepped down into the cabin. "I thought I had a lock on the cabin. Saving my bacon and such."

"Oh, shut up and kiss me."

He did, and they both kept it no more than friendly.

"What're you doing here?" Merchant said. He liked Sarah. Once upon a time, he had even hoped she'd be more than a friend. But considering what she did for a living, now he felt more than a little wary.

She moved back to the stove. "Cooking you breakfast. Now sit down."

"The big boss," he said. "I forgot."

"Shame on you, then." She slid the spatula under the bacon and dropped a half dozen strips onto a plate covered with paper towels. She drained most of the fat into an empty coffee can in the sink, and then ladled the pancake batter into the pan. She nodded to the coffeepot. "Left you a cup."

"Uh-huh."

Merchant poured the coffee, noting the dribble of egg whites, flour, and cooking oil on the countertop. Her cooking skills hadn't improved over time, he could see.

"Only way to keep sane living aboard is to keep everything in its place," he said. "Thought you'd know that by now."

"Yeah, right." She waved the spatula at the small pile of tools, sawdust, and wood strips on the floor of the main cabin. "Give me a lecture, Merchant."

He looked forward. She had a point. He said, "By tomorrow I'll be done. Found some rot along the chain plates, and I had to dig it all out, fill in with strips and epoxy."

"Handy these days, are you?"

"Yeah." He looked at her sharply. "Really, why are you here?"

Sarah flipped a pancake. Gave him a Cheshire cat smile. She said, "You look soaked. Why don't you change?"

She was probably just under thirty now, Merchant figured. Tall, rich black hair, long legs. Heart-stopping body. More fit than he remembered her. Much more fit, actually. High cheekbones more defined, muscle definition in her arms, the way she held herself.

"I'll be right back." He made his way into the forward cabin. He changed into dry shorts and a T-shirt, and then came back to the galley.

He said, "What've you been doing to yourself?"

"The bod? I like to work out."

"I'd say so."

She looked at him critically. "Wish I could say the same of you."

He laughed. "Nice."

"Just look like you could use more sleep, is all. Maybe a shave every once in a while."

Sarah was wearing jeans, boat shoes, a black T-shirt. The shirt was old and faded. A gift from her brother, Merchant knew. It was emblazoned with a promo for the old cult movie *Repo Man*. A car floated on her back, a greenish light glowing from the trunk. Joel had hand-painted the letters WO in the middle of the title, changing it to REPO WOMAN.

That was what Sarah was, a repo woman. Only for boats, not cars.

"So are you here to take my boat or what?" Merchant said.

"All right," she said. "I wish you'd just shut up and let me feed you some breakfast. But yes, I've got paper on your boat."

"Ah, for Christ's sakes," Merchant said.

She put her hand up. "Please. I think I can help out."

"How?"

"I'll get to that."

"You'll get to that?"

"Yep. Meanwhile I want to know why you haven't called me. You've been here how long?"

Merchant paused. Wanting to know exactly how she intended to help out with towing his boat away and leaving him on the dock.

He was only one payment behind.

He said, "You're just going to take it?"

God, was he whining? Sounded damned close to his own ears.

"Shush," she said. "C'mon, why haven't I heard from you?"

He sighed. "I've been here about three months. Believe me, you haven't missed anything. I've been lousy company. You're just going to take the boat?"

She ignored the last. "Yeah, like I ever looked to you for laughs." She tossed the pancake onto a plate. "Here, the first one's always the greasiest. You eat it." She put another ladle of batter into the pan.

Merchant cut the right ear off the bunny, tasted it, found it was indeed greasy on the outside, but light on the inside. He told Sarah where to find the syrup, and she passed it to him.

She said, "Been what, almost five years?"

"About right."

She was silent for a moment.

He said, "I should have been in better touch. But I was under-cover a lot of that time. You tend to get cut off." He looked at her hand. No ring. "So, you're not married."

She looked at him quickly with something going through her eyes. Hurt, anger, he couldn't tell. "My, you *have* been out of touch," she said.

"What's that mean?"

"Later." She flipped a pancake onto her plate and sat down across from him. She looked at him straight on. Dark green eyes with gold flecks. "I missed you."

Merchant smiled at her. He was surprised that he could under the circumstances. But he did like her. Always had. He said, "How you been standing up with it all?"

"I miss the kid."

"Yeah, I'd expect."

"Doesn't seem to make a hell of a lot of difference, the time."

Merchant could imagine. He had a younger sister living up in New Hampshire, just divorced her idiot of a husband.

He loved her like crazy, so he could imagine.

He said, "So the first you heard I was here was the bank paper on *Lila?*"

"No. Last week, I heard. Henriques."

"You're kidding. Where'd you see him?"

"The Stateroom."

Merchant remembered the place. A cinder-block dive right on New Bedford's waterfront without even a window opened to take in the sea breeze. But surprisingly good seafood and barbecued ribs, frosted mugs of cold beer. A big hangout for fishermen.

"You're still being seen in all the right places, huh?"

"Not a glamorous life I lead. The sleazebag tried to hit on me. He didn't get far, and then went on to tell me he'd heard that you were back. Made him happy to tell me you'd done some incredibly screwed up thing. Said I should call you, we were both a couple of misfits."

"Can't argue with him there."

"Uh-huh. He said you should find some landlocked hole, get some dirt, and pull it over your head. Not that I like to agree with Henriques, but I've got to wonder why you'd come back to Charlestown. You got more enemies per capita here than any place on earth."

"I like the view of the Boston skyline."

"Liar. You make an art form of it."

"Besides," Merchant said. "You're behind the times. I've made myself a whole batch of new enemies."

"Now that I do believe."

"Most've them have got southern accents, so it's easier to pick them out up here."

"Long's they talk to you before pulling the trigger." Sarah hesitated, looking Merchant in the eye.

"Say it."

"Henriques tells me you panicked down in Miami."

"He did, huh?"

"Uh-huh. Said he still has friends with the DEA and the story is another agent got killed and it was your fault."

"That's true," Merchant said. "It is my fault he's dead. But as for panicking, no. It was a decision."

"So what happened?"

He sighed. He liked Sarah, had once liked her a lot. But now he didn't know if he was talking to a friend or not. "Look, let's move this along. I'd like to know if I'm going be sleeping in my boat or on the dock tonight."

She withdrew slightly. "Well, let's see. Can you make your payment?"

"I will," he said. "Got my camera up for sale and I have work lined up." Lying about both, but still.

"Do you have the cash *now?*"

"No."

"See?" she said. "The old '*Give me some time, lady.*'"

"Uh-huh. So I'm a deadbeat. Isn't a month short notice to repo a boat?"

"Depends on the bank." Sarah looked around the boat appraisingly. "Even though you're a slob, I see she's got potential. Forty feet right? Custom sloop. Looks like hand-laid glass, got some nice joinery work down here. Your loan on her isn't that big, you'd get at least sixty for her now. She couldn't have been in this shape when you bought her."

"She wasn't. You're looking at a labor of love. Got her down in St. Thomas. She'd been in charter for ten years."

"How'd you pick her?"

"More like she chose me. One morning I was at the mouth of the harbor on Jost Van Dyke taking pictures after a hard blow. I saw her washing up. One thing led to another, and I found myself wading out and getting her dinghy off and rowing her anchor out, and winching like crazy while the tide rose."

"Lot to do for someone else's boat."

"That's what I thought. She was beat long before she ground up on that beach. Hull and decks were sound, everything else pretty much trashed. So the charter company wrote her off as a loss. I told the job she would help my cover, and bought her from the salvage yard myself. They thought I was nuts, but they went for it. I wore a beard and a ponytail back then. I took my gear and posed as a pro photographer with a boat that needed a lot of work who was willing to buy and sell coke to make ends meet."

"Uh-huh. And now you're out of work and my, my the money sure does fly, doesn't it?"

"So I've noticed."

Sarah said, "Some people look at net worth. I look at dock and boat payments. At any given time I know how many months I've got before someone comes with repo paper on me."

"You still living on your dad's trawler?"

"Yeah. Someday I'll get rid of it, but it's so comfortable."

"So how many months before you're on the dock right now?"

"Four. That's assuming I could sell off the assets of the business at a reasonable price. If I got screwed there, maybe I'm already out of a boat. So the trick is for me to stay in business."

She looked around his boat again. "You could sell her, pay off your loan, and maybe even make a little profit. So why don't you?"

"I don't want to."

Sarah laughed. "Good enough then. So we have something to talk about."

He waited.

She said, "You'd make enough to keep you going at least a few months."

"Let's have it."

She said, "You haven't actually sold your camera, right? I might need you to do a little surveillance."

"I've got a couple of them."

"Good. Mainly, the job is to help me find, and then sail a boat back."

"From where?"

"If I knew that, I wouldn't need you."

Merchant thought about the idea of a paid voyage, even on someone else's boat. He balanced that with putting a lot of time in with Sarah. He liked her, but there were warnings going off in his head about her. He didn't know why. The way she was pumped up physically, her nails bitten raw. That edgy look about her eyes. She seemed to be burning too fast.

And he had enough trouble to spare. Of course, being broke was part of that.

He said, "So you'd really tow my boat away?"

"Bet your ass. Leave you on the dock, crying for Mama."

But then she reached out and put her hands on his. Long slim fingers, sun browned and strong. "Truth is, I'd look the other way. Never done that before, but for what you did for me and Joel, I'd look the other way — long enough for you to sail away. I just hope I don't have to."

He thought about his own troubles. About the Randalls. And about his neighbors right here in Charlestown.

He balanced that against the past three months. He'd been looking over his shoulder, but nothing had happened. Far as he could tell, no one was even thinking about him these days.

He turned his palms up, took her hands in his, and squeezed. "So what's the job?"

3

SARAH TOOK A SMALL DAYPACK from the floor, and pulled out a file. "Here she is, the *Fresh Air*. A lot like yours, a custom forty-foot sloop. Owners overdue on payments one month now."

Merchant already felt sorry for the deadbeats.

She laid out an eight-by-ten photo of a single-masted sailboat at dock. A couple was posed in front of it. They looked to be in their early thirties, the man with his arm draped around the woman's shoulders. He was tall and rangy. Craggy features, good smile. Maybe a little geeky. She was a petite woman with short blond hair and nice features. He had to stoop to put his arm around her, but didn't look like he minded. Both of them were sunburned.

"Nice looking couple."

"A lot of deadbeats are."

Merchant looked past them at the boat. "Looks fast."

"You say so," Sarah said. "I prefer my boats with a couple of big engines and a Jacuzzi."

"What's the deal?"

"Got the paper on this from MassBank a week back. The owners, Julie and Paul Baylor. Been making all my calls, doing my usual bit, and I'm getting nowhere. Here's a twist. MassBank is also Paul Baylor's employer. This whole thing is an embarrassment to them. They want Paul Baylor back because he's got some serious explaining to do."

"You know him?"

"No. He was a VP. Not the sort of guy I'd ever run into."

"No idea where the boat is?"

"Turned up nothing around here. Like I said, I did my usual bit, the credit reports, and I've been calling marinas from the Boaters Almanac. It's going to take some time. So far, I've got diddly."

"So you think the Baylors are running."

"Sure looks that way. They took off about a month and a half ago. Supposed to be a two-week vacation up in Maine. Two weeks comes and goes, nobody's heard from them. After a couple of days, both their employers get nervous, make some calls. No sign of them. Bank gets worried, calls the Coast Guard. They start checking around for family. Turns out she's got a sister in Philadelphia. He's got nobody. Her sister's here in Boston now, has been coming up a couple days a week since they were reported missing. I'm supposed to meet with her this evening. Any case, when the company called her last month, she flew up to Bar Harbor right away. She poked around a couple days, tried to stir up the cops. She couldn't find any sign of the Baylors."

"Maine's a rocky coast. Maybe they ran into more trouble than not paying their bills."

"Maybe. But no wreckage, no report of a Mayday, nothing. Coast Guard and Maine State Police looked into it, and in their opinion, these folks took off on their own."

"Based on what?"

"Couple of things. The lack of a Mayday. Decent weather while they were out. Some pretty good winds from a storm further down the coast, but it was basically quite decent from Boston up through Maine."

"Doesn't mean a thing. A good gust at the wrong time can do a lot of damage."

"True. But how about an ATM hit on their account from Manhattan?" Sarah tapped the manila envelope.

"Ah."

"Yeah. Strange way to Maine, isn't it?"

"Got a picture?"

"Sure. The ATM is on the same network as MassBank, so they had no trouble getting hold of it." She took out another photo. This one was murky, blown up from an ATM camera. There was a black teenage boy looking over his shoulder, most likely purposely hiding his face. Other than the Rangers jacket he was wearing, there was nothing distinguishing about him.

"How'd he get the code?"

"He didn't. Tried a bunch of wrong ones, didn't get anything. The attempted transaction was recorded."

"Where was this taken?"

"Around the hundredth block on Broadway. Also far from the lobster tails of Maine."

"Any credit card charges?"

"Yep. Shelly — he's my contact at MassBank — he tells me there are a couple of restaurant bills. Portsmouth, New Hampshire, and Portland, Maine. Which makes sense — these were supposed to be stops along the way up to Bar Harbor. Julie Baylor told her co-workers they were going to Acadia. She said she was looking forward to renting bikes and making their way to the top of Cadillac Mountain for the sunrise."

"How much cash did they take?"

"You ask the right questions, Jack. They withdrew just under twenty thousand dollars. Nine-eight the day before they left, and nine-seven the day they left."

"Jesus. That's a lot of mad money for a couple weeks in Maine. How about the rest of their accounts?"

"Just under a hundred thousand transferred to a Cayman account the day before they left."

"Under," Merchant repeated. "They're paying attention to the drug warning flags."

"Uh-huh."

"Was that everything?"

"Hardly. That left about six hundred thousand in assets. Stocks, mutual funds, bonds, 401k."

"Lot to leave behind."

"True. But they left about a million two in debt on their home and boat."

"Not exactly responsible banker behavior."

"People like the Baylors are usually the kind who keep me in business," Sarah said. "Speaking of numbers, what do you say to three hundred and fifty a day, plus expenses? Twenty-five percent of what I make when we bring her back, and the sale goes through. Total, you'd be walking away with somewhere around three to four thousand for going sailing, and the pleasure of my company. I'll advance you enough right now to cover the current month's mortgage and your dock fees. Sound fair?"

"Sounds like a gift from heaven. Why?"

Sarah shrugged. "Trying to help you out here."

"And what else?"

Merchant waited.

The silence lengthened between them, and finally Sarah gave in. "OK. Truth is, I'm getting my ass kicked. Normally, the banks don't get freaked about a repo. It's business as usual. I find the boat, bring it back, recondition it, and sell it. I take my cut every step of the way, and the bank takes the balance. They go after the owner for the difference."

"And this case?"

"Being it's a senior bank employee, my contact at MassBank, Shelly, tells me there's a lot of heat. The company president has assigned a VP over him to get it done. And Shelly's sweating it, so he's making me sweat it. I got competition now . . ."

"No kidding?"

"Couple of new ones in it now, guy working out of Narragansett Bay and someone in Connecticut. All the time my dad had the business and up until two years ago, there were fifteen East Coast banks on our client list. Now it's down to eight. And MassBank is worth four of them put together. I've got to find this boat."

"So you need a token guy."

"No, I need the real deal," she said. "A guy who can help me find the boat. A guy who can help me sail it back. Most of all, a guy I can trust."

"OK," Merchant said.

"A guy who can understand that I've got to draw the line between business and pleasure. You'd be my employee. And friend, I hope. But nothing more."

"Ah, shucks," he said. "I thought this was a package deal."

"People have," she said, and didn't smile.

The hurt, the anger right there. Merchant said, "OK, Sarah. Just playing with you."

She nodded. "I know. It's just . . . well, just so we understand each other."

They sat there, trying to get past the awkwardness.

Then Sarah nodded toward the camera bag. "Shelly says Radoccia is hot on surveillance. And I promised I could bring someone who could do that."

"Who's Radoccia?"

"The VP leaning over Shelly's desk saying 'Can't you get anybody to find this frigging boat?'"

"Why the photos? Why don't you just slap the chains on the boat and let the courts go after the people?"

"Good question. But that's up for him to explain."

"And when's he supposed to do that?"

Sarah looked at her watch. "About two hours from now."

Merchant thought about it, looked at her directly, and said, "What else?"

He was glad to see she didn't dodge it for a second. Whatever it was, he could feel it on her. Something she wasn't telling. Or hadn't said yet.

"You know, it's been a long time since we saw each other," she said. "It can be a lifetime, everything that can happen in five years. I do have something to tell you, and if you don't want to work with me, I'll understand. I truly will."

"I'm listening," Merchant said, "but I'd say I know you pretty well. The pressure on you, the way you handled it. I know the kind of person you are."

"No." She pushed her plate away. Crossed her arms. Protecting herself.

She said, "You knew the kind of person I was."

4

SARAH HAD MET MERCHANT those five years ago under the worst possible circumstances. And the first time she saw him, he didn't even
register. He was just another man in a suit. Some sort of cop. DEA,
it would turn out, but, again, he didn't really register. Just another
plainclothes cop among the uniformed cops, homicide cops, and
the crime scene techs.

Lou Grasso, a New Bedford cop she knew, had picked her up at
the office. He'd stood in the doorway, fumbling with his hat. The
light from the marina behind him. "It's bad, Sarah. It's Joel. Come
with me."

He told her on the front stoop all that really mattered: that Joel
was dead.

Grasso drove her over to the warehouse. She walked through the
big hangar doors shaking inside. All she really saw was Joel, her
little brother, face down on the concrete. There were five other
men, hands bound behind their backs with wire, clothesline around
their necks.

But Joel was all she saw.

Her nineteen-year-old little brother.

With Joel gone, that was it for her family. Mom dead for years.
Dad gone seven months before. Prostate cancer.

"Oh, Joel," Sarah said. She knelt down to stroke his hair, and

George Henriques yelled at her to get away from him, that she was in the middle of a crime scene.

Go fuck yourself, she said, and she didn't look up. George Henriques she knew. A New Bedford local, he'd been a senior when she was a freshman in high school. Jorge Henriques, then. It was big news when years passed and he was revealed to have been not the worst head in high school but a narc. And now he was back in town with the DEA, his hair short, his anglicized first name, and a reputation for letting people know the depths he'd seen. Her mind had latched on to Henriques at the time, wanting to let loose on him.

But what she was feeling was too big.

The tears blurred her eyes, and maybe she noticed it then or maybe she just remembered it later, but when Henriques started to tell her again to take her hands off her brother, a quiet voice said, "Shut up, George."

That was Merchant.

Two days later, she went to the New Bedford branch of the DEA, and that was the first time she actually met Merchant. He was the quiet guy in the room who listened as Henriques told her Joel was tied in to the smuggling.

"Bullshit," she said.

"It'd be easier to see him as a vic," Henriques said. A phony sympathy on his face, the curls of his black hair combed straight and frozen with some kind of gel. A Portuguese man trying to look like Ken of Ken and Barbie fame.

He said, "From our perspective, Ms. Ballard, it looks like your brother was involved."

She'd tried to keep it together then. *Ms. Ballard,* as if he didn't know her, hadn't tried to hit on her all through high school. She said, "No, George. Joel wasn't like that. He's . . . he was sort of an innocent. Besides, we had paper on the *Melissa.*"

"Did you send him out to repo a fishing boat with crew by himself?"

She hesitated, but shook her head.

"OK, was he the kind of guy to just go out on his own and try it without your say-so?"

Again, she had to shake her head. Joel did very little without her direction. It was the way he was; worse, the way she was.

Henriques lifted his shoulders slightly. "Then, as far as I can see, he looks like the kind of guy that tried to cut into some drug money and got it around the neck. Literally."

He actually smiled for a moment, his little joke, and then the phony professional mask was back up.

Sarah tried hard, very hard to hold herself back. Henriques hadn't been the biggest or toughest kid at school, but if you were a girl or smaller than he was you learned to avoid being alone around him. Someone you didn't turn your back on, ever.

"Ms. Ballard . . ."

"You know my name."

He smiled quickly. "Yes. Well, Sarah . . ." he said. Looking her in the eye. Hitting on her even then, for Christ's sakes. "Just what would you like me to do?"

"Do your job," she said. "That's all I'm asking."

Henriques pulled back a bit. Knowing a slammed door when he heard it.

"Let me ask you this: If Joel was such an innocent, then why did you have him doing repo work? Kind of sleazebags you run into, it was only a matter of time before a guy like that gets caught in it. You must've known that."

That took her breath away.

"George," she said, her voice rising. "Just do your damn job. If you do that, you'll find Joel wasn't involved . . . not the way you're saying, anyhow."

He lifted his eyebrow, and then spoke, as much for Merchant's benefit as for hers. "We'll do our investigation despite your hysteria."

"I'm not hysterical."

"Whatever."

"And you'll let me know what you find out?"

"Of course we will. But I wouldn't go off and start a scholarship fund in Joel's name just yet."

It took just about everything Sarah had not to crack Henriques across the face.

So she looked at Merchant. He had seemed to be listening the entire time, but was offering nothing. She tried to think of something that could make him see Joel the way she had seen him. Joel had been sweet, he'd been a decent kid. But she also knew that he wasn't that smart, that he was easily impressionable, that he wanted money to buy a red five-year-old Camaro IROC-Z. She didn't know what he was doing with the crew of the *Melissa*. He usually did what she told him. She ran the business, she was the boss. That was the way it had always been between the two of them.

Tears tried to fill her eyes, but she stopped them by sheer force of will. She said to Merchant, "And what are you going to do about it?" Her voice sounded harsh to her own ears, and that was not what she wanted. What she wanted to say was that Joel was her brother, her kid brother, and she desperately wanted to believe that he wasn't involved, and couldn't Merchant just be a human being and help her?

But she didn't know how to ask this stranger. Not in front of Henriques, anyhow.

Merchant said, "I'm going to look into it and let you know."

She stared at him, realizing that he meant it, and that maybe she had some help after all. Then the tears came. Without a word, she turned for the door so Henriques couldn't see them.

As she went out, she heard Henriques say, "She always was a stuck-up bitch."

She would like to think she heard Merchant say, "Shut up, George," but she couldn't be sure that she had.

It was almost a week before Merchant came to her boat.

She'd just woken up. She could hear the soft clink of metal on metal, and she knew Owen was in the main cabin lifting weights. The hatches were all open, and the sea breeze was fresh in the boat. He'd put coffee on.

Momentarily, it was all very pleasant, until it hit her fresh that Joel was gone, and the pain took a swipe at her insides with sharp claws and she curled onto herself.

She heard Owen talking to someone and saying, "Yeah, come on in."

Owen came back to the aft cabin. "DEA. Get yourself together, babe."

"Henriques?" she said.

"No. The other one."

She slumped back and stared at the cabin roof. Now that he was here, she didn't want to see him. What if he had proof that Joel was in it up to his ears? What was she going to tell herself after that?

Owen drew a T-shirt on. His chest was matted with sweat, and he looked pumped up from the weights. He laid his hand on her cheek. "C'mon, babe. Let's hear what he has to say. I'll be right with you."

He was so good at that. Making her feel loved and supported.

And why not? He was a skillful man.

Merchant had looked skinny next to Owen. Not that he was, exactly. He had what Sarah had always considered a farmer's build: angular, lean, not exactly bulging with muscles but strong looking anyhow. Big hands. He was dressed in jeans himself, cotton shirt with rolled back sleeves, baseball cap. He looked different than he had in the office, not just the clothes.

"Hey," she said. Her voice was shaky. "You've got some news for me?"

"Are you all right, Sarah?" he said.

"Just took something a while back."

"Valium," Owen said. "She was having trouble sleeping so I gave her a Valium around three o'clock."

"OK," Merchant said. "I just wanted to talk with her."

Owen had taken a protective position between her and Merchant. "Go ahead," he said.

Merchant smiled. "I'm sorry, I need to speak privately with Ms. Ballard."

"No, you don't," Owen said. "We're together."

Owen was an ex-Marine, and back then she had not yet begun to resent what he called his natural leadership abilities. Especially since he seemed to listen to her.

So, at the time, she fully expected Merchant to acquiesce, as everyone did with Owen. It was simply easier.

Merchant was still smiling. It wasn't an apologetic smile. He took out a business card, reached past Owen, and handed it to her. "When you're ready."

He turned to leave.

"Oh, for Christ's sakes," Owen said, and started after him.

Sarah grabbed his arm. "Please. Honey, go to the office and open up, all right?" Owen had been one of her dad's freelance skippers for years, and since her father passed away, he'd been there for her every step of the way.

"I'm staying with you," he said.

"That's OK, really."

He hesitated and then touched her check gently. "If that's what you need." Just like turning on the sunshine.

Joel had thought the world of him. Big brother he'd never had, all that crap.

Owen looked over at Merchant. "She'll tell me the whole deal, anyhow."

"That's her decision."

"Simple enough," Owen said. And then he left.

If only it could've been that easy later.

Merchant and Sarah went up on deck and stood blinking in the sun. "So. What's the big secret?"

"I'm going to be asking you for some help, and I suspect he's the type of guy who would say no for you."

"Maybe," she said. "But I tend to do what I say."

"Good. Look, I found out about your brother. He was being played. They were using him to buy a week or two."

"So it had to do with the repo?"

"The repo and the drugs. The captain's wife told me that he found out Joel wanted to own a boat. Wanted to be a fisherman, right?"

A little energy sparked inside her. Relief, but anger, too. "Like he didn't learn enough repossessing those boats, what a crapshoot it is."

"Well, they needed the boat. They'd been approached by the Colombians about a doing a pickup, and were desperate enough to take it. They were almost four months overdue on their payments. So they figured if they could stall your repo even a week, they could make their pickup. Then they'd have enough to catch up. She said her husband hated doing it, figured this was going to be a one-time deal. She said her husband was going to invite Joel on for a day, talk to him about getting a share on the boat out of sweat equity. That he'd give him a berth, he could work his way up — assuming he could arrange it so that you held off on the repo a few weeks. I guess the captain gave him a line about this catch of tuna they'd been finding and he was sure he'd make enough in the next haul to put off the bank another few months. In any case, Joel was on the boat that night to discuss it. And from what we hear, they were all escorted off the boat into a white van, and taken to the warehouse."

"So he didn't know about the drugs?" Sarah needed to hear the words.

"The captain's wife says no."

"Why were they killed?"

"What I hear is that her husband got to drinking and talked too much in a bar. I guess the Colombians decided to make an example."

Sarah covered her face with her hands.

"Your brother was in the wrong place at the wrong time, really no more than that." Merchant put his hand on her shoulder, and that was all right.

"It couldn't have been easy," she said. "I pushed Joel hard. Working for his big sister. Me always being the boss. Of course he wanted something else."

"He was looking for some adventure. What else is a nineteen-year-old boy supposed to do?"

"Thank you for coming to tell me this. Thank you for pushing the investigation."

"I'm glad it's giving you some relief. But I'm just doing my job."

"More than Henriques would have done. Wait for me, all right?"

"Sure."

She went below and washed her face, and put on some clean clothes. She looked at herself in the mirror and figured there would be lots more crying to come, but she felt better. No doubt about it. She felt better knowing.

She went back up on deck. He was leaning against the bow rail. She stood beside him, looking out at the harbor. "Pretty, isn't it? I've given up a lot for that view. My dad's decision, actually, but mine now."

"Your dad do this repo work for long?"

"About eight years now. We used to have a nice house, go out on his boat on weekends. I was fifteen when my mom died, Joel nine. My dad was the credit manager for J.Walkers, the shoe manufacturer. He was a practical guy, but he wanted a change. Wanted to be on a boat. Moved the three of us down here, cast around for something he could do, and came up with this."

"Tough job."

She looked at him. "Have you got a boat?"

"Not now." He looked out at the harbor with that wistful eye she'd seen so often. "I messed around some as a kid. And I'm ex-Navy."

She said, "So you want a powerboat?"

"Nah. Sail. Something like that." He pointed to a thirty-eight-foot sloop. Fiberglass, but with classic lines. Small transom, good for handling following seas. Small overhangs bow and stern. A beauty, yet fast and practical.

For some reason, she liked it that he had such a good eye. But she said, "Boats. Toys. People get desperate for these toys, think they define who they are. And then run themselves into the ground trying to keep up the image. Their houses are being foreclosed, cars hauled off. Doesn't keep them from making crazy offers. Percentage of their business, cash on the side. All I hear is, 'Gimme me a little time, lady.'"

"So why do you do it?"

"Same as my dad. I'm on the water just about every day. If not on a boat, at marinas. I'm my own boss. Believe me, with my personality, that's important."

She'd felt her eyes well up then. Wondering again if she'd just shoved Joel too much, made him finally run away. But that wasn't what she said. What she said to Merchant was "My dumb little brother . . . I love him, but that's what he was. He listened."

"Maybe. I didn't know him. But maybe he just wanted to go to sea for a while, and it had nothing to do with you. Those fishermen . . . Deadbeats, maybe, but they died, too. They're not the ones who put the rope around his neck. You want to help us find the ones who did?"

"Why wouldn't I?"

"Because it might be dangerous. Right now, you're a grieving sister. To the people who killed your brother, you're incidental, not even on their radar screen. You start helping us out, you might just get on."

"Don't worry about it," she said. "What can I do?"

Merchant laid it out for her. How the Colombians were bringing up coke and heroin in fishing boats. Making drops in New York and then going on to Massachusetts. "New Bedford's hot. So's

Gloucester. We suspect some of it is being off-loaded at the docks, and some is being picked up at sea with smaller boats. Either way, we need to get somebody onboard one of those boats."

"You want me to help point out the replacement for the *Melissa*, right? The Colombians are going need somebody new."

"That's right. Look for someone whose boat is in better shape than their hauls would indicate. Who's driving a new Caddy the same year they had their boat refitted."

"Sure. I know what you want."

"Good."

She liked his face, she thought. Not exactly handsome, not like Owen's. His features were a bit irregular, his nose looked as if it had been broken. But signs of humor around the mouth and eyes. Quiet, yes, but with an energy about him that was very different from Owen's.

She wondered why she was comparing him to her boyfriend at all.

He said, "When did you last eat?"

"Lunch yesterday? I don't know. Owen's been trying, but I haven't had any appetite."

"C'mon," he said. "Let's go below. I'll cook you breakfast, you clean. Then we'll take it from there."

Taking charge in her space. It surprised her and, knowing herself, it should have irritated her. She could be such a bitch, and she knew it. Owen had started letting her know she wanted her way too much.

But to Merchant, she said, "OK."

Maybe it was just that she was hungry again.

They met three times after that, talking about the various leads she was following on the waterfront. She found herself looking forward to their meetings. The fourth time she invited him on her boat, she had something for him. She was feeling somewhat better by then. Like she had regained some control of her life. Like she was doing something for Joel.

Owen was out for the night, and she laid it out for Merchant: "Fisherman. Drives the same ratty old car and his house is nothing special, but he's got a new twenty-two-year-old girlfriend who's spending money like crazy and an *old* girlfriend who's just about choking over it. From what I hear, the wife has no idea about either of them."

"Could be the old girlfriend wants to just make trouble for this guy."

"Oh, she does. But she also says she's got enough detail about his drug running to give you some serious leverage. And she's motivated. Seems the new girlfriend is driving around town in a red Saab convertible, blond hair blowing in the breeze."

Merchant smiled. "Give me a name."

"I've got a condition."

"The DEA's not big on conditions."

"I want to be there. That's all I ask. When they take these bastards down, I want to be there."

Merchant laughed. "A civilian on a bust? Not a chance."

She sat back. Crossed her arms. She liked this guy, but he had no idea how stubborn she could be. "Oh, I think so," she said.

He repeated, "Not a chance."

Two months later, Sarah wasn't there to see exactly what happened, but she was close.

She and Owen were about three miles away on a Coast Guard cutter. Shadowing the fishing boat that Merchant had been working undercover on all the way to Colombia and back.

The boat was the *Juju*, owned by Captain Prada, the fisherman she had identified for them. She'd felt bad about how scared Prada was. She had heard that his wife had broken down in baffled tears when the DEA showed up at their house and informed them both that he was going to help them or go to jail.

But Sarah decided she could live with all of it. Prada had been running heroin. For a new girlfriend.

She could live with it.

For two days, it had been an excruciatingly boring voyage. They'd just shadowed the fishing boat from a distance.

But they had been monitoring the radio messages all along. Reading between the lines, it sounded as if the Colombians in New York didn't want to wait for them to make it all the way to New Bedford. Instead, they might well come out that night and off-load at sea.

It was dark, a hot night with little breeze. The cutter rolled slowly on greasy swells.

The DEA agent in charge on the Coast Guard cutter had agreed that she and Owen could sit in the little communications room with the operator and listen to the transmissions from each of the five agents onboard. The same transmissions were piped up to the bridge for the captain and agent in charge.

Owen resented being on the sidelines. He wouldn't stop talking about it. "God, I wish I was in on this," he said. Hands twitching.

She believed him, but she finally snapped and asked him to be quiet so she could listen. That made him angry, particularly because the guy handling the communications had looked over his shoulder and grinned. Owen smoldered over that, but he kept quiet.

Later, she'd think about that, what sort of restraint Owen must have put on himself.

The DEA had the trawler wired for sound. The Coast Guard had three speedboats with muffled engines waiting to swoop in as soon as the Colombians tried to leave.

Jack — she had long begun thinking of him as Jack rather than Merchant — was on the deck of the trawler. The wire he was wearing was so sensitive that she could hear him breathing. He, George Henriques, and Bill Craig were on the aft deck. Two DEA SWAT agents were hiding on the cabin roof. She could hear their breathing too. Five channels coming through.

But she chose to listen to Jack's, even put the earphones on when the communications agent offered them to her.

And then she heard Jack clear his throat and say, "They're here. Twenty-foot speedboat coming up. Wish us luck."

As it turned out, Prada was too nervous.

Three Colombians climbed onboard and demanded that he bring them the bags of heroin in his hold.

The bust was supposed to happen after the Colombians left; those three muffled speedboats were to sweep in.

But Captain Prada talked too much. He stuttered and tried to joke and generally came across as a man with something to hide. The lead Colombian watched him carefully and then put a gun to his head and screamed they would blow his head off if he didn't explain himself.

Prada said he didn't know what they were talking about.

Sarah couldn't hear what happened then, but she learned later the Colombian kicked Prada in the back of the legs, making him fall to his knees. And then he pulled a length of rope from his pocket and wrapped it around Prada's throat.

Just like the crew of the *Melissa*.

Prada pointed to his three crew members: Jack, Bill Craig, and George Henriques. The Colombian released the rope and let him speak.

"DEA," Prada croaked. "DEA."

The Colombian turned his gun toward them.

The two hidden SWAT team members stood up on the fly bridge and called for the Colombians to drop their guns. Jack and the other two were supposed to fall back behind the big winch, where two AR-15 assault rifles were stashed.

It should've ended right there, but one of the Colombians was carrying a submachine gun under his coat, and he was either very lucky or very talented, because he put the two guys on the cabin roof down, and managed to get Bill Craig in the arm and chest.

Jack and Henriques fell back behind the winch. Jack grabbed his assault rifle.

By then the Coast Guard cutter was roaring to the scene, following the three speedboats. Sarah was straining to hear what was happening.

"Christ," Owen was saying. "Goddamn carnage."

For the next six minutes, Sarah listened to the radio and heard gunshots, and the whistling breathing of Bill Craig, and the thunder of the assault rifle and submachine gun.

She listened only to Jack.

His breath was rushing, too. Then, the crashing sound of the assault rifle before it made a mechanical clacking sound, and Jack simply said, "Empty."

Then there were the individual shots from a handgun. Close up, his gun. And the reply of the submachine gun.

Sarah took off the headphones. "I'm only hearing Jack shoot," she said. "What about the others?"

"Henriques must be down," the communications agent said. He looked perplexed. "I heard him fine . . . but I think he's in the water now."

"In the water?" Sarah put the headphones back on. Squeezed her eyes tight and tried to envision what was happening on that boat. What was happening to her friend, Jack Merchant.

As the cutter roared on the way to the trawler, she heard the gunfire finally go silent. She heard Jack breathing hard, swearing quietly to himself, as if he was hurt. She heard the teams from the three speedboats swarm the decks, heard them shouting, heard them calling clear, and running to check each of the wounded.

They started calling over the status: Billy Craig and Captain Prada wounded. Both of the SWAT guys badly hurt, one of them gasping up blood. Behind it all, Prada was talking a mile a minute, compulsively telling everyone what had happened, what he'd seen. Sarah heard someone speaking to Jack, his voice clear as if he were kneeling right beside him. "Prada says you're a goddamn hero, man."

And then she could hear them calling for Henriques. Beside her, the communications officer thumbed the mike to tell them to look over the side. But first, she heard the voice of the man who was presumably kneeling by Jack. "Hey, where's your partner?"

She heard Jack's voice. "Check the water."

"What?"

"How'd he get there?" the guy said to Jack.

"Ask him," Jack said. Then he apparently remembered he was on the mike. He switched it off.

Owen began to laugh, looking between her and the communications officer. "I gotta hear this. Henriques better have a pretty damn good wound, he ends up over the side while his buddies are in the middle of a firefight."

Minutes later, Henriques was pulled from the sea, alive and well. Not mark on him.

As Sarah sat over the plate of pancakes, the bunny ears soaked in syrup, she thought how incredible it was that such two different men could find themselves in much the same place.

George Henriques had been disgraced from that moment on. He said he had stood on the rail for a better vantage from which to shoot and had fallen over. None of other agents saw what happened. If Jack did, he wasn't saying. But Captain Prada had no compunction about telling everyone, including the local papers, what he'd seen: a DEA agent jumping overboard when the going got hot.

Jack's silence was enormous. He did, however, request and get a new partner. The DEA did what so many institutions do best in such circumstances. Publicly supported their agent. Privately, laid out the realities.

Henriques quit. To the very last, bitterly cursing Merchant for failing to exonerate him.

And now, Jack Merchant himself was enduring rumors of cowardice.

Incredible.

Yet, she'd endured even worse herself. And even if he didn't seem to know what she'd done, he seemed to sense that something was wrong with her. She wondered how it showed, what he saw in her face that made him ask.

Must have been the years of dealing with guilty people.

Almost without thinking, she said the words: "You don't seem to know what I did."

He was watching her steadily. "No. What?"

She took a deep breath. "I killed Owen."

5

MERCHANT WENT STILL. Finally, he said, "When?"

"About two years ago."

"Ah. Is this generally known? Or are you making a confession to me?"

Her lips moved, something approximating a smile. "It's known. Brief headlines. Domestic situation gone wrong. You see it in the papers all the time. Guess it didn't make it down to your newspapers in the Virgin Islands."

"Well," he said.

"Uh-huh."

He shoved the plates to the side. "Did he hit you?"

"Yes."

"Son of a bitch," Merchant said. "When did this start? And why didn't I know about it?"

"The worst of it happened after you left. You'd finished in Charlestown and moved on. His jealousy, it was nothing at first. Flattering, even. Toward the end, I could barely have a conversation with any guy without there being trouble. Including a guy I had working as a captain for me, Raul. Nice guy, about forty-five, wife and kid. Short, friendly. Bald head and one of those awful goatees, and I just liked the hell out of him and we would kid around when he would come to the office. Not flirting, just kidding around. But one night Owen beat him with a tire iron in the parking lot, and I called the cops and they came just in time to keep Owen from killing Raul."

"First time the police were in it?"

"Yes. Up until then, he'd hit me just once. Like all those women before me, I can't explain why I stayed with an abusive guy. He apologized like crazy, even let a few tears show. And I fell for it, feeling as lousy as I was about Joel. Owen was the only constant in my life, or at least that's what it seemed like." She gave a short, bitter laugh. "The fact is, he wasn't just after me, he was after my business."

"Package deal," Merchant said.

"Uh-huh. Not too glamorous, maybe. But he'd been bumming around since the Marines, and then my dad died and then Joel. Here was this woman who wasn't too bad looking and she had a business, a boat to live on. He figured he could have it all, work on the water just like he wanted. If he could only get the wifey in line, he could call the shots. Not a big ambition, but it was his."

"So this thing with Raul brought it to a head?"

"Oh, yeah. Raul wanted to press charges, and I agreed to testify. Owen tells me to lie, and I tell him to move his stuff off my boat, get out of my business, and never come back. He puts me in the hospital. I have him arrested, and he gets out on bail and comes pounding on my door in the middle of the night. I get a restraining order. Blah, blah, blah. You've read this story a gazillion times, you know."

Merchant waited.

"The trial's coming up for the assault charge on Raul. Owen calls me and tells me the kind of man he is, he's meant to be free on the ocean. 'I can't do time, babe, you know that,' he says."

"Telling you his hands are tied."

"That's right. Not his fault if he has to kill me. He's pushing it hard, this, why-are-you-doing-this-to-me attitude."

"Why didn't you call me?"

"What would you have done? Flown home?"

"Yes."

"My mistake. It seems to me you and I were just friends. Not even that necessarily. You were doing your job and I was a victim's sister."

"We were better than that," Merchant said. "You know it. Friends, at the very least."

"Maybe. Because I thought about calling you. I thought about it a lot. But you were undercover someplace, I didn't even know where. Besides, what could you do? Call the New Bedford cops and use your influence to get them to help me better? They were already doing their best. It just wasn't enough."

Merchant thought to argue with her. And then he shut up. He knew the way he had felt about her and how much he had hated to leave her with Owen's arm around her waist. But they'd seemed happy, and he had been on his way to Charleston. After that, the Virgin Islands and Miami. Never really looking back.

Sarah said, "You never know how alone you are until you're in a situation like this. There were people who wanted to help, but when you have someone like Owen coming after you with all the time in the world, it's not like they can watch you forever. Lou Grasso and his partner braced Owen, tried to scare some sense into him. Lou came to me after that, told me that Owen didn't scare. Lou wanted me to apply for a gun. He said that he would try to get the chief to approve it."

"Did he?"

"No. Chief is a political animal, and right then the wind was blowing against vigilante justice more than domestic abuse. He gave me a permit for Mace and suggested I take one of those self-defense courses."

"Jesus."

"Uh-huh. But that's what I did. Started working out in the evening, learning about kicks and gouging eyes. I started riding my bike, and running, trying to get strong. I mean there was no way I could take Owen in a fight. He outweighed me by eighty pounds and every bit of it muscle. But it's what I could do, and I did it."

"So how'd he come for you?"

"I was on the bike. The trial date was about two weeks out, and I couldn't sleep, and it was a good way to get going in the morning. I'd put in about twenty miles before breakfast, come home, take a quick swim just to cool off. He cut me off with his car near the beach. Said he wanted to talk to me. I got back on my bike and tried to take off, but he just pushed me over. Gave me a kick in the stomach, and stomped on the spokes of the bike while I was down.

I had the Mace in the pocket behind my back, and I went for that, and he knocked it out of my hand. I scrambled for it on my hands and knees, and when I got it in my left hand he stomped on my wrist. Broke it."

Merchant didn't say anything. She continued, her voice flat, as if this was a story she had related many times. He suspected she had. To herself, anyhow.

"I got to my feet and ran off toward the beach and he came after me. I mean, this probably wasn't a well-planned thing on his part. I expect he told himself he was just going to knock some sense into my head. And if I'd let him, that's the way it probably would've ended up. If I just took my beating."

"You tell that to the cops?"

"No. I'm telling you."

"OK."

"I'm a fast runner, but the beach was rocky and I was wearing bike shoes with cleats, and between the pain of my wrist, and me holding my left arm in my right, I'm all off balance. I'm just slipping around. He comes up and shoves me off my feet. And he keeps on doing it. Every time I almost get up, he shoves me down on these rocks. He's humming as he does it, showing he's in control, like I'm a dog, some sort of bad pet, and then he starts kicking me. Kicking me in the right spots: my knee, my stomach, a short one to my head. I'm still wearing the bike helmet and you know it's just Styrofoam under a plastic shell. And he has me on the ground and he puts his boot against the side of my helmet and I'm screaming, and, thank God, the helmet cracks before my head does.

" 'I could do that to your skull, Sarah,' he says.

"So I stop trying to get away. He kneels down beside me and puts his hand on my cheek the way he used to do. I'm pretty sure my knee is messed up and I know ribs are broken. And he says, 'Understand me, Sarah. You will get up on the stand and say you made a mistake earlier about Raul and me. That he brought the tire iron and attacked me. You will deny, deny, deny, and when they ask if I coerced you to say this, you will say no. You will say you got these bruises falling down the cabin way. And they will not believe you, but without your testimony, this will all go away. And then you and I will put this behind us. We'll have kids, we'll make the business work. We'll even have a nice house. Someday you'll be glad I put this all together for us. But for now, you're going to get up and get into my car.'"

Sarah looked at Merchant directly. "I hit him then. I got my hand around a rock, and I swung it as hard as I could into his temple. He put his hand around my throat, and then I did it again, and when I took my hand away, the rock stayed, I had shoved it that far into his head."

"And the police believed it all?"

"I was lucky. A lifeguard was just coming on duty then. She saw Owen kicking me and ran to call the cops. She didn't see me hit him."

"Self-defense," Merchant said. "You didn't just get away with it — that was the right call."

"I know that. I also know that there are women in prison with murder charges for the same type of thing."

Merchant nodded. Lot happened under the heading of "Life's Unfair." Something he reminded himself of from time to time.

He wanted nothing more than to put his arms around her and hold her, and tell her that she did everything she could, and that everything would work out fine. But from the rigid way she was holding herself, he could see that she wasn't looking for hugs and kisses.

"So no package deals," he said.

"No package deals. Do you still want to work for me?"

"Sure I do."

"Scared?"

He laughed. "Just a little."

She sat back, looking as if a weight had been taken from her. "This is good, Jack. This is very good."

Merchant looked at his watch. "We better get ready for your banker."

"All right," she said. "After that, I'd like to know what happened in Miami."

"Sounds like we'll have plenty of time in the next few days."

She took his hands in hers again and squeezed. Trying to ham it up a little and not quite succeeding. "Glad to have you on my team, Jack."

6

THOMAS TOOK the stairs.

At the fourth floor, he paused. Still breathing easily, not a trace of sweat on his coffee-colored skin, his heart rate barely elevated. He made his way down the hall to the apartment. The building was hardly the worst dump he'd ever been in. But, then, in his forty-eight years, he'd found his way into a lot of dumps.

Even more since he'd moved here to New York.

The hallway made him feel he was in a low-rent hotel rather than an apartment building: hung ceilings, a dark green wall-to-wall carpeting, and heavy gold wallpaper that did a wonderful job of holding on to dirty handprints. If he had been susceptible to such things, he would've found the place depressing and claustrophobic.

He hoped the girl hadn't screamed.

Then again, it was the sort of place where most people would know to mind their business. And with hookers, screams were a pretty standard part of the repertoire.

He tapped on the door quietly.

Thomas heard quick footsteps on the other side. He figured his new client was peering out at him through the peephole. He could also figure what he else he was going to find in that apartment. Maybe she had laughed or been unimpressed. Maybe she had lost that girl-next-door look his client had been seeking that night.

Whatever the reason, she had done something to cause his client to call Thomas at three in the morning. The man's voice had been surprisingly calm. "You better be as good as I've been told."

Thomas sighed. Part of him thinking he should do himself and the whole world a favor and put a bullet through that peephole right now.

But he didn't.

That was no way to get rich.

7

GENE RADOCCIA KEPT SARAH and Merchant waiting in the third-floor lobby of the MassBank building on State Street for almost a half an hour before he waved them into his office.

Radoccia appeared to be in his early forties, a heavyset man with close-cropped dark, curly hair. He had quick, intelligent eyes. His tie was pulled askew, and there was a damp spot on his leg as if he'd recently sponged something off. He caught Sarah looking and grinned. "Egg salad. Lunch at my desk. Banker's hours aren't what they used to be."

Both Merchant and Sarah had changed into business clothes. He had brought along a small camera bag holding a camera body, short zoom, and flash. Sarah was dressed in a conservative gray suit that still couldn't hide the vibrancy of her body.

Sarah introduced the two of them. Radoccia shook hands with them quickly and then crumpled up the paper bag on his desk and tossed it into the trash can. "So, Sarah — may I call you Sarah?"

"Sure."

"I understand from Shelly you've done a lot of work for us before. I'm calling you up myself, because this one's in the family, so to speak."

"I appreciate the opportunity," Sarah said.

Radoccia shuffled through his desk folders and pulled out a

manila file. He peered into it and said, "Here we go. I understand you were asking for some more information. Here's a printout on the Baylors' credit card purchases that Shelly told you about." Radoccia passed along a statement copy to Sarah before he turned his attention to Merchant.

"So I understand you're being brought in for surveillance?"

"Partially."

"And what's your experience, Jack?"

Merchant quickly outlined his DEA background.

"OK," Radoccia said. "Sounds impressive." He looked to Sarah, then said, "You two seem to have what we need. So why's it taking so long for you to find the Baylors and their boat?"

Sarah said, "As I understand it, neither have the police. Or the Coast Guard. I don't pretend to have their resources."

Radoccia waved her comment away as if it were nonsensical. "Look, if you can't do this, Shelly tells me there's other resources we can bring in." Radoccia held Sarah's eyes with his. "I'll give you one week. I'll want an answer by next Friday."

Sarah said, "I can't guarantee that."

Radoccia lifted his shoulders. "Do you want to pass on this one?"

"No, I would not." Her voice toneless.

Radoccia didn't seem to be too worried about it. "Fine, then." He turned to the calendar on his computer and made a quick note. "Friday it is. I'm sorry I'm pressing you so hard, but believe me, I'm getting it from the top."

He smiled in a way Merchant figured he probably thought was regretful. "Best of luck. You know how it is once someone's got a toe in the door."

"Yes, I know," Sarah said. "You're saying I deliver or screw the past twelve years of business my company has been doing day in and day out for MassBank."

"Twelve years? You must have started when you were an infant."

Sarah's face flushed. "Eight for my father, four for me. I've been delivering —"

"Stop, please." Radoccia held up his hand. "I'm sorry. I don't need to know this. As long as you understand the urgency and the consequences, nothing more need be said."

"I understand the consequences," she said. "And you need to understand, Gene, that I've been delivering successfully in the past years since my father passed away and I fully intend to continue this year, next year, and into the foreseeable future."

"Point taken. And as an incentive, let's say that if you find the Baylors themselves, you'll get a commission not only on the boat but on the home mortgage as well."

"Well, thank you, Gene. But that's a bit down the road."

"Still, it would be significant."

"It's a long ways away," she said, evenly. "At this point I'm sure the bank has issued the demand for payment, but you've got foreclosure proceedings, settlement of their assets — not to mention getting the court to formally determine their status: missing, deceased, running."

Radoccia seemed to relent. "Tell me about it," he said. "But you find the boat, you'll get your fee on that."

"Uh-huh. I just have to do it in record time, with the threat of losing my best customer held over my head," she said.

Radoccia shrugged. "Point taken. OK, you want a real carrot to go with the stick, if you find them in the time frame I gave you, then I'll authorize a fifty percent additional bonus on your fee. How's that?"

"A hundred percent would better."

"Seventy-five," Radoccia said. "Take it."

It was her turn to shrug. "All right. I like carrots. How about expenses?"

"I've got no problem with reasonable travel expenses. Good enough?"

"That's fine," Sarah said

Radoccia turned to Merchant. "I bet you'll find them with the boat. Paul loved that goddamn thing. That's where I see you coming in with surveillance. Because I don't want you approaching them directly, not unless you're going to lose them. Then chain the *Fresh Air* to the dock or whatever you do. I want to talk to Paul myself."

"Why's that?" Merchant said.

Radoccia looked surprised at the question. "I want an answer. And our president, Bill Tyler, he wants an answer. Why'd Paul take off like this? If he convinced Julie it was time for their midlife crisis, more power to him. But running off like this and leaving the bank and his debts behind is just unconscionable. Their home we've foreclosed on, but the boat's security was tied in to their home equity . . : it's a mess."

Merchant said, "What makes you so sure they took off? Sounds like they left a lot behind."

"I may be wrong. Maybe they capsized out there or hit a rock or a whale, I don't know. I'm no sailor. But I'm suspicious about twenty grand in cash, and I'm suspicious about a hundred K wired off to the Caymans. That's just how I see it."

"Was their vacation scheduled all along, or was it a spur of the minute sort of thing?"

"No, scheduled for months."

"So why'd they leave so many assets behind if they had months to plan it?"

"You tell me. Or better, do what I'm hiring you for and get me in front of Paul so I can ask him myself."

"Any question that he took more than his own money out?"

"Lot of questions," Radoccia said. "So far, the answer seems to be no. First thing we looked at when we realized he wasn't coming home from vacation. Paul was the vice president of our venture capital arm. In theory, if one were of a mind to embezzle funds, that's not a bad position to be in. Create a dummy corporation on paper, and invest. In reality, it would be pretty hard, because nobody does anything alone in a bank, and I'm not ready to take on a big conspiracy theory. But for the past month, we've had auditors checking his books and visiting the companies where he made investments."

"Any venture capital between MassBank and his wife's company?" Merchant asked.

Radoccia sighed. Patiently answering these obvious questions. "The very second thing we looked for. No. There's policy against it anyhow, for just this sort of thing. But no. If there's embezzlement, we can't find it."

"Even so, we need to talk to his secretary," Sarah said. "We'd like to look through his office, look into his computer. Maybe there's something that'll at least give us a direction to where to find him."

"Well, the auditors have been doing that . . . but I guess some fresh eyes won't hurt."

He picked up his phone and asked his secretary to have Paul

Baylor's secretary come to his office. "Marcia will be right down," he said after hanging up. "She's very thorough, but a bit on the defensive side. She worked for Baylor for years and isn't thrilled by the scrutiny she's been getting."

"Were you friends with him?"

Radoccia lifted his hands and dropped them on his desktop. "If you'd asked me that before he took off, I would've said, 'Sure.' At those office party things we'd sometimes huddle in the corner and make wiseass comments to pass the time. I never had reason to question his honesty, if that's what you mean. I'd say he seemed to like his job pretty well, but you'll see in his office, all the sailing pictures, his boat was his passion. And his wife, Julie, the guy was crazy about her in a way you don't always see in married couples. From a divorced guy like me, I guess I'd say he was a bit weird in that regard."

"How about money problems?"

"Never said anything about it. He had a lot of expenses going out, what with the boat and house. But he had a generous salary, and I expect Julie was doing OK too. But you never know, not when it comes to money. Not how much people need or how much they *think* they need."

There was a knock on the door and a woman walked in. She was probably in her mid-thirties, dark haired, attractive in a brittle sort of way.

"Marcia, thanks for coming down." Radoccia introduced them all and said, "I'd like you to help them go through Paul's office, show them around."

She looked at them, her lips compressed. But she nodded and said, "All right."

Radoccia looked at his watch, then took out a business card from his breast pocket. He turned it over and began writing on the back. "I've got to run. Here's my home number, fax, and e-mail. If you find the Baylors, keep your distance, get me some photos so I can ID them."

"No problem," Sarah said.

Radoccia looked up. "Can you scan the photos and send them over e-mail?"

Sarah looked at Merchant.

"Sure. I'll bring a digital camera along."

"Ah, it's a pleasure doing business . . ." Radoccia stood up and began to herd Merchant and Sarah politely to the door. Marcia went ahead and waited in the hallway.

Radoccia said, "OK, we clear? You find the boat, call me, and I'll probably ask you to sit on it a day or two, make sure they're not coming back. You find *them*, call me and I'll come day or night, so I can walk up to Paul and ask him on behalf of MassBank and myself, 'Paul, old buddy, old pal, just what the hell were you think-ing?' "

He touched the two of them on the shoulders, checked his watch again, and if Merchant could read him accurately, Radoccia's mind was fully engaged on something else before the door was shut behind them.

Marcia started off quickly. She remained a step ahead on the way to the elevator. Sarah looked at Merchant and raised an eyebrow.

Once the three of them were alone in the elevator, Merchant said, "We appreciate your showing us around."

Marcia nodded abruptly, but said nothing.

"We're primarily looking for the boat," Sarah said.

"OK," she said.

The elevator door opened, and she strode away. They followed.

"Here's Paul's office," she said, taking out a key. "I ask that you go through it neatly, and put things back. I've already straightened up after the auditor's ransack. And I must insist that you don't take anything away without letting me sign it out. In particular, we're concerned about our customer records."

She opened the door to a good-size corner office. The view of Boston Harbor was breathtaking. As Radoccia had mentioned, Paul Baylor's enthusiasm for sailing was instantly apparent. Some of it — the half model of a Nathaniel Herreshoff S-Boat on the wall, the framed America's Cup prints — could have been taken for stock nautical decoration. But the wall to Merchant's right as he walked through the door, the wall that Baylor would have faced from his desk — that wall showed Baylor's passion. There were maybe a dozen pictures in all.

Merchant looked at them with a professional interest and a touch of envy. Damned banker coming up with some shots that would rival his own.

He said to Marcia, "I take it he's interested in photography?"

"Oh yes," she said. "One of his hobbies."

There were a number of candids of Baylor, his wife, and the *Fresh Air*. Julie Baylor coming up from the cabin with a plate of shrimp. A black-and-white portrait of her on a beach somewhere, the sunlight warm on her face. She looked at him with an expression somewhere between wifely indulgence and affection. Someone had taken a photo of Baylor and his wife under sail. Typical enough stern-on shot of the boat sailing away, but Merchant could see she moved sweetly. Early morning scene of fog shot with brilliant sun on the bay. Another from the viewpoint of a boat in harbor, surrounded by a half dozen sailboats aground in a mudflat, their masts canted to the sky, red bottoms showing.

"Cuttyhunk," Merchant said.

Sarah looked over his shoulder. "That low tide surprises a lot of people."

"Not Baylor though. From his view here, he was still in deep water."

Marcia spoke up behind them. "Paul's a very good sailor."

Merchant turned. "Is that right?"

"Loved that boat."

"Have you ever been out on it?"

She nodded. "Several times. My husband and I."

Merchant heard a slight inflection on "husband" but didn't comment. Maybe she didn't want them to think there was anything going on between her and her boss.

"What kind of guy was he to work for?"

"I like him," she said. "And he's smart."

"Lot of ego?"

She shook her head. "Not that kind of guy at all. Good at his job, but not full of himself."

"How was his marriage?"

"I was his secretary, not his sister."

"Still, what do you think?" Sarah said.

Marcia smiled faintly. "I think he was delighted with her. He always lit up when she called. Paul is a fairly introverted sort of guy. I mean he does fine with the clients, and he knows numbers and knows how to smell the value of a company. Loved his work. But for personal stuff, I think Julie was it. She was his world. And sailing his boat."

"You think it was reciprocal between him and Mrs. Baylor?"

"Seemed to be. But again, I'm just his secretary."

"What do you think about him taking off?"

Her eyes narrowed slightly, but she said, evenly enough, "I really don't know what to think. In the beginning, I didn't believe it. I was the first to call the Coast Guard because I couldn't believe Paul would be overdue like this unless they got into trouble with the boat. And I was pretty outraged when the auditors started looking at his records, looking for embezzlement. But what can I say? It is strange the withdrawals he made, the transfer of his assets. The twenty thousand in cash was taken out in two installments just before they left. It looked like he was trying to hide something, you know, keeping it under the ten-thousand-dollar limit. I guess you never know the people you work with. Never really know people at all."

"That's a motto to live by," Sarah said, opening Paul Baylor's right-hand desk drawer. "C'mon, Jack, let's get to it."

They spent the next two hours in Baylor's office, going through his files. They had Marcia open his computer files, and they quickly skimmed folder after folder, looking for anything personal.

Baylor seemed to have a full life. Business meetings clearly noted on his calendar software. Like Marcia had said, dinner dates with his wife, Wednesday night sailing races highlighted for the month. Task file included notes about buying spare clevis pins for the boat along with seeking due diligence reports from companies with investment potential.

Merchant looked back at Baylor's calendar. Saw that two weeks were blocked out under "vacation." He said, "How long in advance was this vacation scheduled?"

"Months," Marcia said.

"He leave right on time?"

"A little early," she said, "one day."

"Was he burning the midnight oil right until he took off?"

"I wouldn't say that, but he seemed to have a lot to do to get ready for his trip."

"Must've screwed things up. Busy guy like that leaves early."

"A bit. But I rescheduled everything."

"That typical of him to cut out early before vacation?"

"No. And he was in a good bit of the time. But not taking meetings. Besides, bosses ask for this kind of thing all the time."

"What kind of thing?" Sarah said.

"Just cover for me," Marcia said.

"Those were his words?" Sarah asked.

"That's right."

"Had he ever asked you to do that before?"

"Never," Marcia said. "First and last."

Merchant and Sarah peppered Marcia with more questions about Baylor. Where he grew up? Did he have a vacation home? Where had he and Julie vacationed in the past? Who were his friends?

She told them what she knew. Some of it she had known already, some of it she had gleaned over the past few weeks in trying to track him down via the phone: Paul Baylor grew up in Michigan, went to school at UMass Amherst. Met Julie about nine years ago when he was at a computer show in New York. He and Julie vacationed almost exclusively on their boat.

"How about friends?" Merchant said.

Marcia shook her head. "He knew lots of people, but I wouldn't say he had lots of buddies. Don't know about her, though."

"Nobody called him to go see a game, grab a beer after work?"

"Not that type of guy," Marcia said. "Go to the marina after work, yes, meet Julie for dinner, yes. I expect they had some couples they hung out with or went sailing with, but I really don't know about that."

"His wife, his boat, his work," Merchant said.

"That's about it," she said. "That's Paul."

When Merchant and Sarah stepped out of the bank, it was just before noontime. They blinked in the bright sunlight, surrounded by the rush of the lunchtime crowd.

"Hate this part of the job," Sarah said. "I make promises like crazy, then scratch my head and say, 'Now what do I do?'"

Merchant said, "How about we start with you buying me lunch?"

"Sure, I've got an expense account." They stopped at a sausage stand, and both ordered subs. Sarah grabbed a Coke and chips; Merchant, a big bottle of iced tea. They found a bench a block away from the MassBank tower and ate in silence.

Merchant looked over at Sarah attacking her sub and would have laughed if he wasn't so busy stuffing himself. He remembered she had a great appetite. Feeding that engine that could work hours and hours, making calls, dealing with all kinds of people, living with confrontation as a way of life, and now, apparently, working out like crazy.

He said, "I thought you athletic types ate healthy. So far I've seen bacon, pancakes, sausage, and chips."

"I just burn it." She licked her fingers with all the delicacy of a cat. "Ready to work?"

Merchant tossed the remaining quarter of his sub into the paper bag and threw it in a nearby trash can. "You bet, boss."

"Ooh," she said, shivering. "Years I've waited for you to come back and call me that."

Merchant took the envelope and laid the contents out on the bench between them. There was more than just the credit card summary. There were ATM and checking charges, including photocopies of the returned checks.

The credit card report included the past month's expenses, just under four thousand dollars' worth. There was a canceled mortgage check of twenty-six hundred dollars, and the credit card report showed lots of household goods expenses, groceries, a number of Boston area restaurant tabs, a fair amount of activity at the marina store. The checking account showed several payments to the marina yard, with just just over five thousand dollars two days before they left. There was a marina charge on the day of their departure for fifty-three dollars.

"Most likely fuel," Merchant said.

"Uh-huh."

The only credit card bills that popped up as out of state were the very last three entries. They looked like restaurant or bar bills: the Seagull in Portsmouth and Rollie's Cajun Kitchen in Portland. The only ATM activity out of state was the attempted New York City withdrawal.

"Eating and drinking their way up the coast," Sarah said. "Sounds like the start of a nice vacation. The Seagull sounds to me like a fish place, maybe a breakfast place. Rollie's Cajun Kitchen, enough said. So it looks as if they were in Portsmouth the second day of their trip, Portland the fourth. Figure something happened between Portland and Bar Harbor."

"Seem weird to you that there are no dock fees along the way up?"

Sarah said, "Maybe. If they were chugging along on a stinkpot like mine, I'd say definitely. But you sailors are such cheapskates. They could be staying on moorings, even anchoring."

"I guess so. And if it's a mooring, it's easier to just hand the kid in the Whaler fifteen bucks in cash rather than rack up a credit card. And with twenty thousand with them, cash is hardly a problem. Couple of days out, they should have enough food onboard without a trip back to the grocery store. So it doesn't have to mean anything."

"And we figure they got the fuel before they left."

"Something was definitely up, though," Merchant said. "The way Baylor cleaned out his office, the computer, that much cash."

She nodded. "Oh, sure. Radoccia's talking to himself, saying there's no embezzlement. Give it time, it'll come out."

"That's not our problem, though."

"Nope."

"It seems to me we've got a couple ways we can go here," Merchant said. "Talk to Julie's co-workers, talk to the sister, check out the house and the marina, see if anybody overheard anything. Maybe whoever pumped the fuel."

Sarah pointed at the five-thousand-dollar marina charge a week in advance of the Baylors' departure date. "Maybe see if they said anything to the clerk . . . After that, well, we drive. Bar Harbor and points in between."

"Long way to go on so little information."

"Welcome to my life," she said.

8

SARAH DECIDED they should stop at Digi.com, Julie Baylor's company, before going out to the house. The company occupied a small redbrick building overlooking the Charles River on the Cambridge side.

They went into the lobby. It was designed to make an impression, with leather couches and armchairs juxtaposed with a freestanding basketball net. A regulation-size basketball sat on a stand on the receptionist's desk with a placard reading: GO FOR IT!

The receptionist had bright orange hair, a pretty face, and a small diamond stud in her left nostril. She was wearing tight leather pants and a red Digi.com T-shirt.

Sarah held back a half step, letting Merchant go forward.

The girl said, "About time I got some company. What's up?"

Merchant introduced himself and Sarah, and said they had been hired by MassBank to help find Julie and Paul Baylor.

The receptionist looked blank momentarily, but then said, "Oh, her. You know, I'm new here. I came in right before she scammed. Do you have an appointment with somebody?"

Merchant apparently chose not to hear her last question.

Good boy, Sarah thought.

He said, "Ah, that's too bad. I guess you couldn't have heard much that would help us."

"I pay attention."

Sarah drifted back to look at the magazines on the coffee table. *Wired, Stuff, Details,* a bunch of web books, a couple of staid *Business Weeks* thrown in there too.

The girl said, "Who are you with again?"

"We were hired by MassBank to find the Baylors," Merchant said.

"Like private detectives? Bounty hunters?"

"Sort of." Sarah saw him grin at the girl. Boyish charm, now. She let her own face grow a little stiff and saw the girl notice it and lean closer to Merchant.

Tramp.

"Cool," the girl said. "So who did you want to see?"

"Maybe you could help me figure that out — who knew her well?"

The girl raised her hands. "That's easy. Cal. He's the boss, and the two of them went way back."

"Is he in?"

"Oh, sure. Where is the question. He doesn't sit still." She picked up the phone, and they watched her make the rounds through the building. "Hi, it's Lia," she'd say. "Cal there?"

Sarah could see her look over at Merchant as she made each of the calls, seeing if he appreciated her effort. Sarah picked up a company brochure. They were clearly trying to distance themselves from the Internet failures of the past: *"Digi.com's infrastructure offerings are fully aligned to enable your business to thrive within the new realities of the marketplace . . ."*

Blah, blah, blah. The stuff made Sarah sleepy. She sure hoped she could make her repo business work out, because God only knew what she'd do if she had to go work for someone else.

On her fourth call Lia apparently found Cal and said there were "detectives, sort of" in the lobby who wanted to talk about Julie Baylor.

She put the phone down. "He's on his way."

"Thanks, Lia," Merchant said.

"D'nada." She looked at Merchant. "You know, I read once how people have their work husbands and wives? Real ones at home, and platonic and sometimes not so platonic ones at work."

"Can't say I've read that," Merchant said.

The girl met Sarah's eyes and raised her voice slightly to include her. "Is that what you two are?"

Merchant said, "I'm not sure what we are."

Sarah said, "No."

The girl pealed with sudden laughter. She put her hand on Merchant's arm and said, "Well then, maybe you and I should share an office sometime. Maybe we could be office mates."

He laughed, and she grinned back at him.

"Made you blush," she said.

"Sure did."

At that moment, a tall, thin man with dark hair came through the double doors behind the receptionist's desk. She turned and said, "Cal, you should give my friends Sarah and Jack a big kiss. They're looking for your sweetie."

"Lia, your mouth runs about triple times your brains," Cal said.

"I'd say that's about right."

Perky, Sarah thought. *Make me yack.*

"No more calls for a bit," Cal said.

"Wow, just like a real executive."

Sarah stepped forward and introduced herself and Merchant. She handed Cal her card.

"So you're the owner of the company?" he asked.

"That's right," Sarah said.

Over Cal's shoulder, Merchant saw Lia widen her eyes at the change in dynamics.

"All right," he said. "Let's go down to Julie's office."

He led them down a wide hallway. The building was fairly new, but it had been trimmed with varnished wood beams, giving it the effect of an old factory. Before a bank of cubicles there was a common area with a pool table to the left and an old pinball machine. Neither was in use.

As they continued on, Sarah noticed that more than a few of the cubicles were unoccupied, save for the detritus of the past owners: blank computer monitors, wall calendars, the occasional small chalkboard.

Halfway down the hall, a black standard poodle stretched across the floor. He didn't move for them, and Sarah and Merchant followed Cal's lead and walked around the dog.

"Casual place here," Sarah said.

"I encourage it."

"So did Jack," Sarah said, looking over her shoulder. "That Lia is a cutie."

Cal laughed. "Yeah, she is. She can also be a pain. Multiply that personality by forty-two employees, and you should see what it's like trying to get anything done around here. Everybody smart as hell, but trying to prove it every minute of the day."

"You look like you have room for a few more," Sarah said, nodding toward one of the empty cubicles.

"Oh, sure. We're down to half of what we once were. Best thing that could have happened to us. Forced us to sharpen our focus and structure around the realities of the marketplace."

"OK," Sarah said. She didn't need the sales pitch.

Cal let them into Julie Baylor's office. It was good sized, with a view of the river. Maybe not as spectacular as her husband's at the bank, but in appearances anyhow, Sarah could see that Julie Baylor was a force within Digi.com. Cal perched on the edge of her desk and waved them to chairs around the small meeting table in the corner. "Anyhow . . . I was expecting you."

"You were?" Sarah said.

"Gene Radoccia called me. Said you'd be looking for the boat. I said I'd be glad to help if it helps us find Julie."

"I didn't realize you knew Mr. Radoccia."

"We've been in contact over the Baylors, of course." He looked at Sarah's card again, and said, "Marine Liquidation. So you're a repo . . . woman?"

"That's right."

"Loved the movie."

"Everybody does."

"No offense, but I've got to say, I'm not too happy that finding Julie is being relegated to this level. Julie's not only a key employee, but also a good friend. I'm thinking they're lost at sea, and I'd like to see her body recovered and buried."

"There's no evidence she's dead," Sarah said.

"Yes, there is," Cal said, looking at each of them. "You don't know Julie. I do. She's grown this business with me from scratch. I don't see any reason why she'd just take off like this."

Sarah said, "I appreciate that. But I've been in this business for a long time —" She saw his skeptical look and managed a winning smile. "Family business. I've been involved since I was thirteen. Anyhow, wives don't know why husbands take off, and vice versa. Never mind office buddies, no matter how good."

Cal shook his head, but didn't argue the point further.

Merchant said, "Did she say anything to suggest she was leaving for longer than two weeks?"

Sarah added, "Extra big hug when she took off for vacation? Advice on how to live your life?"

Cal said, "I was out of town the day she left." He waved around her office. "Radoccia told me you checked out Paul's office, you're welcome to do the same here. Go for it."

Cal stopped back about an hour later. "Made any progress?"

"Can't say that we have," Sarah said. She was behind the desk going through the drawer files one more time. Merchant was at the standing file cabinet.

They had much the same impression that they'd formed in Paul Baylor's office: they seemed to have stepped into the middle of a busy person's life as if she'd just stepped out for the night.

Sarah looked past Cal to the wall. Like her husband, Julie Baylor had lots of photos on the wall.

A couple of them were the same as the ones in her husband's office. The boats aground in Cuttyhunk. The fog scene on the bay.

Cal saw Sarah looking at the pictures. "Loved that boat, Julie and Paul."

"You ever go out with them?"

"Couple times. I have my own. Power. I'm a little too impatient to wait for the wind."

Sarah got up from the desk and looked at the photos more closely. There were more people shots. There was a shot of Julie with a young woman, the Boston skyline behind them. The younger woman had light brown hair, and looked somewhat similar to Julie.

"Her sister?" Sarah said to Cal.

He nodded. "Emily. Her younger sister."

"And these are work related, I'd guess?"

"That's right." Cal pointed to a group shot of about thirty people inside what looked like on old refurbished factory floor. The group was circled around a younger Cal, dressed in jeans and a

T-shirt. Julie Baylor was right beside him, the only one dressed in a business suit. Computers were lined up on long lunchroom-type tables; a thick mess of cables ran under each.

"The original Digi.com crew," Cal said. "Julie goes back to the start-up five years ago."

"What was her role?"

"Sales, at first. She was it. Then we were able to scrape up enough capital to hire a staff of four, and she was the sales manager. Now she's the VP of sales and service. Of course, with a web-based enterprise like ours, service *is* sales. More than half of our employees report to her."

"She good?"

"Made us profitable."

"Really?" Sarah looked at him. "A dot-com actually making a profit?"

Cal laughed. "Damn right. Besides, the name is a bit of a misnomer. We're not a dot-com, we're building and servicing infrastructure for dot-coms."

"Meaning?" Sarah asked.

"Software for streaming video and editing. Important stuff for the dot.coms of the world, particularly after the shakeout in the last couple of years. Most of the companies that survived are trying to bridge the gap between the Net and television, and we've designed some remarkable new enabling technology to make that possible."

"So Julie got venture capital?"

"No. Well, not directly. I did that, along with our CFO. But she kept pulling in the revenue. And not only has that kept us in business but it's a great showcase for investors. They tend to hold every real customer you have under a magnifying glass to see if the same thing can be replicated a couple of million times."

Cal seemed to remember he was talking to a couple of repo geeks. "Any case," he said. "Julie's important to our efforts, and I can't see why she'd just take off." He gestured to the photo of the old factory floor. "We've come a long way. Most of that gang there is gone. She stuck with me — and now's the time to be reaping the profits. That's why it doesn't make sense for her to run. I just don't get it."

"She's got stock options?" Sarah asked.

"Fistfuls," Cal said. "She's a savvy businesswoman and knew how to take care of herself. We're on our way to an IPO."

"Haven't heard anyone say that for a while," Merchant said.

Cal laughed. "No kidding. That's why I can't see Sarah jumping now. If she stuck around she'd have a shot at being rich."

Merchant said, "How rich?"

"Hard to say for sure. Millions certainly. Tens of millions, maybe. *I* wouldn't leave if I were her, would you?"

Sarah shrugged. She wasn't paid to explain why people did what they did.

Merchant moved off to the side, looking at more pictures.

Sarah looked over his shoulder. Julie was posed in grin-and-grip business photo with a tall blond man and another woman. The other woman was simply breathtaking. She appeared to be in her mid-twenties, dark auburn hair, flawless skin, high cheekbones, blue eyes.

"Who's this?" Sarah asked, pointing at the man.

"He's an investor," Cal said.

"And her?"

"That's Michelle Amarro. She was one of our employees."

"She's beautiful," Sarah said. "Was she good friends with Julie?"

"Friendly, I'd say, but not friends."

"Can we talk to her?"

Cal's lips tightened. As if he were steeling himself for something. He said, "God, I wish you could. She died."

"How?" Sarah said.

"It was awful. She committed suicide about three months ago."

Sarah paused. The name clicked. "Didn't I read about this?"

"Probably," Cal said. "The newspapers were all over it for about a week. She jumped off the roof of the Richmond Hotel in Boston. Terrible thing."

"That's right, I did read about that," Sarah said. "But you say she and Julie weren't close?"

"They knew each other, but that's about it. This picture they were just together talking to an investor at some function or other. Doing their jobs."

Cal touched the glass, touching the images of two employees. One dead for sure, the other, quite possibly.

"Jesus," he said. "It's been a hell of a year."

9

"YOU DRIVE THE BEAST, I'll make some calls," Sarah said when they reached the parking lot. They'd changed back into jeans and T-shirts in the rest rooms at Digi.com. She looked like she was comfortably back in her own skin.

Merchant swung behind the wheel. She put her sneakered foot up on the dashboard and pulled her cell phone out of her purse. "Here goes. I spend my life on the phone in this damn truck."

The Beast was a big black Ford with an extended cab, double wheels on the rear axle, set up for towing. No doubt a repo itself.

The first call Sarah made was to Julie Baylor's sister, Emily. She was in. Sarah leaned back and closed her eyes as the sister apparently vented. Once in a while, Sarah would say, "I understand . . . yes, I can see how you'd feel that way . . ."

Sarah hung up. "She's like our friend Cal — times ten. She's bullshit that the only people looking for her sister are a couple of hacks looking to repossess the boat."

"Can't blame her."

"Maybe you'll feel different after she gets in your face," Sarah said. "She's going to meet us at the house."

Then Sarah called her office in New Bedford, took her messages from her office manager, Lenny, and put in another five minutes listening and mollifying and telling him how to manage the boatyard part-timers she had cleaning and refurbishing the boats for resale.

After she hung up from that call, she closed her eyes briefly and laid her head back. "Don't ever hire people, Jack. They make you crazy."

She sighed, opened her eyes, and reached under the seat to pull up a dog-eared copy of the Boaters Almanac. "This is my hobby. Banging through the marinas from Boston to Maine."

She punched in the first number and said to Merchant while the number rang, "Listen up, bucko. Your turn is coming soon."

Someone answered on the other end, and she said cheerfully, "Hi, this is Sarah with Ballard Marine Liquidation. Could I speak to the manager?"

Merchant listened to her make about a dozen calls on the drive over. About half the calls, the marina manager wasn't in or wouldn't take the call. Of those who were, only a few were willing to take the time to look in their visitor logs. None of them remembered the *Fresh Air* out of Boston.

When Merchant and Sarah pulled into the driveway of the Baylors' home in Sudbury, they had yet to learn a thing.

The sister wasn't there yet. Sarah said she was going to call the Baylors' marina in Salem and make an appointment for the next day. Merchant got out of the truck to leave her to it.

The Baylors' home was a good-size colonial finished with a natural wood stain. It was quite new, with expensive windows, skylights, and a three-season porch off to the right. The asphalt driveway led up to a two-car garage. There was a turnaround to the left of the garage with a basketball post and net. An aluminum skiff with a small outboard was parked on a trailer in front of the net.

Merchant walked up to the garage and peered into the windows. There was a new Audi in the left-hand space. The right was empty. He could see two bicycles hanging from the ceiling, nice-looking ones. A well-kept workbench gleamed with tools.

Merchant looked over at the truck and saw Sarah was apparently listening to someone ramble along on the phone. She made a rolling head gesture and sank down into her seat as if she were drowning in quicksand. But Merchant heard her answer politely enough, "No kidding?"

He walked around to the back of the house. There was an in-ground pool with an attached hot tub. Big redwood deck. A sprawling backyard. The grass was neatly cut, but the place wasn't particularly manicured.

He thought about that. The fresh-cut lawn smell. Someone had been keeping up with the grass.

There was a fence surrounding the yard and, beyond that, woods. Conservation land, most likely. There was no neighbor to the left of the house, but to the right there was another home about a hundred yards away.

Merchant went up onto the deck and peered in through the sliding door glass into the kitchen. Impressive — a commercial-style gas stove with a big stainless steel hood. Copper-bottomed fry pans hanging alongside, expensive looking knives on a magnetized wall rack. Marble countertops. An island, also marble topped, separating the dining area from the kitchen. He could see a big flagstone fireplace beyond the dining area, a living room off the main entrance.

In short, the Baylors had a nice place.

Merchant was already getting the feel of a relatively young couple with an ample income, no children, and the ability to surround themselves with nice things. Not particularly ostentatious. Just treating themselves well.

Merchant couldn't fault them for it, but a part of him still did. Nothing but old green-eyed envy, he was sure.

He rejoined Sarah in the front. She was still making calls.

He leaned against the truck. He was hungry and, honestly, a bit tired. It had been a while since he had worked for a living. He checked his watch. It was a little after six o'clock.

He rapped on the truck door.

Sarah looked over at him.

"Going to invite myself over for dinner. The neighbors."

She put her hand over the phone. "Make sure they set a plate for me."

The neighbors' house was a colonial, too. Perhaps a bit smaller than the Baylors', but a far busier place.

Two cars in the driveway. One a minivan, the other a battered Volkswagen. There was a mountain bike lying on the walkway, a plastic basketball stand and hoop in front of the garage. A bright yellow plastic gingerbread house was visible on the side yard. The place said, "Kids."

And when Merchant rang the buzzer, there was the trooping

movement inside the house that meant his assessment was right. "Ma!" he heard someone call. "The door! Someone's here."

More movement. Sounds of footsteps.

"Just a minute, just a minute," he heard.

A redheaded woman opened the door. She was probably in her mid to late thirties, and she looked tired. "Yes?" The smell of cooking, people, and a distant diaper pail wafted out.

He smiled. "Got you at a bad time?"

"Any time's a bad time. What's up?" she said, glancing over her shoulder and then almost stumbling as a toddler, a boy, Merchant thought, slipped directly between her legs and sat on her feet. She said, "Oh, Andy, for goodness' sake!"

She gave a small shake of her head as if to clear it, and then said, "If you're selling, please, don't waste your time and especially not mine."

"I'm not selling," Merchant said. "I'm looking for the Baylors, and I was wondering if I could ask you some questions." He showed her Sarah's business card with his own name scratched in and said he was trying to track down the sailboat.

She made a sound somewhere between laughing and crying. The laugh slightly ahead. "You don't know the Baylors, I guess. Nice people from what I can tell, but we move in different circles. Them in business, me circling around the high school, elementary school, and the day-care center. Throw in the grocery store. You want to know about somebody in those circles, you came to the right woman."

Merchant had the sense she was talking fast to cover something.

"Perhaps one of your kids might know something," he said. "I noticed that the Baylors' lawn was mowed, and I was wondering . . ."

He saw her lips tighten, and then the woman said, quietly, "I've got to tell you something. This really stinks. No, it *sucks*. My son worked very hard on this."

Merchant was confused, but she didn't take the time to see it. She picked up her toddler and yelled back into the house, "Connor!"

"Maybe —" Merchant started, but she held up her forefinger for silence.

"*Connor!*" she called. "I know you can hear me. Now turn off that Nintendo or lose it!"

She said to Merchant, "Now you be fair and listen. The decent thing would be just to forget about it and walk away."

He didn't know what she was talking about, but he kept his mouth shut.

A moment later a boy of about thirteen showed up at the door. He looked at Merchant and said to his mother, "What?"

"Talk to this man," she said. "Tell him about the mower."

She looked back at Merchant. "Paul Baylor said he would help Connor start his mowing business, and now he's gone. I don't see how it's fair for you take the boy's mower, I don't."

"He can't," the kid said. "It's *mine.*"

"We're not here for the mower," Merchant said. "Somebody else will be liquidating the assets of the house. I'm just looking for some help on the sailboat."

The mother stared at him, and then said, "Well, fine. Stay right here for a moment."

She walked back through the kitchen, and Merchant could hear her speaking to someone else. Presumably one of her other kids. "I said *now,* mister."

Connor said, "Ma, I'm fine!"

She came back in the room, a lanky teenager behind her. He was Merchant's height, but about thirty pounds lighter. "Keep an eye on your brother," she said to him.

"Ma," Connor protested. "I don't need a baby-sitter!"

"And I don't let you go off by yourself with strangers. Just do what you can to help the man. I'll expect you and Steve back in fifteen minutes for dinner."

Merchant thanked her.

She had started to turn away, but then she came back. Her two teenage sons stood behind her, and her toddler took two fistfuls of her hair and pulled. She winced but didn't seem fazed otherwise. She said to Merchant, "I'm raising these kids on my own, and I thought it was a good thing, the interest Paul took in Connor. Then he and Julie just took off without a word. It's selfish. I mean, wouldn't we all just like to sail away sometimes? What makes them so special?"

She headed back to the kitchen with her toddler in her arms.

The older kid brushed by Merchant and Connor and went directly out to driveway. He dribbled the basketball and then did a jump shot at the net bolted over the garage doors. The ball hit the rim and bounced off the hood of the Volkswagen.

Connor looked at his older brother, snorted a little. "That's his own car and he doesn't even move it." Connor was gangly, all legs, elbows, and knees. Red hair, like his mother. Lots of freckles. Steady blue eyes.

"So, your own mowing business," Merchant said. "Got many customers?"

The two of them began walking toward the Baylors' house.

"Nine," Connor said. "Four I can walk to. The rest my brother gives me a ride." He smiled. "I pay him."

"How old's your brother?"

"Steve's sixteen. Got his license."

"And you're what, thirteen?"

"Fourteen."

"Not bad. Already your older brother's boss."

Connor grinned. "Yeah. It's pretty cool. He says he's my *partner,* but that's not the way it really is."

Merchant said, "Mr. Baylor got you started on this?"

"Yeah, Mr. B. He's a pretty cool guy. He used to let us play basketball over on his driveway. He's got a lot more room than we have. He'd play with us sometimes. He had a killer hook shot, for an old guy."

Merchant smiled. Baylor was just thirty-six. "How'd the mowing business come up?"

"One day I asked him. We were shooting some hoops and I said I was thinking about trying to make some money doing lawns. He said he'd be my first customer. That worked OK for a while, but then my mower crapped out. He said I could use his, but it was an old piece of shit, too. Didn't last more than a couple weeks."

The boy looked at Merchant quickly to see if he'd object to his word choice. When he saw that no correction was forthcoming, he pressed on. He was an entrepreneur warming to his favorite subject.

"So Mr. B said he might be interested in investing in me." Connor rolled his eyes. "Man, I thought mowing was hard work. But he had me write out this business plan. Like if I bought a new mower, how much would it cost to buy it, how much to maintain it, gas and oil, and then advertising costs to get the customers. Like, if I did a flyer and mailed it out, or if I just walked it around to people. Then how many customers I'd need to make it all pay off, and then how much profit I'd have left. When we did the numbers, he said it would take a long time to pay back my initial investment; maybe a sweat equity thing would work better. And then we figured I couldn't make enough on the five neighbors I could walk to . . . and that's when he said maybe Steve could give me a ride. I said he wouldn't do it, but then Mr. B said, 'Bet he would if you paid him . . .'"

On and on the kid went.

Merchant just listened.

The long and short of it was that Paul Baylor apparently bought a new John Deere mower and retained ownership of it. But he made it available for Connor to use with his other jobs under the condition that he mowed the Baylors' lawn for free and keep up with the maintenance himself. Baylor acted as Connor's consultant, investor, and friend. Apparently he was even talking about buying a snowblower with the same deal in mind.

"Sounds like a pretty generous guy," Merchant said.

"Yeah. She was nice too. Always brought lemonade or water if I was working. And she'd move the car if it was parked under the net when me and Steve wanted to play."

Merchant gestured to the little skiff with his chin. "Guess that's in the way now."

"Yeah." Connor frowned. "My ma won't let us move it. Me and Steve could roll the thing out of the way, but she says no."

"So the boat wasn't always there?"

"Uh-uh. It's new. I mean it's used, but it was new to him. Just before they left, Mr. B brought it home."

The kid stopped to look at Sarah's truck. Sarah herself was still inside, trying to charm someone else.

The kid said, "That's your truck?"

"My partner's," Merchant said. Interesting, he thought. He couldn't quite call Sarah his boss either. Looked like he and big brother Steve had something in common.

"Jeeze, that's *mint*," Connor said. "I could use something like that someday. Put the mower in the bed instead of trying to shove it into the trunk of Steve's Jetta. If I ever do the snowblower thing, I'll definitely need to get a pickup."

Merchant grinned. "Going to have to pull in a few more customers to make that kind of investment pay."

He took a closer look at the boat. It was a fairly heavy-duty aluminum hull with a high freeboard and a flaring bow. A twenty-
horse outboard sat on the stern. Merchant knelt down and looked
at the trailer. He ran his finger along the aluminum. He touched his
tongue lightly and tasted salt. There was a bit of dried seaweed
caught in the leaf springs.

The boat had been in salt water.

No surprise necessarily. It was heavy enough to be used on more
than just a lake. Maybe interesting, maybe nothing.

"You say he just got this boat?"

"Yeah."

"Tell you why he got it?"

"He said fishing. But I didn't ask that much about it. I don't care
about boats."

"No?"

"Uh-uh." The kid looked back at Sarah's truck. "That's what I
like. And Mr. B got this cool old truck that he towed this with. I
wanted that pretty bad."

"You mean a truck other than his Lexus SUV?"

"Oh, yeah. A Chevy."

"Caught your eye, huh?"

The boy looked sheepish. "You know how you get thinking. He's
talking to me about maybe getting a snowblower, and then I see
this old truck, and I figure, hey, maybe I can get him to let Steve
drive that, and I can get a secondhand mower, and we can do twice
as many places. Maybe in a year or two I can buy the truck from
Mr. B, and fix it up myself . . . it could be pretty sweet if I fixed it
up right."

"What color?"

"Blue."

"You say he just got this truck?"

"Uh-huh. Same time he got the boat."

"Where is it?"

"Dunno," the kid said. "I just saw it the one time." The boy
lifted his shoulders. "Maybe he just borrowed it from somebody to
get the boat back, but I don't think so."

"Did you ask him?"

"Yeah. He just said, 'It's not for sale, Connor,' like he didn't want
to talk about it anymore."

"Was that like him? Secretive?"

"Nah. He used to tell me about his work, about how he liked business. Made it sound like fun. I never thought of it that way until he moved in." The kid lifted his shoulders. "But he didn't want to talk about the truck. I could tell. So I let it go. Mr. B was too good a guy for me to push it."

"Sounds like he enjoyed helping you out," Merchant said. "And you've been keeping your part up with his lawn. It looks good."

"Yeah, I do it every week. Tuesdays I do the Baylors'."

"So you still have the mower. Do you have a key to his garage?"

"Uh-huh. But the mower's in my garage now." The kid looked at the ground and fidgeted for a moment. Then he looked up at Merchant. "You told me the truth, right? That you're not going for the mower? Because it really is mine now."

"Connor, you got my word, I've got no interest in the mower. Someone else might come along who will . . ."

"But it's mine now. He left it to me!"

Merchant cocked his head. "He left it to you?"

"Yeah. I didn't realize they were gone for good. I just thought they were going on their vacation."

"Did you see him go? He say good-bye?"

"Nah." Connor looked sad admitting that. "There was a note on the mower when I went in to get it."

"You still have the note?"

"Sure do. It proves the mower's mine, whoever comes by."

"Let's see it."

"Yeah, all right. I'll be right back." The kid loped back to his house.

Merchant went over to the truck just as Sarah put the phone down.

"Got anything?" she asked.

"Maybe." Merchant pointed to the boat. "That's a purchase made just before they took off. And supposedly there's a beat-looking blue Chevy truck someplace that he purchased at the same time. Maybe that five thousand charge at the marina."

"Velly interesting," she said.

A few minutes later, Connor came out of his house and walked over. He handed Merchant a handwritten note on Paul Baylor's letterhead.

Merchant read it:

Connor — Best of luck going into your summer rush. You've done a good job, and I wanted to let you know I'm proud of you. Our books are clear — the John Deere is yours. See you in a couple of weeks.

Paul

Without a word, Merchant passed the note over to Sarah. She read it, passed it back, and said, "Sounds like good-bye to me."

10

JULIE BAYLOR'S SISTER TURNED into the driveway just after Sarah and Merchant were getting ready to pull out. She was a slim, dark-haired woman driving a green Toyota sedan.

Merchant was back at the wheel. He rolled down his window as her car came alongside, and she said, "I know, I know, I know. I'm late. Sorry."

Merchant would have liked to tell her that they were hungry, and bored from waiting for her, and they'd call her another day.

Instead, he said, "Not a problem. I'll back up."

By the time he had the truck parked, she was out of her car and had opened the front door to the house.

"What's her name again?" Merchant said to Sarah.

"Emily Kirkland."

"Married?"

"Divorced I think."

Sarah swung out of the truck and then looked back. "Take your camera, OK? No telling if we'll ever get in the house again. Bang some shots out, get a record of anything that looks good."

Once they were inside the house, Merchant's earlier impressions were confirmed. The place, though not huge, was tastefully and expensively laid out for two people. Lots of photographs throughout. Baylor had talent, no doubt about it.

He turned his attention to Emily. She was staring at Sarah, who was walking around the house, observing, touching things, trying to find her way to some information she could use. "Can I help you?" she said to Sarah's back.

Sarah turned and smiled. "Oh, I'm sorry. Could you talk to my guy here while I look in the office?"

My guy, Merchant thought.

Emily looked back at Merchant. Her arms were crossed against her chest, and she was slightly flushed. Her face was thin, but pretty. Her long dark brown hair was pulled into a loose ponytail that hung over her right shoulder. High cheekbones with a dusting of freckles. Wearing jeans, boots, and a white blouse.

She appeared to be making an effort to keep her impatience under control. "How do we do this?" she asked.

"Well, we're looking for anything that'll help us find your sister and her husband."

"You're looking for their *boat*."

"That's right," Merchant said. "I understand we're a distant second to what you want. But maybe we can find them anyway, and if we do, we'll call you right after we call the bank." He gestured to the couch. "Can we sit?"

She hesitated and then said, "I want some tea." Without waiting she walked over to the kitchen and gestured for him to take a stool at the island. As an afterthought, she said, "You want some? Julie's addicted to the stuff, and she buys only the best."

"Sure, I'll have a cup."

"How about your friend?"

"She's all set."

Emily put the pot on to boil and filled two stainless steel strainers with tea from a ceramic pot on the counter. She reached into the refrigerator. Merchant could see it was practically empty — nothing perishable was there, including milk.

"Oh shit," she said, and suddenly sat down on a stool across from him. A single tear ran down her face, which she quickly and angrily wiped away. "I hardly forgot why I'm here, but then I reach for the milk and I see that it's gone, and that it's not just because they're out of the house for a two-week sailing trip."

Merchant nodded. "Hard not knowing exactly what's happened."

• They were both silent for a moment, and then he said, "So how many years between you and your sister?"

"Three. I'm twenty-nine, she's thirty-two."

"You live in Philadelphia, right?"

"Yes. Just been coming up because of this. Though God knows what good it's been doing."

"But you haven't been staying here at the house?"

She shook her head. "Tried that at first, but couldn't stand it, just waiting for them to walk in the door. So I'm staying with friends in town."

"Were you and your sister close?"

"Not so much lately."

"How come?"

"You need to know this to repossess a boat?"

"Maybe not. But I like to gather everything I can and figure out what matters when I see it."

Emily raised her eyebrows, but after a moment she said, "I married a guy Julie thought was a jerk. My sister is many wonderful things, but diplomatic she is not. It took me a while to come to the same conclusion about my husband that she did."

"Were you and Julie close as kids?"

Emily smiled. "Oh yes. Followed my big sister to Boston. She did Boston College, I did BU. Our mom died when I was in my junior year. My dad was gone so long I don't even remember him. And, tell you the truth, my mom wasn't big in the mother business."

"Where'd you grow up?"

"The Bronx. Foster family."

Merchant knew he looked a little surprised, and she caught it.

"I'll take that as a compliment," she said. "We both worked hard to get out of the life we had there. Believe me, the family we lived with was doing it mostly for the check. Julie pretty much raised me and protected me when I was on the street." Emily put the cup of tea down in front of Merchant. "She's not any bigger than me, but the other kids got the idea sooner or later that she wasn't worth crossing."

"So how'd you get up here?"

"She got a scholarship to BC. And she had me come up and figured it out so I could graduate from high school here. Set it up so I could live with the parents of her roommate until she graduated and could afford her own place. Then I lived with her in Boston.

She and Paul met and got married. They had me out here all the time until I found Seth. Julie overheard him say something nasty to me, and she took it upon herself to tell him exactly her opinion. I was in love and stupid, and I chose to take that the wrong way and left in a huff with my fiancé. And here I am now, couple years later. He's gone."

"What's been happening with Julie and Paul lately?"

"I don't really know. She and I had made up, and we talked now and then over the phone, but still, we lived in different states. And Julie can be a bit of a control freak. I love her, but she's not always easy to be around."

"She and Paul get along all right?"

"Far as I can tell, Paul would walk across hot coals for her and not even complain about the blisters. They're very different. He's kind of quiet, very practical. Easygoing. She was born knowing the way things should be, and you'd better get out of her way if you're messing up the program. Both of them smart as hell. I think he's always been amazed to find a woman as intense as her focused upon him. And he definitely settles something in her, smoothes the edges. They laugh a lot together."

The kettle began to whistle, and Emily got up and poured the tea water. "We'll have to drink it black," she said. "As I've already established."

"I can manage."

When she came back to sit across from him, he said, "Did you know they were going on vacation?"

"She'd mentioned it a few weeks before."

"Any hint that it would be more than a vacation?"

"Absolutely not."

"Was that the last time you talked with her?"

"That's right. I just called her at the office to say hi. She told me they'd be sailing to Maine in a few weeks. No big deal."

"I understand you went to Maine looking for them?"

"That was awful. I flew up there as soon as I got the call from her office that she hadn't come back. I didn't even know where to start The Coast Guard checked their records, said there had been no distress signal from them. They were going to start a search, but then the Massachusetts state cops got the bank to check their records and found there was an attempted ATM charge in New York. Plus

Julie and Paul made some heavy cash withdrawals and this big transfer to the Cayman Islands. Suddenly, these nice Coast Guard officers and state cops officers weren't so sympathetic anymore. They took the missing persons report, but started treating me like I'm some sort of idiot who doesn't know what her sister's gotten into. I end up running from one agency to the other. Because of this *attempted* ATM withdrawal —"

"I've seen the photo," Merchant said.

"Yeah, it looks like somebody stole their card, right?"

"Does to me."

"Well, I call the NYPD, and they say Julie and Paul never filed a report about the robbery. They bounce me back to the Massachusetts state cops. *They* tell me that they're working the case, but they also manage to get across that they're busy trying to find missing children — and a healthy yuppie couple who transferred money to the Caymans isn't their first priority. The Sudbury cops sent an officer here to the house who did about a fifteen-minute walk-through, listened sympathetically, and asked me to call the first thing I hear from my sister."

"Bad case of 'not my department,'" Merchant said.

"Exactly."

"How about the FBI?"

"Same thing: they'll be truly interested if it turns out Paul embezzled money. Otherwise, look to the state cops."

She wrapped her hands around her teacup, as if to warm them, even though the room was stuffy from being closed up for so long.

When she continued, her voice was softer. "What I can't seem to make any of them understand, no matter how many times and ways that I say it, is that my sister and brother-in-law aren't the kind of people who would just run off without telling anyone. Without telling me. It doesn't make sense."

Merchant switched tacks. Too often in the DEA, he had heard impassioned words just like this from some family member who had no idea that little Bobby or Betty had blossomed into a full-blown junkie since the last family reunion. He said, "I understand that a co-worker of Julie's committed suicide a couple months before she left. A Michelle Amarro. Did Julie mention that to you?"

Emily shook her head. "First I've heard of it. How did Julie know her?"

"They worked together at Digi.com."

"Like I said, in the past few years, Julie and I haven't been that close. But if it really bothered her, I *think* Julie would have mentioned it."

Emily moved her teacup around in small circles on the counter. Talking to herself as much as him. "Julie's very tough, very protective. Like I said, I don't see her running away without telling me. But the past few years . . . maybe I just blew it with her." Emily's eyes welled up as she said this.

Merchant couldn't decide if the tears were real or not. He was open to either possibility.

Merchant touched her shoulder lightly, and then left her to cry in privacy while he went to see if Sarah had learned anything.

Sarah was sitting at a desk, looking at the blank screen of the computer. Off to the right were another desk and computer with a scanner and huge monitor. The screen on that one was blank, too.

"Isn't this cute?" Sarah said. "His and hers desks. Looks like Julie had the powerhouse computer, which makes sense, her being the techno geek of this modern American marriage."

"Every family's got to have one," Merchant said. "But keep your voice down. Emily seems to see her sister as her sister."

Sarah played an invisible violin.

Merchant said, "This job has warped your personality, Sarah."

"I *wish* I could blame it on the job."

"Did you find anything?" he said.

"Yeah. Lot of nothing." She pulled the plug for the computer out of the wall. The monitor went black.

Merchant winced.

"I know, I know," Sarah said. "Hurts you to see such callous treatment, even of a deadbeat's property, right? But it doesn't matter." She scooped several small objects off the desk and handed them to Merchant.

He looked at four threaded bolts. "What're these from?"

She took the monitor off the CPU and, without preamble, simply slid the cover off, revealing the inner workings of the PC. "The hard drive is gone. Plenty of other floppy disks, Zips, and CDs around. File cabinets full of business, home, boat stuff. But the disk on Julie's computer is gone, too."

"So they cleaned up," Merchant said. "I think it's clear they're running."

"Yeah. Let's see if your new friend, Emily, can tell us what else is missing around the old homestead."

They spent the next hour walking through the house trying to do just that. Merchant took record-type pictures as they went, the flash flickering across the walls.

It was nearly impossible for Emily to pick out much that was different. "I guess some clothes are gone," she'd say. "I mean, Julie usually just wore shorts and T-shirts on the boat, and some are here, I guess some are gone. How can I tell?"

Sarah looked impatient but not particularly surprised.

Merchant said, "Did you ever go sailing with them, Emily?"

"Sure. Until I got married, I did lots of trips with Paul and Julie."

"Do you remember where?"

"Everywhere up and down the coast. Go up to Maine, day sailing Boston Harbor. We did a lot in Buzzards Bay. The Elizabeth Islands, the Vineyard, Block Island. We'd do Connecticut, even made it to New York sometimes."

"The Elizabeth Islands," Merchant said. "So, did you ever go to Cuttyhunk with them?"

"A few times. We loved it there."

Merchant mentioned the picture he had seen in both of the Baylors' offices of the boats aground. "Do you know which one I mean?"

"Sure. I was there when Paul took it. In fact, he took one of the three of us using the self-timer. Julie kept it in their bedroom."

Merchant and Sarah followed.

Emily stopped abruptly. She looked at three photographs positioned beside the master bedroom doorway.

She frowned. They were all framed the same, but the two below included pictures of the Baylors on their boat with various friends. The one on the top was of a small brown and white dog.

"This wasn't here," Emily said. "It's been a while, but I remember that picture of the three of us used to go here. This one of Ginger — she was Paul's dog before he and Julie got married — he always kept it on his dresser. Julie used to tease him that Ginger was his first love."

Emily brought her hand to her throat and said, "She took the one of us. Of me." Perhaps believing for the first time that her sister had run away and left her behind. "She took it with her."

Emily looked at Merchant, her eyes welling up again.

This time he believed her tears.

11

SARAH DROPPED MERCHANT OFF at the Constitution Marina that night.

"Kinda beat, aren't you?" she said. "This is harder work than lazing around your boat."

"Most things are."

"See you at six A.M. sharp, bucko." Sarah drew out the last word. *Buck-ko.*

She looked as fresh as when they'd started that morning. Her generous mouth, the smiling way in which she looked at him. "So," he said.

"How about I see you in the morning?"

"A simple plan." Merchant got out of the truck. He put the camera bag strap over his shoulder.

"Simple is good." She dropped the Beast into gear and took off.

Merchant headed back to the facilities building before the dock. It was a small gray-shingled structure housing the showers, rest rooms, laundry, and message boards. He was thinking about Sarah.

Seeing himself through her eyes. Or at least trying to. Thinking that, whatever the differences in character, on the surface he and Owen had enough in common so that it was only natural for her to be cautious. Two ex-military types. Both enamored with the sea.

Both at loose ends. Both with histories that included using force as an option.

Too bad.

He had enjoyed his day with her.

As friends. He guessed they could keep it at that.

Merchant heard two car doors slam shut behind him. On some level he noted that he hadn't seen a car pull into the parking lot. But he was fumbling for his keys, not paying attention. Mentally debating issues of lust, love, and friendship.

Then he realized that he was hearing footsteps behind him, coming quite close already. But no conversation.

He turned.

Two guys, his height at least, six-two, six-three, strode directly toward him. Both had something in their right hands. Both wearing jeans, sweatshirts, and sneakers. Sweatshirts emblazoned with sports team's names, Bruins on the left, and Red Sox on the right.

Local boys, Merchant thought.

Both hoods were up, covering their heads like cowls.

It was a warm night.

The two stepped into the light, and Merchant saw that they were carrying baseball bats.

"You Merchant?" the one on the left said.

"Who?" Merchant said, slipping the bag off his shoulder and taking it by the top leather handle. He thought about what was in there: flash, camera body, and lens. About five pounds of plastic, metal, and glass.

"Yeah, that's him," said the guy on the right.

"That's who?" Merchant continued to step forward, looking confused.

The one on the right said, "This is for Charlestown."

The one on the left swiveled, drew the bat back, getting ready for a home run with Merchant's head.

Merchant swung the bag in a tight arc over his shoulder. He caught the man full in the face. It was a good hit. He could feel the weight carry him through, pushing the man right off his feet. Merchant stumbled forward, tangling for a second in the man's feet. He was aware of the other guy winding up and lifted the bag just in time to block the swinging bat.

Though he managed to hold on to the bag, Merchant took some of the weight of it in his face — and it didn't feel good. But it did piss him off.

He went after the second guy. Got him across the face with the bag, which sent him reeling. And then Merchant sidestepped in and kicked him in the kneecap, making him scream. The first guy was on his way up by then, and Merchant stomped him in the face.

He was pretty sure he broke the guy's nose. But they grew them tough in Charlestown, and the man came right back up. The second one threw his bat at Merchant.

Merchant tried to dodge it, ended up taking it on the back of his right thigh. Made him stumble, but he came back up fast, with the bat in his hand.

The thrower turned and ran.

The first one was up. His nose streaming black in the poor light. Swaying on his feet. He raised the bat with sudden strength and tried to bring it crashing down on Merchant's head.

But Merchant parried it away with his own bat, first blocked it and then swept it to the side. Grabbing the middle of his bat with his left hand, he shoved the fat end into the man's jaw like a rifle butt.

The man spun and landed facedown. He tried to get up, and Merchant said, "Don't."

Then the guy reached under the back of his sweatshirt and Merchant recognized that move. He knelt abruptly onto the man's back, knocking the breath out of him, and reached under the man's shirt for the gun.

The guy tried to buck him off, and Merchant swatted him in the back of the head with the gun butt and said, "*Don't.*"

Luckily for both of them, the guy collapsed.

Merchant stood up holding the gun.

So much for idle thoughts about friendship.

Merchant looked around. Surprisingly, or maybe not so surprisingly, no one had come out of the boats to see what the ruckus was about. The marina was still part of the city.

"All right, turn over," Merchant said. He put the gun in his belt and gave the guy a couple of taps on the biceps with the bat. Nothing too painful, just showing his impatience.

The guy rolled over slowly, and then sat up. He held his jaw.

Merchant said, "Is it broken?"

The guy glared at him.

Merchant gave him a hard tap on the shin of his left leg.

The guy clutched his leg and told him to fuck off.

"Good. You can talk," Merchant said.

"Don't have shit to say to you."

"You've done some beatings. You know how ugly this can get if I keep at it."

"I done my share," the guy said. "And I'm gonna do it again with you. You're not gonna be so lucky next time."

"Long as you and your friend are the beaters, my luck'll hold. Who sent you?"

"Nobody."

"See, that's a problem. Because I don't know you. And your buddy said, 'This is for Charlestown.'"

"Just a mugging. Just your wallet, that's all we were going for."

Merchant hit him on the same spot, shin of the left leg. This time, he also mashed the man's right hand as he tried to protect himself.

Merchant sighed.

The guy was hunched over his leg, holding his damaged hand with his left. He rocked back and forth, hissing with the pain.

"This is stupid," Merchant said. "Tell me what I need to know before I cripple you. Who sent you?"

"Wasn't sent," the guy said and then flung himself back, apparently terrified this answer was going earn him another blow. "No, wait. I mean, no one *told* us to go. We heard about you, and then me and Junior, we're having a coupla pops, and we decided to come down ourselves. Teach you a lesson."

"Who'd you hear about me from?"

The guy paused, and Merchant waited. Letting the guy work through it.

Finally, he said, "Kevin. Kevin Wolf."

"Kevin," Merchant said. Kevin had been an up-and-comer back then. He stood up even when Merchant held a bust over him. He wouldn't deal, wouldn't wear a wire in on his buddies. So he was sent to prison for five years. Kevin was a charming, likable guy who had almost certainly killed two men by his twenty-fifth birthday, but Merchant never had enough evidence to prove it.

"So Kevin got parole?" Merchant said.

"Yeah. Kevin's out, and he's got it in for you."

"And you figured you'd do his work for him." Merchant could see it. Wolf had that kind of charisma. Make people want to help him out, figure they'd get on his train. Being sent away was pretty much a rite of passage for someone like Wolf. Merchant doubted prison time had hurt his criminal career a bit.

He said, "Kevin's not going to be exactly impressed with you."

The guy shrugged but, if anything, managed to look unhappier. "Didn't send us," he said, sullenly.

"I see. You figure if you don't tell him you screwed up, he'll never know." Merchant put the bat on the ground and placed his foot over it. He opened the camera bag.

"What're you doing?" the guy said.

Merchant took out the camera and fitted the flash on and powered it up. The filter on the lens was shattered. He unscrewed that and dropped it into his pocket. The lens had a shuddering feel as he focused it on the man, and the camera's viewfinder glass was cracked. Most likely the camera was letting light leak in like a sieve.

"Damn it," Merchant said. "I liked this camera."

He took the picture anyhow. The flash burst into the night. At least that made it look like he was taking a picture.

"Jesus," the guy said, covering his eyes.

Merchant set the camera down and picked up the bat. "OK, take out your wallet."

The guy's voice was incredulous. "You robbing me?"

"No, you're beginning to make restitution."

The guy reluctantly pulled out his wallet.

Merchant took it from him, and looked through it. He pocketed a little over a hundred dollars and took the guy's driver's license. Doug Fogerty.

"OK, Doug. Here's a new concept for you," Merchant said. "You're going to have to pay for what you broke. Two thousand bucks it's going to take me to replace that camera and lens. Flash seems to work OK, and I've got your first hundred. Mail me nineteen hundred care of the marina by the end of the week. That means Friday. I don't get it, the cops and me come to visit you and Kevin. Assault for you, conspiracy for him."

"But Kevin's got nothing to do with it!"

"Not what I heard you say," Merchant said. "And when I throw down the photo of you sitting on your butt wiping your bloody nose, Kevin and the cops are going to believe you said it too."

"Kevin says you got no pull with the cops no more," Fogerty snapped. "They're not gonna buy this bullshit!"

"Think about it, Doug. Do I need pull if I can help them put the screws to Kevin Wolf? Now are you going to take care of this, or do you want to go tell Kevin I'll be around next week to see that his parole's violated?"

Fogerty sat there blinking. Taking in the implications. Finally, he said, "Nineteen hundred, Friday."

"Bank check or cash, Doug. Mail it to me."

"Huh?"

"Express Mail. The point is, I don't want you coming to see me again."

"Yeah. Yeah, OK."

He watched Fogerty get to his feet. Merchant stood, the bat still on his shoulder. Thinking they would be coming with their guns drawn next time.

12

THOMAS FOUND THE BENCH in Central Park and had a seat. He opened a paper bag and took out a cup of coffee. It was nice to be away from the man, even if only for a couple of hours.

Thomas was dressed casually, in black jeans, running shoes, and a gray lambs-wool sweater. His eyes were quiet and watchful. Weariness had begun forming bags under those eyes, and given him the salt and pepper along the temples. Under the casual clothes, Thomas was muscle layered on hard bone, his dark skin stretched taut with a few healed slices and puckered marks here and there.

Thomas wasn't his real name.

Thomas Washington.

Never Tom. He had that presence; few people ever dared to throw Uncle Tom in his face. But with some of his white clients it was there, and he thought it made them more comfortable.

Fine with him.

Thomas Washington enjoyed his coffee while waiting for the girl to come along. He didn't know her, but he expected her to bitch about the time, even though it was her choice.

She showed up about twenty minutes late.

Tall black girl, take your breath away. Short leather skirt, legs and body phenomenal. About what you'd expect given her line of work.

She said, "Goddamn sunshine in the park is not what I do."

"You're here."

She put a boot up on the bench seat and leaned in close. "I got the envelope, so yeah, I'm here. Five minutes, then I go get some sleep."

Skirt opening with her leg up like that, but lots of eye contact, challenging him to dare to look down. Staring right at him, staying above him. He tried to keep from laughing. He didn't care what she felt her expertise, power, or natural dominance would buy her. He could have her bent over the bench with that skirt up around her ears in about ten seconds flat if that was what he wanted.

Instead, he said, "This isn't for me."

She rolled her eyes. "Yeah, OK."

He smiled at her. "Hear that a lot, huh?"

"Uh-huh."

"Really true this time. For a man I know."

"Don't get many ladies, old man. Hurry it up."

"He's an important man."

"Who isn't? That's who come to me. Big boys who don't get told no enough. Part of the psychology." She played with the last word: *psychology.*

"You say so. This is going to be a first for him, far as I know."

"Is he saying this is what he wants?"

Thomas grinned. "He's a flexible guy. He saw your web page, wants to try it. Believe me, he needs to be told no once in a while."

"Whatever. You put enough in that envelope to get me here. I'll give you a code for the door, in he comes. We'll check him out and bring him down into the rooms. Got three of them: the dungeon, hospital room, classroom. I'll figure him out, tell him which one he's going in." She shrugged. "It's no big deal. Point him my way, I'll take care of it."

"Except I'm coming too."

Her lips twitched. "Thought it wasn't for you."

"It's not. But I look after him. I'm sure you got somebody with closed-circuit."

"Bullshit."

He raised his hands. "Don't waste your breath. I make sure no tapes are rolling, that he gets out safe."

"*I* make sure he gets out safe. Trusting me to take him to the edge, then bring him back, that's half the gig."

"Save it for your web site."

She rolled her eyes, then said, "Yeah, you want to watch, that's a kink in itself. He put it up your ass, or is it the other way around?"

"Your ass is more what I like."

She wagged her finger and laughed. "Got the wrong department, honey." Then her smile faded. "We gonna check you for guns."

"That's fine."

"We don't run no free gallery show. You want in, you gotta pay."

"That's not a problem. I'm buying your place for the night. Limit one guy for security, if you have to."

Her eyes narrowed. "Two, or you can just switch his butt yourself. Bet you'd like that."

He let that go. "Fine. Two, then. No other customers."

"I don't know," she said. She looked at him hard, which was hard indeed. "Lot of conditions, and I'm not big on that."

He reached into his coat, took out an envelope, and handed it to her. "For your patience."

She thumbed through the bills and shrugged. Three thousand dollars. Given who she was, he figured she would've been fundamentally incapable of letting herself appear impressed even if it had been a hundred thousand.

But it didn't change the whore in her.

"You got my attention," she said. "But you want the place for the night, I'm turning away lots of regulars. You're talking major cash. Who is this guy? Mayor like his nipples twisted these days?"

"You probably won't recognize him," Thomas said. "But to some people, he's important. And I handle him and make sure he gets what he needs and it's really that simple. Your time, your place, me there to make sure he gets the privacy he needs. Name your number."

She did.

The amount made him laugh.

She didn't get to where she was by being shy. But, ultimately, it didn't matter.

He put out his hand. "We've got a deal."

13

MERCHANT AWOKE just after four in the morning.

Eyes open, wide awake, and unhappy about it. The kids again. He told himself they were just fine. Or at least safe.

They were beautiful kids, even if their father was a suspected drug dealer. Eight and ten, the boy and girl, respectively. Rich black hair, streaming with water. The boy in the dinghy while the sister stood chest deep. She rocked the boat. Both of them were screaming with laughter. Brown eyes. Robert round faced and funny. Justine sweet natured but destined to be a heartbreaker.

Merchant took the pictures.

He was kneeling on the deck of their father's big ketch, using a big lens. Posing as a freelance photographer. Doing his job. Wearing his wire. Miguel, the bodyguard, sitting like a hunk of stone in the cockpit, watching him.

Suspicious.

Merchant never knew why this was the memory he dreamed about. The worst of it came later, the bust that went so wrong. Bobby Lee Randall and his AR-15. Blood and screams and flashes of orange fire.

Merchant stared at the cabin ceiling wondering why, if his subconscious was trying to offer up a nightmare, why didn't it show him the bust?

Instead of these children.

*   *   *

A few hours later, he saw Sarah pull her truck into the parking lot. She had her powerboat in tow. It was a good-size Mako, with a massive outboard on the stern. Probably a former repo like the truck.

The wind was whipping off the water, the skies steel gray. Merchant closed the hatch, picked up his bags, and headed up the dock. He was creaking along pretty slowly.

When he opened the door, the first thing Sarah said was, "What happened to you?"

Merchant stowed his gear and eased himself into the passenger seat. "Let's say we don't talk until after coffee."

"Like hell," Sarah said. "I'm a cheerful morning sort of girl." She reached over and pushed his chin aside, inspecting the bruise on his left cheekbone.

Her brow furrowed. "What happened?"

He told her.

"Just had to dock your boat in Charlestown."

"I like the view."

"Oh, that's funny." She started the truck and took off. She didn't say anything for a bit. He sat there wishing he'd had the sense to take a couple of aspirin before leaving the boat.

After a few minutes, she said, "Hey, we needed that camera, right? We've got to send photos to Radoccia."

Merchant told her it was his backup. "I've got the digital camera and a laptop in the bag."

"Good. Don't want your past life messing up my business, Merchant."

"Yes, boss."

She reached over to touch his hand. "Or you."

And then she pulled away. "Beat them off with your purse, huh?"

"I was wondering when you'd get to that."

Sarah grinned openly. She put her foot to the gas and made the big truck start to eat up the miles. "Beat them off with your purse," she said again. "We run into any other repo men, you keep that story to yourself."

At the junction of Route 128, they headed north and continued on until they saw signs for Salem. They took Route 114, a remarkably twisting and turning route to the center of Salem, home of reputed witches and the location of the marina where the Baylors docked their boat.

The marina office itself was an old building mated to an addition twice the original size: hand-laid gray stone welded to a modern section covered in vinyl siding. The addition matched with the stonework about as well as tennis shoes with a tuxedo.

However, the docks themselves were wide and well laid out. Water lines running onto each boat, telephone and electric hookups. A pretty even mix of sail and powerboats. The yard itself was substantial, with a huge aluminum winter storage barn. Off to the right of the barn was a wood-framed, plastic enclosure. Merchant could see two men inside spray-painting a sloop, which looked to be about forty-five feet long. They wore masks and full bodysuits.

Sarah checked her watch. It was just after seven. "Let's go see the boss."

Just as they were heading into the marina office, a thin man wearing jeans and a dark green short-sleeved shirt came out. He said, "Can I help you?" His voice was surprisingly deep for such a thin build.

"We're looking for Mr. Shadeck," Sarah said.

The man put out his hand. "Got him. You called about the Baylors, right?"

"That's right." Sarah introduced herself and Merchant.

Shadeck said, "Let's walk around, if you don't mind. I've got to get these guys going."

"No problem."

Shadeck walked ahead fast, his boat shoes crunching through the crushed-shell yard base. He said, "I tend to work with people in your business because when someone takes off on their boat, the yard usually gets stuck. Me."

Sarah said, "I hear it every day. Couple repairs, seasonal work, dock fees . . . can add up fast. How much did they stick you for?"

Shadeck looked back. "Nothing, except for this month's dock fees. Paid up beginning of last month. Everything else they paid with their credit cards. So we're fine."

"You had any idea they were leaving for good?"

"Still don't. For all I know they hit a rock out there. The Baylors were nice people, both of them."

"So we hear," Sarah said. "You see them the day they left?"

"Tossed off their lines, told them to have a good time."

"They seem any different?"

"No. But I'm not exactly talking about in-depth human communication here — just a bon voyage."

"How about what they loaded on the boat? Any more stuff than usual?"

"Don't know about that. My days as a dock boy are long gone." Shadeck stopped, turned around, looking, and then put his fingers to his mouth and whistled. A teenager down on the middle dock turned and looked up at them. Shadeck waved at him, and the kid started walking toward them.

Slowly.

Shadeck gritted his teeth. He yelled, "Sometime this week, Peter!"

The kid worked up to a slow lope.

Shadeck shook his head. "Don't expect big things from Peter."

"Could we see what sort of work was done on the boat in the past year that added to the bill?" Merchant asked.

Shadeck looked back at the office, sighed. That was moving in the wrong direction. But he said, "Yeah, OK, you talk with Peter and I'll get Cynthia to pull their file." He started to step away, and looked back. "Oh, with Peter, I'll let you know — he lives for tips. Just don't pay him more than five bucks, all right? He's enough of a pain already . . . customer's kid, you know."

Peter was skinny, sunburned, with pale blue eyes and a shock of dyed black hair. "What's up?"

Sarah asked if he could remember anything about helping the Baylors take off.

"Why do you want to know?"

"We're trying to find them."

"You cops?"

"No, repo."

"Like the movie?" Peter said.

"Just like it," Sarah said, not even glancing at Merchant. "Except no aliens and we do boats, not cars."

"Yeah. And you're a girl."

"You're very observant, Peter," Sarah said. "Now can you remember anything about the Baylors that could help us?"   .

"I dunno, I see lots of boats off . . ."

Sarah pulled out her wallet. "We understand. But I want to give you a little something for taking the time to give it some hard thought." She took out a five.

The boy reached for it, and Sarah crumpled it in her hand and said, "Slow down, Peter. Think first, money after. Anything you can remember about what they said? Maybe something you overheard them say to each other about where they were going?"

The boy screwed up his face. Hard to know if he was trying to remember or just make it look like he was. Either way, he went at it for about thirty seconds or so, and then said, "I *think* they said Maine. I dunno. Is Portsmouth in Maine?"

Sarah's face went blank and Merchant could tell she was trying to keep from laughing. So he said, "Easy mistake to make. Portsmouth is in New Hampshire . . . right on the line, though."

"Yeah. Well, they said something about that. Mr. Baylor did. Come to think of it, he did talk some. He asked me if I liked sailing, if I ever thought I'd take a trip like that. I told him no way, not on a sailboat. Give me something with engines, maybe."

The kid brightened. "He said Portsmouth, and then . . . Port-*land* — that's in Maine, isn't it?"

"Yes," Sarah said. "Portland's in Maine."

"'Cause I remember the two 'Ports' . . . and then he talked for a long time about some vacation place up in Maine. Some arcade place."

"Acadia?" Merchant said.

"Yeah, that's it." Peter's face brightened. "That any good?"

"Well, actually this is all stuff we knew," Merchant said.

"That's not my fault."

"What else can you remember?"

Peter fidgeted. Chewed at his thumbnail. Looked at the bill in Sarah's hand and said, "I'll tell you something, they were better tippers than you. Ten bucks. I worked for it, but not as hard as I am right now."

"What work did you do?"

Peter looked faintly indignant. "Rolled that shit down and loaded it." He gestured to one of the plastic hand trucks. "God, must've taken four trips. Boat was low in the water when they took off."

"What'd they have?" Sarah asked.

"You name it. Lots of clothes. Books. And cans and cans of food. Stew, soup, tuna fish, the works."

"More than they'd need for two weeks?"

"Yeah, I thought so. But I'm not here to complain, you know. Working for those tips, man." He gave Sarah what he apparently thought was a significant look.

Sarah gave Peter the five.

As the kid started to walk away, Merchant said, "Did Baylor always talk with you a lot?"

"What do you mean?"

"I mean was this a regular thing? Him talking to you."

"Naw. I mean he and his wife were all right. Better than a lot of people around here. But we didn't talk that much."

"Who did he talk to? Shadeck?"

"I guess. Tell him what to do on his boat or something. But he talked to Gerard a lot."

"Who's Gerard?"

The kid pointed to the two men under the plastic tent, painting the hull. "The short guy. Gerard. Mr. Baylor was like a nut about his boat being just perfect, and he hired Gerard to wax it. Or he'd have him dive on the bottom to wipe the algae off every two weeks, that kind of thing. They used to have a couple of beers after, which got Shadeck all bent out of shape, because Gerard's an employee. But then Gerard says he wasn't on duty and says the man can invite him to have a beer if he wants —"

"Got it," Sarah said, raising her hand. "Baylor talked with Gerard."

"Yeah." Peter looked positively chipper now. "That worth another five?"

They met Shadeck in his office. He introduced them to a thin woman in her mid-fifties with steel gray hair and a deep tan. "This is Cynthia. She runs the books and keeps us all employed."

"Hah," she said. "Do the office, that's it."

She gave Merchant the Baylors' file.

Shadeck agreed to introduce them to Gerard. "Not too long, though. He's in the middle of a job. C'mon."

When they got outside the shed Shadeck said, "Gerard's a particular guy. A real pro at finishing off boats, though. Make an old bathtub come to life if he puts his mind to it."

He stepped under the plastic sheet and waved the shorter man over. The man came outside, lifted off his mask, and Shadeck talked to him for a moment. Merchant saw the smaller man lift his shoulders, and then he came over.

"What's up?" he said. He was a squat, powerful looking man with mild blue eyes, deeply sun-reddened skin, and a day's growth of beard. There was a faint spray of fresh blue paint on his coveralls, and a line of blue mist along his jaw where the mask hadn't covered him.

Sarah explained they were doing repo on the Baylors' boat.

Merchant saw the man's face grow stony. He said, "So?"

Sarah said, "I was wondering if you could tell us anything —"

"Why you asking me?"

"We understand that you were friendly with the Baylors and did a lot of work for them," Sarah said.

Gerard snorted. "Who said that?"

Sarah told him.

"Peter," Gerard said, shaking his head. "Look, I've had a few beers with Baylor. Told some sailing stories. Talked to him about how to buff the scratches out of his hull. Doesn't make us buddies."

He looked at Shadeck. "I need to get back to work before this sets up."

"Sure," Shadeck said. He made an apologetic gesture to Sarah. "Got to consider the source with Peter."

Merchant watched Gerard as he pulled on his gloves and got ready to drop his mask down. Merchant threw out, "What if these people need help?"

Gerard stared at him and said, "Tell you this. They were decent people. Should have better than a couple of repo jerks trying to find them." He slapped the mask down, and stepped back inside the plastic tent.

"Where have we heard that before?" Sarah said to Merchant.

"Told you Gerard was a particular guy," Shadeck said as they walked back to the office. "He's been with us about three months now, and I bet we won't get much more than that out of him before he sails away."

"Got his own boat?" Sarah asked.

"Yeah. That double-ender over there."

Merchant looked out to the moorings where Shadeck was point-ing and saw a small, well-built sailboat with a canoe stern. A self-steering vane was mounted on the transom.

Shadeck said, "I should've figured it out before I introduced you. A repo man's got to be like the antichrist to him. Gerard lives the life a lot of people around here dream they could have. Ex-Marine. Good with his hands. Sails from place to place, works for a while, moves on. Brings out the Walter Mitty in a lot of the husbands. Of course most of them would want nothing to do with it if they ever got down to the hard work. And the money's got to be real tight."

"Tell me about it," Merchant said. Maybe he and Gerard could start a club.

Merchant looked in the folder Shadeck had given them. Sarah came around and peered over his shoulder. They scanned a printed summary sheet. Most of it was standard stuff. The Baylors had paid off the balance of the winter storage fees, the previous month's docking fees, and a number of spring bills, including bottom paint-ing, engine repair, and the installation of a new heat exchanger.

And then, just before they left, there were a couple more charges, for two, and then three thousand dollars.

"What's this?" Merchant said.

Shadeck looked. "Oh yeah, the boat. Little one."

"The aluminum one?"

"Yeah. With the twenty horse and trailer. Two thousand. We do a little bit of sales here, and that came in on trade. Baylor snapped it right up."

"Say what he wanted it for?"

"Freshwater fishing. Said they were thinking about getting a cabin in Maine, and he wanted it for that."

"Was this a freshwater boat?"

"Nah. The guy who traded it in used it on the bay. Told Baylor the truth, I said he could probably do better. Get a boat and out-board that never saw salt if he looked around up north."

"What's the three thousand for?"

"Truck. Bought my old Chevy truck. Hundred thousand on it, but still decent for towing and snowplowing and stuff."

"He's buying the boat and truck before buying the property?"

Shadeck smiled. "Guys like that, they got money to burn. I see it every day here. Guys buy trucks and boats and the best rods, the best electronics, the best of everything — for all sorts of practical sounding reasons. But the fact is, they're toys. Christ, Baylor had that Lexus SUV. Could've put a hitch on that for a couple of hundred bucks, he'd been done with it. But no, he 'needs' a beater truck."

"Where is the Lexus?" Merchant said.

"Baylors left it here. In the parking lot. About a week back somebody came and repossessed it. Not you guys?"

"Boats only," Sarah said.

Shadeck looked at his watch. "Well, good luck. If they did just take off, a month gone now, they could be in the Virgin Islands, they could be strolling around Big Ben, they could be eating croissants under the Eiffel Tower. Hope this one's not too important to you."

"Just my livelihood," Sarah said.

"Rich people," Shadeck said, shaking his head. "They do have a way of putting it to you."

Merchant and Sarah thanked him, got in the truck, and headed north.

14

THE MORNING SUN was beating down brightly, making Sarah squint behind her sunglasses. It was Merchant's turn to hit the phone, and he kept at it as she moved the Beast along at about seventy. He made cold calls to the boatyards.

Just before they reached Portsmouth, he switched off the phone in disgust.

"Figure out anything?" Sarah said.

"Yeah. For me, the world of telephone soliciting is not a viable career path."

"Poor baby. How about one more call? Buzz the Seagull, and get directions. Don't tell them why we're coming in."

"Yes, ma'am."

Merchant made the call and found that the restaurant was right downtown. They drove along the river, passing a landlocked submarine on display to the right. They continued into the town center and found a small parking lot where the attendant let them park the truck and boat near the back wall.

Portsmouth Center was full of shops, waving flags, rich red brick. Stores with names like Slackers and The Girl Patch across from an old-time hardware store named Pearsy's. Lots of breakfast and lunch places that some people would call self-indulgent yuppie hangouts.

Sarah wouldn't because she was hungry.

The Seagull was such a breakfast and lunch place. It had a hand-carved sign depicting its namesake wheeling over a background of blue sky. With a closer inspection, she saw that the gull was carrying a bagel in its beak. "Cute," she said.

They stepped inside. The restaurant was moderately busy, and breakfast was still being served.

"Maybe it's just hanging out with you, but I'm ravenous," Merchant said.

"Uh-huh. Everything's always the girl's fault."

A chalkboard on the wall proclaimed a steak and eggs special for six ninety-five, corned beef for the same, an elaborate selection of omelets. Wooden booths, lots of mirrors, plants, a number of historical Portsmouth gewgaws scattered about to interest and amuse.

The place was aggressively cozy.

Sarah could see the cook, a hefty middle-aged woman, working behind the long wooden counter. She was dipping slices of fresh bread into egg batter for French toast. Behind her, there were thick breakfast steaks on the grill. The hash was full of chunks of red meat. Even the home fries had gone beyond standard fare, with big slices of sweet potato mixed in with white potatoes and onions.

Sarah said, "Let's say we do this job sitting down."

They took a booth and a young waitress came over. She was slightly heavy, with a round face and a thick black ponytail. "My name's Jenny, I'll be your server this morning. Hope you're hungry."

"Starving," Sarah said.

"Well, you came to the right place."

Sarah started to take the photo of the Baylors out of her backpack, but Merchant frowned at her. The waitress looked between the two of them inquiringly. Merchant ordered the steak and eggs with a side of pancakes. Juice and coffee.

Clog those arteries, Sarah figured. She was impatient, wanted to get right to the photo and some questions. Instead, she ordered the hash and eggs.

After the girl left, she said, "I wanted to get her thinking."

"Food first," Merchant said. "Nothing like waking up after a near beating to whet your appetite."

Sarah made a fist and put it under his jaw. "You slow me down again, buddy, you'll have a great appetite tomorrow morning."

He laughed. "You're scaring me. The photo comes after, when we're laying the tip down."

"Yeah, yeah. You ex-government types know more about bribery than an innocent repo woman."

"You know what an oxymoron is?"

"Yes, now shut up."

A few minutes later, the waitress brought the meal back. Merchant and Sarah ate in silence, and the breakfast was every bit as good as it looked.

When they were finished, Sarah called for the check and more coffee.

By the time the waitress came back with their check, Merchant had the photo and the copy of the Baylors' credit card statement on the table. "That was delicious. Listen, do you think you could help me?"

"If I can," she said, somewhat cautiously.

He explained what they were looking for. Any information about these two customers, maybe a month back?

As soon as Jenny got where he was heading, she started to look at him askance. She said, "I'm sorry, sir, but I don't think you realize how many people we have come through here. If you were talking about a regular, then sure, but if you're talking about a couple who just stopped in one time, there's not a chance I'd remember them from a month ago . . ."

"Understood. And I expect you have other help here."

"Right. I don't even know if I was on. Or if they were here for breakfast or lunch." The girl took another look at the photo. "Nope, can't say I do. What're their names?"

Merchant told her, and again she drew a blank.

"I'll ask Melanie, though," she said, nodding toward the cook. "She owns the place."

Sarah and Merchant watched the girl go back behind the counter. She talked to the woman as she laid out French toast. Sarah could tell from the way the girl was talking that she was strictly going through the motions. The cook rolled her eyes and kept dropping bread into the batter and then onto the hot griddle. She leaned over the picture and then seemed to straighten slightly. She wiped her hands on a cloth, held up the picture and looked at it more closely.

Then she apparently told the girl to watch the griddle, because she came back holding the picture and the bill. She said, "So why are you looking for this lady?"

Sarah took out her card and explained they were looking for the boat.

"Huh," the woman said. "People got to pay their bills."

"So you remember her?" Sarah said.

"Yeah. I thought, No way. How'm I gonna remember this lady from a month ago? But I do."

"How come?" Sarah said.

"Anytime someone douses me in iced tea, I put them right here." Melanie tapped her forehead. "That way I can fry them in hot oil, least in my imagination. Yeah, she was at the counter, and when I was putting her lunch down she knocked the tea all over me. But she was a sweetheart about it. 'So sorry, I want to pay for the cleaning' and so on. I told her the whites get cleaned every night, don't worry about it."

Melanie seemed to think for a moment, and then said, "Hey, wait a minute." She went to the cash register, opened the bottom drawer, and came back a moment later with a card. Julie Baylor's card at Digi.com. She handed it to Merchant. He flipped it over and saw a hastily scrawled note:

Sorry! One ticket, reimbursement for dry cleaning.

Julie B.

"What're the odds of that, huh?" Melanie said. "Remembering a customer a month later. Not bad."

"Pretty amazing," Sarah said. "You remember if her husband was with her?"

The woman closed her eyes, made a slight side-to-side movement with her head. "Nah," she said, finally. "I can't say for sure, but I don't remember a guy with her. So, I'd say no. But, it's been a month."

Melanie flipped her towel back over her shoulder. "That's all I can tell you."

She went back behind the counter.

"It's more than we could hope for," Sarah said

Merchant nodded. "Almost too good to be true."

*   *   *

They decided to launch the Mako. They found their way to a ramp on Pierce Island, which was just outside of town.

"My turn for the boat," Sarah said. "You take the truck and go to the marinas see if the *Fresh Air*'s up on poppits, talk to people."

"Sounds like a plan." He took off.

Sarah put the boat into gear and headed out.

The sky had become overcast and the water turned gray. Though the day was warm, Sarah felt a trembling inside. Nothing she wasn't used to, it was just a little more intense. The dichotomy was there: she was free, on the water, moving along in her boat at one-thirty in the afternoon on a weekday. She never lost sight of how lucky she was in that regard.

Nor how tenuous it all was.

Deadbeats.

Seeing them day after day. People who'd overstepped themselves, their finances, whose life plans didn't work.

And maybe she was on her way.

She got out her cell phone and spent the next twenty minutes catching up with Lenny. Lot of questions that needed answers. A Scarab that needed an engine overhaul before they could sell it. One of their new freelance captains had smacked a repossessed Albin trawler into the dock, and the marina was calling for damages. The boat itself was going to require over a thousand dollars of finish work. Then one of the yard guys hadn't come in and Lenny was bitching that he was forced to clean the boats as well as answer the phones and order parts. He had that whine in his voice as he told her, "And you *know* that's not fair, Sarah."

"No, it's not," she said, closing her eyes. *Lots of things aren't fair.*

But all she said was, "I appreciate your keeping at it, Lenny."

He needed to be stroked for a while. Sarah did it because he was the one who kept the company alive while she was away from the office. The two of them also had a long history — he had been one of Joel's friends. An exasperating kid who had grown up into an exasperating adult. Pipe stem arms, bad complexion, bad attitude. There wasn't much she actually liked about Lenny, but in his way, he was loyal to her. And to Sarah, that meant something.

But she also wanted to scream at him sometimes that she was the one who made payroll every two weeks, and she'd never missed it.

Even through everything with Owen, she'd paid her bills. Sometimes she'd like to scream that didn't he know — didn't any of them know — how hard that was to maintain?

But she didn't.

She went back to looking for the *Fresh Air*. Knowing what the odds were, she was probably wasting her time. She looked at the chart and found the first marina coming up, and she swung into the small cove and circled inside. She scanned for masts and then quickly looked down to the hulls. Going for size first, hull shape next. Color and boat name could be changed.

Lots of boats, none of them the *Fresh Air*.

She left the cove. A mile or so to the next.

That trembling inside. It had been there since Owen. It kept her from sleeping more than five or six hours a night, and that was if she'd put some time in on her bike or swimming, pushing her body hard enough to exhaust her. Now it'd been almost a week since she'd got any real exercise, and she'd eaten all that feel-good but fatty food with Jack.

Jittery. She found herself tapping her hand against the polished aluminum wheel. Realized part of it was that she wasn't with Jack. She'd felt better when she was with him.

Girly girl, Sarah thought. Need a man to make you feel confident. She didn't like that.

Her mind flew with quick suspicion, probing to see if he was purposely trying to bring her too close. Just as quickly she pushed it aside. He'd been doing exactly what she asked of him. Working hard, and being her friend.

In a few hours, they'd be back together again. It infuriated, amused, and scared her that the idea made her feel good. "You're a mess, Sarah," she said out loud.

The next marina came up, and she powered down. Started looking at the masts.

God, she needed a swim.

Both of them looked at lots of boats, none of them the *Fresh Air*.

Afterward, they loaded the Mako onto the trailer and continued on to Portland, reaching downtown just about seven o'clock. They found Rollie's Cajun Kitchen. It was a small place on Market Street right on the waterfront.

They took the same approach as they did at the Seagull. Eat first, talk later. Same drill with the waiter, too.

Nothing.

But when the waiter brought the owner out — he remembered. "Yeah," he said, holding Julie Baylor's picture. He was probably in his early thirties, worried looking. Even though the food had been excellent, the place was practically empty.

Jittery, Sarah thought. Small business owner disease. She wondered if she was so transparent.

"I remember her because we got to talking," the man said. "She seemed to know a lot about marketing." He had a soft southern accent. "Marketing" was "Mahketing."

"So she was by herself?" Sarah said.

"Yes, ma'am. Said her husband was off picking up something for their boat. They'd sailed in, she said. So I guess she was kinda lonely, and it was quiet that night . . . like now. I came out to ask her if she enjoyed the meal. We got to talking. She seemed like a smart lady. Lot of ideas. Talked about how I should get a band in on Friday nights, do some work on the menu. Start letting some artists place their art . . . how if I catered to the right crowd the restaurant business would follow. She also said she could help with a web page — not that she'd do it herself, but she'd know someone who would. How I could list the events, and special meals, how I could put coupons on the page, people could print them out and bring them in . . . and she said I should do a highlight on my background . . ."

The guy grinned self-deprecatingly. "I mean, I used to be a name chef in New Orleans, and when I came here with my girlfriend, everybody gave me all this advice, told me I could make a fortune opening my own place. Well, I know food, but I don't know how to build a crowd. She seemed like she could help."

"Quite the conversation you had," Sarah said. "She say where she docked her boat?"

"No, ma'am. But I assumed it would be at Coughlin's." He gestured out the window toward the north.

The owner stepped back behind the bar and opened the register. "She left this for me too."

He came back and put Julie Baylor's card on the table.

Sarah said to Merchant, "Jesus, after a month we get two hits. Incredible."

Merchant flipped the card over.

Call me about the web page!

— Julie B.

"Unbelievable," he said. "Unbelievable is a lot more like it."

Sarah said to the owner, "So, did you ever do it?"

"Make the call?" The owner shook his head. "Decided she was a flake."

"How come?" Sarah said.

"Saw her 'boat.'"

"At Coughlin's?" Merchant asked.

"No, sir. About fifteen minutes after she leaves, I headed across the street to get some change. I see her go by . . . *driving* by. What she told me, I understood her to be docked on a sailboat. You know, I'm figuring forty, forty-five feet or something. I'm thinking she's made some money giving out all this advice, she knows what she's talking about. Instead . . ." The guy laughed.

"What?" Sarah said.

"Instead, I see her driving this old truck. Towing a little aluminum boat with an outboard. Man, I figure, if this is her *yacht . . .*"

The owner gestured to the empty restaurant. "I've already taken enough bad advice to last me a lifetime."

15

AS THEY LEFT THE RESTAURANT, Sarah said, "How about a little dessert at Coughlin's? Something with foam on top."

"Hops in the middle?"

"That's what I was thinking."

They went into the big parking lot and walked down to the old ferryboat that had been converted into a restaurant. On each side of the ferryboat were docks filled to capacity with sail and power-boats.

At the front desk, they asked to talk to the marina steward and were sent back to a small office near the gift shop. The steward was a rail-thin middle-aged man with dark frame glasses.

He was sucking on a lollipop.

When Sarah showed him her card and told him what they were looking for, he grinned and said, "Repo woman, huh? Sounds like something in a comic book."

"My life is like something out of a comic book," Sarah said.

"Well, then, wouldn't want to get in the way of those super-powers."

He pronounced "super" as "soupa."

Sarah smiled her dazzling smile, and the guy grinned around his lollipop stick. He said, "We keep pretty good records. When would you be talking about?"

She gave him the approximate dates, and the steward got up and pulled a black three-ring binder from the top of his file cabinet. He ran his tobacco-stained forefinger through the list.

Midway through, he crunched down on the small candy, and took a few moments to throw away the white stick, unwrap a new lollipop, and put it in his mouth. "Quit smoking," he said. "Candy keeps me civil."

He bent down over the guest log again.

A moment later he spun the book around. "That them?"

Merchant and Sarah leaned over, reading, "Paul and Julie Baylor, *Fresh Air.*"

There was a penciled notation alongside their names: "NS."

"What's that for?" Merchant asked.

The steward looked at it and said, "No show."

"So they were never here?"

"Doesn't look that way. People make reservations for dock space, don't always show up."

"You ask them for credit card numbers when they call to reserve?"

"If it's over the phone, we'll usually write it down. If they're calling over the radio, you can't ask that."

"How about the Baylors?"

The steward lifted his shoulders, but he flipped to the back of the notebook and went through a sheaf of handwritten yellow receipts. "Yuh, OK. It was written up. Telephone call, two days in advance."

"You bill them if they just don't show?" Merchant asked.

"You got a problem if I do?" The man's mildness was now replaced with a little edge.

"Not at all," Merchant said. "Just curious as to why their credit card bill didn't show at least a cancellation charge."

The steward grunted. Clearly he liked bantering with Sarah better than answering Merchant's questions. But he said, "We take the number, don't usually run it through until they're here. I got to decide if I bill them, it's not automatic. Not getting my bills out ain't the worst of all the things I done wrong since I quit the coffin nails."

They went onto the ferryboat for that dessert. Sarah ordered a light beer, Merchant an ale. They sat at the corner of the long bar. Behind them was a bank of windows. The last of the evening light had faded, and night was upon them.

Now that his meal had sat for him for a while, Merchant was feeling full. He sipped his beer, thinking that if they stayed he would switch to scotch.

Sarah looked over at him. "Still sipping, huh? Didn't your dad ever teach you to drink like a real man?"

"Sure he did." Merchant thought of his father, glassy-eyed in the living room while the television blared. Never missed a day of work, never raised his hand to Merchant's mother or sister. But he had checked out of their life, as far as Merchant could remember, long before he died of a liver infection at age forty-eight.

Between that, and the amount of addiction Merchant had seen in his years in the DEA, he was a cautious drinker. Liked the taste, liked the effect to a degree. But he held back.

"So what do you think we've got here?" Sarah said. "Are we going to find this boat, or should I start looking for gigs as an exotic dancer?"

"An easy job for you to get," Merchant said. "But ultimately, unfulfilling."

"Well, I'm screwed then. Because that's the only other thing I'm qualified for, far as I can tell."

"I'll tell you one thing — I don't think we're going to find the *Fresh Air* here in Portland or up in Acadia."

Sarah sighed. "It doesn't feel likely, does it?"

Merchant pulled a notebook from his back pocket and laid it on the bar. "OK, let's see what we've got, in no particular order." He began to jot down impressions as fast as he could. Sarah threw in comments while nursing her second beer.

- Two hits at restaurants/Julie alone — *Don't believe it*
- Julie in truck towing boat. Boat back at house.
- Where is truck? (Truck & boat bought just before they go)
- Mower/Kid — note — goodbye
- Julie walks away from big $$ stock options at Digi.com
- Girlfriend — Michelle Amarro — suicide
- Paul — Straight arrow. Embezzlement??
- Paul talks up storm with Peter — hard work
- NYC ATM charge??
- Boat painter — Gerard — lying??

Merchant pushed the list between him and Sarah, and they stared at it for a few moments, then sat back. He said, "Looks to me like we're following a false trail."

"Looks like amateur hour. Wife drives north, tries to leave a trail, husband sails south?"

"Something like that. Well, they've never done it before. Julie Baylor didn't need to dump iced tea all over that poor cook. The credit card receipts alone would've been better. But everything about this says, rush, rush, rush. Even the boat and the truck, bought just before they left."

"Yeah. With the boat — the little one — I bet they were trying to fake the sinking of the *Fresh Air*. Put in a distress call, dump some oil and identifiable junk overboard . . . What more do you find, usually?"

"Could be enough, given a little time."

"But that didn't happen. No distress call. No junk . . ." Sarah grinned. "These amateurs, it would have been a life ring with the name *Fresh Air* stenciled on it, like in the movies."

"Yeah, well, what do bankers know about true crime?"

Sarah pealed with sudden laughter. "You child."

She looked at the list more closely. "This Michelle Amarro. The suicide. I went on the web last night and looked up the headlines in the *Globe*. This was a bigger deal in the news than I remembered. She was at some cancer research fund-raiser. Lot of people involved in the Internet in some way. Including that blond guy in the picture with her and Julie. I forget his name. Vance. Something Vance."

Merchant shrugged. "Suicide of a business associate. Even if she was a friend, it's a sad thing, but doesn't mean quitting your job and running off to sea would solve anything."

Sarah put her forefinger on the last notation on the list. "This guy, Gerard. He's the only one who didn't want to talk to us. He couldn't get away fast enough."

"Yeah. He's worth another talk. If you know you're going to be taking off on your boat — running away — a guy who can repaint it and put a new name on it would be a good guy to know."

Sarah downed the rest of her beer and said, "Maybe we should make Gerard our first stop on the way back. What do you say we do one more round, and then find ourselves some rooms some-place?"

*   *   *

The problem was that somewhere into that "one more round" Sarah asked Merchant what had happened down in Miami, and Merchant was feeling tired and loose enough to tell her.

"I got him killed," he said. "The long and short of it."

"I know that much from Henriques. Tell me why."

Merchant sighed. "It was my next assignment after leaving the Virgin Islands. Considered a promotion, a move to the big leagues. I was to help chip away directly at the Columbian cartel in Miami. And the cover I'd been using fit to a tee. I sailed into Miami as a freelance photographer looking for work."

"So you were undercover from the start?"

"That's right. The job had been seeing to it some of my photos got published. Plus a number of shots were bought from pros and published under my name. I had a good portfolio and looked the part. And the Miami DEA thought I'd be perfect at gathering evidence against the head of the cartel, Victor Rodriguez, by getting close to his cousin."

"This would be Gacha?"

"I thought you didn't know anything about it."

She blushed. "While I was on the Net last night, I went to the archives in *The Miami Herald*."

He took a moment to digest that and then said, "Guess you've got the right to keep an eye on your employees."

"It's not like that," she said. "Sometimes I reread the news articles about me and Owen. Try to make sense of my story as if it happened to someone else."

"How's that working for you?"

"About as well as you'd think. So tell me what happened."

Merchant went through it quickly: How Carlos Gacha, the cousin of Victor Rodriguez, wanted to publicly distance himself from his cousin. He wanted a book written. A book that would show that, although he was indeed the cousin of one of the most violent criminals in history, he was simply an honest businessman.

"You've got to understand," Merchant said. "On the face of it, this was ridiculous. Gacha lived in a small palace. Back in Colombia, his cousin is at the very top of the cartel — he's placed bounties on the heads of Colombian cops and anyone else who's given him trouble. He's estimated to have been responsible for the deaths of thousands of people over a ten-year period. *Thousands*."

"Did you think there was a chance Gacha was innocent?"

"Hell, no. I went in the same as everybody else. We'd flipped this writer, Hadley Pearson, who'd done a couple of pretty good biographies — pretty good in that they managed to look objective while basically making heroes out of his subjects. We had him in our pocket because of a cocaine bust. We saw to it that he applied for the writing job. Gacha liked Hadley — and Hadley brought me in as the photographer."

"Gacha accepted you just like that?"

"No. Fact is, he pretty much assumed that I was DEA or FBI. Kept after me when I was taking photos, 'Hey somebody actually teach you how to use that thing? We're really going to need to those pictures for the book.' That kind of thing. Showing he didn't care, we could stare at him all we wanted, that he had nothing to hide. He was like that, thought he had a sense of humor. The only thing he got serious about was his kids. His wife had died years before. He said to me that he didn't want the kids coming out looking bad."

"But you thought he was dealing anyhow?"

"Didn't know. What we suspected him of was laundering money. We knew somebody had to be orchestrating the cash pickups from drug sales all over the world. Our theory was he was responsible for shuffling the money through bank accounts and brokerage firms, and eventually purchasing U.S. equipment — anything from computers to raw steel — for legitimate Colombian businesses. When those businesses paid their bills, they paid them in pesos — directly to the cartel accounts in Colombia."

"OK," Sarah said slowly.

Merchant smiled. "See, the U.S. currency never left the States and was never directly exchanged for pesos . . . the money the cartel received was clean."

"All right, sure. So was he involved?"

"Certainly not according to him. According to him, he was living proof that a Colombian man could grow to be a success without being entwined in the drug trade. And this book was to be 'an inspiration to my son and to other young Colombians.' "

"How much time did you spend with him?"

"A lot, actually. Hadley had to spend a fair amount of time over a couple of months interviewing him. I came along for a number of those visits, but not all of them. Still, I was there a lot. Took a sailing trip with them over the weekend."

"That's close," Sarah said. "You end up liking this Gacha?"

"No. But his kids, yes." Merchant thought of them in the water again. Playing in that dinghy. Justine and Robert. Or later, when they were back at the house. Robert playing hide and go seek and jumping out at his father from behind the couch. The bodyguard, Miguel, losing his stony-faced mask then, and grabbing the little boy, and swinging him around the room. The handgun visible under his coat.

Gacha off on the sidelines, a little worried looking but smiling. Not stopping his bodyguard.

"No," Merchant said again. "I can't say I liked Gacha, but I didn't particularly dislike him. And the kids were just that, kids."

Merchant paused. Sipped his beer and thought about that time. Something he did every night before he fell asleep whether he wanted to or not. During the day he could focus on his lack of money and career, and let himself fret over whether or not the *Lila* would stay afloat. But at night this all came back to visit like an acquaintance who doesn't know when to leave.

Merchant began to tell Sarah about Miguel. The bodyguard.

Miguel. That deference Gacha seemed to pay him. It made no sense to Merchant from what he had seen of a Colombian's typical treatment of subordinates. At Merchant's request, the agency had searched their files and sent photos to the Colombian government — but weeks passed without anyone even recognizing the man.

The more Merchant and the agency looked, the less they found. Nothing incriminated Gacha. Merchant had begun to wonder if there was anything to get.

They tracked Gacha's tax returns for fifteen years back. His wealth, at least on paper, was explained by his family's substantial real estate holdings bought over thirty-five years before.

About two months into Merchant's involvement, Lester Titus, the head of Miami office, called him into a meeting.

"Got him," Titus said, standing at the front of the large conference room. "The sanctimonious son-of-a-bitch. Your instincts were dead-on about Miguel Dominguez, Merchant."

"How so?" Merchant asked. Around the big oblong table, there were two members of Merchant's surveillance crew and the leader of the DEA's SWAT team. The SWAT officers were dressed in jumpsuits and black boots. All of them were white, mostly clean young men with sun-reddened faces. Hard looking. One stood out more than the others did. B. L. Randall, according to his name tag. Small red mustache, bright blue eyes. Wound tight, and ready to do something.

Or maybe that was just the way Merchant remembered him.

"Tell us about it," the SWAT leader said.

"We got the family cook," Titus said. "Her son is up on a heroin charge, so we got her right where we want her. She says Miguel is more than a bodyguard. Around the house when they're alone, Gacha listens when he speaks. And there's a computer in the den, and Miguel is on it more than Gacha."

"What about the phone?"

"Nothing specific," Titus said, shrugging. "He's careful."

"I've seen the PC," Merchant said. "How do we know he's not just using it for his taxes? Or surfing the Net?"

Behind him, Randall said, "Ah, for Christ's sakes."

The SWAT leader said, "Shut up, Bobby Lee."

Titus said, "'Listen, when we were following Gacha on that trip of his to the Glades about a month ago? It seems Miguel had a guest. And he and that guest spent most of their time huddled in that office."

Titus grinned triumphantly and laid down an artist's sketch.

Merchant and the others crowded around. A heavy-faced man with a broad nose, dark bags under his eyes. Thick mustache. Possibly Victor Rodriguez.

Possibly not.

"Rodriguez in Miami?" Merchant said. "I thought he was under surveillance around the clock in Bogotá."

"Supposedly he is," Titus said. "But they could've been running a double. Wouldn't be the first time. Besides, the cook, she grew up in Bogotá. She's seen Rodriguez before."

"She's certain it's him?"

Titus said, "That was her gut reaction on it, when he walked in. Scared the hell out of her."

Merchant stared at the sketch. "You offer her kid a walk if she came up with something good? Because looking at this, I'm really not sure."

"You don't have to be," Titus said. "The judge was. Enough to charge Gacha and Dominguez with harboring a fugitive. We're taking them in and seeing what we can shake loose."

He addressed the room in general. "Gentlemen, we want what's on that computer. If we can key in on the purchases made on behalf of the Colombian businesses and have their government shut them down, we've done a day's work."

"Like they'd move on that," Bobby Lee said.

"Shut up," the SWAT leader said, with weary patience.

Titus went on, "If we get the distributors at each major U.S. city, *we* can nail them ourselves — then we've done at least a coupla weeks' worth."

He grinned, almost rubbing his hands in satisfaction. "OK, I'm going to ask Special Agent Merchant to come up to the board and sketch the layout of the house. We want that computer intact, we want the same with the people."

Merchant paused and then said, "I don't think we have enough."

Titus said, "Noted. In the meantime, get to it." He gestured to the blackboard.

So Merchant went through it all. The house, the placement of the office, the number of people usually there. One of his surveillance team members went back to the lab and returned with his photos. He passed these along to the SWAT team and taped up identifying shots of everyone in the house.

Despite his reservations, Merchant had been a cop long enough to believe that where there was smoke, there was fire. Maybe this would be worthwhile. Gacha had never spent a night in jail; maybe he'd fold.

He said, "We've got to be careful. Chances are the kids will be in there."

"So go baby-sit them," Bobby Lee said.

It was meant as an insult, but Merchant said, "I should."

Titus nodded. "You go in first. Say you've got to take some more photos before Hadley gets there. If the kids are downstairs, try to find a way to get them upstairs. Then protect that PC. If it's what we think it is, they're gonna try to destroy it the second we come in."

So Merchant rattled through the presentation on automatic: "This is the foyer. Left in through the dining room. Sunken living room behind that. Bath to the left, open sliders to the rear onto a deck. The den here to the right . . . foot of the stairs ending just in front of the doorway. So if you're flying into that doorway, you got to be ready for an attack down the stairs."

"I'll run it from here," the SWAT leader said, getting to his feet. "Speak up if you think I'm missing something."

Merchant sat down. He was just a few feet away from Bobby Lee.

Bobby Lee smiled at him, not a particularly nice experience. "The baby-sitter," he said.

Miguel let Merchant in.

"Where's the writer?" he said. He looked over Merchant's shoulder.

"Be on his way," Merchant said. "He said he wanted me to set up some shots in the office with Mr. Gacha."

Miguel nodded. "He called. I thought he'd be here at the same time."

Merchant lifted his shoulders. "Maybe twenty minutes behind me."

Miguel stood aside, waving him in. He didn't check Merchant's bag; hadn't for the last few visits now. Good thing, too.

Gacha came down the stairs to meet him. He was wearing a cream-colored pair of pants, a tailored shirt with the collar open, tie loosened. He put his arms wide. "What do you say? The casual businessman, yes?"

"That'll do it." Merchant smiled.

"I'll be watching you," Gacha said. "You take the pictures of me, not the papers on my desk, got it?"

This was a constant now, this banter.

Merchant could imagine the way his tone would change minutes from now when the team came charging in.

Because Miguel was armed, the judge had given permission for them to storm the room. Merchant was to disarm Miguel before-hand.

"Where are the kids?" Merchant said.

Gacha jerked his thumb over his shoulder. "Upstairs glued in front of a video game, like every good American child. You need them for the photograph?"

"No, that's fine. Just you today."

They went into the kitchen, where Merchant had Gacha pour a cup of coffee as a prop. And then Merchant moved them along into the office. He asked Gacha to sit at the desk, then had him do some poses that involved keeping his hands on his desk.

Merchant listened carefully as he sighted through a wide-angle lens. He could hear the sounds of an electronic game upstairs. Miguel was off to his left, in easy view. The bathroom door was open, and Merchant glanced in. Clear. He'd managed to check out each downstairs room while walking them from the kitchen.

Also clear.

Merchant moved so he was standing between both men and the hall door.

"Hold on a second," he said. "Got to change lenses."

That was the code phrase for the listening team.

Merchant took the lens off the camera and put it in his bag. He came out with his gun and badge, and said to Miguel, "DEA. You're both under arrest."

He kept the gun facing down, the badge held out first. Kept his voice easy. Letting them be confused for a moment, letting the idea seep in.

Then there was the pounding of feet outside, and Miguel reacted.

"Freeze!" Merchant said, bringing the gun up. "Right there!"

Gacha yelled to him also. "Stop, Miguel."

Merchant heard the front door slam open, heavy footsteps in the foyer. Three members backing him up, he knew. The rest containing the house.

Miguel reached under his coat for his gun.

In one stride, Merchant was on him. With the flat of his hand, he shoved Miguel's pistol against his chest and put his own gun to the man's forehead. He shoved his face inches from Miguel's and yelled, "Drop it! Take your hand off right now!"

Miguel stared at Merchant but would not release the gun.

Gacha was beside Merchant now, and he spoke rapidly in Spanish. Merchant could understand only enough to realize that Gacha was also telling Miguel to drop the gun.

And perhaps he would have.

But Bobby Lee burst in and Miguel shoved Merchant away and raised his handgun.

Even in Merchant's memory, everything went extremely fast from there. Hard to believe how much could change in such a short time.

Bobby Lee shot Miguel in the chest twice.

Then he turned and shot Gacha, whose hands were free of weapons, who, as far as Merchant could tell, was only trying to calm Miguel.

And then the bathroom door moved behind him, and Bobby Lee whirled. Merchant had a millisecond to see that it was Robert, eight-year-old Robert. Stepping from where he must've been hiding behind the open door.

Apparently playing hide-and-seek. His favorite game.

Coming into the middle of confusion and mayhem to see his father being blown against the wall.

That millisecond was more time than Bobby Lee had.

Merchant screamed for Bobby Lee to stop, that it was the kid, that he had to stop.

But he could see Bobby Lee swing the gun around, the first bullets pock the wall beside the boy.

Merchant grabbed Bobby Lee. Tried to swing the gun up to the ceiling.

Succeeded at that. The bullets ripped plaster out of the wall over Robert's head. The boy screamed and ducked.

Then a gun erupted to their left, and Merchant felt Bobby Lee jerk in his arms and then stumble.

Merchant looked over, saw that Gacha had gotten hold of Miguel's gun and was pulling the trigger as fast as he could. The barrel was swinging toward Merchant now. Merchant felt the wind of the bullet against his sleeve.

Merchant raised his own gun. But then the next team member was through the door, and he fired instantly. Gacha was thrown back against the wall again, and this time there was no question of him recovering enough to reach for a gun.

Little Robert began screaming.

Merchant stood there. Blood on the walls, his ears ringing. The room filled with cordite, empty shell casings all over the floor.

He realized Bobby Lee was clutching at his leg. Merchant bent down.

"You bastard," Bobby Lee said. "You gutless bastard, you've killed me." He was jerking spasmodically. His left leg was bloodied.

"Take it easy, Randall," Merchant said pressing him down. "It's just your leg. Your vest took the worst of it."

But Randall knew what he was talking about.

His face turned white as paper. Beneath him, the blood spread fast, very fast. Merchant would learn later that the bullet had hit his femoral artery.

The rest of the team was in the room by then.

One of Bobby Lee's team members — Merchant could never remember which one — stepped forward screaming, "What'd you do, what'd you do?" He hit Merchant across the face with his gun butt, knocking him out.

Merchant learned later that Bobby Lee Randall died before he reached the hospital.

16

"**HUH,**" Sarah said.

"That's what everybody says." Merchant took a sip of his beer.

Sarah sipped her beer, too.

Lot of sipping going on, Sarah thought. She looked up and down the bar. Place had really emptied out. She said, "What turned out to be on the computer?"

"Plenty. But not a byte that proved Gacha was dirty."

"Nothing?"

"Last I heard they never tied any criminal activity to Gacha himself. As far as what happened after, Victor Rodriguez probably would've done the same whether or not Gacha was actually working for him. Gacha was family."

"What happened after?"

"Henriques didn't go into that?"

"Didn't give him the chance. I walked out."

"Well, it only got worse from there. The SWAT member who actually shot Gacha was killed. A sniper's bullet through the window of his living room."

"Oh, no."

"And then Lester Titus's wife awoke at two in the morning to find her husband sitting alone in the kitchen. A turkey sandwich was laid out before him. His hands were bound behind his back and his throat was cut."

"Jesus," Sarah said. "Jesus Christ. Did Rodriguez come after you?"

"In his way. A package was left outside the door of the Miami DEA office. Long white box, with my name on it. They cleared the building. Miami Bomb Squad was called in. They used a water cannon to burst the box."

Sarah cringed inside.

"It was designed for the maximum damage," Merchant said. "Inside were flowers — and a thank-you card to me from Victor Rodriguez."

Sarah closed her eyes momentarily. "What a spot."

"You could call it that. It was my word against the team members coming in after Randall. Me saying I was protecting the boy. Them saying I panicked and it cost Randall his life. The job was looking for somebody to blame. So I got a lawyer, which pissed them off, too. Ultimately, the job backed me. Saving me also meant saving them a huge settlement with Randall's family. Unofficially, they let it be known that no one trusted me and they wanted my resignation. I didn't feel like sticking around."

Sarah slid her glass in slow circles on the bar. "Makes me proud of this country sometimes."

"Hard to look me in the eye right now, isn't it?"

That startled her. "Christ, no." She turned to him full on. Seeing a defensiveness that was unlike anything she'd ever seen in him. "Jack, I understand why you did it. You couldn't let him shoot the kid. I'd like to think I would've done the same thing . . ."

"But?"

His defensiveness was still there, and he was reading her just fine. She said, "It's not you. It's just . . . those people — those drug people — they killed Joel."

"Not this boy."

"What about ten years from now? Position he's in with his uncle? What're the odds he doesn't go into the family trade?"

"Not good. But I couldn't let him be shot."

"No, you couldn't."

They drank more of their beer. Not sipping now, but taking deeper drafts.

She broke the silence. Tried again. "Jack, you had no choice. What you're feeling off me isn't about you." The anger was right there, and it came out: "Those *fucking* drugs," she said. "Those fucking drug people."

The bartender looked over at them.

She lifted her hand in apology.

She wanted to drop her hand onto his. But she didn't know how to do that kind of thing anymore. Instead, she just sat there feeling miserable. Feeling the rage boil inside her. These people came along and just ruined her brother. Ruined *her*. She tried another sip of beer. Seemed to be her only way of relating at the moment. Maybe she'd just become an alcoholic, sit on her tub of a boat and feel sorry for herself.

Merchant looked like he was considering similar thoughts.

Sarah tried a smile. Felt more like a grimace. "Tell me about these enemies with southern accents you mentioned before. Who're they?"

"Sure you want to learn any more?"

"Anger management," she said. "Got to practice it to make it perfect."

That made him smile a little, which eased the temperature inside her a few degrees. God, she wished he'd just put his arm around her. Knowing at the same time that, if he did, she'd probably withdraw.

Merchant said, "Randall's family."

"His wife and kiddies packing for you?"

"Didn't have either. But he did have four white trash brothers, plus parents, and an assortment of cousins. Most of them in a little town called Orlee, south of Miami. One of the brothers is in Starke on assault charges. Far as I can tell, Bobby Lee's the only one who made it to the right side of the law. They apparently considered him a black sheep, but they sure didn't like the idea of a fellow cop holding him back to get shot. Especially with the lousy settlement offered by the DEA. So I've been told, in more than one way, that they were coming after me."

"Like what?"

"Three of the brothers tried to surround me at night. Tire irons and chains."

"You have your gun?"

He shook his head. "I told you, I don't carry one anymore."

Sarah looked at him incredulously. "With this kind of trouble going on?"

"No."

"You telling me you're going to stand there and let them shoot you?"

"So far, no."

"What'd you do then with the guys with the tire irons?"

"Kicked the smallest one in balls, ran over him, and kept going. Worked surprisingly well. Another time, a pickup truck tried to run me off the road. Shotgun out the window. I hit the brakes and slammed back into them, and they took off."

"The cops any help?"

"Some. Told me where I could find the oldest brother who was out, Jarvy. I tracked him down once. Figured I'd let him try me one-on-one, see if I could end it there."

"He go for it?"

"I decided against it."

"He's that big?"

"Not that. Figured it wouldn't end. Then there would be the next brother, and then the next. Best to leave that family alone. I'd already done enough to them."

"So you got out of town."

"Short of me showing up at the Randalls' various trailers and shacks and killing them all, that seemed my best option."

"And so you sailed to Boston."

"That's right."

"Jack, you should have a gun."

"No. Besides, I'm not licensed here anymore."

"You still know people here. You could get a permit," Sarah said.

Merchant lifted his palms. "I'm out of that business."

"You've got to be able to defend yourself!"

"So far, so good. Those two with the baseball bats last night — I figured it was the Randall boys found their way to me at first. I was happy to hear those Boston accents."

"You want to die?" Sarah's voice was harsh enough to make the bartender turn again.

"No. I'm just not putting myself in a spot where the only option is to pull a trigger. If I don't have a gun, I can't do that."

"And if *they* do?"

"Hasn't happened yet."

"Jesus, you're further gone than I thought."

"Certainly possible. But don't I think the Randalls are that likely to make it up here. Leaving the state and making it all the way up north would be a much bigger act of bravery on their part than killing me. The boys in Charlestown, yeah, they can be a problem for a while, anyhow. But Boston feels as close to home as I'm going to get. And as long as I'm on the road, I think I'll be all right. That's one of the reasons I agreed to do this with you. But if you're not comfortable traveling with me —"

"I didn't say that."

"Maybe you should." Merchant swirled the remaining beer in his glass. "I probably haven't been giving the situation all the thought I should. Not fair to you."

He downed the last of his beer and dropped cash onto the bar.

"I've got that," Sarah said. "I'll put it on MassBank's tab."

"Nah, no reason the bank needs to pay for my confessions. Listen, what do you say we split up tomorrow? I go back and see Gerard. You do a harbor sweep tomorrow morning, and then go up to Acadia."

"I'm not asking for that."

"I know you're not."

He put his hand on her back.

Not his arm wrapped around her, nothing but the touch of his hand between her shoulder blades. Close to what she wanted.

But she froze. She could feel herself do it and hated it, but she couldn't change herself. She arched her back slightly, avoiding him.

He dropped his hand. "Sorry."

"No," she said. "Don't say that . . . it's just me being nutty. Look, Jack, I'm your friend. I want you to keep working with me on this job."

Jack nodded. "I will. But right now I think the best way to do that is go our separate ways."

"All right. That's what we'll do." Her voice cool now, the distance between them fully established.

As if that was what she really wanted.

17

THE NEXT MORNING, Sarah dropped Merchant off at a car rental office right outside the airport.

They were being outwardly friendly, nothing more. She was wearing reflective sunglasses, and Merchant could see his own face in her eyes as she said, "Call me on the cell phone once you've got something."

"You bet."

He rented a mid-size sedan. It took him about two hours to reach the marina in Salem. First he went to the office, looking for Shadeck. He wasn't in, but Cynthia was.

She recognized him. "How can I help?"

Merchant told her what he was looking for.

She frowned. "I don't know, that's a little different than just looking at our bills. Employee records. Whose exactly are you looking for?"

"Gerard's."

He saw her make a face. Just a quick downturn of the mouth, a flash of irritation. She didn't like the man, he decided.

She began to work away from her previous position. "Well, Gerard isn't exactly an employee. So I suppose in his case it's a little different . . . he's more like an independent contractor, and he's leaving us high and dry at that."

"He is?"

"Just going to sail away," she said. "Mr. Shadeck says he worked out fine while he was here. *I* say the guy's a boat bum."

"I see," Merchant.

"And Mr. Shadeck did say to help you."

"He did."

She smiled quickly. "But I certainly don't feel like I can on my own authority. Mr. Shadeck will be back tomorrow . . . but if you'll excuse me, I have to step out and grab a soda."

She winked.

Merchant said, "I understand."

Silly stuff, but it worked sometimes.

She pulled a manila file out of a steel gray cabinet and dropped it on her desk. As soon as she left, he opened the file and flipped through a half dozen subcontract labor time sheets until he found one with Gerard Drummond's name. Underneath was a listing of work dates and the amounts paid.

Merchant quickly turned Cynthia's desk calendar around so he could match the dates.

Two days after the Baylors sailed away, Gerard took three days off. Merchant went through the rest of his monthly log. Gerard often didn't work weekends, and he missed other weekdays here and there in the course of a month. So the fact he missed a few days right after the Baylors took off was hardly conclusive.

But it was a place to start.

He made a call to Sarah then, and asked her to make a call to the bank. "No problem," Sarah said. "Shelly could find out."

Merchant waited in the office for about ten minutes, and then Sarah called back and told him what he'd hoped to hear.

He went out and looked for Peter.

The boy was at the end of the dock, sneaking a cigarette.

The gas dock.

Merchant said the boy's name, and he whirled around and threw the cigarette into the water. It took a moment or so for him to realize he wasn't going to get in trouble, and he let the smoke drift out of his nostrils.

Peter said, "You looking to buy some info?"

Merchant held back a smile. "You got some?"

"Like what?"

"Nothing complex today. Just tell me where I can find Gerard."

"I think he's on his boat. He's getting ready to take off."

"Can you take me out to see him?"

"Well, I'm not supposed to run the launch. And it's too early for the service. About an hour, somebody should be here."

"But can you do it anyhow?" Merchant smiled his most disarming smile. "I won't sue if you crack us up."

"Does Gerard know you're coming?"

"Oh, yeah. Called him from the road yesterday."

"Maybe I could take you out in the workboat. Sucker leaks though."

Merchant pointed to his boat shoes. "Not a problem."

The kid waited.

Merchant took out his wallet and found two fives. "Luck's with me. A ticket for each way out."

"Well, sure," the kid says. "Long's you don't mind the leaking."

They made it out to Gerard's boat in just a few minutes. The kid hadn't been exaggerating. The wooden workboat had a good inch of water sloshing around.

"You ever bail this thing?" Merchant said.

The kid made a face.

Merchant turned to look at Gerard's boat. Custom, about thirty-five feet long. Beautifully finished. Sitting fairly low in the water, as if it were loaded for a voyage.

Gerard was kneeling in the stern, working on the steering vane.

He turned to look at them as the workboat pulled alongside. His face was grizzled with a day's growth of beard.

Merchant stepped onboard without waiting for permission.

"What the hell are you doing?" Gerard said.

"Coming for a visit."

Merchant turned back to Peter. "You keep an eye out. When I wave to you, come back."

"You can get back on that boat right now," Gerard said, standing. "I didn't invite you aboard."

The kid looked worried. "Hey, Gerard, he said you two talked on the phone yesterday."

"Yeah, bullshit. Now take him out of here."

"Mister . . . ," Peter began.

But Merchant held up a crumpled twenty. He balled it up and tossed it behind Peter's head. The boy tried to catch it, but he missed. The bill landed on the water's surface and floated.

"C'mon!" the kid said. He immediately threw the outboard into reverse and started to back his way down to the bill. He snatched it out of the water just as it began to soak and flatten.

He turned to look questioningly at Merchant.

Merchant had another bill crumpled in his hand. "Now take off and wait for me to give you a signal. I'll put the other one in your hand."

"Deal," Peter said.

"Get him out of here," Gerard said.

Peter lifted his shoulders as if to say it was beyond his control — then twisted the throttle and took off.

Merchant turned to Gerard and thought about how mad he'd be if someone intruded on his boat the same way.

He hoped Gerard also had a no-gun policy.

Merchant said, "We've got to talk . . ."

"Like hell we do."

". . . about your mortgage on the boat."

Gerard's head jerked. "What're you talking about?"

"I checked. You've got a mortgage with MassBank. And it seems you've got a spotty record with payments."

"Check again, asshole. I'm up to date."

"I know you are. Took care of last month and this month — did it right after the Baylors left. Nice to have a little peace of mind for a while, isn't it?" Feeling quite the hypocrite saying this.

"My bills are none of your goddamn business. Now call that idiot boy back and get off my boat. I'm leaving."

Instead, Merchant sat down in the cockpit. Gerard stood, his hands on his hips.

"Look," Merchant said. "I really don't like starting off this way. But the fact is, you know something that I need to know. If you don't come through, I'm going to have to make trouble for you. It could be as simple as flagging the bank to pay attention to your loan. Sooner or later you'll screw up, and I can arrange it so they drop you the instant you're in default."

"Not gonna happen."

"Or," Merchant continued. "Depending upon what you give us . . . maybe I can scare up enough cash to cover you for another month, maybe two."

Gerard smiled. "I don't need your money, *repo man*."

"Guess not. Here they leave, and now you're all stocked and ready to sail away."

"I've got nothing to do with them."

"How'd it go? We know Julie Baylor headed north with the little boat in tow behind the truck. Did he sail south? You met him somewhere . . . maybe Red Hook? Or did you go on to Block Island? Maybe the Elizabeth Islands — Cuttyhunk? And you were waiting and had it all set. To pull the boat, and repaint it. Can't be that many yards able to do that. I start looking around and showing your picture, we'll find out who you set it up through."

"You're smoking something," Gerard said. But he looked uncomfortable.

And, if Merchant had read his face right, he'd looked most uncomfortable about Cuttyhunk. Not a practiced liar, Gerard.

Merchant was struck by that. Gerard seemed to be a pretty good person. Same could be said of the Baylors, from what he had been able to read about them. Amateurs, trying to be sly and making a lot of the wrong moves. Like possibly sailing to their favorite anchorage, Cuttyhunk. Where they may have gained close enough friends, they figured they could trust them to help change the boat.

"Where are they, Gerard? Where are they headed?"

"Don't know." Gerard backed behind the wheel, slipped the gearshift into neutral, and started the engine. "I'm leaving," he shouted over the clatter of the diesel.

"What color did you paint their boat?"

Gerard laughed. It looked forced. "Jesus. You are a pain. But a very lucky man."

"Why's that?"

Gerard rolled up his sleeve. Showed a U.S. Marines tattoo. "There was a time I would've kicked your ass just for getting on my boat without permission. One of the things I gave up when I gave up the booze. Now you better call that boy over and get away from me before I forget all my good intentions."

"Shove your good intentions," Merchant said. "And tell me what the new name is on the Baylors' boat."

Merchant didn't really want to fight. But he knew he'd never learn anything while Gerard was remaining cool and collected.

Gerard moved around the wheel faster than he would have thought possible. Merchant scrambled to his feet.

Gerard was a good five inches shorter than Merchant, but maybe thirty pounds heavier. He'd be tough to tackle in the confines of the small boat. His eyes narrowed, and he stepped in closer.

Then he seemed to catch himself. He said, "Her name? You go look for it, you repo jerk. It's the SS *Get Stuffed*." He bulled past Merchant and headed up to the bow. He dropped off the mooring line and the boat was free.

He came back, took the wheel, and shoved the boat into gear. He powered over in the direction of Peter, who was drifting near the docks. Gerard said, "Get your ass off my boat now. You stick around, I promise you, you're gonna be swimming. What's it gonna be?"

"Well, Jesus, you put it that way," Merchant drawled.

Gerard didn't smile.

Merchant waved to Peter to come pick him up. The kid came out immediately and swung alongside the sailboat. Gerard put his boat in neutral and said, "Scratch my boat, Peter, I'll be getting down there with you."

Peter kept his head down. "Yeah, no problem, Gerard." He held the workboat away with his hands.

Merchant stepped down, and Gerard pushed his throttle forward. The sailboat surged ahead. He took a moment to give Merchant the finger, then turned his attention back to steering out of the harbor.

"Everything work out?" the boy said.

"Oh, yeah," Merchant said. "I handled it beautifully."

18

MERCHANT DROVE DOWN to New Bedford, his old stomping grounds, and caught a small single-engine seaplane to Cuttyhunk.

Cuttyhunk was the southernmost island of the Elizabeths, a chain of small islands between the mainland and Martha's Vineyard.

The plane circled once and then swooped in to land outside the harbor. The pilot revved the engine, and they powered along quickly to the dock.

Merchant got out of the plane, feeling the heat, the sunshine. Wishing he was there to play.

He walked down to the small harbor. He was wearing jeans and a short-sleeved shirt, and was beginning to wish he'd worn shorts.

The little harbor was as crowded as could be with moored and anchored boats. There was really just one place, as far as he could tell, that would've been capable of hauling a boat the size of the *Fresh Air*. It was about three quarters of the way inside the small cove. A marina with a big H-shaped boat hauler leading down to a track in the water. The office was a gray weathered building poised at the water's edge.

Merchant saw two men in green yard clothes power-sanding a sailboat hull. He went to them directly, avoiding the office.

He figured if Gerard had set up something for the Baylors, he would already be tied in to the yard manager. And Merchant had to assume Gerard had made it to a phone by now.

Assuming, of course, that the uncomfortable look Merchant had seen on Gerard's face when he mentioned Cuttyhunk hadn't been just the result of indigestion.

The two men noticed him approaching and put down their tools.

"Hi, guys," Merchant said. "Maybe you can help me. I was wondering if you've seen these people?" He held out the picture of the Baylors.

"Talk to the office," the heavier one said. He kept his goggles down. He was covered with red paint dust.

"What's up?" the other man said. He was skinny, with black hair, and a narrow face. He shoved his goggles up with the back of his hand.

"Just wondered if this guy was around a month or so back. Getting his boat repainted most likely."

"No," said the heavyset guy.

Merchant smiled. "See, you're supposed to look at the picture first before you say no."

"He's right," the black-haired man said to his friend. "That's how you're supposed to do it."

The black-haired man glanced at the picture, then looked Merchant in the eye. "Never saw them, and the boss is coming up right behind you to tell you so."

Merchant turned.

Indeed a big, florid-faced man was walking up from the office. "Hey, you! These guys are working."

Merchant introduced himself and put out his hand.

The big man had pale blue eyes and muttonchops sideburns. Merchant couldn't remember the last time he'd seen those.

The man kept his hands by his sides. "What do you want?"

Merchant showed him the picture of the Baylors. Muttonchops was shaking his head before he even saw it.

"You guys are quick studies around here," Merchant said.

"What's that supposed to mean?"

Merchant looked over his shoulder at the black-haired man, who rubbed his mouth to cover his smile.

Muttonchops glared at him. "You got something to say, Northup?"

"Not a word," Northup said. He turned on the sander, making it whine. "I don't see, hear, or do *anything* unless you tell me to, Mr. Bouchard."

Bouchard stared at the man's back.

"Mr. Bouchard," Merchant said. "I'm just doing a job here myself. These people left a financial mess behind —"

"Take off," Bouchard said. "We can't help you here."

He positioned himself between his men and Merchant, and crossed his arms over his chest.

Merchant left.

Merchant went to a nice B & B up the street in time for a late lunch. He watched the road outside the marina for a while, at least as long as he could make the meal drag out. Chicken breast sandwich. Salad after that. Dessert, then coffee.

All told, he dawdled for about an hour and half. In that time, he saw Bouchard himself walk up the hill to a small sandwich shop, pick up what appeared to be a bag full of subs, and then walk back down the hill.

Merchant sighed.

Lunchtime on the boss at the marina.

Merchant drummed his fingers on the table.

The friendly waitress was beginning to appear a little strained when she said, "Can I help you with anything else?"

"Got a local phone book?"

"For the island?"

"That's right."

"Sure." She came back with a tiny thing, couldn't have been more than a couple of dozen pages. He went through it and found four Northups. He asked the waitress over. She came quickly, and seemed a little dismayed to see the bill was yet to be paid.

He asked her if she knew which of the Northups listed was the one who worked down at the marina.

"Sorry," she said. "I'm just here for the summer."

Merchant knew the answer to this one. "The owner in?"

"Nope, she stepped out."

"The cook?"

"He's from Providence. He won't know."

"Anybody else local?"

She looked around the restaurant, apparently thinking through each of the four or five employees there. After a moment, she made a face. "Sorry. All of us are from the mainland. Can I get you anything else?"

"Guess not."

He paid the bill and left. Figuring he'd finally have to do some detective work.

But it wasn't that hard. The island simply wasn't big enough.

He would've gone to the sub shop, but with Bouchard having just been there, he figured they might call him. Although that might not have been such a bad idea. If Bouchard got angry enough, he might blurt something out.

But Merchant learned what he wanted to know at his fourth stop, a little variety store up the narrow road.

The owner was a blue-eyed man in his sixties with close-cropped gray hair. "That'd be Axel Northup," he said. "Why?"

"I ran into him last time I was here a few weeks ago. Now I need some work on my boat, but the guy with the sideburns — Bouchard — he says they're booked. Last time, this guy, Northup, told me he might be free for after-hours work, but I lost his name and number. He said I shouldn't approach him at the yard, it'd get him in trouble with Bouchard."

The shopkeeper snorted. "Yeah, that'd be Axel all right."

"Is he any good?"

"Sure. When he's not tanked. Used to own the yard. He can do anything to a boat needs doing, if he's not drunk. Last part's the problem."

"The yard used to be Axel's?"

"His family's," he said. "Northups used to be big around here. Till Axel piddled it away." He shook his head.

"Not a very responsible guy, huh?"

"He's a shitbird," the man said. "With a big mouth."

Perfect, Merchant thought. He said, "Do you know where I could buy a bottle of scotch? I think I need to show up with a present."

The shopkeeper's eyes glittered. "Presents are good. Just make sure you give it to him after he does the job. Hold it in front of his gawd-damned nose."

"You've got something like that for me?"

"We're a dry island."

His idea of a joke.

Merchant reached for his wallet. He took out a fifty. "Got something in your private stock?"

The man said. "Wait here."

He went into the back room and came back a few minutes later with a brown bag. He put a bag of potato chips in the brown bag and handed it to Merchant. He could feel the fifth inside.

"Don't drop them chips," the man said. "They crunch."

Merchant spent the rest of the day at the beach.

By the time six o'clock came around, he was feeling tired, useless, and weary of the beautiful scenery.

He hiked through the island, following the shopkeeper's instructions, until he found Northup's house. It was a small place, with classic lines, a beautiful view, and clearly a lot of hard times in recent years.

Rusting bed frame in the back. A dishwasher. A Jeep with huge wheels that probably hadn't run within the last decade.

He sat on the steps and waited. Resisted opening the bottle of scotch. Even though he wasn't much of a drinker, he was bored, and it would've been something to do.

Northup came home an hour and forty-five minutes later.

He stared at Merchant as he drove up, and then slowly started to grin. He got out of his pickup truck and swatted his leg with his baseball hat a couple times. Apparently to get the red paint dust off. Comical in a way, since he managed to clean a little of his hat and knee, but the rest of him was practically dyed red.

"How the hell about this," he said.

"Got a present." Merchant held out the bottle.

Northup scowled. "Who you been talking to?"

"Do you really care?"

Northup thought about it. "Guess not."

He took the proffered bottle and cracked the seal. He took a sip. "Jesus, welcome home."

He sat on the porch steps next to Merchant. "I'd invite you in but the place is a mess." He took another sip. "Mean to say, the place is a *shithole*. That'd be a little more accurate."

"So you used to own the marina, huh?"

"You been talking," Northup said.

"Sure. It's what I do."

"You got some reason that I should care what you do, mister?"
Pronounced *Mistah*.

"How many of them do you need?"

The man laughed. A dry sound that left him hacking a moment later. He spat out a patch of red, and then another. "Don't worry. Just marine paint, not blood." He wiped his mouth with the back of his hand. "Don't get me going on the subject of need. When I talk money, I need a lot. I sold enough of my damned legacy to know that."

He looked at Merchant. "I'm sure whatever bird you talked to told you that."

Merchant nodded.

"And here you are with your bottle and some money. Hoping I can tell you what you wanna know."

"Give that man a cigar."

"I'd take one if you had it," Northup said. "Good health not the top of my list."

"So they were here?"

"He was. Not the cutie. I'd remember her, and even Bouchard would've had a hard time forgetting her."

"You paint their boat?"

"No. They had this outside guy, Gerard. Some buddy of Bouchard's. He come over, did the job himself. I'm just a fucking yard monkey for them. They were all hurry, hurry, treating the guy like royalty. Must've paid them real good. I got an extra hundred just to keep my mouth shut."

Northup chuckled, spitting again. "Not enough, I guess."

"Who paid you?"

Northup put his finger on Paul Baylors' face. "This guy. Said his name was Coburn."

"How long ago was this?"

"About a month."

"What was the name of their boat?"

"You must know that."

"I want to make sure you do."

"*Fresh Air.*" Northup took another swig of the bottle. "Light blue custom sloop."

Merchant felt the first real breath of excitement.

"What color is she now?"

"Painted it a nice jade green. Boat was sweet, I'll say that."

"How about a name?"

"How about I see some money?"

Merchant took out a fifty.

Northup said, "Double up on that, boy."

"Prove to me I got something."

"*Wildest Dreams,*" Northup said. "That's the name of it. Put a Delaware registration on it. Don't know if that's real or not."

Northup put his hand over, and Merchant gave him the bill. Northup said, "Show me what else you got in your wallet."

"How about you tell me what you've got, and we'll take it from there."

Northup shook his head, grinning. His teeth were yellowed, streaked now with the red paint. Not a wolf, not a fox. Carrion eater. "My daddy raised a fool, but no reason I got to be a poor one. Show me the cash. I got something you're gonna be happy to pay for."

Merchant opened his wallet and thumbed through the bills. Altogether about three hundred dollars.

Northup grunted. "Hoped for more, but you'll like this."

"What's that?"

"I know where the boat is."

Merchant just looked at him.

"Marina called and I was in the office. Said that they were doing repairs on a forty-foot boat called *Wildest Dreams.* Wanted to match the paint, and found the plate we put inside the hull. Little sticker, you know. It seems the hull took some storm damage not more than a night after your guy sailed her away from here."

"You know which marina this was?"

Northup nodded. "I know. Better still . . . I know something else."

"Which is?"

"The owners. They took off when the boat needed to be repaired. But it seems they're coming back to pick it up."

"When?"

"How's tomorrow for you?"

Merchant took out three fifties. "You get these now. I'll mail you the same tomorrow if your story turns out accurate."

"*Mail* it?" Northup seemed as confused by the concept as the guy from Charlestown.

"Trust me."

Northup stared at him, maybe getting ready to try something. But then he apparently decided it wasn't a good idea. He shuffled through the two hundred dollars in his hand and shrugged. "Like I said, my daddy raised a fool."

19

HOGDON'S MARINA, Green Harbor, Connecticut.

Merchant pored over the map. He was at the dock, waiting for the pilot to finish his checkout of the seaplane.

He used his cell phone to call Sarah, and got her in the truck.

"Got some news for you," Merchant said. "Where are you now?"

"Acadia."

He told her.

Sarah let out a whoop. "I *knew* I did the right thing hiring you!"

"We haven't got her yet," Merchant said. But he felt pretty pleased himself.

He said he would go to the marina first, see if the boat was indeed there. He could hear the rustle of paper. A map probably.

"OK," she said. "I see it. Just remember to keep your distance. I'll see you in six, maybe seven hours."

"I'll be there," he said.

He saw the pilot waving, and he hurried to catch his flight.

It was full dark when the plane landed in New Bedford. Merchant was yawning heavily by the time he picked up his rental car. He was also ravenous.

He checked his watch. Just after eight.

The Stateroom was nearby. The dive he used to frequent with Sarah five years ago. The dive with cold beer and good barbecue.

He drove down to the waterfront and went inside.

The place hadn't changed. Lime green walls on the outside, cheap wood paneling on the inside. Chilly air-conditioning fighting against a heavy smoke odor.

But big steaks, creamy bowls of chowder, and fresh lobster.

He took a stool and told the bartender that he'd do the lobster chowder, a small steak, and a glass of soda.

The bartender didn't recognize him, which was just what Merchant would have expected. He looked at himself briefly in the bar mirror. One of those patterned mirrors that added to the dullness of the image. His image.

Merchant thought about it. How he felt pretty good. Not ecstatic. But there was a quiet satisfaction . . . assuming the boat was indeed there. He was getting ahead of himself.

It was just that it was good to be doing work of some kind, even as limiting as what this was.

And then there was Sarah. He liked being with her. Liked it a lot. Maybe he even cared what she thought of him a bit too much.

Because he didn't know if he could honor the "no package deal" if they kept spending time together. He could feel how scared she was underneath the attitude. That she needed just what she said, a friend.

He needed that, too.

Only problem was the physical part. The emotional too. He wanted his arms around her.

He wanted her close.

Merchant sighed. Sipped his beer. Told himself it was good to be working.

It was good to go out and find something that was lost.

Someone came up behind him.

Merchant spun out of his stool and was on his feet before realizing it was George Henriques.

Henriques backed away, and then regained himself. "Jesus Christ, Merchant. Frigging hair trigger."

Henriques had changed. Before he had been reasonably fit. Now he'd bulked up. Good-size gut along with his still powerful chest and heavy arms. Purple birthmark just under his right eye. His dark skin was further shadowed with burst blood vessels in his cheeks and nose. But his face was nicked from shaving, and his suit was well tailored and working hard to cover his bulk.

Merchant said, "How goes it, George?" and didn't wait for an answer. Hoping that George would get the point and walk away. Merchant sat down on his stool.

Henriques pulled one out beside him.

"I don't know that we have much to talk about," Merchant said.

"Sure we do. Old partners in crime. Can be civilized, right? 'How you, George, what're you doing these days?' That kind of thing too hard?"

Merchant waited.

Henriques said, "Well, thanks for asking. I've gone private. Best move of my frigging life. Thanks, Jack. Never would've done it if you hadn't fucked me over way back when."

Henriques snapped his fingers at the bartender. "Hey, I turn invisible here? Give me a draft."

After a moment, the bartender drifted over with the beer. He said, "How's it going, George?"

"Now that's nice." George jerked his thumb at the bartender. "That's manners. You could learn some like that."

The bartender's face remained impassive, and then he moved away.

Henriques said, "So what're you doing in this dive?"

"Why don't you take off, George."

Henriques made a snorting sound. "I don't think I need your permission to drink at the Stateroom. I figure my bar tab covers their mortgage." He spoke up loudly to the bartender. "Hey, don't I just about pay your mortgage around here?"

The bartender took Merchant's meal from the kitchen window and said as he walked over, "We say a prayer for you every month, George. But keep it down, OK?"

Henriques ignored that.

"You know, Jack, it's funny seeing you here. I was talking about you and your . . . southern adventures . . . to that chick. Sarah Ballard. Just a couple of days ago. She get in touch?"

"Do you want something?"

"God, she's a body to die for. Guess her last boyfriend found out, huh?"

"Shut your mouth, George."

Merchant looked at him dead-on and Henriques lifted his hands. "Jesus, you got balls now, huh? Could've used those in Miami."

Merchant turned to his steak. It was good, but the taste no longer mattered. He said, "George, what do you want?"

In the mirror, he could see Henriques's smile.

"You must lead a nerve-racking life these days. Made some real enemies, I hear."

Merchant waited.

"I mean, any time, any day. Pow." Henriques laughed. "Just wish I could be there to see it happen."

Merchant signaled to the bartender. The man came over, his face worried now. Eyes flickering over to Henriques.

"Do me a favor and wrap this up to go," Merchant said.

"You bet." The bartender smiled. He took the plate away.

"Aw Jesus," Henriques said. "Did I spoil your appetite?"

Merchant turned to face Henriques. The angry eyes that he remembered, his face blurred by alcohol.

Merchant said, "You did it to yourself."

"Screw you. High and fucking mighty Merchant, you did just as bad yourself. You caved and a man died for it."

"Wasn't the same thing, George. And you can pump yourself up all you want trying to make it so. But it wasn't."

Henriques's face flushed. "If you weren't carrying, I'd kick your ass." He reached over and slapped Merchant's side with the back of his hand.

Checking him for a gun.

Merchant shoved him away.

Henriques looked startled. "What, couldn't even get a carry permit?"

Merchant stood up.

Henriques danced back off his stool. Surprisingly fast, considering his bulk. The stool fell over. He'd once done some boxing, Merchant knew, and it seemed like he still had something on the ball.

The bartender yelled, "Hey, hey, take it outside!"

The room had gone silent.

Merchant took a step forward. He was a good twenty pounds lighter than Henriques, but they could see eye to eye.

Henriques started to come forward, then something sank out of him. Hard to say what. Maybe he could just see into the future far enough to know that he would lose. Or maybe it was just a fundamental lack of heart.

The place was full of fishermen. Guys sitting at their tables, beers in front of them, waiting for a fight.

They were going to be disappointed. Henriques started motoring his mouth. "This guy's a killer on fellow officers."

He made a shooting gesture with his thumb and forefinger.

The bartender said, "George, for Christ's sakes."

A couple of fishermen laughed. They knew it was over.

Merchant put money on the bar. The bartender slid him his meal in a white Styrofoam box.

Merchant made sure not to turn his back on Henriques. It was all there, all that rage on tap.

Just a little touch of cowardice.

Merchant walked around him and started for the door.

"Yeah, now you're running," Henriques said. "Doing what punks like you do best."

Merchant ignored him.

The fishermen were already beginning to talk among themselves again, Henriques's fury already dismissed as entertaining noise, nothing more.

Merchant closed the door behind him.

20

BEACH TRAFFIC was still surprisingly heavy on the way through Rhode Island. His run-in with Henriques had soured Merchant's optimism, and the stop-and-go didn't help with what he was feeling. But around the Connecticut border, the traffic eased up. He set the cruise control at seventy, and along with a few cars behind him, sped along the coast, the darkness of the ocean visible from time to time on his left.

He reached Hogdon's Marina just before midnight. His headlights swept over a No Trespassing sign, and a warning about a dog.

"Great," Merchant said aloud in the empty car. "Bow wow."

He liked dogs just fine, but he'd had his right calf chomped by a neighbor's German shepherd as a kid, and still remembered what it felt like.

He drove inside the marina parking lot.

There was a forest of masts just past the low marina building. It would do him a world of good to see that one of them was stepped to the Baylors' sloop.

He parked, took out his camera, and slung the strap over his shoulder. He walked directly out onto the lighted deck just in front of the marina office. There were four ramps going down to floating docks.

Merchant began methodically looking up and down each row of boats. He was aware that, just off to his left, the night watchman was walking up to him.

"Sir?" the man called. "Can I help you?"

He had a dog on a leash. Big rottweiler mix.

Merchant said, "Hi there," in a friendly voice, and kept on looking up and down those rows.

She wasn't in the first.

Nor in the second.

The man was upon him now, and the dog was solemnly sniffing his pants. "A big fellow," Merchant said, offering his hand to the dog.

The guard said, "I'm sorry, I don't recognize you, sir."

Merchant looked directly at him. He was wearing one of those franchise security uniforms. Young, mid-twenties. Short blond hair. Taking himself and his dog seriously.

"No, I'm not a member here," Merchant said. He hoisted his camera. "Just scoping out the marina for a shoot."

"Is this something you've authorized with management?"

"The shoot?" Merchant looked into the third row. There was a dark-hulled forty-foot sloop midway down. He stepped closer. Lots of forty-foot sloops, but the majority of them were some variant of white.

"Sir?" The guard was becoming irritated. "I asked if —"

"No," Merchant said. "How am I going to know if I'm going to do the shoot here until I scout the location, right?"

The boat was named the *Daliah*.

He continued, "So I figured I'd drop by tonight, get at least a sense of the layout. Won't really know anything until I see it in the daylight . . ." He pointed to the roof overhanging the porch. "That wouldn't be bad," he said. "Good shade from the sun for me shoot from."

"Shoot what?"

"Catalog. Women's clothing. Two models, 'summer daze' kind of thing. It'll be fun, you'll see."

Merchant looked back at the fourth dock.

"That's not what I was asking. I was asking if you were authorized to be here tonight."

Merchant saw another dark sloop, about the right size. Fourth row, midway down.

He stepped forward, saw *Wildest Dreams* emblazoned on the stern quarter.

Lights glowing from the open cabin way.

Somebody was home.

Merchant felt a surge of relief.

Got them in time.

As if in counterpart to that thought, Paul Baylor stepped out of the cabin and into the cockpit. Even in the poor light, Merchant could recognize him. He stepped lightly off the boat and onto the dock. He headed up the ramp.

Merchant set the auto tracking on the focus. Leaving the camera at about stomach level, he idly pointed it toward the head of the ramp and waited until Baylor reached the top, underneath one of the lamps. Baylor paused for a moment, and Merchant squeezed the shutter. Being digital, it took shot after silent shot.

All the while, Merchant kept up an idle line of chatter to the night watchman. About what a pretty location this was, that he was certain it'd be a perfect site for his shoot.

Baylor walked by them toward the marina building. He didn't look their way.

He had a towel over his shoulder and a toiletry kit in hand. Cleaning up for bedtime.

Merchant checked the frame counter. He'd taken seven shots. Who knew how well composed they were, but chances were fair he had something that would identify Baylor.

He turned back to the night watchman, who was on his way to becoming genuinely pissed off at Merchant's distracted line of bullshit. Merchant said, "You know, you're right. I should've started with the manager first. What's his name?"

In a comfortable area now, the night watchman gave him the name. A Mr. Christopher Howland. Merchant asked when Mr. Howland would be in and for his phone number.

"He'll be in at seven."

"That's great. I'm an early riser myself."

Merchant felt a little bad about the Baylors, who'd be losing their cozy boat as soon as he and Sarah could arrange it.

But he'd get over it. They were deadbeats, after all.

He checked the LCD on his camera as soon as he got into the car. The shot of the boat itself was dark but acceptable. Three of the seven shots he'd taken in the vague direction of Paul Baylor came out fine.

Baylor was caught, towel over shoulder, toiletry bag in hand.

Tall, skinny guy. Looked pretty harmless.

Busted.

Merchant found a motel a few miles up the road. He downloaded the image to his laptop, hooked up the modem, and sent the e-mail with a brief cover note to Radoccia.

That done, he took a shower, put on shorts and a T-shirt. Settled down to watch cable TV until Sarah arrived.

She got there around two in the morning.

When he told her his plan, she said, "I'm your *assistant?* Why not a model?"

"You've got the looks but not the clothes."

"You're an idiot, Jack. Your big chance to flatter the boss, and you make me an assistant." She struck a pose, and then laughed.

He could see she was exhausted and a bit giddy with relief.

Merchant said, "The photo shoot gig will give us an excuse to keep an eye on the Baylors until Radoccia gets here." He told her he'd sent the e-mail.

She checked her watch. "Like he's going to see it now."

"You want to wake the client, go ahead."

"No, you're right. I'll call him in the morning."

She put her arms out to Merchant, just draping them casually over his shoulders. And kissed him.

She meant it to be chaste, a friend congratulating a friend. He could tell, the way she held her body away from his at first. But tired, happy for the moment, the two of them relaxed into each other.

"Hhmmnnn," she said, pulling herself away. "Too good, Jack. Girl's got to have rules."

"Too bad," he said.

She picked up her bag and headed for the door. She looked over her shoulder. "No more kissing up to the boss."

"Hey, it's not that," he said. "I'm just after you for your body."

She laughed and continued on to her own room.

21

JASON VANCE WAS SITTING in the back of the rental car. "Goddamn car. Don't know how people can live like this."

Thomas looked back in the mirror. There was nothing wrong with the car as far as he could tell. It was a new Chevy. Plenty of people would've been happy to make due with it. And it was a lot more innocuous than the limo. Vance was wearing a baseball cap, his leather jacket, and dark glasses. His idea of a disguise, but probably good enough this time of night.

Thomas said, "Nothing says you got do this."

"It was your idea."

They both knew that wasn't true, but Thomas didn't say anything. Vance had showed him some S & M shit on the web, stayed on it long enough for Thomas to say he could set it up if Vance wanted to try.

Well, trying time was here.

That black girl with the short leather skirt. Vance looked scared. "She knows not to leave any permanent marks, right?"

"She knows."

Vance rolled his shoulders and sighed. "Really, if this works for me, all the better. I recognize the liability as well as you do."

"I'm sure you do."

"Hey, it'd be *my* ass," Vance said. He liked to swear when it was just the two of them. With all the politically correct doublespeak in his business, Thomas couldn't really blame him.

"Not just yours," Thomas said. "They'd cook us together like black beans and white rice." He adopted a hominy sound for this last.

Vance tried a smile. "You must think I'm a goddamn freak."

Damned straight, Thomas thought. He said, "Don't you worry about what I think, Mr. Vance. Fact is, this'll be a lot safer than what you've done."

Silence from the backseat now. Vance wasn't in the mood to talk. Sometimes Thomas couldn't get him to shut up.

Vance cleared his throat. Then offered, "I'm open for experience. I guess that *does* make me a freak in this world."

Thomas glanced back at his client and said in a confidential voice, "Hey, Mr. Vance? Shit I seen, what you're doing tonight is *nothing*."

Vance chuckled. Embarrassed to need the opinion of his employee, the freak. "I guess you have seen the darker side of humanity, haven't you?" He liked to talk like that sometimes, too. *"The darker side of humanity,"* as if he did voice-overs for PBS on the side.

"That I have," Thomas said. His twenty-two years of covert work with the CIA had given him a close-up view of the various diseased passions of his fellow man. He had been part of a little cell that moved from place to place, primarily doing the domestic work the agency wasn't supposed to do. Unlike his cousins in the FBI, who might help find your kidnapped daughter, Thomas had been one of the team members who'd see to it that your teenage son followed his baser instincts and that your complicity was needed to assure he had a future outside of prison bars. This was assuming you were in a position where your cooperation was judged valuable. Vice president of a import-export business, perhaps. Or assistant to a U.S. ambassador. Maybe a senator who needed to get behind the administration on some facet of foreign policy.

Certainly a job that required planning skills, people savvy, ruthlessness and, yes, intelligence. When the Cold War ended, he hung on for a few years until they fired his ass. Since then, Thomas had made his living with corporate security work — sometimes the other way, espionage. It paid his bills but offered nothing that really tapped his abilities. Until a couple of months ago, when he was directed by a former client to this man.

Thomas knew he didn't hold a candle to Vance in sheer intelligence. Not in technical intelligence, moneymaking intelligence. People called Vance brilliant, people called him a visionary. Mainly because a lot of people hoped, trusted, and were desperate to believe that he could recoup their enormous losses and make them a lot of money.

And, in fact, he had made Thomas a lot of money. His salary was better than decent, but the real money was in the special services. Like taking care of that dead hooker in the dumpy apartment.

The money made Vance brilliant enough, as far as Thomas was concerned. As for the people savvy, Vance operated pretty well on the surface. Just under that, he was a squalling, destructive baby, whose appetites required constant management and protection.

It was a damn good job for Thomas.

The dungeon was on the Upper West Side, off West End Avenue. Basement of a very nice building. No doorman, but there was a video camera in the corner.

"You see that?" Vance said.

"What'd you expect?" Thomas said. "I'll take care of it."

Thomas pressed the intercom, and a male voice answered. Thomas gave him the code the girl had told him: "Sunshine in the Park."

"Second basement level," the voice said.

They took the elevator down. Vance was humming under his breath. He was a big guy, late forties. Taller than Thomas with a sunburned face and a thick body. Fat, but Thomas knew how strong he was. Light blue eyes, whitish eyebrows and lashes. Friendly enough look on his face. Would be a pleasant looking guy aside from a softness about the mouth. Pouty lips, babyish.

He repelled Thomas, but then again, Thomas had seen what he did to that hooker. Most people found him charming, especially when he was talking about making them money.

The elevator reached bottom.

The door opened up to a surprisingly sterile waiting room. If anything, it looked like a doctor's office. There was a buzzer on the desk, and Thomas went over, pushed it.

Nothing happened.

They stood there for a moment, and Vance said, "You screw up the time, Thomas?"

"No. Let's sit."

Vance wasn't used to waiting rooms. In his professional life, people were always falling over themselves to make his time run smoothly, effortlessly. To show their respect.

Vance looked at his watch, a thirty thousand dollar piece of jewelry. "Where the hell is she?"

"Part of the game," Thomas said.

"I don't like it."

Thomas shrugged. "So we can go."

Vance paced back and forth, ignoring Thomas's answer. After a few minutes of that, he sat beside him. "I'm not good at waiting, have you noticed that?"

"I noticed."

Vance looked at his watch again. "Do you know how much my time is worth?"

"Couldn't begin to guess." Actually, Thomas had once listened to Vance pontificate on this at some length, calculating his rags-to-riches story into a stratospheric hourly value.

But this time, Vance seemed to accept Thomas's answer as appropriate. "You know, I might not be psychologically suited to this kind of service."

Thomas pointed to the elevator door, but Vance shook his head. He closed his eyes and leaned back in the chair. Trying to be patient.

He managed it for a surprisingly long time, almost five minutes. In fact, Thomas began to wonder if the man had gone to sleep, so still had he become.

But when he opened his eyes, he checked his watch again. He shook his head and said quietly to himself, "Well, OK, then."

"What's that?"

When he spoke, Vance had adopted the studied casual tone that Thomas knew to listen for. "I've just been thinking about what I like and what I don't and what I can afford and where you fit into all of that."

"OK."

"Thomas, you did well with my previous situation. And you certainly were paid well, correct?"

"Paid well for an important service."

"I agree." Vance looked at Thomas directly, revealing the reptilian persona behind the blue eyes, the smooth, well-fed face. "You're my boy, aren't you? For the money, I can count on you?"

"You can count on me, Mr. Vance."

Vance smiled. "Good." He touched Thomas on the knee, an intimacy Thomas truly didn't like. But he let it go.

Vance said, "You have your good pen, if we need to write an extra big check tonight?"

"You want that, you should've let me set up something safer."

"I just want to know if my options are fully open."

Thomas paused, then said, "If my compensation is."

"Well, not necessarily at the same rate . . ."

"This ain't no time to bargain."

Vance seemed to think about it, and then lifted his shoulders. "Whatever."

"Uh-huh. Well, I've got my pen. If you've got the checkbook."

"That's fine, then." Vance looked at his watch again. "Just knowing that makes the wait so much easier."

It was another ten minutes before the door opened and two men followed the black girl out.

She was naked.

Naked except for a gold necklace and anklet, the briefest of black bikini panties. Her breasts were taut and full, tilted upward. Large, erect nipples. If Thomas were any judge, her breasts were real.

The two men were in full leather garb, with leather face masks and studded leather collars around their necks. Only their genitalia and hands were exposed. They flanked the girl on each side, the smell of their sweat pervading the room.

Her effect, spectacular though she was, created distance. Thomas was surprised to feel his own physical response: equal parts lust and trepidation.

Made him think maybe she was too much for him.

Astounding.

And Vance did what so many guys do when they are intimidated — he became a clown. He slapped the shoulder of the guy nearest him and whooped. "Leather Man," he said. "Gimme one of those suits."

Vance went right into goofing with the girl, calling her mistress, and laughing and fawning, and looking back at Thomas to see if he appreciated the humor.

She seemed bored by his antics.

Thomas studied Vance carefully. Not knowing how much he was putting it on, not knowing where he was really headed with this.

Because unpredictability was truly his greatest asset.

One of the big guys came over to pat Thomas down for weapons.

Thomas felt distinctly uncomfortable. Being touched by another man who was exposed like that was disconcerting at the very least.

He almost lashed out right then, but it was the wrong time. The second option was to appeal to her, to ask her to call them off.

He almost did, and then shut his mouth.

Almost had him begging for her permission already. She apparently did know her business. Thomas took an envelope from his coat pocket and tossed it in her direction.

She didn't even glance at it. The slave with Vance did, though. He knelt down, opened the envelope, and pawed through the cash quickly. He nodded to her.

Thomas gestured with his chin to Vance. "He's all yours."

She said, "He most certainly is."

She jerked her head at the other slave, and he abruptly kicked Vance in the back of the legs, sending him to his knees. She kicked him in the stomach, knocking the breath out of him. He curled over, gasping for breath, and the slave got behind him, put his hand on the back of his neck, and pushed his head to the floor.

The woman put her foot on his face. "Keep your mouth shut until I say otherwise."

"Don't mess up his face," Thomas said.

She spread her arms wide at Thomas. Like Thank you very much for telling me my business.

Those breasts were real. Thomas was certain of it. He said, "I want to see the rest of the place. Before you do another thing to him, I want to make sure we're alone like I paid."

"Whatever you want, sweetie. I'll hold off on him till you get in the viewing room. You won't miss a thing."

Thomas had the Leather Man walk him into the back rooms, which included four small bedrooms, a cramped little office, and a dressing room with a wall of neatly hung costumes, a small gas stove, and a single shower stall surprisingly decorated with pink nonskid flower petals.

The Leather Man walked him through the three primary rooms: a basic dungeon with some sort of rack, plus chains on the walls; a doctor's examining room with shiny aluminum table and a tray of clamps and clothespins; and a small classroom with a desk, chalkboard, and a couple of kiddie desks with shiny wood-laminate tops. Leather strap hanging on the wall.

Wordlessly, Leather Man pointed to the video cameras. The cables were easy to follow: they were simply stapled along the junction of the wall and ceiling. The man led Thomas back into a booth. It was a paneled room with four video monitors. There were no video recorders in the room.

"My, my," Thomas said. One monitor displayed the street front, the other three covered the rooms they'd just left: dungeon, doctor's office, and classroom. Thomas looked over at Leather Man. "Can't you people come up with anything more original than this?"

Leather Man's head turned his way, but there was no answer. His breath whistled through the nose guard. The mouthpiece was wide open, so Thomas could see his lips and the fringe of his mustache.

Pretty goddamn obscene, Thomas thought.

The mask covered just Leather Man's face. Straps held it on with two big buckles from behind. Looked uncomfortable as hell. That studded collar was thick and wide, but not too tight.

Thomas drew his pen from his pocket and sat down in an easy chair beside Leather Man. Thomas idly clicked the pen in and out, and settled down to watch the monitors. Watch the show.

"Don't tell me there's no popcorn," he said.

Leather Man didn't answer.

The video quality was for shit. It made Thomas think of some of the stuff he'd seen on the web with Vance.

In the past months with Vance, Thomas had seen more porn sites and general weirdness on the web than he had in the past five years. Vance was enthralled with it all. Maybe because he had so much to do with making the Net work himself, he felt some ownership.

Either way, looking at three video monitors, Thomas could see Vance had made his way completely into one of his web fantasies.

The girl took her time. Thomas would give her that. She had Vance strip down, his body big and pink in the monitor. First she had him do the dog bit on his knees, following her.

Made him be a student for a while, threatening a strapping but not delivering. He had an erection; his penis was a skinny little stick protruding past his thick thighs. She shook her head, smiling like an indulgent teacher. "You are *so* disobedient. I'm afraid you've got a medical condition that needs controlling."

Thomas yawned. Third-rate acting. Yet Vance seemed to be taking it seriously.

She rode him into the doctor's room and left him there. He put on a johnny and waited obediently. She came back as a physician, white lab coat, clipboard, naked underneath.

They went through a game. Man comes to the doctor complaining about impotence. She has him expose himself, and demonstrates that he needs to be punished to feel pleasure. Vance revealed his skinny little dick as if it were the Empire State Building.

Thomas felt embarrassed for him.

Vance went along with being strapped down to the table, and Thomas began to feel that it all might work out just fine. Maybe Vance's impatience about being kept waiting was just a passing thing.

Maybe it was all the guy needed, his weenie whacked by the right woman. If that worked, God bless.

After all, pay as well as it did, Thomas hadn't exactly enjoyed meticulously washing that dead hooker. He had worked on her and the apartment until just before sunrise to obliterate any DNA evidence.

Thomas shifted in his seat. Thinking about how getting Vance set right wouldn't help his own portfolio too much, but it would be safer. Telling himself he had already come out fine. His portfolio was already sitting at five hundred and seventy-six thousand, which was five hundred thousand greater than it had been before he took care of that dead hooker for Vance.

Still, Thomas felt a little disappointed. It was peanuts compared to what Vance had.

He looked back at the monitor. She was using the leather whip.

Thomas yawned again.

Then he heard through the cheap speakers a different tone in

Vance's scream. Fury. Sheer fury. He guessed her whip had traveled a little too far southward.

Whether that was a mistake or intentional, Thomas didn't know.

But she laughed, and hurt Vance again.

And then she began using some of the toys from the silver tray, the various clamps. Vance started blubbering and begging for forgiveness.

Thomas considered stopping it right there. It would be safer, he told himself. And then he thought about more his portfolio. About how nice it would be to bump it up again.

Eventually, the woman called the other Leather Man in and told him to unfasten Vance from the table. He began to release the straps.

Thomas twisted the center band on his pen and felt rather than heard the soft snick. He pushed the top button, sliding a stainless steel blade out the end of the pen. The little blade was just an inch long, razor sharp, and once engaged, locked.

He held the pen alongside his leg.

On the monitor, the woman's back was to Vance as she said that she felt he was ready to go back to the classroom now, that she suspected he knew how to behave.

So she didn't see it when Vance kicked the Leather Man in the crotch, but she heard, and reacted instantly.

"Rollie, get in here," she screamed, and the Leather Man to Thomas's left jumped to his feet, knocking his chair over.

Thomas rose behind him silently, grabbed him by the spiked collar, and plunged the pen into the back of his neck. Thomas pulled and twisted the little blade back hard, working at the spinal column.

The guy shuddered, and then his legs went out from under him and he collapsed. Thomas stood over him. The guy's arms and legs didn't work, but his lungs sounded fine and he screamed, that mouth a red hole inside the black leather mask.

"I'll be back to finish you," Thomas said. He wouldn't leave a dog to live like that. He hurried off to the doctor's office to dispatch the other Leather Man.

The girl, he knew, Vance would want for himself.

22

SARAH PUT ON DARK SUNGLASSES as she left her room the next morning.

They barely helped. "Poor me," she said. Hamming it up to herself. It made her feel better.

Merchant was waiting for her in the truck.

Six-thirty A.M. Normally she would've been about ten miles out on her bike, but normally she would've had more than three hours of sleep. Goddamn Owen had been back last night. That little bit of flirting with Jack; that kiss. It raised the old fear, that Owen would be jealous and coming after her.

"What happened to my morning person?" Merchant said as she got in.

She said, "Shut up."

He grinned.

She scrunched against the door of the truck and pulled her baseball cap low. "Soon you'll have my usual devoted love and attention. But for now, just give me some peace."

Merchant stopped along the way to the marina and picked up bagels and coffee. Sarah sipped hers slowly, holding the cup between two hands.

She looked over at Merchant. He seemed happy, apparently looking forward to finishing the job, getting his pay. She was going to miss him.

Poor me, she thought.

*   *   *

They pulled into the marina parking lot a little before seven.

Merchant walked her to the head of the dock, and she saw the boat. "*Wildest Dreams*," she said. "You've worked out beyond my wildest dreams, Mr. Merchant."

He put his hand on her shoulder, gave her a squeeze. "I can only say the same." He gave her a little shake, jumbling her up. Made her laugh.

Then she disengaged herself. She enjoyed that, his arm around her. He also made her nervous.

Owen had provided the same comfort, once upon a time.

"C'mon," she said. "We've got a steward to bribe."

They went into the marina office to find Howland.

He was a weather-beaten man in his early fifties. He let his eyes travel up and down Sarah with frank interest. "She your model?"

"No, my assistant. We'll be figuring out the shoot today. If this is the right site, we'll be back tomorrow with the models."

"Christ. She's your assistant, can't wait to see the models."

He stared at Sarah, waiting for her to say thank you.

She didn't.

Instead she smiled blankly and thought about how satisfying it would be to kick him.

Apparently that wasn't the reaction Howland wanted, and he began to make noises about not being sure the marina was insured for "models and such." Merchant took out his wallet and said he realized there would normally be a "permission fee" of a hundred dollars or so, and would that go to Howland?

"Yes, it would," Howland said, and the money disappeared. Then he went on to say the permission was specifically for today, to set up the shot. They agreed if an "actual shoot" with several models was decided upon, there would be another permission fee necessary, most likely in the two-hundred-dollar range.

On the way back to the truck, Sarah took out her cell phone and called Gene Radoccia.

His secretary answered and said he was out and she'd take a message. Once Sarah gave her name, the secretary said, "Oh. He said if you called to let him know immediately. Hold on a second."

It was more like three minutes. Sarah sat on the pier watching

Merchant turn the truck around and start backing the Mako down the ramp into the water.

Radoccia came on. "Hey," he said. "I just checked my e-mail, saw the picture. You got them!"

"That's right, Mr. Radoccia. We're at the dock now, and I can go make the repossession any time."

"No," Radoccia said. "Just like I called it before, wait for me to get there." She heard him rustling around, and then he sighed. "Damn. I do have a board meeting I've got to present to Bill Tyler. That'll go through lunch. Where are you, exactly?"

She told him.

"Ah, Christ. It could be as late as three, maybe even five before I get down to you. I'm sorry, but I'm going to have to ask you to wait. Figure out a reasonable day rate, and bill us. I'll authorize it."

She sighed inwardly. But keeping MassBank happy was what this was all about for her.

She saw Merchant had the boat in place, and he got out to push it off the trailer. He moved with that easy energy of his; he stepped lightly onto the trailer, and then he shoved the Mako into deeper water and did a small sideways vault, getting his butt onto the rail. He swung his legs over into the cockpit. He smiled back at her as he got behind the wheel and lowered the outboard. She smiled back.

"Sure," she said to Radoccia. "We can wait. It's beautiful here."

They played at photographer and assistant throughout the morning and early afternoon.

If anyone were near, dock boy or Howland or other marina guests, Merchant and Sarah would discuss their fictitious shoot and fictitious models, Dana and Jennifer, with intense energy:

Merchant would say, *"I'll want Dana here in the white one-piece and I'll want the reflector here, and she's just going to be looking over her back shoulder, warm skin, just blinding high key-tones on the suit, you know, with that skin of hers and suit together, you know what I'm talking about . . ."*

And then once the person was past, Sarah would start in on Dana, saying that would be a terrific shot really, if the poor girl didn't eat those chocolates and break out in pimples, and the only reason Merchant was so hot on a pimply girl like Dana was because she was blond, but Sarah had definite proof that Dana wasn't really. . . .

Bored silly, passing time. All the while, they kept an eye on the Baylors' boat.

Around one o'clock, Sarah asked Merchant for the camera and took a few photos herself. Out of her peripheral vision, she'd seen movement on the *Wildest Dreams* and swung the lens that way just as Julie Baylor had stepped out on deck.

She was a pretty woman, though she seemed a bit older than her pictures. Not quite as tall and elegant as Dana and Jennifer, but, after all, she was real.

She looked up at Sarah.

Sarah immediately began tracking a seagull from just over Julie's head and followed it up to the piling in front of herself, actually capturing several good midflight shots. "Not too subtle, huh?" she said.

"I think it's time we got off this dock," he said.

"Good. I'm sick of discussing those two tramps with you."

"Tramps, are they now?"

Sarah took the camera strap off her neck and handed the Nikon to Merchant. She leaned in close. "It makes me sick how they throw themselves at you."

For the next few hours, they puttered around the harbor in the Mako. They'd drop the anchor from time to time and go through a charade of lining up shots on the boat with different backgrounds.

Finally, around midafternoon, they went back to shore, picked up a lunch at the marina, and then puttered out to a free mooring several hundred yards off the dock where the *Wildest Dreams* was docked. They'd both changed into swimsuits at the marina.

"Yuck," Sarah said. She considered her tuna sub on a white roll, the little bag of chips, the diet soda. "I eat like this when I'm on the road, and then I have to work out like crazy to get back in shape."

"I can see it's a problem," Merchant said.

"Well, you know," she said.

She liked her body pretty well herself. Long legs, smooth muscle. Definition in her arms.

What she liked was the strength. She liked feeling it in her, liked that at one hundred and forty pounds and five ten, she was stronger and faster per pound than most men.

I can run away really fast, she thought.

She liked what she saw in Merchant, too. Laying back with his shirt off. A big guy, well-muscled arms and chest. No beer belly, but not ridged with stomach muscles like Owen.

Or herself, for that matter. She knew what it took to make that happen, and didn't like what it said about a person.

Wouldn't date myself, she thought.

She wanted Merchant's arm around her, liked having him beside her on the bench seat. The nearness of him, the scent of suntan lotion, the brush of heat when her bare arm touched his. It was having its effect, feelings she hadn't felt in a long time.

But she told herself that wanting him around was scary enough. As for the physical stuff, cool your jets, Sarah.

He raised the camera, focusing through his longest zoom lens at the Baylors. "Still there," he said. "Mechanic with them now, and Howland, too."

She raised her binoculars. Howland was appearing to explain something, and Baylor was nodding. Probably discussing work that had been done.

Sarah sighed. She wrapped up the wax paper and stuffed the remains of her lunch into the paper bag.

Checked her watch. Just after three-thirty. Few hours to go.

She stretched and yawned. Boredom on top of the lack of sleep.

She laughed and he said, "What?"

"Nothing."

"Uh-huh."

She looked at him directly. The attraction she was feeling for him. Wondered if it was just the walking-wounded thing. If all they had between them was a history of bad judgments and worse timing.

"What're you thinking?" Merchant asked.

"Mmmm." She stretched again. Felt him watching, and she enjoyed it. "Nothing," she said.

"Want to share?"

She almost did. But she chickened out. "No. What I'd really like is to conk out for a while."

"Yeah, you didn't get much sleep last night. Go for it."

She went to the bow and pulled up the small awning, threw in some of the cushions and a beach towel. Merchant sat back in the sun and watched the Baylors some more while she twisted around, trying to get comfortable.

The sunlight was still bothering her, bouncing off the white fiberglass. He came around the console and knelt down in front of her. She smiled up at him warily.

He put his baseball cap on her head and tugged down the brim, covering her eyes. "Sleep tight."

But it wasn't that easy.

No matter the cushions, the towels, and her lack of sleep — the Mako was a little boat on a hot, brilliant day. Plus she was aware of Merchant just a few feet away, and as time passed she became more aroused, not less so.

She imagined him kneeling back down beside her and without saying a word, putting his hands on her back and just touching her. Touching her legs, her neck, her arms. And then she would roll over and he would continue. His warmth superheating the languor of the day.

She kept her eyes closed, her mind letting him touch her. It awakened her even more for a while, and then, when she at last realized that it wasn't going to happen and that she didn't really want it to happen, she let it go.

After that, she felt drowsy and happy that she was having such feelings again.

It had been so long.

She fell into a half sleep. She was aware of the motion of the boat, that she was in the bow. In the dream, they had made love, and they were both naked and Merchant had left their little bed.

Now Owen was on the boat too, and though she knew she was asleep, she felt her hand swinging that rock and the wetness in his temple when she hit him, and then again when she swung the rock again. It became an ugly little repeat for her: hit once, hit twice. The second time going farther into his head. The blood under her fingernails. The nurse at the hospital took a swipe of them and put the cotton swab into a plastic bag for evidence.

Only now when she was sitting on that hospital bed with the white paper underneath, she was naked and it was embarrassing, with people coming in and seeing her, and there was blood all over her and she was naked.

Merchant was still in the boat. He didn't seem to be aware Owen was there. She was incredulous. Goddamn, it wasn't that big a boat, didn't he see what he was getting into? Didn't he see Owen right there? Was he going to let him climb out of the water and get onto the boat?

Blood was streaming down Owen's face as he climbed up the swim ladder. The salt must've hurt the wound in his head, must've hurt like a bastard.

Owen's going to be furious, she thought. *And I'm naked.*

She woke up.

Merchant was still sitting behind the console. "Hasn't even been a half hour," he said. "Go back to sleep."

"It was enough." Her voice was croaky, and the taste of her tuna sub was something she'd rather be doing without.

She looked over the side of the boat, eyes blinking in the harsh light. Just making sure Owen wasn't really there, she supposed.

She tossed Merchant's hat onto the console. "Be right back." She stood up on the rail and dove into the water.

Oh my God, she thought. My God, my God. That rush of water. Even though it was harbor water, not the cleanest. But she was free and fast in the water, and that cleansed her.

She stayed down, doing a scissors kick, keeping at it until the pressure on her lungs sent her up. And then she took off with a medium crawl, just getting her stretch in. She kept at that for about ten minutes, steady speed, passing by the moored sailboats surprisingly fast. Never minding the mild chop, that was part of the fun.

Once she was loosened up, she started doing sprints. Pouring it on from one boat to the next. Feeling herself rise out of the water, practically planing, at least in her mind.

She felt good.

It'd been too long. Still had it. Still had the strength and endurance waiting there on tap.

She stopped at a twenty-five-foot sloop and held on to the mooring line. Looked back to see Merchant a distant figure on her little boat. Sarah hung there, breathing deep, hiding under the overhang. Feeling good again in the cold salt water. Feeling refreshed and independent and strong. And thinking that maybe it would be best to just keep things that way.

23

SARAH'S CELL PHONE sounded. Merchant flipped it open and answered. It was Radoccia. "Just got out of that meeting," he said. "I'm leaving now. They still there?"

"Yep."

"Good. Keep an eye on them. I'll be there as soon as I can, but the traffic on 128 is miserable already. Must be an accident up ahead."

Merchant checked his watch. It was already four-thirty. "All right," he said. "We'll be here."

Another couple of hours, minimum.

He saw the mechanic was just leaving the Baylors' boat. He looked back at Sarah and saw she was on her way back as well. He figured if the Baylors took off, he could always swing by and pick up Sarah in the water. But he saw Paul Baylor talk briefly with his wife and then head up to the dock. A few minutes later, he returned with a cart full of supplies.

Merchant sat down and sighed.

He put the lens on Sarah and watched her while she kept at it, the flash of her legs, the smooth reach of her arms. Eventually, she pulled herself up easily on the swim ladder. Her breathing was steady, and she was smiling. "That cleans out the cobwebs."

He found a jug of fresh water near the transom, warmed by the sun.

"Here," he said. He began to pour the water over her, but she took the jug from his hand.

"Thank you," she said. "I'll do it myself."

"Sure." He stepped back. Good to keep things clear. Keep business and pleasure separate. He should know that.

He told her about Radoccia's call.

"Then take your turn," she said, gesturing to the cushions. "We've got time to kill. I'll keep watch now."

Why not, he thought. He was tired. Aroused, too, but it didn't seem they'd be doing anything about that. "All right. Wake me when something happens."

He lay down where she had been. She tossed him his baseball hat, and he covered his eyes and let the heat wash over him. He shifted around awhile, the testosterone keeping him awake, and it wasn't until he was finally asleep that Sarah came to him.

And that, he knew, was just a dream.

Sometime after that, he awoke to find Sarah standing over him.

But this was no dream, and she wasn't happy. She was saying, *Damn it, damn it, damn it,* as she shoved the awning down.

"What?" he said.

"I slept," she said. "Fell asleep after my swim, God damn it, and they're gone."

He rolled to his feet. "I'll get the mooring."

She hurried back to the console and turned the key. The outboard coughed twice but started.

Merchant looked at the dock. The sun was just down; it was hard to see. But there was no doubt, the Baylors' boat was gone.

Merchant dropped the mooring line.

Sarah backed the Mako down hard, spun the wheel over, and shoved the throttle forward. "I'm such an idiot. I just put my head down for a minute, *damn it!*"

They quickly toured in and out of the other four docks, making sure the *Wildest Dreams* hadn't just been moved for some reason.

And then they booked it out of the harbor.

Sarah put the throttle all the way down as soon as they were in the main channel. The Mako's bow rose and quickly flattened out onto a plane. Merchant flipped through the chart pack and said, "We've got a shot. This channel takes over three miles to get out. Only one way to go, and we can do it a lot faster than they can."

It was about twenty minutes before eight o'clock. Night was almost fully upon them.

The big outboard roared, and Sarah's hair was whipping about her face. Merchant went to the bow and knelt with the binoculars. Hard to see much, between the chop of the small waves and the poor light. But he kept the binocs sweeping to each boat they passed.

They rounded the first buoy, then the next, and then the next.

Plenty of boats, many of them sail. None of them the *Wildest Dreams*.

They were past the mouth of the channel, into the Atlantic, before they found her.

Fifteen minutes more, she would've slipped away in darkness.

As it was, Merchant almost missed her. With her dark hull, she was now almost invisible in the fading light.

He pointed her out, and Sarah banked the Mako for her.

"You're the right man for the job, Jack," she yelled.

She cut the engine to idle as they pulled close to the sloop.

They could see the Baylors in the cockpit, staring back at them. Merchant found it hard to read their expressions. He would've expected fear, maybe resignation, but there was something else.

"Let me do this," Sarah said.

"Be my guest." Now that they were at it, Merchant felt how intrusive and ugly this job could be. Time to put a towrope on and tell the Baylors' their boat was no longer their own.

Sarah pulled a file folder from her backpack. "Mr. and Mrs. Baylor," she called. "I'm Sarah Ballard of Ballard's Marine Liquidation. I'm sorry, but I have to inform you that I have authorization to repossess your boat for nonpayment of your loan."

"There must be a mistake," Baylor called back. "Who do you want?"

He didn't sound convincing.

Sarah ignored his response. "I have to ask you to lower your sails. I'll tow you in."

Baylor said, "You're making a mistake."

"I'm afraid not, sir. Please let's not make this more difficult than it need be."

Baylor paused and then looked forward into his cabin, as if thinking. He said, "You should come aboard and we can discuss this. You have the wrong people."

"That's fine," Sarah said. "Lower your sails please."

"Something's screwy," Merchant said.

"It's like this all the time. They think they can talk me out of it. I've gotten pretty good at convincing them they can't."

Paul Baylor spun their boat into the wind and dropped the sails.

Sarah eased the Mako alongside, and it wasn't until Merchant was tying them off that he realized there was tangible evidence that something was awry.

There were two dinghies. One on the stern cradle, poised above the water. The one that had been there all along.

And an inflatable being towed behind.

Someone else was onboard.

It was a nightmare.

Bobby Lee Randall emerged from the cabin.

On some level Merchant understood that it wasn't Bobby Lee. That it must be one of his family, if not one of those brothers, a cousin, somebody.

But Merchant could think of him in that instant only as Bobby Lee.

Bobby Lee had a gun in each hand, and he was grinning.

He shot Sarah.

Merchant had already grabbed her right arm by then. He had grabbed her as she started to step onto the Baylors' boat. As Bobby Lee raised the gun in his right hand and made it spit fire, Merchant had pulled at Sarah with all his strength. Off balance, she'd virtually flown off the railing, clutching her left arm.

He swung her down into the forward area.

He spun around and scrambled over the rail, fully expecting that Bobby Lee would be waiting, poised and ready to finish the job with him.

But Paul Baylor threw himself on the man.

The gun flashed again. Only this time it was the gun in Bobby Lee's left hand. Baylor stumbled back clutching his stomach, and Bobby Lee reached out and aimed between Baylor's eyes and even as Julie screamed, Bobby Lee finished that job.

Merchant got to Bobby Lee, got his hands on both wrists.

He realized that this man was bigger than Bobby Lee. Taller and heavier than Merchant. He was immensely strong.

Merchant kept both guns pointed down; one of them went off, and he felt a scrape, no more, along his left leg.

How long he could've held both of those guns down, Merchant didn't know, but he knew it wouldn't be for long.

But there was movement behind him. Sarah had somehow gotten to her feet and climbed over onto the boat, her left arm hanging limp.

"Hold him, Jack," she said, her voice half-crying. "Hold him."

Bobby Lee's eyes turned to her and he tried to tug the guns away, but Merchant held fast.

Sarah sucked air through clenched teeth, drew her good arm back and chopped Bobby Lee on the neck as hard as she could with the knife edge of her hand.

That made him wobbly, and maybe forced a decision on him, because he dropped the gun in his left hand and concentrated both hands on his right.

Merchant covered Bobby Lee's hands with his own.

Sarah hit him again.

Still didn't put him down. Bobby Lee began to twist the gun up, against everything Merchant had. Merchant butted him with his head, and that made the guy stumble, and Merchant got his finger inside the trigger guard. He told himself — mentally babbling — really, that he'd be able to wrench the gun free as long as Sarah could keep delivering those blows to Bobby Lee's neck.

But he didn't believe it. The gun barrel was moving up again, and the guy was squeezing the trigger hard enough to break Merchant's finger bone.

Luckily, Julie Baylor picked up the other gun. She stood beside Merchant and pressed the barrel against the forehead of Bobby Lee's brother or cousin or whoever he was.

She pulled the trigger.

24

MERCHANT TOOK THE GUN from Julie Baylor.

For a moment, none of them said a word.

Merchant grasped Sarah by the hand, pulling her to the cabin roof. Her hand, her whole arm, was covered in blood.

"Sit," he said. "Lay down, in fact. Let me get your feet up."

The enormity of it was sweeping over him, threatening to engulf him. What he had brought on these people.

Jesus God.

He tried to shake that away for the time being. Told himself the best he could do for Julie Baylor and Sarah was to keep moving, keep thinking.

Julie began shivering. "Oh God," she said, kneeling down in front of her husband. Blood all over the white cockpit, his face distorted by the bullet in his forehead.

"Oh God," she said again, a hiccuping sound. Barely able to catch her breath. "Paul. Oh, Paul, no."

She touched him, clasped his hand in hers, and shook it as if to implore a favor of him. "Don't. Please don't."

"Julie," Merchant said. "Mrs. Baylor."

She turned on him wildly. "Who are you?"

She backed away from him as if afraid he might hit her.

He took quick stock of the situation. Radio on both boats. The Mako much faster, obviously.

Sarah shot.

"OK," he said. "We've got to get her to a hospital. Both of you."

He took a glance at the depth gauge on the bulwark and saw the digital readout was at forty feet. The seas were calm.

He went forward and let the bow anchor off. He didn't take time to do it very well, just dumped off enough line so that the *Wildest Dreams* would probably catch once she drifted a bit.

It was all the time he had to give her, anyhow.

He hurried back and said to Sarah, "OK, Sarah girl, we're going now."

"OK," she said. Her eyes were closed. "Good idea."

He picked her up, stepped onto the Mako's rail, and then quickly into the bow section. She helped him set her down, and he put a cushion under her head and the cooler under her legs. He rummaged around the boat until he found her white cotton shirt, and he ripped off a strip to wrap around her arm. The cloth was immediately soaked with blood.

He stepped back onboard for Julie Baylor.

"Mrs. Baylor. You need to come with me now. I'm taking both of you to the hospital."

"You can't just leave him," she said. She was still holding her husband's hand. "You can't just leave him with that man."

For the first time, Merchant took a good look at the other man. His face was much like Baylor's, misshapen by the effect of the bullet. He was sprawled across the cockpit beside Baylor, his head cocked at an odd angle the way it was wedged against the genoa winch.

Definitely part of Bobby Lee's clan.

Merchant knelt beside Julie Baylor. "I'm going to call the Coast Guard the second we get on the boat. Now come on, my friend is hurt, I've got to get both of you back."

"I'm not going."

"Julie, I'm sorry. It's not your fault. God knows, it's not your fault. But if you don't come, I'm going to pick you up and take you. You've got to get on my boat, and now."

"You brought this on us," she said. "You bastard. He said he was doing this for the man following us, that he wouldn't hurt us."

Inside, Merchant flinched.

She lunged past him, and he saw that she was going for the gun, the one that had killed her husband.

Merchant grabbed her by the shoulder and pulled her back, being as gentle with her as he could. He scooped the gun up in his right hand, and held it behind him.

He kept his arm around her. "Please, Mrs. Baylor," he said. "We've got no choice. Now get in my boat."

On some level, she seemed to recognize the comfort of his grip, and she sagged against him briefly before standing straight, and withdrawing.

"You can let go of me," she said.

He did.

She stepped onto the Mako.

He turned to put the gun down. Put it back where it had fallen. Years of training about not disturbing a crime scene.

But the familiarity of it in his hand made him pause.

It was a revolver, looked like a thirty-eight.

It was much like the one he had in the bow of his boat. The one he had taken from the Charlestown punk Fogerty.

In fact . . . looking at the oiled blue steel more carefully, at the nick just behind the sight, the thick rubber bands around the wooden grip, Merchant realized with sudden and appalling clarity that this didn't just look like the same gun.

It was the same gun.

25

MERCHANT PUT IN A CALL to the Coast Guard over the roar of the outboard. It was dark enough now that he had to concentrate fully just to make out the buoys.

The Coast Guard officer answering the Mayday wanted to know the location of the *Wildest Dreams* and Sarah's condition. He asked Merchant twice to confirm that not only were two men dead but the weapons that had made them that way were still on the sailboat.

"You're telling us you're now unarmed, is that correct, sir?"

"That's correct."

"All right then, sir. Proceed back to Hogdon's Bay Marina. You'll be closer to the hospital, and we'll have the ambulance crew waiting on the dock by the time you arrive."

"On our way, Sarah," Merchant called after putting the mike down.

She nodded. After a moment, she roused herself to yell, "Who was that guy?"

Julie turned to look at him.

Merchant kept his focus on the next buoy, and then, after he rounded it, he yelled back. "My trouble. I'm so sorry, Sarah. Mrs. Baylor."

Merchant could barely read Sarah's expression, so dark it had become. But she said nothing.

Julie Baylor looked at her, seemingly for the first time. After a moment, she moved beside Sarah and sat there for the rest of the short journey, not touching her, not talking.

The police were waiting on those docks, as well as the ambulance crew. Merchant knew the drill and kept his hands visible as two cops came down on the dock, their guns drawn.

"Step off the boat, please," one of them said. He looked at Julie. "You, too, lady." Big tall guy, with a crew cut. The other was smaller, dark-haired, built like a weight lifter.

Merchant stepped onto the dock and let them search him quickly. Julie did the same.

Satisfied that they were unarmed, the cops relaxed visibly. They made way for the ambulance crew. One of them got into the boat and knelt beside Sarah. The other led Julie off to the other end of the dock, had her sit on the portable stairs for a big cruiser, and began to examine her quickly.

The lead cop rounded on Merchant. "OK, let's see some ID."

Merchant gave it to him, and told him that he and Sarah had been approaching the *Wildest Dreams* for repossession. He gave them Sarah's card and told them the Baylors' names and address.

The cop took the information down, then looked up the dock as an older uniformed officer started down the ramp. "All right, there's Chief Konig. I expect he'll want to take your statement."

Merchant saw that the ambulance crew was getting ready to lift Sarah out of the boat. He and the cop went over and helped them. Merchant looked down at her face, almost as pale as the sheet on the stretcher. He leaned close. "How're you doing?"

"Don't worry about me." She moved her arm, trying for a smile, but it came off more as a grimace. "They've given me drugs."

"No one deserves them more."

"Mmmhh. Coming from a former DEA man . . ." She looked past him. "You should go check on her. He's probably over there serving her an eviction notice."

Merchant turned.

Gene Radoccia was standing over Julie Baylor.

Merchant kissed Sarah and said, "I'll be along as soon as they let me."

They hustled her up the ramp.

He started over to Radoccia. Julie was crying, her face down. Radoccia put his hands on her shoulders, bent his head, and talked quietly to her. She looked up at him sharply, her face pale.

He whispered to her some more, and then he apparently saw Merchant coming and frowned abruptly.

The police chief stepped between them and said, "Mr. Merchant, let's talk."

"Sure."

Konig followed his gaze and saw that Julie was still at the end of the dock. He snapped at his uniformed officer, "Pierce, what've I told you? Keep people apart at this stage. Take the lady up to the marina office and get her a cup of coffee or a Coke, whatever. I'm going to need to talk to her in a minute."

"Yes, sir." The cop hurried over to Radoccia and Julie Baylor. He offered Julie his hand, but she stood up and walked ahead of him up the ramp. Radoccia stood where he was.

The banker said, "Just what the hell happened, Merchant?"

Konig said, "Keep the conversation with me, sir. Who are you?"

Radoccia introduced himself. He kept his attention directly on the chief, as if Merchant were no longer there.

"So the MassBank was the client in the repo, that right?"

"Correct," Radoccia said. "However, Ms. Ballard's firm is an independent company. Fully responsible for their own actions."

Konig said, "I don't care about that, Mr. Radoccia. I want to find out what happened here."

"We have strict guidelines for our repos," Radoccia said. "No conflict. This . . . this is absurd."

"Yeah, that's murder, Mr. Radoccia. Usually a bunch of dopes. Now I'd like you to sit upstairs if you could, no more conversations with Mrs. Baylor until I say it's OK."

"Why is that?"

"Because I told you so. Could you have a seat up at those tables on the main deck?" Konig pointed to the ramp at the end of the dock.

Radoccia looked affronted, but at last he said, "That's fine." He made his way up the ramp.

Konig looked at Merchant. "How long you been doing repo?"

Merchant told him he was just helping Sarah with her business.

"Huh. You got a record? Or you ever a cop?"

Merchant said he'd been with the DEA.

"Figured you for one or the other." Konig pulled out a pad from his back pocket.

Merchant had made some quick assumptions about Chief Konig. Maybe all of them wrong, but what else did he have? Konig's uniform was neatly pressed, and he held himself like he was on the balls of his feet, balanced but ready to swing forward whenever the mood struck. Probably in his late fifties, his face a bit on the bloated side.

Merchant would have guessed Konig had been a big city cop who had retired to Green Harbor for the fishing. That he had years of experience in listening to evasions, partial truths, and outright lies.

Let's see how the truth works on him, Merchant thought.

He and Konig stood at the end of the dock, looking out at the dark water, waiting for the lights of the Coast Guard vessel. Konig checked his watch. "Should be in any time now."

He turned and looked fully at Merchant. "OK, Mr. Ex-DEA. You know the way this works. What've you got for me?"

Merchant took a deep breath.

He told Konig about everything — including the gun.

In as abbreviated a version as Konig would allow, Merchant described his last days in the DEA. He said he suspected the man on the boat was a relative of Randall's. He talked about how Randall had come out of the cabinway with a gun in each hand — and how one of the guns had last been in Merchant's possession.

Konig's face took on that interested, nonjudgmental look cops so often wear when a suspect is confessing and they don't want to slow him down.

"I see. How do you figure your gun ended up down here?"

Merchant shrugged. "It must've been stolen from my boat." He knew how that sounded.

Konig cocked his head to the side. "Great conspiracy theory, huh?"

"I'm just telling you what I know."

"Who'd he shoot with it?"

Merchant thought back. It was clear in his mind. The big revolver with the grips was in the man's left hand.

"Baylor," Merchant said. "He shot Baylor with it."

Konig stared at him. "Sure that you didn't just bring the gun along? Something went wrong, and the reactions got the better of you?"

"No," Merchant said.

"So you think this guy was kin to a cop?"

"Sure looks like him."

"Christ," Konig said. "Who can I talk to about this Miami crap?"

Merchant gave him the name of the new head of the DEA's Miami office. Konig wrote it down.

"Will the two ladies agree with the way you told the story?"

"I don't see why not."

"You say you had your hands on both guns?"

"That's right."

"Go through it again, from the time you pulled alongside."

Merchant described how the fight had taken place.

"So you're sure Mrs. Baylor actually killed this man?"

"Positive. And a good thing she did. I couldn't hold him any longer."

"Jesus," Konig said. He looked out over the bay and stood. "Well, here comes our floating crime scene."

The flashing lights of the Coast Guard boat were visible as they rounded the last buoy on the way into Hogdon's Cove. Minutes later, they pulled up to the dock with *Wildest Dreams* in tow.

The two bodies were covered with tarps. The blood in the cockpit was black in the fluorescent light of the dock lights.

Konig took rubber gloves from his back pocket. "Here's why they pay me the big bucks."

Konig had Merchant run through it once again. He drew a quick stick figure sketch of the relative positions for each of them. A police photographer captured shot after shot of the boat, the bodies, and close-ups of the head wounds.

The medical examiner hadn't arrived yet, so Konig looked at the bodies, but didn't touch them. Afterward, he picked up the guns with a pencil. They were both cheap weapons, little more than Saturday night specials.

"So which is yours?"

Merchant pointed out the one with the rubber bands on the grip. Konig looked at it carefully under the flashlight beam. "Registration numbers filed off. You could've just said your hands had been all over it fighting the guy, explain the fingerprints."

He looked up at Merchant, met his eyes. "You a Boy Scout once or something?"

Merchant said, "You going to make me regret telling you?"

"Dunno yet. Thing is, the story kinda works, the guy stealing it off your boat, comes in to set you up. But it also works that you brought it onboard and things got screwy." Konig watched him, his mild brown eyes steady.

"First one's the truth."

"Uh-huh."

Konig got a flashlight from one of the officers and went down into the cabin. Merchant knelt in the cabinway looking down. There was a yellow and red bag on the galley counter with a zippered top. It looked waterproof.

Konig opened the bag and pointed the flashlight inside.

He reached in with his gloved hand and moved something around, shuffling through paper.

Merchant could see it then and recognized it.

Money. Lots of money.

Konig looked up at him, eyes hard. "You got something else to tell me?"

An officer took Merchant to police headquarters. Two other cars brought in Julie Baylor and Gene Radoccia. The headquarters was a small, modern building with silvery cedar shingles.

Merchant and Radoccia were put into separate interview rooms and Julie Baylor into Konig's office. Then he started to make the rounds, comparing stories. Altogether, Merchant saw him three times over the course of as many hours.

Around midnight, Konig came back. Merchant said, "Have you made the ID yet?"

Hoping that somehow the man was connected to the Baylors' — that the similarity to Bobby Lee Randall was just coincidence.

But Konig said, "It just came through. You had it right. A brother. That was Richard Kyle Randall. R. K. Randall. Oldest of the Randall boys. Just got out of Starke two weeks ago."

Starke.

Merchant sat back heavily in his chair. The brother he hadn't seen. The big brother.

Konig continued, "Mrs. Baylor says he came onboard while she was alone at dock. Came up in the little inflatable — which turned out to be stolen — and started making conversation with her about their boat and then got onto the dock and put a gun on her. Kept her below until her husband came back onboard, and then told him to motor off or he'd kill her. She said he found their money, which was a god-awful lot of money to be traveling on, but from what Radoccia says, it was theirs."

"Did Randall come in looking for the money?"

"She said not. Said from the get-go he was talking about a guy who was going to try to repossess their boat. That he was after that man — you, apparently — and that he'd let them go free later."

Merchant sat thinking.

The obvious question hung there, and Konig asked it: "So why'd he go to the trouble of hooking in the Baylors? Why not just shoot you on the street and be done with it?"

Merchant had been thinking about that since before placing the Mayday. He said, "Randall was trying to make it look like me. He went to the trouble of getting what he thought was my gun from the bow of my boat. He shot Sarah with the one in his right, Paul with the one in his left."

Konig seemed to weigh it. "Sounds right. Especially when you put it together with what else we found — he had another gun on him."

Merchant was surprised.

"Yeah," Konig said. "Didn't find it until the medical examiner turned him over. Thirty-eight in a holster, small of his back. Better quality than the two pieces of shit that were used. Registration filed, too. That make any sense to you? Three handguns?"

"No. It doesn't."

"You still want to stick with what you're telling me?"

"It's the truth. The way I see it he was going to kill us all and take off in his inflatable. Leave it looking like I came on, maybe Baylor waves a gun and we kill each other. Sarah and Julie caught in the cross fire. Make it look like I panicked."

"Possible, I suppose. Assuming he put the guns in each of your hands and squeezed off a round. Got the powder marks on your hands, fingerprints, all that. But has he been following you for the past week, and you didn't know it?"

"I wasn't looking for him, but that's not likely," Merchant said. "Especially when I was over on Cuttyhunk. First of all, I flew over there, and even if he did get the next flight out, I'd sure notice him tiptoeing around behind me. Just not likely."

Merchant retraced that mentally. Flying in, flying out.

"I dunno," Konig said. "We found his car."

"Where?"

"Couple blocks from the marina. Stolen Chevy from Miami. Connecticut plates on it. His prints all over it. R. K. Randall wasn't exactly a neat kind of guy. Backseat pretty much his trash can and clothes hamper combined. Soda cans, beer bottles, porno mags, dirty socks, the bit. Lots of takeout food trash bags. Near the top of the heap, we've got a balled up bag that reads "Harley's Roast Beef.""

Merchant knew it. "That's outside of New Bedford."

"Uh-huh."

"Anything from Maine?"

"Can't tell. Lot of trash from Burger King, McDonald's. No addresses on those. Either way, it's a pretty good assumption he followed you here. How long he was on your tail exactly, I don't know."

Merchant took that in.

Konig said, "You might as well go back to your motel room. I'll want you back here in the morning. By then I should have the reports by the Miami cops. They hauled in the remaining Randall boys for questioning."

"That should be interesting."

"Oh yeah. Sound like nice folks." Konig paused. "I also had a couple of conversations with your former colleagues back there."

"What'd they have to say?"

"One told me you're a fuckup and should've been up on criminal charges. Another says you saved a kid, and he might've done the same." Konig shrugged. "I wouldn't have wanted to be standing in the spot you were in. Clear record like you had before that, I'm giving you the benefit of the doubt."

"I appreciate that," Merchant said.

He felt distracted. Cuttyhunk. New Bedford.

Konig said, "R. K. Randall is not a loss from this world. Assault charges all his life. Three of them aggravateds, couple of rape charges, one which stuck, and suspect in at least three murders . . ."

George Henriques and R. K. Randall, Merchant thought.

Running into George Henriques at the bar, and then going on down to Green Harbor. Henriques's hand slapping at his jacket.

Checking him for a gun.

Made a lot out of it, him not having a gun.

Merchant thought about telling Konig and decided not. He felt as if he were grasping at straws. Not a half hour ago, he'd been hoping that the big redheaded man had been someone from the Baylors' past rather than his own. Now was he looking to lay his guilt off somehow on George Henriques?

Merchant said, "I'd like to go to the hospital now."

"Visiting hours are over. I saw Ms. Ballard about an hour and a half ago. Got her statement. She's doing fine, in a private room. They gave her something to sleep. How about I drop you off at your truck now, and then you get in to see her in the morning. And then we'll all sit down with the ADA after that."

"All right. How's Mrs. Baylor doing?"

"She got a lawyer, but she's been telling me everything I want to know."

"What about the gun that shot Sarah? Maybe the Baylors had that onboard."

"Mrs. Baylor says no. It was a real piece of crap. From the look of the rest of the equipment on that boat, I figure if Baylor wanted to buy a gun, he'd probably have had the best."

Merchant thought about their house, the boat, everything about them he'd seen. All quality. Still, three guns.

Konig said, "Fact is, as far as the law, I think Mrs. Baylor is going to be all right."

"She should be. The guy came after me, and the Baylors were caught in the middle. She didn't act, we'd all be dead."

"So you said. So she said." Konig stood up.

"Can I talk to her?"

Konig shook his head. "I told her about you and Randall's brother. She knows why her husband was killed. She doesn't want to see you."

Merchant couldn't trust himself to speak.

Konig opened the door, and as Merchant walked through ahead of him, Konig said, "Hell of a price to pay for not keeping up with your boat payments."

26

THOMAS HATED these sessions.

Jason Vance in his robe. Sitting in front of the computer. Dark in his suite, the shades drawn against the lights of the place. Big beautiful hotel suite, best ventilation available.

Place still smelled fetid when Vance got going with his computer. Hand disappearing under his robe now and then, giving himself a tug.

Thomas didn't like it, but it was part of the job. Figuring out what the man wanted.

Vance's fingers rattled over the keyboard. Moved the mouse with the speed and surety that some people reserved for real skills. He kept talking the whole time, using this jocular, instructive tone, like maybe there was a white paper that was going to come out of all this.

"The web's made a fundamental change to human sexuality, my friend," Vance said. "You can download bits of imagination and lust that'll do more to make one human understand another than all the do-good crap about valuing differences ever will."

"You a humanitarian now, huh?"

"No. Human being." Voice getting rich, comfortable in his lecturing. Images on the screen moving fast; no slow modem time for this guy. Upskirt pictures of young women. Flashing breasts. Bunch of blow-job shots. He went fast through those. Basic stuff for

Vance. Full intercourse, anal intercourse. Moved right over to some gay stuff. "Looks much the same, doesn't it?" Vance said. "You squint a little, you see skin and penetration, and it's not all that different. Lubrication, penetration, friction. All it comes down to. Iction, iction, iction."

He continued to click the mouse. Voice droning on. "Transvestites. Autoerotica. Boys with wigs, girls with toys, girls with fruit. Girls peeing on men, men peeing on girls. Old ladies doing it with young men, girls doing it with old men. Men with dogs, women with dogs, women with ponies. You name it, we provide it. . . ."

Click of the mouse, occasional slap down to the enter key.

"And race relations," Vance said. Fruity, infuriating voice. Like he was above it all, but Thomas could see he was squirming in his leather chair. Thomas was faintly nauseous. Some of the colors and friction he saw there may've appealed to him, but not in the presence of this man.

"Yes, sir," Vance said. "Black on white. Black *in* white. Asian women servicing white men. Here we have a Asian girl, can't be more than fifteen I'd bet, with one of yours. Big black guy, look at that thing."

"Yeah," Thomas said. "I seen dirty pictures before. You saying that made you do it?"

"No. That didn't make me do it." Vance clicked the mouse again. Videos. Leather and rubber. A woman over a bound man.

Vance waved his hand. "Well *that* turned out just fine, now, didn't it?" He logged out of the porn sites and got in on a different set of files. Shots taken by some morgue attendant in the city, putting the more attractive women's bodies on display. Showing them in as graphic detail as possible. Showing the stillness and emptiness of death in a way Thomas himself had seen all too often. At least that was what he saw. He suspected Vance saw something different in the same images.

"OK," Vance said, with real pleasure. "Look at this, she passed the screen test! Here she is."

The hooker from the dumpy apartment building. Thomas's first job for Vance, where he spent all those hours sanitizing the dead girl and her apartment. Thomas said again, "You saying the web made you do it?"

Vance shook his head. "Didn't *make* me do it." Tapped his forehead. "Helped what was in there come out. Shrink once told me Plato said something to the effect of an insane man does what the sane man only dreams."

"So you insane now?"

The big man turned to look over his shoulder at Thomas. Dead girl on the screen behind him. "No. Not insane. A new paradigm. Or, I should say, my own interpretation of a very old paradigm."

"Uh-huh. What's that?"

"Sane man does whatever the hell he wants as long as he can get away with it." He winked. "And that's what I have you for, right?"

Back in his own room, Thomas turned on the laptop. It was a gift from Vance. Always a bit of a technical geek himself, Thomas frankly loved the device the way he would a favorite weapon. Which, in his hands, it was.

Thomas also loved access to the best and brightest minds. Of all the companies in Power. Share's fold, Vance was closest to the crew at RyDak, a San Jose-based company that made firmware for television and web interactivity. Vance had a substantial personal share in the company and had seen to it that some of their emerging competitors never received funding so that RyDak could buy up their patents for a song. Because Vance had that kind of pull, and Thomas often spent what idle time he had asking one expert or another, How could we do this? What if I wanted to do that? His interest perplexed some of the software experts. After all, he was a "security consultant."

But in the couple of months that Thomas had been onboard, people quickly learned that he spoke for Jason Vance — and that was all they really needed to know. Together, they'd figured out some interesting things about the use of computer viruses as offensive weapons, and Thomas was looking forward to trying some of his ideas in the field.

Now, he was doing something technically prosaic but, nevertheless, something he truly enjoyed. He was going over his portfolio.

Something he did at least twice a day if he had the time. Reveling in the fact that his was growing while just about all the rest of the country were watching their paper wealth disappear.

Vance's payment for the dominatrix job had come through a few days before: $2 million in the form of stocks wired directly to him.

He marveled, looking at the bottom-line number.

Goddamn.

He worked for his pay, but he sure couldn't complain about the amount — even if Vance did. They'd had to burn down the dominatrix's building to help cover some of the evidence. Rang the fire alarm, everybody got out except for some geezer who had a heart attack in the stairwell.

And then Thomas had to orchestrate a fall for Vance when he got out of the limo in front of the hotel, because he'd gotten a whopper of a scratch and bruise on his face from the fight with the Leather Man, and that needed some explaining. The hotel management were shitting bricks, thinking they might be sued.

Bad news was that it got in the media, that Vance appeared at a news conference with his face damaged. What with the thing in Boston before Thomas's time, he hated to have any attention like that directed at Vance. Thomas didn't want them looking at Vance as a person — just what he stood for.

Jason Vance. The head of Power.Share. The only leading U.S. incubator of Internet start-ups to not only survive the burst bubble but come out with a select list of companies that actually made money.

Making Vance well worth protecting. At least until Thomas made $5 million.

That was what he'd decided. Here he'd made $2.5 million in just these few months. Nice, very nice. But he wouldn't really be rich, and able to retire in the style he desired, until he had $5 million.

Working with Vance's appetites and his ability to pay, $5 million seemed like a very reasonable number. Not reasonable to Vance, of course. He *screamed* about the cost. Before the latest market-wide plunge, Vance's personal worth had been in the area of $800 million. Now he was probably worth about $100 million.

Still a lot of money, the way Thomas saw it. A lot of money to cover up murder.

Thomas opened the calculator file on his computer. He could do this in his head, of course, but he liked to see the numbers pop up on the screen.

Let's see, first the girl Vance had been gazing at in the morgue photos. Thomas had charged $500,000 for that. And now Thomas had just killed two men himself, and covered up the death of the woman. Turned up the gas on the little stove in the back and blew up the basement floors. And, oh yes, the one old geezer who died from a heart attack trying to get out of the burning building. So that made five people for $2.5 million. Certainly not cheap, at $500,000 apiece, but Vance was getting away with it all.

Getting away with murder.

Thomas tapped the keyboard and quickly went to a chart that extrapolated the rate of growth of his portfolio in the past few months to reach $5 million. The math was obvious, but he still enjoyed seeing it chart out.

He sighed: equal parts satisfaction and anxiety. If he could just keep the golden goose from landing himself on death row. Thomas would do anything within his considerable powers to keep that from happening.

"Damn," he said out loud. "I'm a rich man."

Just then, the phone rang. It was Vance. He was upset and worried, and Thomas said, "Downstairs. We're going for a walk."

He kept at his portfolio a few minutes longer, giving Vance time to get dressed. Then he closed the file but left the computer on. He slipped a snub-nosed revolver into a holster at the small of his back and pulled a sport jacket over it. He checked himself in the mirror, making sure the bulge wasn't obvious.

When he got down to the lobby, Vance was waiting. Some kid talking to him, teenager, looking impressed that he had the ear of the big man. Talking some technical nonsense that Thomas couldn't understand, and he was no slouch as a layman.

"It's been done already, son," Vance said. "But you keep at it, you'll make it someday."

They left the kid looking crestfallen.

Thomas said, "God, you attract them."

"Kid's got some ideas."

"Hire him then."

"Why?" Vance grinned, proud of himself. "I got all I need from him. Before we get back to the hotel, I'll have a better angle on it, and then I'll make some calls and we'll work it into a package we already got going with RyDak. We'll be making money on the bastard eighteen months from now, count on it."

Thomas shook his head slightly. Vance was such an ass. But everything he'd just said was true. Or *might* be true. Not only would he rip the kid off without compunction, but by tomorrow he'd genuinely think the idea was his own. That was another one of Vance's assets. Knowing how to pick up what was around him, decide it was his. How to throw away anything or anyone he didn't want without a hint of shame or remorse.

Way back when Thomas was a little kid growing up on the streets of Washington, D.C., before he even thought about getting a job in one of those big white buildings, he knew guys like this man. Not rich white guys: mainly violent black men who pushed coke and heroin or ran girls. They too had it all worked out in their heads that they were "businessmen." They would pose and strut in front of the younger gang kids and talk their way into believing whatever they wanted about themselves.

Not Thomas.

He always knew who he was screwing and who he was setting up to take the fall. He knew what he could do and what he couldn't. Knew when to hit and when to run. Knowing things as they *were*, not the way you wanted them to be.

Thomas's eyes moved over the crowded street restlessly. He didn't usually let Vance free on the streets like this. Even though the man caused a lot more damage than he took, the risk was there.

If they only knew.

If the people around him only knew how much money this man to his right represented . . .

Vance was still talking about what had happened in Boston. When Thomas figured he could get a word in edgewise, he said, "Quit bitching at me. This was before my time and you told me this wasn't a problem."

"I thought it wasn't," Vance said. Aggrieved. "I was assured that it was a done deal."

"Shut up," Thomas said.

Vance's face flushed deeply, but Thomas didn't care. He had him by the short ones, and Vance knew it. Thomas had Vance follow him to a narrow traffic island and said, "OK, let's hear it."

Vance continued, laying out the story as he'd heard it.

Thomas groaned out loud. He said, "Amateur hour."

"Obviously."

"Why didn't he call you sooner?"

"Didn't know I had you in place. And he was trying to kiss my ass. Take care of the problem himself. Because it's not clear we're taking them public. He's after me for help with some patents with RyDak. It's not clear at all that I'm going to help him."

Thomas snorted. "Is now. Either I kill him or he's on."

"Yeah, no shit."

Tough guy with his tough words. Thomas sometimes wanted to backhand Vance across his fat white face, and this was one of those times.

Vance said, "So what're you going to do about it?"

"Looks like I'm getting on a plane. Get your ass out of the sling one more time."

He could see Vance relax. He looked over his shoulder, saw that the lights were with them. They were alone.

"How much is this going to cost me?"

Thomas thought about it. The risks sounded high this time. Too many people involved. Could be the last one. Damn. Lucrative gig like this, and it could be over already.

"Two point five million," he said. "That's for me. Plus I'm going to have to hire some talent."

Vance sounded shocked. "After what I just paid you?"

Thomas snorted. "It's going to seem like a hell of a deal to you when they're hooking up the electrodes to your head. This time, I want cash."

"Cash!" Vance's voice actually squeaked. "Look, we've got to do this as a stock option. I'll transfer some stock your way, just like before."

"Forget it. Cash. I'll give you a Swiss account."

"Like hell." Vance settled in, talking to Thomas if he was an idiot, the "cost of cash" in terms of what it would take to pull it out, the upside of leaving it in. One of his favorite phrases: "the upside potential."

It was something he could get quite passionate about. "This is all going to turn around, a year tops. I can multiply what you've got tenfold, but just hang with me now, don't pull out my own seed money!"

Thomas prodded him hard on the chest with two rigid fingers. "Shut up. I said cash, and I mean cash. One million up front in that Swiss account by tomorrow."

"You blackmailing bastard!" Vance actually took two steps into Thomas, crowding him.

Thomas didn't back off. He put his face right in Vance's. "Listen to me, you sick tub of lard. I don't stop you from the mean, vicious shit you like to do. I set it up — and I clean it up. Now you want to screw with me about money, or you want me to get to work?"

Vance didn't say anything for a minute. His face was stark white now, his breath whistling in and out. Standing back with his hands on his hips, the trench coat open. Looking at the traffic rush by on each side, the view of the Times Square lights. A king infuriated that he must negotiate with the court assassin.

"Take care of it," he said, at last. Waving his hand. "Get to work."

"Cash in my account, tomorrow. You clear on that?"

"There's very little I'm not clear about."

"Uh-huh," Thomas said. Thinking that was true, except maybe in matters which depended upon kindness or common sense.

Back in his hotel room, Thomas logged on to his computer to book a flight out of LaGuardia and then took a moment to add to his portfolio the amount he had just demanded.

He wouldn't get the full payment until the job was done and Vance was once again safe. Assuming Thomas could arrange that.

If not, well, he expected to have that cash in the Swiss account in case it all fell apart. One million in advance. The rest of his portfolio was in the form of stocks. Those were "a gift" directly from Vance, and they were restricted. Thomas couldn't sell them for another few months. But if he pulled this off, $2.5 million in cash, $2.5 in stocks. Thomas would be at his $5 million goal. He could retire.

"Damn," he said under his breath. *I'm a rich man.*

27

WHAT A NIGHT.

Sleep was not an option. A videotape played in Merchant's mind that connected Carlos Gacha and the Baylors, that depicted gunfire and blood spilled, and Paul Baylor's head now misshapen.

He had been a good man, Merchant knew it.

The tape would run, rewind, run again.

Merchant ended up sitting out by the pool. Old habit from living aboard a boat, seeking some sort of solace from the water. But he found none in the glow of the underwater lights, the smell of chlorine. He found only himself, and pretty sour company he was.

He thought about what he had brought on others, with only the best of intentions. The road to hell, and all that.

What a night.

Sarah was awake when he arrived that morning. "There you are," she said.

Her face was pale under her tan, and she was propped up with an IV bag dripping fluid into her right arm. Her left hand was bandaged and lay on a Formica board that had been clamped to her bed rail.

He had to work his way past the IV stand to kiss her on the cheek, but he managed.

He asked about her arm. She told him the doctors were saying her wound was clean, that she could probably leave in two days.

She asked him if he had talked with Julie.

Merchant told her he hadn't and filled her in on everything that Konig had told him. He also told her about the gun, stolen from the bow of his boat.

Sarah turned away from him. "That poor woman," she said. "What we brought down on her."

"What I brought down on her."

Sarah nodded. "OK," she said. "But it was my responsibility to pick up the boat. I hired you, the heat comes back to me."

He reached out to touch her head and she moved away. She said, "I'm struggling here, Merchant."

"I know."

"I mean, I know this isn't your fault . . ." She put her hand to her face. "That poor woman," she said again.

"I know," Merchant said.

The two of them repeating themselves left and right.

Merchant offered to leave.

Sarah told him no.

But minutes later she told him she was tired and needed to sleep.

He headed for the police station.

The assistant district attorney was a slim blond man in his late forties named Whitfield. He looked like he had lots of hours on the tennis court behind him.

They were all in the interview room — Merchant, Konig, Julie, and Gene Radoccia. Julie's lawyer was a well-fed man named Beech in a tailored thousand-dollar suit. Julie's sister, Emily, wasn't there. Merchant wondered where she was.

Beech had spent a little time pontificating about how his client should never have been questioned in her state of mind. But once he saw things were heading in the right direction, he shut up.

Whitfield and Konig were apparently satisfied, at least at this stage, that the Miami police interviews of the remaining Randall brothers had established R. K. as being motivated by simple revenge. The forensic evidence was clear: ballistics, flash blowback, blood splatter all supported the testimony of the three survivors.

R. K. Randall had killed Paul Baylor.

Julie Baylor — in imminent fear for her life — had killed R. K. Randall.

Self-defense. There would be no charges against her.

After running through it all, Whitfield looked over at Merchant with unconcealed dislike. "With the hell you brought on these people. I wish I could go after you for that . . ." He seemed to have a thought and turned to Julie Baylor.

"Mrs. Baylor, did Merchant board without your permission? There may be some action we could take if so. Boarding at sea without permission constitutes piracy . . ."

She shook her head. Her voice was barely audible. "No," she said. "We gave them permission. And it's what the man told us to do. This Randall."

Julie's face seemed etched with at least ten years since the day before. "Leave him alone," she said. Her voice was toneless. "Just let me go home and bury Paul."

Radoccia said, "Once again, Julie. My personal condolences and those of the bank. Any help we can give . . ."

She stared at him, and then shook her head abruptly.

Merchant watched Radoccia. The sympathy on his face. The sort of look a good mortician might acquire.

Merchant said to Julie, "Why were you running?"

She said, "We just needed out . . . out of the rat race. We took off."

She didn't even seem to be trying to convince him.

Merchant said to Radoccia, "Is that the way the bank sees it?"

"Just what are you implying?" said Beech.

Radoccia said to Merchant, "Anything of that nature is between Ms. Baylor and us. Certainly not you."

Konig said, "Excuse me, gentlemen. If there's an issue of embezzlement, then it most certainly is not just MassBank's business. What have you got to tell us?"

"Nothing," Radoccia said. "Just that our audit is continuing." He turned to Julie. "However, if there's something you want to tell us, Julie, I'd certainly be interested."

"Just a moment," Beech said. He laid his hand on Julie's arm and stared at Radoccia. "If you've got an accusation, make it."

Radoccia stared back at him. "Like I said. Nothing at this point. But our audit is continuing."

"Who else did you tell?" Merchant said.

"What?"

"I said, who did you tell that we had found the Baylors? I sent you the photo over e-mail."

"Is there a reason you're asking?" Radoccia said.

"Consider that I asked," Konig said.

Radoccia turned toward him. "Didn't tell anyone."

"You said you were in a meeting with your company's president. You didn't tell him Paul Baylor had been found?" Merchant said.

"It was an executive staff meeting. Not the place to make such an announcement. I wanted to talk with Paul myself first."

"Let's get this straight," Konig said. "You didn't say a word to anyone? Not a secretary?"

"No." Radoccia shook his head. He made a kind of shamefaced smile. "Wanted to come back with the whole story, I guess . . . I told you I was coming down." He looked over at Merchant. "And when I got there, both the Baylors and these two from Ballard's Marine Liquidation were gone. I almost left myself, until I saw the ambulance come down to the marina and heard that there had been an incident."

Julie Baylor was staring down at the table, as if the conversation meant nothing to her.

Radoccia said, "So why do you ask, Merchant? Trying to figure out some way to sue the bank for your troubles?"

"I just don't know how Randall found me."

"I'm damned if I know," Radoccia snapped. "Maybe he followed you."

"I didn't see anyone."

"Were you looking?"

Merchant thought about that night. That drive through heavy beach traffic, his pissed-off mood after his run-in with Henriques. Distracted as he was, he could've been followed and he wouldn't have noticed.

Julie looked up from the table. Merchant felt a lancing inside him. He said, "No."

Radoccia rolled his eyes. "Oh for Christ's sakes. Why are we wasting our time?"

Whitfield said, "Enough of this, gentlemen."

He stood up and said to Konig, "I've heard as much as I need. I'll be in touch."

Radoccia wouldn't let it go. He jabbed his finger at Merchant. "From what I've been made to understand from Chief Konig, you've had this kind of trouble before. People get hurt, people get *killed* around you, and it just isn't your fault, is that it?"

Merchant said nothing.

Radoccia shook his head. "I'll tell you what, you tell your girl-friend there that she better not show her face around MassBank again. You tell her that I'm going to make some calls, and the two of you are never going to work again in repo."

Konig said, "Shut up, Mr. Radoccia."

Radoccia's face turned red. "Just who do you think you're talking to?"

Konig stood. He pointed to the conference room door. "You and Merchant, take off. I've got your numbers."

Beech stood up as well.

Julie's eyes met Merchant's for a second. He expected anger, hatred even. He steeled himself to take it. He thought she was going to say something to him, but then she looked away.

He said, "Mrs. Baylor, I know how this sounds . . ."

He couldn't think of the right words. So he just said, "If there's any way that I can help. Any way at all."

Konig spoke up. "She's gone through enough, Merchant. Don't ask her to make you feel better."

Merchant turned for the door. He felt he was choking. He looked back to see that Konig had put his hand on Julie Baylor's shoulder. Konig's voice was gentler now, but his message was just as clear.

The case was all but closed.

He said, "Whenever you're ready, Mrs. Baylor."

28

MERCHANT DROPPED HIS RENTAL CAR OFF at the local branch and got a ride from them back to the motel so he could pick up Sarah's truck. He threw his bags onto the floor and headed back to Boston.

Sarah was going to be in the hospital for at least two more days. He figured that would be enough time if he handled it right.

Back in Charlestown, he checked his mail before heading down to the boat. Nothing but bills.

He went right to the *Lila* and climbed aboard. R. K. Randall had been fairly careful getting the gun. Merchant could tell the boat had been searched, but he doubted anyone else could.

Merchant went into his closet and made a few selections. Leather jacket, jeans. Gray muscle shirt. A wrist chain. Wallet with a chain attachment. Biker boots. Scraggly black wig with gray streaks. Wire-rim glasses.

He took a spring-loaded sap from the bottom of the closet. Something he'd taken off a dealer in the Virgin Islands. About as dangerous a weapon as he had ever hoped to carry again.

Merchant walked through the streets of Charlestown. A biker without his bike. He had Fogerty's license, and he remembered the streets well enough. There were some changes, but he found the address. It was a redbrick building that needed to be repointed so badly it seemed as if any one brick could be pulled by hand to bring the whole thing tumbling down. He hit the buzzer. No one answered.

He tried the front door and it was open. The hallway smelled of boiled cabbage, sweat, and stale beer. Someone had left a case of long-neck empties by the door. The place had probably been redone somewhere in the early eighties and wasn't holding up well. The brown laminated paneling up the inside stairway was separating from the wall.

Merchant knocked on Fogerty's door. Cheap hollow core, an inside door. When he didn't hear anything, he drew back a step and kicked hard just over the knob. The door flew open. No one in the other apartments bothered to come into the hallway. And Merchant knew from experience that no one would call the police. Charlestown residents knew how to mind their own business.

It took him about ten minutes. In the toilet tank, he found a thick packet of cash, just under twenty-five hundred dollars. He took the nineteen hundred he was owed and left the rest on the sink counter. Merchant found a blue athletic bag under the bed and stuffed in some of Fogerty's clothes and the cash.

The gun was in a shoe box under the kitchen sink, a cousin to the cheap .38 he had taken off Fogerty before.

Merchant paused, the weight of blue steel in his hand.

Ugly thing with only one purpose. Last resort of the weak.

He thought about the promises to himself. The way it could go if the next eight or so hours went wrong.

He thought about Sarah in her hospital bed and Paul Baylor lying dead in his boat.

And about his own part in putting them there.

Merchant put the gun under his belt at the small of his back, so the shirt hung over, and left the apartment.

But it wasn't going to be that easy.

A teenager was standing in the hall. He was a big kid with a dirty white T-shirt, bad teeth, and a baseball bat. The apartment door behind him was open.

Baseball bat.

"What is this?" Merchant said. "Fogerty some kind of role model for you?"

The kid said, "What're you doing in there?"

"Collecting a debt."

The kid drew back the bat. "I'm gonna collect your frigging head, you don't put the bag down."

Merchant took out the gun, letting it point to the floor. "Don't push this, kid. Fogerty wouldn't do it for you. Now just go back in your apartment and close the door."

The kid eyed him, eyed the gun. The bat held high. More balls than brains.

"Give Fogerty a message," Merchant said. "Tell him I've collected his debt on the camera."

"The camera?"

"He'll know what I mean."

The kid looked at the gun. Apparently thought about the message.

"He rip off your camera?"

"Smashed it," Merchant said. "It got in the way of my head."

The kid let the bat down along his leg. "He's gonna be pissed that you came here."

Merchant said, "I was sort of pissed myself."

The kid backed into his apartment, and Merchant walked by.

The kids said, "He's gonna be on your ass."

"He knows where I live." Merchant continued out to the street.

Merchant used Fogerty's clothes, cash, and one of his own sets of false IDs to buy a plane ticket. He checked his bag with his handcuffs and Fogerty's gun inside, wrapped in a lead film pouch.

On the plane, Merchant didn't order any drinks, but he ate the meals and accepted the free sodas, and said please and thank you. He made no other contact with the flight attendants or the people sitting near him.

He arrived in Miami just before six o'clock and rented a car. He went south for an hour, pulled off at a big shopping center, and drove through the lot until he found a red Ford with the windows down. He parked his rental, took his bag from the car, strolled over, and dropped his bag into the front seat of the Ford.

He popped open the hood, took from the bag a five-foot piece of wire he'd brought and a long screwdriver. It took him a moment to find the coil at the rear of the engine block. He attached his wire to the positive end of the coil and then to the positive battery post. He found the starter solenoid in the passenger side fender well and laid the screwdriver across the terminals. There was a spark, and the engine cranked over and started.

He slammed the hood shut and got behind the wheel. He jammed the flat blade of the screwdriver at the opening along the top center of the steering column and pushed hard against the locking pin.

The wheel turned freely.

The whole operation took less than four minutes and he was on his way with the stolen car, and a potential felony charge for the first time in his life.

Merchant continued for three more exits, then pulled off when he saw a big national hardware chain. He went in and bought a shovel, duct tape, and clothesline. He used cash.

He continued south in the direction of Homestead. Even though the sun was low in the sky, the heat was still stultifying. The Ford's air conditioner was broken, but Merchant couldn't bring himself to steal another car.

He took the exit for Orlee about forty-five minutes later. He'd been there once before, waiting for Jarvy Randall.

Back then, a local cop had told him he could just about count on finding Jarvy at Baby's Ribs any time after six, any day of the week. "He ain't there for the food," the cop had said.

Back then, Merchant had ridden away without making contact. He'd decided that leaving the family alone was the best decision.

Live and learn.

Merchant drove past the restaurant. It was a long ranch-style roadhouse backed by a swamp.

Just like before, Jarvy's old black Plymouth was parked out front. Back end jacked up, faded black plastic moldings added to the hood to make the car look like a high-performance machine. Merchant continued down the country road and found at least two places that would work, maybe three. He turned around and passed Baby's again, checking it out from the other direction.

Couple of places there, too. Not as good, but he could make them work. Then he found another roadside restaurant about five miles down and bought some fried chicken, corn bread, grits, and lemonade. He sat at the picnic table and thought about the Randall family. Bobby Lee a cop, if not a good cop. The third kid in his family.

And then R. K., the oldest, jailed for assault, suspected of murder. Now a confirmed murderer and dead as a doornail.

Jarvy. Next in age.

Presumably the head of the family now that R. K. was gone. Jarvy had been the one taking aim from the pickup truck three months back. Would've gotten him too, if Merchant hadn't rammed the truck. Two more after that, Luke and Roy. Merchant thought about his own role within that family. He must be their personal bogeyman. Killed the black sheep, the cop. Now R. K. coming home in a coffin. Merchant thought about his own sister, Anne, the only family he had left. How what he felt for her must be different from what these Randalls felt for each other. Brutal as they were, it couldn't be the same. Could it?

Merchant did his best to shove these thoughts aside. Thinking instead of Sarah lying in that hospital room.

Around ten, he parked in a dark corner of the Baby's Ribs parking lot. He pulled his baseball cap low over his eyes and waited. He had to keep the engine idling because he couldn't be fooling around with screwdriver and solenoid when Jarvy came out. He quickly got a headache, between the fumes and the heat, and he hoped that the gas would hold out. But he'd started with a full tank, compliments of the Ford's owner, so he thought he'd be OK.

People came and went, and if they noticed him, they didn't say anything. Merchant figured he looked like a jealous husband waiting outside the bar. That was fine. Unless Jarvy came out with someone else's wife on his arm. But from what Merchant could remember about Jarvy's looks, that didn't seem likely.

Jarvy came out just after midnight.

By then, Merchant's joints had frozen in place, and he'd begun to obsess that maybe Jarvy's car had died in the parking lot months ago and he wasn't inside.

But Merchant recognized him as soon as he walked out. He was big, at least a few inches taller than Merchant. He was going bald on top, with a ponytail gathered together from the sides and back. Tight jeans and T-shirt. A powerful build, long arms, bowed legs, a small chin. He staggered slightly on the way to his car. Jarvy fumbled with his keys but finally made it behind the wheel.

Merchant followed him out of the parking lot, and they took off down the lonely road together. Jarvy was driving like he was drunk. Moving too fast, and letting his car wander to the side before jerking it back into the lane. Merchant stayed a half dozen car lengths behind but kept his speed up, too. Jarvy cruised past the first spot Merchant had selected.

But then the brake lights showed on Jarvy's car. He slowed to a crawl at a spot where the road had been washed out to bare dirt. The mufflers on his car were low.

Merchant floored the big Ford. He looked over to see Jarvy staring, his eyes and mouth black hollows in the poor light.

Merchant pulled in front of him and jammed the brakes on. He threw the car in park, jumped out, and walked back to Jarvy's car, holding the gun in his right hand behind his leg, the bag in his left. He kept the hat brim low.

Jarvy was too drunk at first to realize he was in trouble. He fumbled with rolling down the window and was shouting the usual what-the-fuck-are-you-doing nonsense, and he apparently didn't recognize Merchant or see the gun until it was right in his face.

"Get out, Jarvy."

Jarvy recognized him then, and he paled. "What do you want?"

"What do you think? Now get out." Merchant opened the door.

Jarvy got out slowly, bracing himself against the door. Telegraphing his rush a mile ahead. When he went for it, Merchant simply backed up a step and smashed him in the face with the gun butt.

Jarvy howled. He grabbed at his face, and Merchant spun him around. Merchant hit him behind the ear, and the new leader of the Randall family fell to his knees. Merchant shoved him to the ground, knelt on his back, and put the cuffs on him.

Jarvy found his voice again. Saying, "Can't do this, can't do this. You're no law down here."

Merchant shut that up by wrapping duct tape across the man's mouth.

And that, not surprisingly, terrified Jarvy. He kicked and rolled, and thrashed on the ground. Merchant got off him and let him wear himself out.

He reached in and popped the trunk in Jarvy's car, then hauled him to his feet, walked him over to the trunk, and shoved him in.

Merchant parked his own car by the side of the road. He got the shovel and the paper bag out of the backseat, then strode back to get behind the wheel of Jarvy's Plymouth.

He took off.

Jarvy was now kicking in the trunk. About a quarter mile up, Merchant found the dirt road he had scouted earlier. It was little more than a weak spot in the solid wall of brush along that road. He drove Jarvy's car through it, the branches slapping at the sides. He was unable to see more than a few feet ahead, and he kept on, the bright lights of the car reflecting back on the stunted trees and saw grass. Knowing what Jarvy must be thinking back there in the dark, as the car rolled through mud, bouncing over roots and small logs.

Hearing himself brought deeper and deeper into the darkness.

After about a quarter mile, the road disappeared entirely. Merchant left the parking lights on, and got out. The ground was mushy underneath his feet. Swamp water nearby. Mosquitoes singing around him. He opened the trunk and stood back.

Sure enough, Jarvy tried to kick him, but Merchant was ready. He let the man thrash about until he had rolled himself out of the trunk. No easy feat.

Jarvy lay facedown, exhausted, breathing hard through his nostrils. Merchant waited.

Suddenly Jarvy tried to roll over and lash out at Merchant's knee. Merchant simply stepped back and fired, letting the bullet slap into the mud just beside Jarvy's face. The sound, flat and hard, silenced Jarvy instantly.

Merchant took his pocketknife out, unlocked the blade, and slid it just behind Jarvy's ear, cutting the tape. He yanked the rest of it off, ripping away hunks of Jarvy's long wispy hair.

Jarvy gasped for air, his eyes scared.

Merchant got the shovel out of the back seat. He nudged Jarvy with his toe and said, "Roll back onto your stomach."

After a moment, Jarvy did.

Merchant knelt on his back and took off the cuffs. He stood up and said, "Now go over there. Start digging."

"What for?"

"Shut up and dig."

Jarvy stood up and took the shovel. The car's parking lights cast him in an orange-yellow glow. He stared at Merchant and said, "You think you're just gonna run through all of us?"

"You haven't left me any choice. Now shut up and get to it."

He pointed the gun at Jarvy's face, and the big man spat and began digging. The work went slowly. Mosquitoes feasted on both of them. Merchant stood out of swinging range of the shovel.

Jarvy dug a shallow grave, about three feet deep, six feet long. Water kept seeping into the hole, so before long Jarvy was ankle deep in water, slopping mud. His breathing was labored, and he was still stumbling drunk.

But as the exhaustion began to overtake him, he sobered up. He seemed to become less frightened than angry.

"You son of a bitch," he said. "How much that spic pay you to kill Bobby Lee?"

"It wasn't like that."

"You're gonna kill me. Least tell me the truth."

"I grabbed him to save the kid. What you heard at the inquest."

"You're full of shit."

Merchant said, "I tried to leave you people behind and let it end there. But you followed me, and an innocent man got killed and a woman I care about is lying in the hospital now with a bullet wound. It's got to end."

"It's not gonna." Jarvy shoveled a slop of water and mud aside. "Maybe you get me. You did R. K. and Bobby Lee. But there's two more to come, and we'll get you, motherfucker."

"You're not leaving me any choice."

"Tough titty. Didn't leave us none either." Jarvy kept digging, slopping the dirt and mud even faster.

Merchant figured Jarvy was getting ready to swing the shovel any time now. He said, "Who told him about the money?"

"Huh?"

"R. K. Who told R. K. there was money to be made?"

"He wasn't just doing it for that. That was nothing but icing on the cake, man."

Merchant felt a brief jolt. But he kept his voice steady. "I know that. But who was it that told him?"

"Some guy. Sounded like a cop."

"You meet him?"

"Phone. R. K. went to see him."

Merchant noticed Jarvy had moved closer to him.

Jarvy went on in an almost casual tone. "Yeah, he and R. K. got together. This guy told R. K. that he knew he was just out of Starke and how would he like to make some money and take care of some family business? Way me and R. K. looked at it, twenty thousand was just a pisspot amount of money, compared to what the state shoulda paid out for Bobby Lee."

He stared at Merchant. "Put it this way. I'd pay twenty thou just to see your ass in jail. Cowardly shit like you got Bobby killed. That's what we're owed. The money, shit, we'd take that, but it ain't nothing to what we're owed."

The man's lower lip was trembling. Fear, rage, it was all coming together. Merchant braced himself. Abruptly, Jarvy bent to dig another shovelful.

He threw it at Merchant.

Merchant rolled to the left and came up on his feet. Jarvy was out of the hole now, raising the shovel overhead. Merchant charged him, getting him in close. He cracked Jarvy on the forehead with the gun butt, hard.

Jarvy staggered back.

Merchant reached up and grabbed the shovel and tried to twist it away. "Let it go," Merchant said.

Jarvy wouldn't. He was barely conscious, but still he struggled, trying to regain control of the shovel.

Merchant hit him again, not so hard this time. The man crumpled, and fell into the shallow grave. Merchant leaned over him, his hands on his knees, taking in big gulps of air. Looking at the mud slopping in the man's face, blood flowing off his forehead.

This wasn't going to end.

Best to put a bullet in his head now. Best to cut the competition down by one more, because they weren't going to stop.

Merchant sighed. He pulled Jarvy out of his muddy grave so he wouldn't drown. He put his ear down to the man's mouth, made sure he was still breathing. Checked his pulse, found it was strong.

He dragged Jarvy over to the car and put him back in the trunk.

Then he started the engine and backed away. Once on the road, he dragged the man out, checked his pulse again. And shoved him into the passenger seat. Put the flashers on.

Jarvy was breathing steadily.

Merchant got into his stolen car and headed back to his rental car, and his life back in Boston.

29

THE FOLLOWING NIGHT, Sarah was wide awake when Merchant arrived at the hospital.

Her left arm was heavily bandaged, and she wore it in a sling. Her eyes were clear and she had brushed her hair.

"Clothes," Merchant said. He put her bag on the dresser beside her bed. "I stopped by your boat on the way back. Couple of my shirts in there, too. Big enough to fit over your bandage."

"You look like hell," she said.

"We can't all lounge around in bed all day."

"What've you been doing?"

"C'mon. Get dressed. Leave us something to chat about on the drive home."

They hit the road just after dark. They didn't say anything at first, just let the miles accumulate.

Sarah rolled down the window. Her hair whipped in the wind, and she closed her eyes. She'd been awake most of the day, and feeling pretty good. Now that it was evening her body was reminding her she was hurt. "Somebody just pulled my plug out of the wall," she murmured.

"So sleep," he said.

But she couldn't let go of how she'd acted when he had come in before. How she blamed him for everything that happened. How she couldn't, even with life and death on the line, forget about her business and what it all meant to her. She was feeling selfish, and a little sorry for herself. Sorry for him, too.

About twenty minutes in, she gave in to what she was feeling and let her hand brush his. He took her hand, and she moved alongside him, and rested her head on his shoulder.

"Glad you're back," she said. Within minutes, she was asleep.

When she awoke, the lights of the oncoming traffic made her eyes hurt, and she shifted to get comfortable. He patted her leg, and she sat up and rubbed his arm for him. "You must be sore," she said. "Let me sleep here the whole time."

"I'll live."

She yawned and said, "So tell me."

He said, "Wake up a bit."

"Mmmnn. Sounds ominous."

But she waited a few minutes more and then said, "OK. Tell."

So he did.

She listened carefully, her eyes on him the whole time. When he was done, she was silent.

Merchant drove, silent himself. One mile, then another.

She said, "Would you have killed him?"

"Wasn't my plan."

"How do you know he's not dead now? Sounds like you hit him hard."

Merchant smiled faintly. "I called Baby's Ribs just before I picked you up. Asked the bartender if Jarvy was in. Said he was right there at the bar and called him over. I hung up when he answered."

"Ah, well that makes it all right."

"No, it doesn't. I just didn't see a lot of options. I had to know who was driving this thing and I got my answer — somebody other than R. K. Randall."

"I thought you were turning into a pacifist. No guns."

Merchant looked over at her. "That bullet that went through your arm came from Randall's brother."

"I just . . ." She shook her head. "I just don't know what to think. And I mean that every which way. Part of me is glad. Glad you went and faced them directly and learned something we needed to know. You're so calm on the exterior; you just seem to float along accepting what comes your way. . . . But then, this. The other side of it is, what do I want with you in jail? Or dead?"

"Neither happened. I'm right here."

"But for how long?"

"We'll see."

That answer yielded yet more silence.

Finally, he broke it. He said, "Tell me about Henriques."

"What about him?"

"Tell me about when you ran into him at the Stateroom."

"You're thinking he was that guy on the phone to the Randalls?"

"Certainly has that cop sound to him. And he hates me."

"Way you've told it, there's a line of cop-sounding guys who hate you."

Merchant ignored that. "And when I ran into him the night before, he checked me out for a gun."

"You sure?"

"Definitely."

"So you say he didn't find it on you, he sends Randall to your boat to find your gun?"

"Could be."

"I'd think they'd check your car first."

"Maybe he did. Either George or Randall would know how to break into a car without making a mess. George could've checked it before coming into the Stateroom or either one of them could've followed me to the motel that night and searched the car in the parking lot."

"And then what? They didn't find it, so one of them had to go all the way to Boston and hope to find your gun on the boat?"

"That's what I think. Maybe George followed me to Green Harbor and Randall went back to my boat. George was good at surveillance and traffic was heavy on the way through Rhode Island. I wasn't looking for anything, so he could've followed me and I wouldn't have noticed." He shrugged. "Lot of driving, but so what? Big reward, for Randall. Kill me, you, and the Baylors, makes it look like they pulled a gun when we were trying the repo and I let loose. Then he leaves in his dinghy with twenty grand in cash. Take care of family business and earn the kind of money that'd take him a good part of a year robbing mom-and-pops and breaking legs."

"Huh . . .Yeah, George found me in the bar," Sarah said. "I was having lunch and he came up to me."

"You a regular there?"

"I'm there too much, let's put it that way. You think he set you up through me?"

"Who brought me up in the conversation?"

"He did, of course. I wouldn't have brought you up to him."

"He suggest I go work with you?"

"No. But it came to the same thing. Him cackling about how you were disgraced, living alone on your boat in Charlestown. But why?"

"I'm sure the way he sees it, I cut him loose, let him take that slide into his miserable career."

"He's seen it that way for a long while, I'd expect. Why'd he move on it now? How'd he know about the Baylors and the twenty thousand?"

"If not from you . . ."

She gave him a look.

". . . then there's only one way to find out."

"Go ask him," she said.

"Right after I let you off."

She shook her head. "Right now."

30

MERCHANT ARGUED BRIEFLY with Sarah, but she wouldn't budge.

"You need me anyhow," she said. "I know where he lives."

"He moved out of the condo?"

"Oh, he lost that place years ago."

"Then where?"

"I heard he was so broke he had to move home with his mother. You ever meet her?"

"No."

"Lace curtain Irish married to a Portuguese man, and she never let anyone forget it. A real shrew. She passed away last year."

"Damage seems to have been done to her boy."

"I'd say so," Sarah said. "George certainly qualifies for damaged goods."

They found the house. It was a sagging Victorian, about ten minutes from the waterfront. It had been painted a bright yellow once upon a time, but now the paint was faded and peeling. An old Ford Taurus with rusting back panels was parked half on the curb, half on the street. It looked as if Henriques had come home on a tear.

"You want to wait here?" Merchant asked.

"No."

She got out and followed him up the sidewalk.

"He's likely to be a bit unpleasant," he said.

"Gee, I never ran into that in my business."

They could hear the TV blaring. Some sort of hospital drama it sounded like. A woman was yelling that she needed oxygen.

The steps sagged under their feet. The porch was a wraparound and a big bow window protruded out to the right. Merchant could see the glow of the TV screen through the curtains.

He pushed the doorbell and waited. Over the sound of the TV it was impossible to hear if the buzzer had sounded or not.

He knocked.

They waited.

Knocked again, and waited longer.

No answer.

Merchant tried the front door, and it was open. He got ready to call out Henriques's name, and then the smell hit him.

The place smelled like shit. Literally. A sweetish smell underneath that. It made Merchant's insides clench. He felt himself go rigid, the muscles along his face, back, and stomach all tightening. The urge to simply walk away was almost overpowering.

"Get back," he said.

"No, I'll —"

He turned on her. "You go to the car, don't touch a damn thing on the way out. And wait for me. Please."

She nodded. "OK."

He watched her go. Following her seemed like the best idea. But he turned around and headed for the living room.

Part of him scanned the place, maybe looking for something else to do instead of going into that room and finding what he expected to find. The place was dark, with faded flowery wallpaper, lots of pictures. An old woman's home, layered with the mess of a man. A leather jacket on the floor. Beer can sitting on top of an upright piano to the left. Ring marks left by God knows how many earlier cans. French doors led to the living room. Between the French doors he could see the big blaring TV and stereo speakers obscuring half the entrance to the dining room.

The old woman gone, her drunk of a son left behind.

Too lazy, too self-involved, too screwed up to make the place his own. Just move in with his unhappiness and let it rub off on the place around him.

Merchant stepped through the doorway and saw Henriques's body.

He was lying in a leather lounge chair, blood and brain matter on the wall over his left shoulder. The smell of feces was stronger near him; apparently his bowels had let go. He had begun to swell. The blood was dry, and the flies had been at work for some time.

There was a nearly empty fifth of scotch on the coffee table in front of him and a shot glass. The gun was in his lap, held loosely by his right hand.

Merchant stood over him, unconsciously breathing out of his mouth. Trying to keep himself clear of any blood splatter, trying to figure out what he should be looking for, what good he was really doing there.

He realized that what he was looking for were signs of himself. Was there anything here that pointed to him? Had Henriques truly done this to himself or had someone else? Had Merchant been implicated in any way?

He had never seen the gun in Henriques's hand. A short-barreled revolver. There was no note that Merchant could see.

He walked around the downstairs, looking in the dining room, the dingy kitchen. He went upstairs and stepped into the first room to the left at the top of the stairs. It was a small bedroom, the window shades drawn. Probably Henrique's room as a kid. Single bed, the covers tangled. As if someone had been sleeping in it recently. Merchant went on to the master bedroom. Henriques apparently now slept in what was once his mother's room. A new water bed overwhelmed the room. A huge television set perched on top of the rather feminine dresser. The room was sour with the smells of sweat and alcohol. If despair could not be identified as an individual smell, it was nevertheless prevalent in this room.

Henriques's wallet was on the dresser. Merchant went into the bathroom and unrolled a handful of toilet paper. He came back in the room, wrapped his hand carefully, and opened the wallet. There was about fifty dollars in cash, a small packet of receipts, and bank ATM charge slips. The receipts told him nothing valuable — most were for miscellaneous purchases around New Bedford, for anything from gasoline to hot dogs. But the ATM receipts told him something.

George Henriques had about $40,000 sitting in his checking account. Most likely part of his mother's estate.

But she had been gone for a year. Even a lush like Henriques should've been able to figure out a money market fund, something a little more intelligent than letting forty grand sit in a checking account.

New money? Merchant wondered.

But that was speculation, and there were safer places to do that. He replaced the contents of the wallet.

He walked downstairs and out the door, taking a moment to wipe down the doorknob and the buzzer button with the wad of toilet paper. He walked out to the truck, aware that neighbors could very well be peering out their windows now and taking down Sarah's license plate, that police forensics could later find carpet fibers on his shoes, that whether or not it was intended by Henriques — or someone else — Merchant was digging his way into deeper trouble.

Henriques would've liked it that way.

31

"WE SHOULD CALL THE POLICE," Sarah said as they drove away.

"Yes, we should," Merchant said. "But we can't. *I* can't."

"Why not?"

"It's like this: I think George died sometime yesterday or early this morning. About the third or fourth question the police will ask me is where was I around the time of death. And I don't think I can count on Jarvy providing me with an alibi."

Sarah slumped back. "Oh, Jesus."

"That's right. Oh what a wicked web, and all that."

"You think this is funny?"

"Not even slightly."

"Don't you think they'll come to you anyhow?"

"That's the question. We don't know if George was the guy on the phone to the Randalls, but this makes me more suspicious, not less. For now, the Connecticut cops don't have any reason that I can think of to connect him. As for his little performance in the Stateroom with me, yeah, there's a risk all right. But I didn't recognize anybody, so maybe nobody recognized me. He made references to you . . . but whether the bartender was listening close enough to relay that to the cops, I don't know."

Merchant rubbed his face, thinking. It all came down to how hard the cops would be pushing. It came down to whether they thought Henriques was murdered or had committed suicide. Merchant didn't know himself.

But he did know that there were questions he couldn't answer if he called in the police right now.

"No," he said, shaking his head. "I've got to sit tight on this. And ask you to do the same."

"You don't ask much, do you?" Sarah lay back against the seat, closing her eyes again. Even in the low light, he could see she was pale and exhausted. "Jack, do me a favor and take me to my boat, put me to bed."

She added, "To sleep."

Her trawler had been closed tight for more than a week. The day's heat was still trapped inside, and Merchant opened all the hatches and set up a fan to get some air in.

The shore power was hooked up, so it didn't take long to have the boat bright and looking comfortable. The trawler was positively palatial compared to his sailboat. A huge aft cabin with a queen-size bed in the stern, private head with a bathtub, a built-in stereo system. There was a big main cabin with windows — forget portholes, these were windows — all around. And a very decent cabin in the bow just beyond the galley.

Merchant opened the refrigerator door and found nothing but condiments, jelly, some bottled water, a half-full jug of a sports drink, and a few beers.

The beers were layered with condensation though. He took one, rooted around the galley for an opener, and finally found one in the last drawer. He downed half the bottle. The cold beer exploded into his empty stomach, and he considered feeling ill but decided against it. All that he'd seen of George Henriques in those minutes might have sickened him, but it also made him very happy to be alive on the most basic of levels.

He checked the cupboards and found there were canned soups, boxes of rice, pasta, jars of spaghetti sauce, beans, cans of tuna fish. He looked at his watch. It was just after midnight. He went back into the main cabin, to see if Sarah wanted anything to eat.

She was already in bed, wearing a T-shirt. Her bandaged arm was propped up on pillows, and she looked very pale.

"You hurting?"

"Of course, dummy. I've been shot."

"Can I get you anything?"

She paused and then said, "A little company. Nothing more."

"Happy to oblige." He turned out the lights, stripped down to his underclothes, and lay down beside her. He was exhausted. The first real rest since getting on the plane to Florida.

He put his arm around Sarah carefully, making sure not to bang her arm. She eased back into him, careful, but wanting to be close.

In spite of how tired he was, his body responded. But there was so much else in his head: that Florida swamp, the old woman's home with her dead son.

"Just this," Sarah said. "Just this."

Merchant buried his face in her dark hair.

Minutes later, he was asleep.

Hours passed.

Merchant's eyes opened in the dark, and he lay quiet. Wondering if he'd heard something outside the boat.

But it was Sarah. She'd moved away from him. Her shoulders shook ever so slightly, and he realized she was crying.

"What?" he said. He leaned against her, and she curled tighter onto herself.

"Nothing. Go back to sleep."

"How can I with you bawling here in the dark? Tell me what's wrong."

He felt her shake her head. "Girls get to be weepy. Now go back to sleep."

He slipped his arm around her, again careful for her arm. And pulled himself close. "Maybe we didn't make wild passionate love yet, but I am the man here in your bed here at — " he looked at her clock " — three-forty-five in the morning. So I get to be nosy."

She didn't say anything, but she didn't pull away either.

He reached over and rubbed the tears from her cheek with the back of his hand. "What?" he asked again.

"Henriques," she said.

"You're crying for Henriques?"

"Yeah."

"He's not worth it."

"I know," she said. "Never was. Always mean. Selfish. A misfit. But I went to school with him."

"I see."

"No you don't."

But he thought he did. "You're not a misfit, Sarah. You're not going to end up alone in a room with a gun on the floor."

"Tell Joel that. Tell Owen that. Christ, tell my arm that."

"Owen deserved it."

"Maybe. But I'm the one with blood all over me."

"I've got my share."

"I know you do." She rolled over and looked at him. "Do I want a man in bed with me who's got that, too?"

"That's your choice to make, Sarah."

She didn't say anything.

"Fine," he said. He sat up and threw the covers off. Ready to get dressed and leave. He felt less angry than enormously tired.

She reached for him, her hand warm on his neck.

He said, "If you want someone different, wait for him."

"Shut up," she said. "Please, shut up."

She pulled him down to her.

He kissed her eyelashes, her cheeks. She put her hand alongside his face and when he kissed her mouth, she made a small sound deep inside, as if a small but fierce resolve had just broken.

He helped her off with her panties and shucked off his shorts. For this first time, they were too anxious to go slow. Both were trembling as he carefully entered her and began to move slowly. Sarah's breathing grew harsh, and she pulled him close with her good arm.

Her bandaged arm remained an independent presence beside them, an inflexible reminder of violence done.

32

MERCHANT WOKE AROUND SIX. He rolled over quietly and watched her sleep.

Sarah's lips were parted slightly, her dark eyelashes trembling on her cheeks. Dreaming, he supposed.

He wondered if he was in there.

He stayed like that, simply taking her in. Feeling smug that she was sleeping so well. Something she supposedly never did.

Finally, Merchant got up and went about the boat, drawing the curtains closed against the morning light. He dressed in the main cabin and left her a note saying that he would be back soon.

He found a convenience store and picked up coffee, eggs, cereal, milk, orange juice, sliced turkey, cheese, and a loaf of whole wheat bread. He poured a cup of coffee.

He was stalling, of course.

The primary reason for his shopping excursion was to pick up the morning papers. He bought *The Boston Globe* and the New Bedford *Standard Times,* and went out to the truck. The sun was brilliant now, beating off the small asphalt parking lot. He looked at the posters plastered on the glass inside the store, shouting for him to come back in and buy some more: a Styrofoam cooler for $9.99; potato chips and paper plates by the crate; hot dogs and buns. A four-color poster of a woman skater falling back into the arms of a man, both managing to hold on to their cigarettes. Life sure was full of potential here at the ShopRite.

Merchant sat behind the wheel sipping his coffee, knowing that the newspaper would make it all real again; would end the refuge that Sarah's bed had provided.

He found a small article in the *Globe* about George Henriques. *"Former DEA Agent Found Dead."* A larger article in the New Bedford paper with a fairly recent photo of Henriques staring out from a head-on shot.

Both stories read much the same. Henriques was found alone, a gun by his side. He was single and living in his recently deceased mother's home. Police would not comment on whether or not they believed it was suicide, but the reporters for both newspapers had clearly come to the same conclusion: loser kills himself, let's move on to something important.

Then Merchant turned to the *Globe's* obituary page. There it was, a picture of the young, and distinguished Paul Baylor. Company photo, no doubt.

The funeral was for ten o'clock in the morning.

Three hours, fifteen minutes.

"Do you think Julie wants you there?" Sarah said when he told her he was going.

She was still in bed, but sometime since he'd left, she'd put on her T-shirt and panties. She'd yet to mention their lovemaking the night before, and Merchant was just taking in how completely she could compartmentalize.

He didn't know exactly what to think about that, but it wasn't good.

He said, "Hold on. I'll get us some coffee." Showing he could do it, too, he supposed.

On the way back, he got his notebook and a pen from his computer bag. She moved over, and he sat beside her, leaning back against the headboard. They sipped their coffee for a few minutes, not talking. Shoulders not touching.

After a while, she said, "You didn't answer my question."

"No," he said, "I didn't. On the other hand, I think you should spend the day here. Resting. Eating the groceries."

"Join me." She colored just a bit. Very nice to see. She said, "I could make it worth your while."

"Sounds nice," he said. "Thought you weren't going to say anything."

"Yeah. I can be like that." She took his hand and squeezed. "I don't know what to think about what we did last night other than it was great and I'm buzzing and scared and don't want to talk more about it now."

He laughed. "Well, that's succinct."

She grinned at him and leaned close. They stayed there for a moment, and she said, "So . . . you with me today or not?"

"I've got to go."

"Why?" She pulled away. Exasperated, but no more than that. "We found the boat. Every other aspect of it is a tragic mess. But the job we were hired to do is done. So let it end there."

"I'm not sure it will, even if we want it to. Look what happened to Henriques."

"As far as we know, he killed himself."

"Maybe." Merchant opened the little notebook and turned it to the page they'd drafted together sitting at the bar at Coughlin's.

- Two hits at restaurants/Julie alone — *Don't believe it*
- Julie in truck towing boat. Boat back at house.
- Where is truck? (Truck & boat bought just before they go)
- Mower/Kid — note — goodbye
- Julie walks away from big $$ stock options at Digi.com
- Girlfriend — Michelle Amarro — suicide
- Paul — Straight arrow. Embezzlement??
- Paul talks up storm with Peter — hard work
- NYC ATM charge??
- Boat painter — Gerard — lying??

"OK," he said. "Some of this makes some sense now. We have a pretty good idea that Julie and Paul were running. Her going north to set up a false trail, him going south. Gerard to help repaint the boat. For some reason, they're apparently in New York City long enough to at least get a wallet stolen. Whole thing is very amateurish, very rushed. It seems like they weren't just running but running scared. Of what, we don't know."

He started scratching new notes:

- R. K. Randall — up from Fla. to kill me & possibly Baylors
- R. K. took phone call from "cop-sounding" man who told him about Baylors' cash onboard.
- Henriques — grudge against me
- Henriques played matchmaker between Sarah & me. Why?
- Henriques is "cop sounding." Dead now — suicide or murder??

Merchant stared at the list. Looked up at the older items on it and circled Michelle Amarro's name. "Two suicides. Related or not, another question mark. But interesting. Especially because I don't think Henriques killed himself."

"He wasn't the happiest man in the world."

"Yeah, but he was always pretty good at laying the blame someplace else."

"Late at night, few too many drinks? Reality comes crashing home?"

"Sure, it's possible. But there's other stuff." He reminded her about the cash sitting in Henriques's account. "Plus I had the feeling someone else had been there. The bed in the guest room was messed up. Put it this way, if it *is* murder we're dealing with, then someone was a pro at making it look like suicide. Tell me again about Henriques coming to see you at the Stateroom."

She sipped her coffee quietly, thinking. She said, "I was there for lunch. Truck parked out front. So I expect it wouldn't have been too hard for him to know I was inside. He came in, sat beside me at the bar."

"Sounds familiar."

"It didn't take him long to get to you," Sarah said. "Enjoyed telling me about you in Miami. Also managed to imply you'd panicked back on the deck of the *Juju* without actually saying it. Hard case for him to make seeing as he was swimming most of the time."

"Uh-huh. But he didn't recommend that you hire me?"

"No. But George was pretty good at reading people. He knew I liked you."

"That obvious, huh?"

"Shut up. Anyhow, so for him to tell me you were back in town — and under a cloud — it's a pretty fair chance I'd go see you. And then, not long after that, I got the paper in on your boat."

"A one-two punch," Merchant said. "I'm back, you're my friend, and you get handed paper to repo my boat. And you've got a problem assignment and need help. It's not a sure bet, but the odds are good you'd ask me to come work for you."

"It could still be coincidence."

"Could be," he said. "But the paper on my boat just one month overdue? That sounds awfully fast."

"It happens."

"How often?"

"Maybe . . . two in ten? Probably less, actually. One in ten. Most banks will let a couple, maybe three months go before they call in a repo."

"OK. And both the Baylors and me got the royal treatment. One month. Bankers. Different banks, though."

"I'll make some calls," Sarah said. "But you haven't answered my question."

"Which one's that?"

"Julie. Do you think she wants you showing up at the funeral?"

"Probably not," he said. "And if I told you why I was, you'd probably say I was presumptuous and self-deluding."

"And that is?"

"Because I think she needs my help," Merchant said.

Sarah lifted her eyebrows. "You called it," she said.

Merchant waited outside the gates of the cemetery until the procession arrived. He saw Julie Baylor go by in the limo. He thought she looked his way briefly, but the glass was so dark it was hard to be sure.

After that, the line of cars continued. Even if Paul Baylor supposedly had few friends, he apparently had a lot of acquaintances. Many of them drove expensive cars: BMWs, Audis, Porsches, Lexus and Infiniti sedans, a number of big SUVs, a smattering of midlevel cars. All clean, well kept. Presenting a nice crowd with solid or better prospects. Coming to say good-bye to one of their own.

Merchant followed them in.

*   *   *

He would have liked to have melted into the crowd around the grave. But enough people seemed to notice him: Cal Leland, Julie Baylor's boss, looked his way. Gene Radoccia was standing just off to the right side. He shook his head slightly, as if amazed by Merchant's gall.

And Julie Baylor herself looked at him.

She turned away and seemed to be trying to hold herself together as the minister said his prayers. Her shoulders shook as her husband was lowered into the ground.

Merchant followed along with the prayers. Said good-bye to the man he'd never actually met. Made some promises that sounded a bit foolish, but that he meant nonetheless.

After that, they all filed away, and aside from a few glares from those who recognized him, Merchant was left alone.

He assumed he wasn't invited back to the house afterward. But he went anyhow.

He drove past first, saw that there was indeed a gathering. He did the same again an hour later, and then again an hour after that. The cars were beginning to dwindle down.

He found the library in Lincoln, a beautiful redbrick building just past an expansive green lawn. He parked and went inside.

He had vague plans for reading magazines for a while before heading back to the Baylors' house. But he found the reference room just off to the left, noticed the computers on varnished wood tables. He remembered Sarah's search of the *Miami Herald* headlines in the newspaper archives and figured there was maybe a better way for him to kill time.

He logged on to a newspaper search engine and highlighted a half dozen newspapers in Massachusetts, Connecticut, and Florida. He typed in his own name. Moments later, he received a listing of a depressing number of articles where his name was linked between the Gacha and Baylor incidents.

Next, he put in Paul and Julie Baylors' names. The same articles appeared as his, plus Paul's obituary.

He tried Gene Radoccia's. Nothing.

R. K. Randall's. Numerous New England accounts of his attack in Connecticut, all saying pretty much the same thing. The Florida papers had news of his death and, before that, a short story about the assault that had put him in prison.

Merchant drummed his fingers. Thinking about each step along the way. He punched in Julie's sister's name, Emily Kirkland. Nothing.

Then he tried Henriques's name and included the New Bedford paper along with several other southern Massachusetts newspapers in the search. He came up with just a few small text links going back years, and then the recent news of his death and obituary.

Merchant read them and didn't find anything he didn't already know.

Then he typed in Michelle Amarro's name, hit the enter key, and started reading.

Killing time.

He headed back to Julie Baylor's home and rang the bell.

There was no answer.

He waited a few minutes and rang the bell again.

This time, he saw movement behind the narrow vertical window beside the door. But the glass was pebbled, and all he could tell was someone was there. He rang the doorbell again. "Mrs. Baylor, it's Jack Merchant."

The door opened. Julie stood in the doorway.

She seemed to pause, as if she didn't recognize him. He wondered for a moment if she was drugged. Then she said, "What do you want, Mr. Merchant?"

"I'd like to talk to you."

Again, she waited. As if expecting something else from him. Finally, she said, "I've had a long day, as you know. So please leave."

"I'm sorry. But it's not that simple."

Julie's eyes narrowed. She said, "I'm not blaming you for what happened, Mr. Merchant. But I'd like you to go."

"Why aren't you?"

"What's that?"

"Why aren't you blaming me?"

"Please . . . if this is your conscience bringing you here, I've got other things to worry about. Please just go away."

"Mrs. Baylor, I'm very sorry for what happened to your husband. I'm very sorry for any part I played. But from what I've learned, there was more to it than my part."

"I don't know what you're talking about," Julie said. She backed away. "But I do know I buried my husband today. Now please leave, Mr. Merchant. If you have any respect for me, you'll do what I ask."

"I think you're still in trouble," Merchant said

She started to say something but instead began to close the door. He put his hand out to stop it. "Just take a look at this. If you don't call the police about it, I will."

She hesitated. "What're you talking about?"

He held out a printout he'd made from *The Boston Globe* at the library.

She opened the door, scanned it quickly, and said, "So?"

But she didn't meet his eyes. He knew she wasn't a very practiced liar, and it showed.

"Julie? I'm only trying to help you."

She stared at him, her eyes meeting his now.

He simply waited.

After a moment, she turned away but left the door open. He followed her in.

33

THEY WENT INTO the office.

She offered him a seat in front of Paul's computer and sat across from him. Her desktop computer had been pushed aside, and her laptop was in its place, the screen glowing.

Julie was wearing a pair of faded blue jeans, and her hair was wet from the shower. Her face was scrubbed free of any makeup, and under her sunburned skin she was pale and shaken. She was strung even tighter than he'd realized: skin pulled taut over wire.

It felt odd, sitting across from her. The days that he'd spent looking for her and her husband, he'd come to feel he knew something about her.

He realized he didn't.

The questions were all there for the asking. Topping the list, the one she had deflected back at the police station: *Why were you running?*

But he started slower than that. "I had a conversation with the brother of the man who killed your husband."

"I thought the police already did that."

"They did. I wanted my own."

"You went down to Florida?"

"Yes."

"And?"

"I found that R. K. Randall knew about the cash you had onboard. That someone convinced him to come up. Somebody who sounded like a cop. Someone who wanted to set me up to take a fall for killing you. It looks to me that R. K. may've been onboard as much to kill you and your husband as me. The way I see it, I was to be left with a gun in my hand, set up as the one who killed you."

"The way you see it," she said.

"Three guns. The only way I see that makes sense is that he came onboard with two: the one he'd taken from my boat, another one to hold on you. And then he found the third on your boat. All the better, he'd actually use your own gun."

"I don't see it that way," she said. "Neither does anyone else."

"They will if I talk with them some more. Is that why that kid had your ATM card in New York? You go to buy a gun in the wrong part of town and get ripped off?"

She ignored that. A little too easily, he thought.

She said, "What is it you want? If you're looking to be absolved of any influence in getting my husband killed, I'll give it to you."

"Again, why? Why are you so ready to forgive?"

She started to say something else and then paused. Then said, "Mr. Merchant — "

"Call me Jack."

"All right, Jack. Let me ask you something. Why are you trusting me with this information?"

"I know you're good at keeping secrets."

"Meaning?"

"Meaning I know about you in the little skiff out there. Towing it behind that Chevy truck up the coast to Maine, leaving a false trail. Getting ready to call in a fake Mayday, I'd guess. What went wrong?"

"I don't know what you're talking about."

"You're not a very good liar, Mrs. Baylor. Speaks well for you in the long run. The false trail played way too obvious. You didn't need to dump iced tea on that poor cook."

A dull bit of color had grown on Julie's cheeks but at this last, she broke into laughter. A sad, tearing sound; she put her hand to her mouth as if to stop it. Then her face crumpled and she began crying for good.

He waited.

Crying didn't seem to come easily for her. She fought it, rubbed at her face with her palms. She stood up and banged her hip against the desk as she reached for a box of tissues on top of the filing cabinet. She kept her back to him as she wiped her tears away.

Merchant waited while she sat back down across from him. When she turned back, her eyes were red rimmed.

She said, "I told Paul I did that. And even as scared as we were the past month, we both got how silly it was, me dousing that woman. We had no experience. No experience at all, dealing with this sort of thing. We only had two days to put it together, and ideas from books and movies as to how to do it. I can't say we were doing our best thinking." Julie touched her eyes with the tissue, and said, "You seem like a good man, Jack."

"It's been debated."

"Did I understand you have some police background?"

"DEA. But I'm retired."

She looked at him carefully. Assessing him.

He said, "Do you need help, Julie?"

"Why are you offering?"

"I owe you."

"I don't know about that," she said. "You've been used."

"You didn't think so on the boat."

"I didn't know for sure then. I thought maybe it happened just the way it looked, and I hated you."

"So who used me? And what were you running from?"

"I wouldn't be doing you any favors telling you."

"I wasn't asking for any."

For a moment, he thought she would continue. Then she said, "Really, I've had a long day . . . ."

Merchant held up the New Bedford paper. The one with Henriques's photo. "Do you know him?"

Julie's face went white. She reached for the paper, and stared at the photo. At Henriques. She grasped Merchant's arm, her nails biting into him. She said, "Do you know this man's name?" Her hand was trembling, and there was no deflection in her eyes now. "Could you find him?"

"Why?"

"I think he's the one that's got my sister. He's got Emily."

"What do you mean he's *got* her? Kidnapped?"

"Yes, yes. If you know who he is . . . I'll hire you to help me get her back . . . if you'd only help me."

Merchant was trying to take it in fast. Emily hadn't been at the funeral. She hadn't even been at the police station in Connecticut. He said, "Jesus, why didn't you tell the police? How long has she been gone?"

"As soon as I got off your boat. As soon as you brought me in after Paul was killed. Gene Radoccia whispered it in my ear that they had her."

"Radoccia?"

"Yes. On the dock. Before I even spoke to the policeman."

"Radoccia's in this?"

"He said they'd kill her if I didn't keep my mouth shut. They want the photo."

"What photo?"

But she was talking as much to herself as to him. "Don't you see? It's my only leverage. They'll kill her unless I can swap it just right."

"Julie, listen to me. Henriques is dead." He opened the article, let her see the headline.

She put her hand to her mouth, and he quickly filled her in on what he knew. That he'd found Henriques's body. And that his guest bedroom appeared to have been used recently. "There's every chance she was there."

"When did you do this?" Julie said.

"Last night."

"But I got this e-mail just this morning!"

She turned to her computer and opened a saved e-mail message. She opened an attached photo file.

And there was Emily. Sitting alone on a small bed, holding up a newspaper. That morning's *Boston Globe*. The same one that held her brother-in-law's obituary. Emily looked glassy-eyed, as if she'd been sedated.

Merchant said, "Julie. It's time you tell me just what the hell is going on. Me and the cops."

He reached for the phone. "No!"

She snatched it away. "I'm not going to lose her. They say they'll kill her if the police are involved."

"Who's they? Gene Radoccia?"

"No. If it was only him, I'd have called the police long ago."
She set the telephone on the desk behind her. "Here, give me those
articles," she said.

She stood up and spread them across the desk. Merchant suddenly had an image of her at work: fast thinking, capable. She said,
"What do you know about Michelle Amarro's death?"

"Just what I read. That she supposedly jumped out of her bedroom window at the Richmond and landed in the alley below. That
the forensics showed she'd had intercourse some time that night.
And that it turned out she had a more exotic past than your aver-
age high-tech employee."

He pointed to the *Globe*'s third-day coverage of the suicide.
When it was revealed she once ran a porn web site, Luscious-
Ladies.com. Then another flurry of articles when it was discovered
Digi.com owned LusciousLadies.com. Interviews with Cal Leland
defending the nature of "an early investment." More articles about
how the bad publicity might tank Digi.com's bid for an IPO.

Merchant said to Julie, "So were you at the Richmond that
night?"

"All of us were. It was sort of a who's who of the Boston area
Internet and banking. Me, Paul, Cal. Gene Radoccia — "

Merchant interrupted. "Those two know each other for long?"

"Cal and Gene? They should, they went to school together. Gene
personally fronted a lot of the start-up money five years back."

Merchant remembered when he and Sarah had met Cal Leland.
The impression Merchant had taken away was that Leland and
Radoccia knew each only in that they coordinated over the Baylors'
disappearance.

Julie pointed to a heavyset blond man. "Jason Vance. It's got to
be him behind this."

The caption under the picture says, *"Top Internet Names
Shocked over Suicide."*

"This is the guy in the photo in your office, isn't he? An investor,
right?"

"That's like saying Rockefeller was in the steel business. And
that's why the stakes are so high."

"Did he kill her?"

"I can't know for sure what happened. But what I do know is dangerous enough for him that my husband has been killed, my sister

taken, and I don't expect to make it through the week if I can't get it resolved somehow." She took the articles, shuffled them together quickly, and put them in a file folder.

"Paul liked to take pictures," she said. She gestured at the photos on the walls. "He always had some sort of camera with him, and he had one that night at the Richmond. But he didn't always get the rolls in for developing right away. Every once in a while he'd put them in an envelope and mail them off to a specialty printer he used in New York. He'd get the film, prints, and a CD back. So a couple of months after the fund-raiser we were getting ready for our vacation, and he dumped a bunch of exposed rolls of film from his camera bag into an envelope and sent them out. And when the prints came back, we saw he'd taken a shot of Michelle that night."

Julie turned to her laptop and Merchant moved closer. She opened up a JPEG file on the desktop, and a photo filled the screen. In the foreground Julie stood close to another woman, smiling. Typical grin-and-grip shot.

She said, "We were at a reception on the sixth floor when Paul took this picture. The elevator door must've just opened and he caught this." She pointed to the top right corner of the photo. The background.

Merchant could see Michelle Amarro in an open elevator. There was a big blond man with his arm around her, whispering in her ear. She was laughing, her head thrown back. Lovely neck exposed. Cal Leland was behind, off to the right of them.

Merchant looked closely at the blond man and back at the newspaper printout. "Jason Vance."

"That's right."

"Let me guess. He said he never so much as talked to Michelle that night."

"Uh-huh," Julie said. "The police questioned everybody. And I heard him deny even seeing her that night. But then this picture . . . When I saw this, I knew Vance lied for some reason."

"So did you got to the police?"

Julie shook her head. "You've got to understand. Jason Vance is huge for us at Digi.com. He's the key to investment money. He's the key to getting patent clearances with a competitor, RyDak, in San Diego. I did what people do . . . I went to my boss."

"You went to Cal Leland."

"That's right."

"Your friend."

"Never my friend. I've worked for him for five years, but I know that at heart he's a mean bastard. Still, I never thought he'd be up for something like this. But there he was in the elevator with her and Vance. And so I asked him what it meant. Asked him why he and Vance had lied to the police."

"What'd he say?"

"He brushed it off. Said it meant nothing. That Vance had been with her in the elevator, nothing more. And that naturally Vance denied knowing her — he didn't want to get tied up in any bad publicity because of her death. 'And neither do we,' Cal said to me. He said the company had already taken a big enough hit because of Michelle's death and the porn site. And that if my stock options meant a damn thing to me, I'd better let it go with Vance. That it was just bad publicity and nothing more. 'Go on your vacation,' he said. 'This is nothing to worry about.'"

"Did you buy that?"

"I tried to. I *wanted* to. I had worked for those options. So I didn't want to believe what I was seeing — that he was lying."

"So you kept quiet?"

"Wouldn't you? I stood to lose my shot at somewhere between ten and twenty million dollars. On what? A photo that showed a man had lied about who he was with that night, not that he was a killer."

"Did Paul agree with you?"

"Absolutely. He knew money. He knew the forces it would bring to bear. He looked at Jason Vance's fortune — probably a hundred million now, possibly into the billions someday — and put that against us. And he did the math. 'We'll lose,' he said. 'One way or the other, we will lose if we go up against this.'"

"Did Cal press you for the photos and negatives?"

"No. I saw this man." She put her finger on the picture of Henriques.

"He approached you on the photos?"

"No. The night after I met with Cal, Paul and I went to the boat. We were due to leave on our trip in two days, and even though it was late, we were wound up from talking about the picture and we decided to make a run to the marina to drop off some supplies. And when we were pulling into the parking lot, I saw this man walk under a streetlight. I didn't recognize him at first, but he seemed familiar. All the time we're bringing the stuff down to the boat, it's nagging at me, and then I got it — I'd seen him at the office a couple of times before over the years. He'd come in to meet with Cal. I assumed he had something to do with the porn web site. When I told Paul where I'd seen the man before, his face goes white, and he says, 'Get off the boat.' I thought he was being over-cautious on me. But I got off and went up to the marina deck. And he turned on every light on the boat and started crawling through it with a flashlight. And he found something."

"A bomb?"

She nodded. "Under the engine mount. Paul came up, and we sat on the bench and talked in the dark." Julie raked her fingers through her hair. "I've been over that night again and again. The choices we made . . . the choices *I* made. Paul went along with me. Tried to figure it out for me. I just couldn't let it go. I'm supposed to give up millions of dollars because these *jerks,* these two men and this girl screw up? It's not like a few years ago, when I might have signed up with some other Internet start-up. This was my *shot.* Michelle was practically a hooker, the things she'd do on that web page. Why should I give up all that for her?"

Julie flushed as she said this. "Paul was a sweet, wonderful, smart man. He'd do anything for me. And I told him to figure it out. Figure out how we could get past this. I was an idiot, Jack. I was greedy. I knew if we went to the police, whatever chance I had at that money was over. I wanted what I was owed." A tear streaked down her right cheek. "Paul didn't care about that. But with that kind of money against us, he didn't think we'd live long if we went to the police. Somehow Cal or Vance would get at us. So Paul agreed to figure out something different. To at least give us some time."

"By making it look like they'd succeeded?"

"That's right. Let them think we sailed to Maine, the boat blew up and sank. We're dead."

"You didn't just get back on the boat with the bomb on it?"

"We weren't that crazy. No, Paul called a man at the marina — "

"Gerard?"

Julie looked surprised. "Yes. Did he talk to you?"

"Just barely," Merchant said.

"Well, he helped us. You know he's an ex-Marine and very capable. And he and Paul had always hit it off. Well, Paul called him right then on the cell phone and said, 'How'd you like to not have to worry about money for the next year?' Gerard came and picked us up at the dock in his boat. We went back to his mooring. We talked until about three A.M. and told him what was happening. We figured out my trip north while Paul sailed to Cuttyhunk and Gerard repainted the boat. The idea was that we'd buy ourselves some time, maybe sail to the Carolinas or Miami. We told Gerard we'd pay him ten thousand dollars, plus the boat painting."

"Gerard disarmed the bomb?"

"He said he'd look at it. He said he'd go that far because he was pretty sure no one would put some sort of motion-sensitive detonator on a boat because even the wake of a passing boat could make it blow. He said it was more likely to be on a timer or set for when the engine was turned on."

"And was it?"

"Yes. A timer. We had fallen asleep on Gerard's boat. At about five-thirty, he and Paul left in the dinghy. I sat there in the cockpit. Thinking about what Paul was doing for me, how dangerous it was, but not willing to stop them. And when they came back they said they'd disarmed it. Dynamite placed right under the engine mount and a smaller detonator linked to the propane tanks. I guess in case anything was salvaged to make it look like it had been a propane explosion. This bomb was enough to send the engine itself up through the cockpit floor and to blow a hole out the bottom. It was just about guaranteed to bring us and the *Fresh Air* to the bottom. It was set to go off right about the time we'd be sailing up to Acadia from Portland."

"So what went wrong?"

"Everything, really. What sounded like a plan when we were talking about it on Gerard's boat began to fall apart when we actually tried it. I drove north, Paul sailed south. I made sure I was visible in Portsmouth and then in Portland. But when I got to the ramp at Acadia, this young guy was there fishing and he wanted to help me put the little boat in. Wanted to know why I was going out alone. Just being friendly, but there was too good a chance he'd remember me if there was any publicity about the *Fresh Air* sinking. So I just left. And then I met up with Paul in Connecticut. Prescient Cove. He wanted to stay that night because of the storm. But I insisted we leave — I was scared. And he did what I wanted. We didn't make it ten miles down the coast before running aground."

"Did you take the photo and the film with you?"

She shook her head. "No. Left that here in our office. We kept the CD. Paul and I figured they'd break in, find the prints and negatives, and think they were safe. They even took the hard drives on our computers to be sure."

"Where'd you stay when the boat was being repaired?"

"We took the train and stayed in crummy hotels in New York until the boat was ready again . . . and I got a taste for what we'd signed up to do. To be hiding. Our money just being eaten into day after day. Paul met a man in a bar who said he could sell him a gun. He had to go into Harlem. He came home looking like he'd been through a war. After he bought the gun, someone mugged him, stole his wallet. He pulled the gun and they ran off. I wanted to cry and I wanted to scream. Everything I'd given up for that job. Paul had wanted children and I always held him off, saying there was time for the kids once the options paid off. It just ate at me. Cal and Jason Vance get to live their lives, while we have to hide out for what they did."

She gestured to the laptop, to the photo. "So I sent this. Paul was in the shower, and I put the CD into the computer and sent an e-mail to Cal. Told him that I was alive and expected my options to be paid."

"Blackmail?"

"I didn't look at it that way," Julie said. "It was getting what I deserved."

"I see," Merchant said.

"I'm sure you do," she said, bitterly. Julie gestured to the empty room, to Paul's picture up on the wall, his arm around her. "And you'd say I got it."

"No, Julie."

"But Emily didn't," Julie continued as if she hadn't heard him. "She did nothing but come back to look for me, and now she's terrified, and God knows what else is happening to her. You said you wanted to help. Well, what I need is help getting her back."

"Just her?"

Julie looked confused. "What do you mean?"

Watching her closely, Merchant said, "The money. I want to know if we're going for the money as well as your sister."

Julie tried to strike him.

He caught her hand in time, felt the wiry strength of her arm. "Don't test me," she said. Her voice thick with anger. "I've gone through enough, don't test me."

"Taking a swing at me hasn't passed any test. If you mean what you say, let me call in the FBI. They're going to offer the best hope of getting your sister back alive. But they're not going to have anything to do with getting some cash settlement for lost stock options, believe me."

"I don't care about that anymore," she said. "It's just that I don't know who to trust."

"Start with me. And I still know people at the DEA in Boston that I'd bet my life on. They'll get me to the right people at the FBI."

"Bet your life on," she repeated. "But it's not your life, it's Emily's."

"Still the right people," Merchant said. He picked up the phone. Waiting to see if there was another objection.

But what he saw on her face was relief. Relief that someone else was taking charge.

Merchant put the phone to his ear — only to hear dead silence. No dial tone.

He swore. "Do you have a gun in the house?"

She picked up the telephone herself, listened. Confused.

Then she seemed to take in his question. "A gun? No. Just the one the police have."

Merchant headed to the door. There were sharp knives in the kitchen, he remembered.

But there was a muffled sound of glass breaking from the other room.

Julie sat down in front of her computer. "I'll do it," she said. She turned and yelled at the door. "I'll send it to the police!"

Merchant hesitated. No time for the knives. He locked the door. "It's too late," he said. "The lines are down, Julie."

She didn't seem to hear him. She kept trying.

Merchant looked out the office windows. There was a big sedan parked next to his car. The lights out. But he could see the shape of someone behind the wheel.

He heard footsteps coming closer. At least two people coming fast. Making no attempt at silence.

He pulled Julie away from her laptop and said, "Get down." She snatched the little computer to her chest, as if it still offered some protection.

He pushed her behind the desk and stood off behind the door himself.

And waited for it to be kicked open.

34

AS MANY BUSTS as Merchant had been on, as many kicked in doors, he'd never been on this side of one before.

And these weren't cops.

But they hit the door like pros: it slammed open, missing Merchant by inches. A bull came through. Not a cop, maybe, but a bull nonetheless. A heavyset man with broad shoulders, a big square head.

A slightly smaller man behind him took a position to the left. Smaller, meaning about Merchant's size. He was leveling a sawed-off shotgun.

The bull turned direction without a word and plowed into Merchant.

Merchant tried to pull him in, roll him over his hip.

The bull was having none of it. He altered his charge, scooped Merchant up off his feet and drove him into the wall.

The bull put his head and shoulders down and got to work. Swung deep hooks into Merchant's ribs and gut, and left nothing for Merchant to hit but a rock-hard head and shoulders armored with layers of muscle.

The guy with the gun was talking. He said to Merchant, "Just take it, man. He's gonna keep at it until you're down anyhow."

It seemed he knew what he was talking about.

*　　*　　*

Merchant came to probably just a couple of minutes later. The man with the shotgun was over him now. Bandy-legged guy with red hair, freckles, blue eyes. Cheerful face, but mean eyes. The bull was beside him. Blowing heavily. Big square face, pocked skin. "He need any more?" he said.

The man with the gun said, "Naw, he's perfect. Take her out to the car."

The bull grabbed Julie by the arm, and picked up her laptop in the other hand.

Merchant tried to get up, but Red Hair tapped him lightly on the head with the gun barrel. It sent Merchant back down, and for a moment, he thought he was going to be sick.

He heard the front door close.

"Get up," Red Hair said. "You're coming with me."

Merchant got to his feet. There was blood in his mouth. It hurt to breathe. He stumbled on the way out of the hallway.

And Red Hair crowded behind him and shoved him along. Felt like he turned the gun sideways and shoved him with that. A sloppy move.

Merchant did it again and got another shove for his clumsiness. "Move it," the guy said.

"Give me a break," Merchant said. Putting a whine in his voice. Looking for another shove.

And when it came, he was ready. He pivoted to the right. Away from the direction of the gun barrel. He got his right hand on the gun, and though Red Hair tried to tug it away, Merchant wouldn't let go.

Instead, he kneed the man in the balls.

Merchant yanked the gun away and hit the guy across the face with what remained of the butt.

Red Hair slid to his knees. Merchant kicked him in the stomach. Then he ran for the front door and out onto the driveway, the shotgun leveled.

Would've been something to be proud of except that the car with Julie in it was already pulling away.

Merchant took aim and saw her looking back at him from the rear window. There was someone in the back with her, a man, but it was too dark to tell anything else, or who was driving. And then the car was around the hedge and out of sight.

"Damn it!" Merchant said.

He ran back into the house. But Red Hair was gone. The back door out to the deck was open. Merchant walked over to it cautiously. Thinking the guy might be waiting for him right around the corner.

But he wasn't there. Merchant stood on the deck, looking back across the darkened lawn into the woods. And then, faintly, he could hear the sound of an engine starting.

Merchant ran back through the house into the driveway. He ran up to the road. About a hundred yards away, a car pulled onto the road, the lights off.

He hurried to his truck. Put the shotgun onto the floor and fired up the engine. By the time he got out of the driveway, the second car was already out of sight. Merchant stood on the gas pedal, and the rear tires shrieked on the asphalt.

He wasn't certain what he could do if he caught up with either car.

Minutes later, his cell phone rang.

Concentrating on the road as he was, he almost didn't answer it. He'd pushed the truck up to over eighty. He had yet to catch up to Red Hair.

The phone continued to sound.

Finally, he put it to his ear. "What?"

"Merchant?" a man said. "I hear you're screwing around with our plans. Ms. Baylor wants to talk to you about that."

Julie's voice came on. "It's me."

"Are you all right?"

Stupid question, but somehow he had to ask it.

But the man's voice came back. "OK, here's the situation — if you call the police, not only does Ms. Baylor die but so does Sarah Ballard. That clear, Merchant?"

Merchant went cold. "You have Sarah?"

"She's on her boat, doesn't know a damn thing. They told me she had a shower not long ago. So, hey, you keep screwing around with me, at least she can pass her last moments clean and fresh. But her telephone lines are cut, and I know for a fact you're holding her company cell phone. So she's going to be just fine unless you get in my way. Now do what you're told, and I'll be in touch."

Merchant took his foot off the gas. The big truck immediately began to slow down. He said, "Who are you?"

"I'm the fellow who came late to the party," the man said. "But I'll put things in order. Head out to Route 2. Continue east toward Boston, and wait for your next call."

Then he hung up.

35

SARAH WAS TURKEYED OUT.

She'd put turkey in her omelet for lunch, had a small sandwich around four, and then a massive one for dinner, complete with some canned cranberry sauce she'd found in the cupboard.

She'd kept at the coffee throughout the day and had the jitters to prove it. She'd made a number of the calls that Merchant had asked her to make. While she didn't have anything definitive, she did learn that MassBank owned his bank. And, therefore, Merchant's bank followed the criteria for loans outlined by MassBank. Whether or not MassBank had specifically flagged his, she didn't know. She'd left a call with Shelly, but as the hours passed by she became fairly certain he wouldn't be calling her back.

And he'd once been her best customer.

She went through the accounting software on her laptop again and again to confirm what she already knew: there was no way she could stay in business beyond the year if she didn't get MassBank back or fill in with equivalent new business.

And a lot of luck she'd be having getting new business with Gene Radoccia out there bitching about the liability of having Ballard Marine Liquidation work for you.

Gets the boat back but kills the owners. Not the makings of a good slogan.

She had also been poised all day for the police to step onto her Grand Banks with questions about why her truck had been seen outside George Henriques' house while he was inside letting the flies gather on his face.

Most of all, she wished Merchant had returned. And needing him and knowing consciously that she *should* be happy did very little to make her *feel* happy, and that pissed her off, too.

Plus, her arm hurt.

This sucks, she thought.

"I'll tell all my friends." Listening to the sound of her voice alone in the boat. "Getting shot *sucks*."

That got her to thinking about her friends. Who exactly were they?

She'd never had many women friends. She'd had a bunch of high school girlfriends, but they'd faded fast when her father moved her and Joel out of their home onto the boat. When the office at the repo yard became her place to play, do her homework, and keep Joel from knocking the poppits out from under the boats with the tractor.

Sarah looked in the mirror, giving herself an appraisal. She was wearing a T-shirt and boxer shorts. A good body, pretty enough face, tired looking, though. She had a bandage on her arm and a history of being beaten.

Dark smudges under her eyes. Hair clean. She'd showered with a bag around her arm to keep the bandage dry. That was a good sign, clean in body and mind. But how did freshly washed hair stack up against killing a man a couple years back? Doing repossessions for a living? Recovering from a gunshot wound?

She summarized: *Has potential, but quickly fading. On her way to trailer trash. Floating trailer trash.*

Friends.

A few restaurant and bar owners who knew her by name. Nice to her, but then she had a good appetite and paid with cash, so what was not to like?

Lots of skippers of the local fishing fleet who hated her on sight. Repo woman, what'd you expect? Didn't stop them from whistling when her back was turned, yelling what they'd like to do to her. Not friends, certainly.

Friends.

There was Allie Gale, a graphic designer in town. She and Allie were pretty close, even though they seemed to have nothing in common other than they made each other laugh. Allie was a friend, definitely.

There were other women down at the gym. People to chat with, maybe have coffee with after, but nothing more, really. Who else? There had been a bunch of male friends, guys she knew in the business, guys like Raul who she could kid around with. Owen had certainly cut a path across friendships with those guys. Bad enough when he was around to stare them down, but after she'd killed him, she found lots of her buddies still didn't want to hang with her.

Wussies.

And there was Lenny and the other part-timers. Lenny, well, dysfunctional as their relationship was, she supposed he was a friend. As for the others, she liked most of them pretty well, but she was the boss. Who knew what they really felt about her?

Lou Grasso. He was a friend. Tried to help her with Owen. He was there for her when Joel died. But since he'd made detective, he was so busy she almost never saw him.

Joel had been her friend. Her best friend, even though she had been hard as hell on him sometimes. Harder than a friend or sister should be.

Her eyes welled up briefly, and she wiped them dry, angry with herself.

Christ, she was doing something wrong. Pushing thirty and Merchant was her closest friend.

And now her lover, *shit!*

Wide open, she thought. *Left myself wide open.*

Before last week she hadn't heard from him for five years.

And now she wanted his touch. Was already counting on him to come back and treat her well, and for her to do the same thing and not screw it up.

Which was her usual mode of operation with men. None of them lasted.

Hell, she even *killed* the last one.

She laughed out loud in the empty boat, but it wasn't a joyful sound.

Sarah picked up the phone. Figured she'd give Allie a call and maybe they'd meet for a glass of wine. Plenty to talk about, as long as she avoided the topic of George Henriques, dead in his mother's house.

But there wasn't even a dial tone. Damn it, Shelly could've been trying her all afternoon for all she knew.

She sighed, and then went down into her cabin to pull on some jeans.

Merchant could've been trying to call, too.

And now she cared.

Pathetic.

She grabbed her keys on the way out and flipped on the deck lights. Padding outside in her bare feet, she first went around to see that the phone line was still connected.

No problem there.

She stepped down to the dock, holding her arm carefully as she did. The light was OK on the dock itself, and she knelt in front of the little pedestal near the bow of the boat where the phone and electricity hookups were set. No problem apparent there. The plug was snapped in.

She headed up the dock to the ramp. She flicked her thumb under the little Mace canister on her key chain. Carrying the Mace was just a habit now. Press the button and it would squirt a mess for the eyes and nose of the attacker.

Hadn't done her much good with Owen, but this was a different kind of canister. Shaped so it was easy to hold it the right way.

She didn't see that she needed it exactly, but it was hers.

As she passed the *Jambalaya,* a custom wooden cruiser, she saw the owner, Grace Eli, inside the cockpit on the phone. Grace waved to her and then held up her arm as if to say, "What happened to you?"

Sarah smiled and waved back. Tell her later.

Thinking that *her* phone worked.

She climbed the ramp up to the gate, turned the knob — and it turned too easily in her hand. Someone had put a piece of black tape over the sliding bolt — the gate was left unlocked.

Suddenly, Sarah felt cold.

Standing there in her jeans and T-shirt, barefoot. Her arm in a sling, that little canister of Mace her only defense, which had done nothing but earn her a broken wrist last time.

But he's dead, she thought.

She exhaled slowly, opened the gate, and stepped through. The parking lot at the end of the ramp was darker. She was standing right under the lamppost, feeling exposed.

She almost peeled the tape away from the lock and ran back to the boat. Maybe would've if it didn't feel so foolish and cowardly.

Because maybe the phone company had just screwed up. What next? Hide under the covers if the lights went out?

That thought gave her another chill. She didn't like the thought of the lights going out, didn't like standing under *this* light.

She felt that someone was watching her.

She told herself to keep moving. The utility box was to her left, a gray metal cabinet with a locked panel that housed the circuit breakers for electricity and telephone hookups for each boat. What she needed to do was simple: walk through that dark parking lot, and get whoever was on night duty to come out with the key and make sure everything was working there. If not, call the telephone company.

She looked at the panel box, stalling really, before stepping out of that pool of light.

The padlock was in place on the panel.

She swatted at it, irritated with herself. And the padlock swung open.

Sarah felt sick.

She stood there staring for a moment, and then knelt down.

The lock was open. But it had been turned to look as if it were still closed.

Her back was to the parking lot. The feeling of being watched was overwhelming.

She took off the lock and opened the panel. Each slip was numbered. The plug on hers was pulled. Everyone else's just fine.

Behind her, a car door opened.

She tried to think.

If you run to the marina, you'll have to run past whoever it is.

If you run back down the dock, you'll have to peel off the tape and slam the gate behind you. How long for him to get the gate open again? Enough time for you to start the engines, get the boat off the dock?

Didn't seem likely with her arm in the sling.

She slipped her thumb under the little Mace canister. Told herself that she'd wait until he was close, that she'd act like she didn't know he was coming upon her, that she'd shove it in his face and push the button, and God help her if she nailed some new boat neighbor, but she'd wash his decks for the next year to make it up to him.

Sarah stood up and turned around.

The lamppost was between her and him, and even though she shifted to see him better, the glare made it impossible for her to see more than a shape. The shape of a good-size man walking directly to her.

"Hey, there," she said, in a friendly voice.

The man kept coming.

Sarah told herself to shut up and wait. That if she needed to use the Mace, she had to wait until he was close. Very close.

Shut up and wait.

But he stopped outside the light. She could see over his shoulder that his car was a white midsize sedan. And the door was open, but the interior lights were off.

Her breathing was rushing, and her instinct was to attack, to close the distance. But there was her stupid arm in a sling, and she was barefoot, and her little can of Mace that had proved so useless against Owen seemed even more puny and ridiculous now.

The man said, "Sarah Ballard?"

She didn't say anything.

s

And then a car swept in behind the man. Lou Grasso's car. A blue light swirling on the dashboard. High beams on.

Revealing a man Sarah had never seen, a tall guy with close-cropped hair, dark clothes — and holding a gun.

The guy turned instantly and fired three shots into the windshield of Lou's car. The noise was unimaginable. Orange flame.

Sarah spun and pulled the gate open. There was a flash of sparks on the doorjamb, and a bullet whined. She recoiled, and then forced herself to run anyhow.

She waited for him to shoot her in the back as she ran down the narrow ramp, high handrails on each side. If she had the use of both her arms, maybe she would've vaulted into the water, but she didn't, so she just ran.

Good enough, apparently.

Because by the time she got down to the bottom of the ramp, she heard an engine come to life, and more gunfire, as Lou apparently shot back. The engine screamed, and Sarah turned to look up at the parking lot. She couldn't see from that angle, but she heard spinning tires, the sound of metal on metal, and then more peeling rubber.

Sarah ran back until the angle improved and she could see Lou's car was still there. The blue light swirling.

"Oh my God," she heard behind her.

She whirled. Grace. Grace standing in the stern of her boat, her telephone in hand.

"Call the police," Sarah said. "Call them right now. Tell them one of theirs has been shot."

Grace immediately dialed the phone.

Sarah turned, and ran back up the ramp.

36

MERCHANT DIALED LOU GRASSO'S cell phone number for the third time.

This time, someone answered.

Merchant barely recognized her at first.

Sarah. Her voice was so quiet. Not subdued, but held in check.

"It's me," he said. "Are you all right?"

"I guess," she said. "Was this you? Did you call Lou for me?"

"I couldn't get to you myself. I got him at home. What's happened?"

"Lou's shot. Hit just over his collarbone and there's blood all over his face. But he's talking. Glass cuts. The windshield is shattered."

Merchant could hear him the background. Saying, "What the Christ, what the *Christ*."

"What've you done for him?"

"The ambulance is coming. And there was a blanket in the trunk. I've got that over him."

"Tell me what happened."

So she did. About the phone line. The man standing outside the glow of the lamppost. Lou coming in, the blue light swirling on his dashboard.

"So the man got away?"

"No. Lou shot back. The guy's car is still across the street."

"He cracked up?"

"Yeah. He got out of the parking lot, didn't finish the left turn. Hit a van."

"Lou must've wounded him."

"No. Worse than that." She laughed, her voice tinged with hysteria. "Better than that, maybe. He's on the street. He got that far. The door's open, I think he tried to crawl away. But he's laying out on the street. I think he's dead. I ran up to him, couldn't make myself get closer than about ten feet. But he looks dead."

"You recognize him?"

"No. Never saw him in my life." He heard that she was shivering now, though it wasn't cold where he was. "Jack," she said. "Just what the hell is going on?"

Merchant was pulled over in a gas station parking lot. The light traffic on Route 2 rushed by him. He breathed deep, finally taking it in that Sarah was safe for the moment.

Time for some help.

He could hear through the receiver the sirens were close. He said, "That a cop or ambulance?"

"Both," she said. "Fire truck, too."

"Good," he said. "Tell them I'll call back in about ten minutes, I've got to call the State Police for Julie."

"What about her?"

Merchant realized he hadn't even gone into it with Sarah yet. "When I call back," he said. "I'll tell you all about it when I call back."

He hung up and sat still for a moment, organizing his thoughts.

State Police instead of FBI.

Roadblocks.

It'd take a little doing to convince them. Man calls in saying a woman's been kidnapped. They'd react, but they'd be skeptical.

He was reaching for the phone when it rang.

He picked it up, thinking it might be Sarah. "I've got to call," he said.

"Oh, don't do that," a man said. The man. The one who'd taken Julie. "Merchant, did you bring your computer with you?"

"What?"

"Your laptop. Do you have one in the car?"

"Yes."

"Fine. Is it a good model? Good clock speed, RAM, and storage? Video card? I've got one of the best myself, and sometimes I underestimate the capabilities of others."

"It's fine," Merchant said. Couldn't believe he was having this conversation. "Is Julie all right?"

"Well, log on. Use your cell phone. Check your e-mail. See if I can answer your question that way."

Merchant was in the middle of telling the man to just answer the damn question when he hung up again.

Merchant walked around to sit in the passenger seat. It took him a few minutes to hook up the cell phone, boot up the computer, and log on.

Indeed there were two new e-mail messages sitting at the bottom of his long list of unread junk mail. The two were untitled but had icons showing that files were attached.

He downloaded both files onto the desktop and double-clicked on the first one. His video software application opened automatically, and he saw a crude little movie open in a box on the middle of his screen.

It was Julie.

The barrel of a shotgun was taped around her neck. She spoke toward the camera. After a moment's hesitation, the sound on his computer delivered her message: "Mr. Merchant, please do what he says, or he will kill me."

Merchant closed that file and opened the next. His hands were shaking.

It was a different scene. The quality was poor, harder to see than the previous video. Darkness, flashing lights. At first, the image moved slowly, jerkily. Blue light in darkness, red lights, too. A bright light near the top of the frame. A streetlamp, he realized. Then as the system began to manage the file better, Merchant realized he was seeing police and ambulance lights. Then he got it, and it was like somebody had buried a fist in his stomach.

It was the marina. Sarah's marina.

There was an exposure adjustment in the video, and the blacks became gray. He could see Sarah.

Cops and ambulance crew surrounded her. She was walking

around a car with a blue light flashing on the dashboard. Something in her hand, the cell phone probably, but it was too small for him to be sure.

The camera moved, shaking hard. As if whoever was holding it had just set it down. And then Merchant saw that was indeed the case.

A man had set the camera down so he could be seen.

A man in black, almost impossible to see. A man with a mask over the lower part of his face, holding a high-powered rifle with a scope. He waved slowly at the camera, mockingly.

And then the camera returned to Sarah.

Merchant's computer sounded to indicate a new e-mail message. He opened it, and read:

> She's not safe. Go to the address below. Do this without calling Ms. Ballard again. If my man sees her lift that phone to her ear, if he sees the police begin to escort her to her boat or to their car before you make it to your destination, she dies. A bullet from that distance would be nothing for my marksman. Here's the address and directions. I strongly urge you to memorize the instructions right now. <u>I repeat, memorize them now.</u> We'll expect you in twenty-five minutes. As soon as you get here, my gunman will walk away and Ms. Ballard will never even know that a gun had been pointed at her head.

Merchant read the directions and memorized them. A street right off Beacon Street in Brookline.

The address seemed familiar.

He went through his wallet, found the card. Found Gene Radoccia's card, complete with fax, phone line, e-mail, and home address.

The same address that was on Merchant's computer right now.

He held the little card up to the monitor to compare them . . . and the file closed suddenly. So did the two video files. The computer began clunking quickly, clearly processing some data fast.

He tapped on the return key; nothing happened.

Then the screen froze.

He swore, and started the car, and took off toward Gene Radoccia's place. Once he settled at eighty, he reached over to restart the computer. Figuring he might want those files for evidence later.

But the computer didn't restart; it simply got to a flashing question mark and held there.

Virus, most likely.

The man on the phone had wiped out everything.

37

THEY WERE SITTING in the back of Thomas's car.

Not exactly his. Stolen, but with fresh plates, so close enough. Just down the street from Radoccia's house. Waiting for Merchant to show up.

Thomas looked over at the woman. Julie Baylor.

She stared back at him but didn't say anything. Not surprising since she had tape over her mouth. He'd taken the shotgun from around her neck shortly after the performance for Merchant's video clip. The shotgun hadn't even been loaded — Thomas didn't want any sloppy mistakes.

The driver sat behind the wheel. The big guy with the pocked face.

He didn't like working for a black man, Thomas knew. Especially one that got one of his buddies dead.

Thomas didn't care. These were hired help, locals farmed out from Connolly, one of the big Irish players from Southie. He'd have to pay Connolly for the one killed down in New Bedford. The man apparently had a family; his driver had spoken up to tell him that.

So Connolly's fee would be steep. But it was all in the cost of doing business. Jason Vance would pay.

Now the guy spoke up again. "He's here."

Thomas leaned forward between the seats to get a better view. Merchant had just pulled up.

They were far back at an angle to Radoccia's house, and Merchant didn't seem to notice them. He got out of the car and stood on the sidewalk looking in.

Light on in Radoccia's house. Just a couple of table lamps pretty far back in the study.

"You think he'll do it?" the driver said.

"One of them will."

The driver twisted around. "Doesn't it matter who?"

"Not really. I can make it work either way. I'm going for confusion, not perfection."

The driver raised his eyebrows. "Whatever you say."

Something Thomas had learned early on in his business. To throw the blame elsewhere, you didn't need tightly constructed indictments against the poor sap you put in place to take the blame. Like the legal system itself, you didn't have to prove your man didn't kill anyone. All you had to do was throw enough mud onto someone else so that your man wouldn't even be considered.

Thomas saw Merchant knock on the door.

The door was open, of course. No one came to answer his knock.

So eventually he walked into the dark house himself, calling out.

Thomas smiled. Merchant had the shotgun in his hand.

So it'd turn out messy no matter which one did it.

Messy was good. Messy was real. *Looked* real, anyhow. And, in Thomas's business, that was all that mattered.

38

MERCHANT MOVED THROUGH the dark house. It was a Victorian, high ceilings, expensively furnished. He didn't notice more than that.

Before him was a narrow hallway that passed alongside the stairwell. There were two closed doors at the end, one straight ahead, the other to the left. To the right at the end of the hallway was an open arch, to the kitchen most likely.

There was light coming from under the doorway to the left.

He crept forward.

Outside the door, he listened, holding his breath, trying to envision what was on the other side.

He thought he heard small movements.

Merchant stood to the right of the door. He twisted the knob and pushed the door open.

There was an immediate and thunderous reply as a gun was fired three times.

Merchant crouched down, sliding backward until he was against the door at the end of the hall.

He heard someone coming and took a deep breath.

Gene Radoccia came around the door.

The light was behind him, and Merchant took in only that the gun was extended in both hands, and it was shaking like crazy. Radoccia was breathing hard, most likely hyperventilating. Apparently terrified. He aimed the gun at chest height about a foot over Merchant's head.

Merchant almost shot him.

Should've, really.

But he saw the chance and took it, erupting from the floor with all his strength. He shoved Radoccia's arms up into the air with the shotgun.

Radoccia's gun went off. Plaster showered on them from the ceiling.

Merchant dropped his own gun, grasped Radoccia's chin with his right hand, and shoved his head back against the doorjamb.

He did it twice more, his adrenaline rushing so fast that he was about to do it a third time when he realized he was almost fully supporting Radoccia's weight.

Merchant twisted the gun from the man's hand and let him go.

Radoccia slid to the floor, moaning. There was blood on the doorjamb all the way down.

Merchant knelt beside Radoccia. "Where's Julie?"

His own breath was coming pretty ragged. Merchant barely resisted the most tangible urge — to crack the man across the face with the revolver and shout the question again.

But he could see Radoccia's eyes were glassy. Radoccia shook his head, muttered something incoherent. When he looked toward the light in the study, Merchant could see the left pupil was dilated more than the right.

"Where is she, Gene?" he said. "Where's Julie Baylor?"

Something touched Merchant's head. Cold and hard. "She's with me," a man's voice said. "And I'll let you see her in just a moment. The gun please."

Merchant froze. He knew the voice.

The gun was cocked behind him; he heard the solid click of the hammer being pulled back. "Gently now," the man said. "Hand me Mr. Radoccia's revolver with the grip up first."

Merchant hesitated.

The man moved the gun barrel to the back of Merchant's neck. "I cut a man here not too long ago. Bullet would do much the same. He had to lay there paralyzed until I came back and took him out of his misery. Are you looking for the same experience?"

Merchant handed the gun over. A middle-aged black man, someone he'd never seen before.

"That's good," the man said. "Now just stay there. This will be a bit shocking."

There was the sudden explosion of the gun once again, right over Merchant's head. Radoccia grabbed at his chest, his eyes bulging wide. He seemed to see Merchant then, and tried to say something, but coughed blood instead. It continued for just a moment longer, the man's choking attempt to say something to Merchant.

And then he stopped.

Merchant scrambled back, moving on revulsion more than any plan. He tried to sweep the black man's legs out from under him.

But the man had backed away into the kitchen archway.

He aimed the gun at Merchant's head, yet kept a good five-foot distance. He said, "That's enough, Mr. Merchant."

In the light from the open door, Merchant could see his shirt was covered with a fine spray of blood.

He said, "Where's Julie?" His voice sounded hoarse and alien to himself.

"Waiting to see you," the man said. He tossed Radoccia's bloody gun over Merchant's head into the study. It landed on the carpet with a soft thud. Merchant could see that the man was wearing rubber gloves, and he realized dully that his own fingerprints would be on the gun that killed Gene Radoccia.

"Who are you?" That same alien voice. His ears were ringing, too. And why the hell not, he thought. *Gun went off right over my head.*

"That doesn't matter," the man said. "What matters is that you stand up, lace your hands behind your head, and walk over to that desk. Behind it, you'll find a black bag filled with a substantial amount of cash."

"Is that what this is all about?"

The man shrugged. "Hardly. But cash is cash, Mr. Merchant. Go get it."

Merchant got to his feet slowly. The man backed away just a bit, the gun steady. Merchant stepped over Radoccia's body, went into the room, and found the bag. He held it up. "What now?"

"Now, you get to be the hero, Mr. Merchant. You get to rescue the sister."

*   *   *

She was in the basement.

The man had Merchant walk before him down the stairs. He had both the sawed-off and his own gun.

It was a big old basement. Smelled slightly of heating oil.

Emily was on a cot in the middle of the floor. Her mouth had tape over it. Her hands were tied behind her back, her feet tied as well.

She rolled over wearily when they came in, and then her eyes widened.

Thomas waved Merchant off to the side. He pulled a knife from his pocket and gave it a quick flick of his wrist. The blade snapped open. He sliced through the rope binding Emily's legs, and then the one between her hands.

"She'll need help standing up, Merchant. Help her up the stairs so we can reunite her with her sister."

The man smiled, showing coffee-stained teeth. "Spreading joy wherever I can."

39

THEY WERE ANGRY. All the cops pumped up that one of their own had been shot.

Sarah had waited outside Lou's hospital room. A Detective Rossi was right beside her then, buying her coffee at the machine, talking in a quiet voice, trying to find out who had been trying to kill her and for what reason. Rossi was a small man, balding, with a too-large mustache. Patience clearly wasn't one of his virtues, but he seemed to be doing his best to cover.

Two hours passed before a doctor came out to tell all of them Lou would be just fine.

After the first wave of relief, Sarah kept turning to the double doors, willing Jack to walk through them. Wanting to share the good news, wanting him to be safe, too.

Then they'd taken her to the station. Rossi put a photo of her assailant in front of her and asked what he was to her. It was a head shot, taken as the man lay in the street. There was a smudge of blood on his cheek and an abrasion on his forehead. But mostly, his face was slack, his eyes empty of any light.

"I never saw this man before," Sarah said.

"Really," he said.

"Really."

"Huh."

She asked him if he'd heard from Jack.

Nothing.

Later in the night, he told her the man's prints had come through and he had a record of assault, and was a suspect in several murders. "You repo some boat belonging to the Connolly clan?" Rossi asked her. "You find something on it you weren't supposed to and maybe didn't give it back?"

No. Nothing like that, she told them.

She went through it again. Her voice toneless now. About the attack down in Connecticut, where she was wounded. She told them about R. K. Randall. About Merchant's call to Lou Grasso. That Jack had said he was going to call the State Police about Julie Baylor.

"What about Julie Baylor?" Rossi said.

"I told you, I don't know. He said he'd call me back."

"It's been four goddamn hours. Where is he?"

"I don't know! Maybe somebody came after him too. Is anybody looking for him?"

"You tell us where."

"Have you gone to Julie Baylor's house?"

"We've done all that. We get no answer from her house, the Staties got no record of a call by any Jack Merchant, and we can't raise him on the cell phone. Boston Police been by his boat. Sudbury Police been by her house. Nobody home, either case. So you tell us what's going on."

She went over it again.

Rossi's eyes grew harder. "OK. Now tell me what you're *not* telling me. What don't I know that I should? Because there's something."

She shook her head.

That was when he slid the picture of George Henriques across the table. George, his face bloated beyond recognition. Which had saved her, because she actually didn't recognize him at first but just recoiled naturally when Rossi pushed the rather horrific photo at her.

"Who's this?" he said.

By then, she had known. But she said she didn't.

Jack's secrets. About going after Jarvy, using a gun. Stealing a car. All enough for prison time if it came out. If he was in serious trouble she should tell. But so far, she had only the phone call he hadn't made.

Rossi sensed her hesitation. "C'mon, Sarah, right now. Who is this?"

She shook her head. "I don't recognize him."

Rossi said, "George Henriques. Used to be a DEA agent here in town. Used to be Jack Merchant's partner way back when. But you'd know all that."

"I know George," she said. "But I didn't recognize him like that. I didn't know he was dead."

"Uh-huh," Rossi said. "It was in the paper this morning."

"I didn't read it," she said. Too quickly.

"You didn't read it," he repeated.

She was shivering inside now, not knowing if she was doing the right thing. But though he kept at her, he couldn't get her to say anything substantially different and so he finally said, "Time for you to go home. You got anything else, you come see me."

Sarah called Allie Gale and woke her up.

It was after 1:00 A.M., after all.

But she was good about it, even though Sarah knew she would be getting up early for work. Said that of course Sarah could come over. "You're always welcome," she said, yawning heavily. "Always."

Yes, Sarah decided. She was a friend.

The cop who drove her wasn't so easygoing. "Lou and I are tight," he said, glancing back in the mirror. "He's a good personal friend."

Sarah was exhausted. She lay back against the vinyl seat, her eyes closed. Her arm was throbbing.

The cop said, "I thought you and he were, too."

"We are." She didn't open her eyes.

The cop said, "How come I'm hearing you're not being too help-ful?"

Sarah opened her eyes. "Who's saying that?"

"Everybody," the cop said. "Listen, I'm supposed to be doing drive bys all night, watching out for you. How about you have the decency to tell us everything you got? Make it easier for us to help you."

"I have," she said.

I haven't, she thought.

They pulled in front of Allie's apartment building, and the cop stared at her. "You want to talk, you come see me. I can get you to Rossi anytime."

"OK," she said.

And waited. So did he.

"Do you mind?" she said, gesturing to the door. There were no handles in the back.

The cop shook his head, got out, and let her free.

Allie was waiting for her. She had a bathrobe wrapped around herself, and she thanked the officer for bringing Sarah upstairs as if he were returning a wayward child.

"Whatever," the cop said, and left.

"Cheerful," Allie said. She hugged Sarah, being careful about her arm. "My God, what've you done to yourself?"

"I'm too tired to tell you."

"Then how about a shower?"

"Sounds like a dream come true." But instead, Sarah sat on the arm of the couch and turned the light off. She looked out the window, down at the police car.

The cop got in. He slouched back in his seat, his hands behind his head. As if he was settling in for a while.

Sarah sighed.

"What?" Allie said. "I've got a guest room, you know."

"Sweetie," Sarah said, in her best wheedling voice. "You have any coffee?"

In spite of the caffeine, Sarah fell asleep on the couch. But she didn't stay that way long, about an hour. She came awake suddenly, found she was still dressed and there was a blanket over her. Allie had gone to bed.

It was the dream that had awakened her.

A man stepping through that darkness around the ring of light and lifting his gun and shooting her.

In the dream she felt the bullet enter her chest, she felt herself being lifted back against the fence. There was no sensation of pain, but the fear and sudden weakness felt real.

Sarah stood up, swaying for a moment. Her arm was stiff and hurting dully.

She went over to the window and saw the police car was still there. Or maybe it had just come around. It was idling. She could see the small plume of exhaust.

Taking the cordless phone, she went back into the guest room and tried to get through to Merchant. The cell phone message said the user had left the area or the phone was not turned on. At his boat, she got his answering machine.

From the number of beeps, she could tell he had lots of people calling for him. She dialed information and got Julie Baylor's number. She called, but there was no answer at all, just a constant busy signal.

Sarah was completely awake now. She wasn't exactly feeling chipper, but she could tell she was hours away from being able to sleep again. She found herself pacing in Allie's small apartment, back and forth from the kitchen to the window.

"No," Sarah said to herself. "Not worth it. Not worth it at all."

She couldn't see how Henriques fit in. Couldn't see it, but she just didn't know enough. Should've told the cops no matter what Merchant had asked her. Whatever heat Merchant might take for abducting Randall's brother down in Florida, Sarah figured by now it must be worth it. If Merchant was all right, somehow he would have gotten word to her. To the cops.

She checked the window again, making sure the police car was still out front.

She went to the bathroom and washed her face. Told herself in the mirror that she should've done this before. Should've leveled with Rossi.

She left a note for Allie, slipped on her coat, and left.

As the front door closed behind her, she realized the police car was no longer there. "Oh for God's sake," she said. She stepped out onto the sidewalk just far enough to see the car turning a corner about three blocks away.

She was sure he'd be coming back around, but whether in ten minutes or forty, she had no idea. She turned back to the front door and found it was locked. Of course. She had no key. She'd have to buzz Allie, wake her up again.

Christ. She checked her watch. It was a little after 3:00 A.M. She knew Allie had to be up at six.

Sarah's boatyard was just a half dozen blocks away. It was a warm night. If she hadn't been shot at recently, she would have felt very comfortable walking down these streets. Not that they couldn't be dangerous; the town was hardly crime free. But these were her streets; the smells of the sea and faint hint of diesel fuel were smells she was familiar with.

She took off on foot, figuring she could take the yard truck to the police station.

Within fifteen minutes, she made it to her block. The little bakery on the corner already had a faint light inside, and she could see the baker moving between his two ovens. She could smell bread baking, the sweet Portuguese bread. She had smelled that just about every day since her father had bought the yard, and though she knew logically someone could still be after her, at that moment, she felt safe.

She opened the combination lock to her gate and walked down the tarmac alongside her office building.

The yard truck was old, but it was registered and inspected for street use. She opened the door, but the keys weren't in the ignition — which was fine, she was always after Lenny to put the keys away every night, even if the gates were locked.

She let herself into the office and turned on the lights.

God, it seemed like forever since she'd been there. She turned on the rest of the lights, walking through the office. Her office, her business. Looked good. When her dad had run the place, "functional" was the best that could've been said of it. Now that it was hers, she'd done more. Repainted the walls, left red brick exposed where it made sense, hung some original photography. She even had a small waiting room for customers, complete with listings and photos.

She took a moment to call Merchant again from her office phone.

She got the answering machine.

Part of her wanted to sit down in her leather chair and start doing some paperwork. Knowing in a short while that she would get tired and move over to the big couch across from her desk. It wouldn't be the first time she had taken a nap in the office, and God knows, she had the right to take some sleep.

But she kept moving.

She found the key to the truck on the hook behind Lenny's desk.

Shut down the lights, locked the door behind her.

She was on the way to the truck when she saw there was a car parked on the street outside her gate.

A car that hadn't been there five minutes ago when she had walked in.

She whirled to go back into the office, but a man stepped out from around the back corner of the building. She screamed once before he was on her, and he clamped his hand around her mouth.

Sarah was about to do more, to stamp on his instep, to see if she could roll him over her back. To do some of the things she had been taught.

But he found her wound, her gunshot wound, and he dug his thick thumb right through the cloth into her.

The pain was enormous and paralyzing. Though she screamed he kept his hand tight over her mouth. And instead of all the clever things she was going to do to hurt him, she collapsed to her knees for a moment, and he finally released her arm.

And then he hit her behind the left ear with something hard.

That was all she knew for some time.

40

THEY WERE ON DIGI.COM'S small loading dock. The sliding aluminum door was down, and Thomas had all the privacy he needed.

And he'd come to appreciate just how tough Julie Baylor was.

He'd tried the direct approach first.

Told the two thugs of Connolly's to hold down Merchant.

And Thomas went to work on Julie Baylor himself.

Nothing too psychotic. He just cuffed her around with an open palm. Figured for a lady from the suburbs that would do the job. Merchant was trying like hell to get past the muscle and not having much luck between his bound hands and legs and the fact that the red-haired guy felt he was owed some payback.

Fact was Merchant took a worse beating than she did.

But still. Little blond lady, Thomas was impressed. He knocked Julie Baylor off her feet twice, and she just got back up. Hands bound behind her back, blood pouring out of her nose, and she was still telling him squat. Telling him to fuck off, as a matter of fact.

So he switched off to the sister, and Julie spilled pretty quickly after that. The three of them now, tied back up, the sister crying. Merchant and Julie Baylor still looking like they could kill.

Looking like they could kill *him*.

Ah, well, he thought. *It's not a popularity contest.*

He told the red-haired guy where to go and what to do. He said, "Call me when you're done."

* * *

Cal Leland had left during the beating. Thomas called him back afterward. The lights were low, and Cal looked over at Connolly's thug and the three people tied up and said, "Did you have to hit her like that?"

"Yeah, I did," Thomas said. "We're gonna do worse than that later, you understand?"

"I don't want to see that."

"Not that you don't want it *done*, you just don't want to *see* it," Thomas said. "I understood that from the get-go."

"Can't we at least talk someplace else?"

"Don't worry about them."

"But they can hear!"

"But they won't be able to tell." Thomas touched his lips. "Telling. See, that's the important part. Now let's try this again. Who else — if anyone — is out there walking and talking, and still able to tell secrets we don't want them to tell?"

"Nobody," Cal whispered. "Jesus. I mean there's Gene, but he's tight with me."

"Taken care of already," Thomas said.

"What do you mean?"

"When we picked up the sister tonight, he and Merchant had a disagreement and Merchant took him out."

"What?" Cal turned and stared at Merchant. Then he turned back to Thomas. "You set that up."

"If you say so." Thomas nudged the bag of money at his feet. "But as far as the world is concerned, it was a fight over money. Embezzled money."

"For Christ's sakes," Cal said, appalled. "He was my friend. There was no need to do that!"

"The way I see it, if I'm to protect you and my client, there's every reason," Thomas said. "You do want me to protect you, don't you? Clean up the little program you put in place before it bites your head off?"

"Yes, but — "

"But nothing. The way I've got it going now, it'll look like an embezzlement gone wrong. An embezzlement from MassBank. Nothing to do with Digi.com. Pretty much what you set up . . . only instead of everyone looking at Paul Baylor, with Julie just along for the ride, now there's some mud stirred up that maybe it was

Radoccia. Since it *was* him, that should work. Either way, Merchant went after it, killed him. That's not so far from your first plan, right? That *was* your idea."

"Yes, but I didn't know it was going to go this far."

"Then I don't know how such a stupid man ever got to be president of *any* company." Thomas looked around at the immaculate loading dock and shook his head. This wasn't a place of work.

He'd seen some of the offices, big swoopy desks like airplane wings, the massive monitors on every desk, hoops up on the wall, the framed mountain bike and skateboard posters — intermingled with a lot of empty cubicles. "Goddamn children."

That pissed Cal off, and *that* made Thomas laugh.

The guy'd been stumbling around and using what few contacts he had to set up murder and embezzlement and try to pawn it off on someone else — Thomas's kind of work, basically — and that didn't embarrass him, but a little critique of his business did.

After Thomas stopped chuckling, he said, "Listen. Fact is you did all right, Calvin. Can I call you Calvin?"

The guy paused and then said, "It's Cal."

"Fine, Calvin it is. You know, all I'm trying to do is finish up what you started. And the idea wasn't bad, getting Merchant over here to take the fall for killing them. But you were dreaming that this Henriques wouldn't suck you dry. How'd you ever hook up with him?"

Cal stared at Thomas for a moment, his eyes trying to bore through him. But there wasn't any competition.

After a bit, he shrugged. "He busted me for coke once on my boat. Years ago. I offered him money and he took it. He's done things for me since."

"Like what?"

Cal shrugged. "Stuff on the porn site. Tough crowd. Michelle managed the day to day, he took care of any problems."

"And at this party, Michelle, *she* was the problem, that it?"

"She came along willingly enough, it just went wrong. Baylor dinking around with his little camera got me and Jason with her."

"A photo of you all together doesn't prove murder."

"Proves that me and Jason lied though. And if it got to DNA and all that stuff, we'd be in a spot."

"DNA," Thomas said, grinning. "Vance finally kept it up long enough, huh?"

Cal looked offended, which really struck Thomas as funny. He said, "Yeah, well, Ms. Baylor here just told me where the CD is. I sent Red down to Connecticut to get it. It's in the water tank of their boat. He'll destroy it. And we'll take care of this one right now." Thomas opened up Julie Baylor's laptop. He turned it on and spent a couple of minutes opening files before he found what he was looking for. He clicked on the picture, and it filled the screen. He looked at it carefully. First he'd seen of it. Yeah, with this and some DNA samples, the cops could apply some real pressure on Vance.

And he'd never stand up to that.

Thomas deleted the file.

He then dropped the computer onto the concrete floor and stamped on it until it was a broken mass of metal and plastic. He told the big guy to sweep it into a plastic bag, that they'd find the right place to sink the remains later.

Thomas was feeling fairly satisfied with how things were moving along. He had gotten a lot of what Calvin told him from Henriques while making him drink shot after shot. Merchant with a reputation for panicking under pressure. R. K. Randall to make it look like Merchant lost it while repossessing their boat . . . and R. K. to take the fall if anything went wrong. Drunk and scared as Henriques had been, he hadn't been making sense toward the end when he passed out — and Thomas put his gun in his hand and blew his brains out.

"Not a bad plan," Thomas said. "But if I'd set it up, I would've gone for something a little simpler."

"Yeah, well, you weren't around when the accident happened. Henriques was."

"That what you calling it? An accident?"

Cal shrugged. "Believe me, the people and things Michelle was into after running that site? It was just a matter of time before something bad happened to her. That asphyxiation thing was her idea. Supposed to make it more intense for her. It was Jason that couldn't control himself. Broke her neck."

"*Sounds* like my guy," Thomas said. "So what, you two are standing around her room bare assed wondering how you're going to get out of this, and you call old Henriques up and he figures out a way to dump her off the roof? On her head?"

"What else were we going to do?"

"God knows," Thomas said. "Confess? Well, now you're gonna pay. You and Vance. Pay me to clean up your mess."

"Why do I have to pay?" Cal said. Managing a little outrage. "I've been covering for your boss. I need that patent clearance and I need the IPO to fly. Jason's the key to both, and *he's* the one that killed her. Now he's saying he can't touch us because of our links to porn. You get what I'm saying?"

"Life sucks sometimes, Calvin. How do you think these three feel?" Thomas jerked his thumb over his shoulder. "Buy cheap, get cheap. Now you've got to pay your tab. The good news is you'll be able to afford it."

The dark cloud that had just passed over Cal's face held back for a second. He said, "What?"

Thomas said, "From what Vance tells me, the Power.Share investment in Digi.com's gonna sail right through. We're clearing that firmware patent with RyDak, too. And we're taking you public."

For the first time since Thomas had met him, Calvin Leland smiled.

41

THEY PUT MERCHANT, Julie, and Emily in the back of the black man's car.

Thomas. That was what Merchant had heard Cal call him once. Didn't know if it was a first or last name. Or know if the information would ever do him any good.

The big guy drove the car. Cal drove Merchant's truck. They took the Boston University Bridge across the river to Boston. For a time, it seemed they were just circling aimlessly, going up Boylston Street to the park, and then coming back down Beacon Street and doing it over again.

Thomas looked back at the three of them. "I'll make it as easy on you as I can. No reason to do otherwise, unless you give me one."

Thomas's cell phone rang, and he listened and said, "Yeah, they just go by? All right, meet you there."

He switched off the phone and said to the driver, "Cops just did a pass by. Figure we're good for a half hour or so. Let's do it now."

They pulled into the parking lot of Merchant's marina. It was around four-thirty in the morning by the dashboard clock. The sky had yet to lighten, but it wouldn't be long.

"C'mon," Thomas said, getting out.

He held Merchant's door open. It was difficult for him to get out with his hands bound behind his back, but Thomas simply stood back and waited.

Once on his feet, Merchant saw there was an old truck in the lot, too. Vaguely familiar.

Then a big man got out from behind the wheel and walked around to the passenger side, opened the door — and pulled Sarah from the front seat.

Merchant began moving before he'd even figured what he was going to do. Problem was, Thomas seemed to have anticipated that.

He spun away from Merchant's rather clumsy charge and kicked him in the back of the right leg. Nothing particularly hard, but Merchant's knee buckled and he fell. Without the use of his hands to protect himself, he took the brunt of the fall on his shoulder and face.

Thomas said, "Just seeing how bad you screwed up, huh?"

He grasped Merchant by the elbow and heaved him to his feet. It was disconcerting how strong the man seemed.

He hustled Merchant around the front of the car. They all paused there for a moment: Thomas and his two men, Merchant, Julie, Emily, and Sarah. Cal stood off to the side of both of them.

"Are you all right?" Merchant asked. The words sounding ridiculous.

"I'm peachy," Sarah said.

Cal was trying to keep his distance. An employer who wanted to be spared the details of a particularly dirty assignment. "I've got to go," he said.

"And what, catch a cab?" Thomas said. "No. You're staying with me. I'll take you home afterward."

"I'd rather not."

"I don't give a damn what you want," Thomas said. "I want you to see what cleaning up the mess looks and feels like. Maybe you'll behave yourself a little better in the future."

Thomas then turned his attention to the man who'd brought Sarah along. "You got a GPS on your boat, right?"

"Sure."

"Know how to use it?"

"It's my boat, I know how to use it."

"OK." Thomas took a piece of paper from his pocket and

handed it to him. "OK, longitude and latitude. Just west of Georges Island. Got it?"

"No problem."

"Then go."

The man got into Thomas's car and took off.

Thomas looked at the other man, his own driver. "OK. Let's get these people down."

"Frigging boat's gonna be loaded," the guy said. "Seven of us."

"Don't worry about it," Thomas said. "We won't all be staying."

Cal had Merchant's car key ring, and he fumbled around trying to find the gate key. He eventually got it, then stood aside while Merchant headed down the ramp first. Once on the dock, Thomas had Sarah, Emily, and Julie walk behind him and Merchant. The big guy brought up the rear.

Merchant looked to the other boats. But there wasn't a light on in any of the half dozen boats. Everyone asleep, apparently.

Merchant said, "So what's it going to be? Propane tanks?"

The man held his arms out wide. "Happens often enough, it's still plausible. Besides which, have I given you my little theory on confusion rather than perfection?"

"I must've missed it."

Thomas held up the little satchel. The bag of money Radoccia had embezzled. "Money to burn. Few hundred thousand of this charred and floating around the wreck will make it real."

"You're shitting me," the hired help said from behind. "You're gonna burn that?"

"Don't worry, you'll get a bonus from it."

"A bonus? Why don't we just split it?"

"Shut up," Thomas said.

Merchant looked back at Sarah. Julie was just behind them, whispering to her sister. They looked over to him and looked away.

Hope. They were looking for him to do something.

Problem was, he was drawing a blank. Hands tied behind his back. Plus there was no gun onboard, nothing more dangerous than the usual kitchen and steak knives. If he had the use of his hands, maybe once onboard he could go for the winch handle. That was what he'd done that time before he'd realized it was Sarah on the boat, came natural to reach for that . . .

His hands.

Maybe ask them to release his hands so that he could run the boat. But that would only get him the answer no.

As they reached the boat, he realized the answer would present itself.

He'd never bothered to request steps for his boat. He always just swung himself aboard. High step, hand to brace himself on the stanchions, and up he went.

Just about impossible to do without your hands.

Merchant walked out onto the finger pier alongside his boat. Stood in front of the cockpit, and waited while Thomas reached by him to unbuckle the two stanchion lines that served as a gate.

And then he waited some more.

Thomas sighed. "Here's where you figure you're gonna get tricky, huh?"

"Can't levitate myself up there."

Thomas said to the other man, "You know how to run a boat?"

"Not a frigging thing."

"It's just as well." Thomas took hold of Merchant's hands and cut the rope binding them. "They're not going to be found with their hands tied." He held on to Merchant's left wrist and carefully cut away the ring of rope remaining, then took his right and did the same.

Thomas pulled Merchant away from the cockpit and said to the big guy, "You first. Stand on the cabin roof and shoot him in the knee if he causes any trouble, and then do his girlfriend in the head as punishment."

The big guy climbed up quickly. "C'mon up," he said.

Merchant pulled himself onboard and stepped into the cockpit. Immediately he noticed something was different.

It took him a second to get it. A smell.

The night air was fresh and still. Over the sharp scent of the sea and the fainter smell of diesel fumes, there was something else.

Gin. The boat reeked of gin.

And the washboards to the cabin were gone. The cabin was wide open.

He looked over at Sarah. Thinking of finding her in his boat, making breakfast. The smell of bacon coming from his galley.

Now there was the smell of gin.

And before Merchant could question it any more, the answer became clear.

Fogerty, the punk from Charlestown, came out of the cabin. He was drunk. Drunk on Merchant's gin presumably.

And he was holding a gun.

"About time you came home," Fogerty said. "Brought yourself a mess of friends."

He pointed the gun at Merchant. "Broke into my place, I broke into yours, asshole. You and your buddies pull out your wallets or I start pulling the trigger."

There was a long moment of silence.

No one did anything except for Thomas, who pulled Sarah in front of him and reached around her with his gun. "We don't have time for this," he snapped.

That was when the big guy spoke up. Probably figured that since he was a local, this was a simple problem that could be fixed. "Hey, nitwit," he said. "This is a Connolly job. Put that — "

Presumably he expected a little back-and-forth. A discussion of who knows who.

But Fogerty shot him.

Fogerty had probably been too drunk even to know there had been someone standing behind him on the cabin roof. Because when the big guy spoke up, he had just turned around and shot him, and then stood there looking astounded at what he'd done.

He didn't have long to look that way.

Two forces converged on him. Thomas aiming, his gun flaming once. Fogerty was hit, but Merchant grabbed him before he could fall. Took him by the collar and belt, shoved him across the cockpit, and heaved him off the boat onto Sarah and Thomas.

Merchant jumped down onto the little pier. It was rocking crazily now, with the weight of all of them. Merchant's landing shook Thomas's balance just as he was getting back onto his feet.

But Thomas regained himself fast.

Merchant saw him taking aim. Even as he charged forward, Merchant could feel that the bullet would plow straight into his chest before he could put his hand on the man.

And then the gun barrel lifted.

A look of annoyance crossed Thomas's face. He fired, but the bullet tugged at the cloth of Merchant's shirtsleeve and didn't touch him.

Sarah had grabbed Thomas. She was still pinned under Fogerty's body, but she'd reached out and grabbed Thomas's foot and held on stubbornly as he tried to pull back.

Merchant butted Thomas in the gut with his head, sending them both sprawling. He scrambled on top of Thomas and reached up for the gun.

He got Thomas by the wrists.

Merchant had the weight advantage over Thomas; it still took everything out of him to keep the gun pinned above Thomas's head.

Below him, Thomas was breathing hard through clenched teeth, otherwise silent.

He reared upward abruptly, trying to knee Merchant in the groin.

Merchant caught it on his upper thigh, and Thomas just as quickly changed tacks, letting go of the gun with his left hand and trying to plunge his thumb into Merchant's eye.

Merchant quickly bound his right arm around Thomas's forearm and then grasped his biceps, effectively trapping Thomas's left arm with his right. But it left both of them locked, one arm fighting for the gun, the other bound.

Merchant reared back and shoved his head down at Thomas's. Trying to crush the man's head between the wood of the pier and his own bone and gristle and gray matter.

But Thomas used Merchant's downward momentum. He rolled abruptly and tugged Merchant's arm along with his. He swung on top.

And then Sarah was back into it. She kicked Thomas in the head.

Braced herself against the boat on the other side of the finger pier and let him have it again. A hard kick to the side of his head.

That knocked the man off Merchant.

Merchant took Sarah's lead. He pulled his leg back and then pistoned his heel into Thomas's chest, knocking him into the water.

Sarah grabbed Merchant's hand and said, "Go, go, go," to Julie and Emily.

Merchant was trying to catch his breath. Confirming that there wasn't anyone else. Fogerty was down. He looked dead.

And Cal Leland lay on his back, hands at his throat, his legs drumming the dock. Blood pouring from between his fingers. Merchant hesitated, remembering the tug on his shirtsleeve, the round that had missed him.

"Let's go!" Sarah said, pulling at his arm.

Suddenly there was a cracking sound, and it was like Fogerty was alive and swinging his baseball bat. The bullet took Merchant high and hard in the back of his left shoulder.

He staggered forward.

Sarah cried out, wrapped his arm over her shoulder, and kept him moving. He could feel how strong she was underneath him. That was a good thing. Given his sudden wobbliness in his knees, his sudden weakness — the enormous pain that he could feel just waiting in the wings — it was a very good thing indeed.

42

THOMAS SAW THEY WERE GONE. He rested his gun on the dock and sank back into the water.

It was going to be hard to get up on that dock. It was a good couple of feet high, and those soaked clothes didn't help. Neither did the broken rib.

Thomas figured that was what it was. Maybe just a bad bruise. But it hurt like a bastard. He handed himself along the dock until he found a cleat. Grabbed the rope going to the boat, to Merchant's boat, and then hauled himself up that.

Practically screaming, the way he was torquing his rib.

When he finally made it onto the dock, he lay there for a moment, his breath whistling in and out. Dumb bastard who'd been hiding on the boat lying there dead. Same with Calvin Leland and Connolly's punk. Couldn't remember his name at the moment.

Christ, what a mess.

Thomas got to his feet and stepped over the punk and then stopped at Cal. Knelt down, checked his pulse. He was dead. Thomas slapped at Cal's front pockets with the back of his hand, found the keys. Went into the pocket, tugged them free. Keys to Merchant's truck.

And the keys to the girl's old truck were gone with the other guy, the one who was going to be circling around in his boat, staring at his GPS.

OK.

They were on foot, and he had a car. And he was pretty sure he'd hit Merchant in the back.

Thomas got up, keeping himself from screaming out loud through force of will. That goddamn Merchant had a kick. Her, too. Neck felt creaky, like something was grating. Definitely a broken rib. He spat, came up with some blood. But he still figured he was better off than Merchant, that bullet in his back.

Thomas started after them.

Good.

Car and truck were still there. Apparently no hidden keys.

Thomas saw a bloody handprint on the hood of the truck.

He decided he should leave.

The cops would be along any minute, he knew that. Gunshots down on the water, somebody would be making a call. And when the cops heard that gunshots were coming from a place where they'd assigned drive bys because of a cop shooting, the response would be very fast.

Take the truck or not?

Thomas winced. His judgment on this one wasn't the best. He was hesitating, doing what chumps usually do.

It was the money. So much money at stake.

He told himself he already had a lot. He had the million that he'd insisted upon in Swiss accounts. But he'd lose the balance on this job, the second million and a half. Plus the stocks, his paper wealth. The $2.5 million he had — not worthless, but just about. Couldn't sell them for months because they were restricted, and if Thomas failed here, Jason Vance would tumble. The stocks would plummet with the news of his arrest.

Thomas told himself he was already a rich man.

A millionaire.

One million anyhow. More than he'd ever come close to accumulating. Cash, sitting in those Swiss accounts.

But the *potential*. If he kept sweeping up after Vance, there were millions more to be made. Tens of millions. Keep what he'd already earned and keep bleeding Vance without even tapping the potential of what was there. Maybe $30, $40 . . . even $50 million. Fifty million had a nice ring.

Thomas shook his head. Rubbed his temples. Jesus, he was as bad as them. Bad as Vance and Leland. Greed keeping him from facing the facts.

Time to cut his losses and run.

From the blood trail, he could see Merchant and the women had headed toward Paul Revere Park. He hadn't walked it, but he'd seen it on the map. It led to a pedestrian bridge over the locks of the Charles River Dam. They'd be running into the North End. He couldn't follow them in the truck; he'd have to go after them on foot. Follow them, kill them, and then keep moving that way himself and escape through Boston, keep walking until the subway opened or steal a car. Yes, steal a car.

Fifty million. The upside was simply too great to ignore.

Thomas shook his head, angrily. Told himself that he couldn't spend the money on death row. He took the keys out of his pocket, and once again made a firm decision to get in the truck and leave. Time to disappear, change his name again. Time to make his $1 million last into retirement.

He told himself he would use his head like he had all his life. *Don't confuse what you want with what's possible,* he thought.

And then he put the keys back in his pocket and began to follow the trail of blood.

43

MERCHANT WAS STRUGGLING.

Blood soaked his whole left side. Big exit wound just under his collarbone. Sarah was hustling him along. Had his right arm over her shoulders.

"You OK, Jack?" she said. It was about the fifth time she'd asked.

"Peachy." About the third time he'd said that.

She was walking in front of them, but she kept turning back to see if Thomas was following.

It hurt Merchant's neck to turn, hurt a lot. So he didn't.

They were almost through the park, past the playground. The pumping station for the Charles River locks was just ahead of them. Once they got around that, there would be a path leading to the pedestrian bridges over the three locks. Three narrow water-ways with gates at each end. Get across those locks and then the first building to the left was the Massachusetts State Police barracks for the Marine Division.

Merchant couldn't think of a better destination. It made him practically giddy to think of stumbling in on all those cops. Or maybe it was just the loss of blood. Either way, he knew he wasn't thinking that well.

"You see him?" he said to Julie and Emily.

Emily stopped dead still. "Jesus," she said.

Merchant and Sarah turned around.

They could see someone walking through the underpass. The underpass that led from the marina.

He came under the streetlight.

Medium-size black man.

The light was poor, but they could see him looking their way. Moving pretty fast, but not as fast as you'd expect. Not as fast as you'd think if he was trying to chase them down.

Then he apparently saw them. And started to run.

Still not so fast, but a hell of a lot quicker than Merchant could move himself.

Merchant did the math: how fast Thomas was running, how slow the four of them were moving. How slow *he* was making them move.

He put on what passed for a burst of speed, leaning heavily against Sarah but willing his legs to keep up with her. They got around the pumping station and started down the path toward the locks. The lights of the city were reflected in the water to the right, interrupted by the shadows of the old double-decker bridge, the construction equipment, and the new cable stay bridge. About a million years ago, Merchant had drifted in that little basin in his inflatable.

"Not drifting now," he said.

"What?" Sarah said.

He shook his head. He was starting to babble with the blood loss.

But still, he thought his head was clear enough to judge the distance to the station. He thought they'd make it.

Over those lock bridges, police station just a few hundred feet to the left. They should make it.

Then he saw the moving lights. To his right, something moving in the water.

A murmur of voices.

He blinked, hustling along. Not wanting to think what this might mean. It was a boat. Not too big. He could see it coming in, silhouetted in front of the city lights. Red port lights on the bow, the white light on the stern. About twenty feet long, dual outboards. Fast.

"Oh, Jesus," Merchant said.

"What?" Julie looked over his shoulder.

"Hurry," Merchant said.

But then the boat sounded its horn. Two long blasts and two short.

They were calling for the gates to open, like Merchant had himself a half dozen times over the past few months. All it took was to blow the horn. Twenty-four hours a day, seven days a week, the gate operator opened the gates.

And when the gates were open, the bridge parted.

The pedestrians had to wait.

Merchant pushed at Julie and Sarah. "Run! They're going to open the gates!"

They tried to hustle him along.

"We're not making it," Merchant said.

"Shut up," Sarah said. "Doing our best."

"No." Merchant pulled away his arm. "You three run ahead, get the cops."

"Jack, don't you dare start this leave-me-behind *shit*!"

"Go," he said to Julie and Emily. Desperate to make them move. "Run now, damnit!"

Julie said to Sarah, "You too."

"No!"

Julie hesitated and then grabbed Emily's arm, and they turned and ran.

The narrow bridge was just beginning to part. The two sisters went running down the ramp, and for a moment, they hesitated. But Emily took Julie's hand and they jumped. Julie tripped when they landed, and they both went down.

Then they were up again, running in between the narrow guardrails onto the other side. Merchant saw Julie look back at them once.

The powerboat motored inside the lock, and the guy behind the wheel screamed after Julie and Emily, "Jump in here, girls!"

He sounded drunk. Merchant turned to Sarah. "You could've made it."

"Just be quiet. We can get over at the other end." She pointed to the gate at the far end of the lock, the harbor side. "The lock's not going to fill that quickly."

She grabbed him under the arm, and he hurried along as fast as he could.

It beat waiting around for Thomas.

44

AS THOMAS ROUNDED THE CORNER of the pump house, he saw movement on the other side of the pedestrian bridge. The bridge itself parted. But he saw just two of them: the sisters.

He was pissed. Pissed with how sloppy he'd become.

He considered turning back, but all his best considerations weren't being listened to these days. It was the money.

Besides, he was fairly sure he'd seen other movement as well. Definitely movement on the water, as a boat slipped into the lock, the gates now closing behind it.

He hurried, jogging along the path, each footfall sending a jagged-edged knife up into his side. That goddamn kick of Merchant's.

Thomas kept his breathing easy, exhaling the pain. Ignored the fact that he was coughing up more blood. It looked like a lung had taken some damage and his running was just making it worse. He tried to push the pain into a specific bit of pulsing heat. Isolate it, surround it in black tar, and then set it aside in one corner of his brain.

Yes, it's there. Yes, you can handle it.

Keep moving.

He got to the lock and stopped. The gate to his right was completely closed now. The motorboat was puttering in front of him.

He kept the gun back behind him, so the three men onboard couldn't see it. They looked up at him, three white guys dressed warm, drinking from mugs, but he didn't think it was coffee. He could smell schnapps. Guessed it was time for morning fishing.

One guy nudged the one at the wheel, and Thomas heard the word, "Spooky" come up.

Not sure if it was a comment on the way he was standing or a racial thing. Either way, Thomas didn't care.

He turned to his left, and there they were. Two of them, anyhow. Merchant stumbling along. They were beside the locks, heading for the second bridge. The harborside bridge. Must've got caught on this side with him and now they were trying to get down to that second bridge and get away.

They were going underneath the big glassed-in walkway where the lock operator almost surely would be poised. A walkway leading to the pumping station on the left and crossing the three locks to another building on the right.

The operator can see me, Thomas thought.

Keeping that clear. That he couldn't just shoot them from there if he wanted to get away with it. And he certainly wanted to get away with it.

He took off after them, walking fast.

45

SARAH LOOKED OVER HER SHOULDER. "He's here."

"Then why's he not shooting?" Merchant notched up the speed a little, but it wasn't much. The end of the locks was about two dozen yards away. The gates were still closed.

If they made it over that bridge, they'd be at the back door of the State Police building.

He turned around and saw how close Thomas was. He was walking toward them a hitch in his step but his eyes on them. His hand close along his side, the gun just visible.

They wouldn't make it.

"He's waiting until he's under here, out of sight of the operator," Merchant said. "That's all."

He and Sarah were directly under the glass-enclosed walkway where the operator sat, about twenty feet up.

Merchant looked to their right.

And saw a door. Locked or unlocked, he didn't know. Most likely a door up to the walkway, to the operator. To the walkway that connected the State Police and the pumping station offices.

Sarah saw it too.

"Take it," Merchant said.

*   *   *

It was unlocked.

The stairs were metal, a spiral straight up. Sarah pulled the door shut.

"It's got a lock," she said, and twisted the button on the knob.

Merchant started up the stairway.

But it was too much. With the blood loss, he stumbled and fell. He stepped back. "Now go."

"Jack!"

"No," he snapped. "Just do it. He's locked out. Now go bring back the cavalry, will you?"

She stared at him and abruptly kissed him. "Be here when I get back or I'll fire your ass."

"Yeah, yeah."

She took off up the stairs.

46

THOMAS GOT TO THE DOOR and pulled at it. The goddamn thing was locked.

He tugged at it a couple of times, sheer frustration.

Put his ear to the door. Could hear them running up the stairs. Clatter of steps on metal. Some kind of metal staircase.

Think they have me, he thought.

And he had to admit, maybe they did. There had to be people in these buildings, at least the operator upstairs. If he shot the lock off the door, that sound was going to reverberate all over these concrete walls.

Operator had to have a phone.

The cops were probably already responding to the gunshots at the marina. It wouldn't take them long, not long at all.

Thomas looked back at the lock.

The gates on both ends were closed now, the water filling up the lock so the boat was lifting to meet the harbor level. He could get over either pedestrian bridge now. Get out into the North End.

Thomas bit at his lip. Indecisive. Which was not him. The money, now the pain.

It was clear what he *should* do: run while he had the chance, if he still did.

Instead, he put the gun up to the lock and fired three times.

*   *   *

He pulled the door open, and stepped in.

The light was bad.

He took a small penlight in his pocket and held it up in front of him, the gun out in his right hand. Metal stairs, solid plates on each step. He heard a door close up at the top.

He saw blood on the stairway, going up.

I can still do it, he told himself. Knowing that it wasn't a good bet, a good risk.

But the upside was just too great to let them go.

47

MERCHANT HAD HEADED DOWN when it became apparent he wasn't going far climbing. He kept his left arm cradled in his right, making his way down the stairs precariously. Trying to keep the blood from dripping. He'd just gone down the spiral another level past the door when he heard Thomas rattling the knob.

Then the gunshots had erupted, virtually deafening.

Merchant jerked back, put his head down. He went as fast as he could down another level.

Not exactly a surprise, but he'd hoped Thomas would've done the numbers and run. Maybe Thomas didn't know the State Police were housed next door. The sign wasn't visible from here.

Or maybe he was just crazier than Merchant realized.

He heard Thomas step onto the grate, two turns above.

Merchant kept his head down.

And waited. If Thomas came down, he figured he'd slide down the stairs on his butt as fast as he could and hope he could lose himself in the rooms below.

If Thomas came down.

If he went up — if all went well — Thomas would meet a group of cops coming back with Sarah.

If all went well.

Merchant felt his bloody arm, the deep shaking inside himself.

Not much had gone well.

Other than the fact he and Sarah were still alive in that moment. That was certainly a good thing.

But what if things weren't going so well upstairs? What if Thomas chose to go up and found her talking with a terrified or incredulous lock operator, who was just now getting around to calling the police?

And where were the cops by now, anyhow?

Merchant heard Thomas start up the stairs.

The shaking inside Merchant only got worse.

He closed his eyes, gathered his strength. Thought about what he had to do next. And then did it.

He climbed up the stairs as fast as he could. Made plenty of noise.

Up above, he could hear Thomas stop.

The clatter of his feet coming down the metal stairs, fast.

Merchant got up to the doorway, his breath rushing hard. He opened the door and made what passed for a run to the little bridge over the harborside lock.

He kept running even when he saw that things, indeed, weren't going well on his end. Not only could he hear Thomas catching up fast but he saw the pedestrian bridge in front of him — his escape — was slowly separating.

The lock was full.

The boat was ready to leave.

Once again, he was trapped on the wrong side.

48

THOMAS CAME OUT OF THE DOOR and saw Merchant at the gate. Saw that the bridge was opening, that Merchant was screwed. Merchant had his hands on the chain-link fence ringing the lock. Tugging at it as if that were all that was standing in his way to a long and happy life.

Bad arm hanging there.

Thomas said, "That's it, man."

His own breath was rushing in and out. Damn stairs. Damn stairs with a broken rib. Girl wasn't here. *Damn.* He raised his gun.

Then the cops started yelling.

Thomas turned, incredulous.

Cops on the other side of the lock. About four of them. Julie Baylor off to the side. All four cops pointing guns at him, yelling for him to freeze, to drop the weapon. One of them yelling up to the lock operator, "Close the lock, close the lock!"

Behind him, he could hear sirens wailing. Cops filling in from behind, rolling into the driveway of the little park.

Thomas had never had a cop point a gun at him in his life. Killed more than a dozen men, but never got close to being caught.

Never screwed up that bad.

Some upside.

Something like panic crawled through Thomas, and he took a

sharp breath and quickly set his fear to the side. Told himself to think.

He saw the boat.

The three guys on the boat. The gate open in front of them. It was just beginning to close now. The open harbor, the big dual outboards on the stern.

He did what any other desperate man who'd boxed himself in a corner would do.

Started to run.

He saw how it could work out. Played it out in his head. Jump down into the boat, shoot the guy at the wheel, slam the throttle down.

Hope the cops didn't nail him. Get the boat through the gate and into the harbor before popping the other two.

Yeah, it could work.

Thomas saw all that in his head within the first few steps, and he was just about past Merchant and ready to jump the low chain-link fence when Merchant hit him across the face.

Blinding pain.

Thomas stumbled and fell to his knees. Blood in his face, stinging his eyes. He raised his gun, and Merchant hit his hand.

Hit it with something incredibly hard and fast, and then Thomas got it that Merchant hadn't been fiddling with that chain for nothing, that he'd unhooked a length and was now hitting him with it.

Thomas got to his feet, tried to ignore the third lash of the chain, one that cut open the back of his head. He stepped over the chain link and poised himself for the jump, poised himself to land in that boat. His right hand wasn't working. He switched the gun to his left. The wiseass fishermen were just getting it, and scrambling, falling over each other.

Thomas could still see it all working out: his escape into the bay on this fast boat, finding a dock, stealing a car — somehow making it all work — when the cops fired. Four bullets. Two of them missed, one hit him in the gut, but the last one took him in the right cheekbone and blew out the back of his head and that was that.

49

Nine months later

ON HIS THIRD NIGHT IN MANHATTAN, Merchant finally caught a break.

Vance went out at night. And he was going solo. No bodyguard shepherding him along like during the day.

It was a beautiful night in the first week of May. It had been a warm day, and there was just a touch of spring chill in the air.

Vance left his hotel, said something to the doorman, and walked down the street. He was dressed casually, far different from his usual suits. Dark jeans, a silk shirt, maybe, and a dark leather jacket. Expensive, certainly, but dressed down.

Maybe ready for some fun.

Merchant surely hoped so. He was sick of following the man, and there was no telling how much longer Vance would be staying in Manhattan. The conference he was attending would be ending the next day.

Vance caught a cab, and Merchant was lucky enough to get another one to follow him.

About a half hour later, Vance's cab let him out in the Village. Merchant followed him at a discreet distance, and almost missed him when he went down the steps to the basement entrance of a small brownstone.

Merchant waited about twenty minutes, then walked slowly in front of the building. He stopped and turned as if he was looking for a cab in case anyone was watching from the window.

But he doubted anyone was. There was a steel grate over the windows, and through them he could see heavy maroon drapes.

The doorway to the right was painted black. There was a cheap mechanical buzzer in the middle of the door, right below a peephole. Black mailbox beside the door with the street address number stuck on with cheap hardware store laminates. No name on the mailbox.

He decided he didn't care if someone saw him or not. He was disguised in bicycle messenger gear this time, loose slouchy clothes, backpack, glasses, bike chain looped like a bandolier.

Merchant continued down the street, then crossed over and found a coffee shop that sold bagels and croissants and had a good view of the street from the table in the front window.

He took the *Business Week* article from his backpack. It was dog-eared, folded over many times. Been out for a couple of weeks at that point, yet Merchant had read it maybe a dozen times. An inside article headlined "The Comeback Kid."

Jason Vance has weathered all sorts of personal rumors — including whispers of a rather sordid sexual past and even accusations of being behind several murders in Boston. Pitch the killings of a beautiful porn star/Internet executive, two Boston bankers, the president of Digi.com, and a couple of Boston's seedier thugs at Jason Vance — and Vance and his lawyers pitch right back.

Vance wasn't even in the same state for all but the killing of the porn star, Michelle Amarro. In her case, DNA samples proved inconclusive for Vance, but not for Calvin Leland, president of Digi.com. And as for the supposed pictures of Vance with Amarro? Never found.

The rest? Vance contends they were the activities of a "crazed" employee who was found to be working under an assumed name. Vance states that his own involvement goes only as far as, "My poor judgment in hiring him — but I can't be responsible for his actions in these tragic circumstances."

The truth? Who knows?

Certainly not Boston's district attorney, who has yet to file charges.

However, the continued accusations by the wife of one of the bankers, Mrs. Julie Baylor, have not been without impact. Due to the bad publicity, the board of Power.Share asked Vance to step down as CEO.

A blow that would have permanently felled many a senior officer, but Vance has come back like a Teflon-coated politician. Six months ago, RyDak of San Jose, one of the many start-ups in Power.Share's fold, stepped forward to offer Vance the role of CEO.

It turns out Vance did not come to the party empty-handed. Just last week, Vance announced that they would be releasing a new streaming video and editing package that has the potential to make the current Holy Grail of seamless Internet-television interactivity a reality. This technology uses some concepts from the now defunct Digi.com — which raised more than a few eyebrows. But Vance has stated that RyDak's version of the technology is unique enough to clear any patent infringement questions. From the first reports out, he may well have succeeded.

Proving, as anyone from Boston could tell you, that Jason Vance is a tightrope master. Because now, long after the Internet bubble has burst, it seems there are rumors of an early buyout by Time Warner. If so, the implications to Internet-television interactivity, RyDak — and Jason Vance's personal fortune — will be profound. Look out, Bill Gates, Vance well may be the next billionaire on the block.

Crowning all of this was a highly manipulated picture of Vance himself. Grinning, thumbs up.

Balanced on a tightrope.

A smaller inset of picture of Julie Baylor, her face drawn and exhausted. Merchant could only wonder how many times she had read that article.

About an hour and a half later, Vance came out. He looked right and left, and then quickly strode away. Merchant left a tip on the table and made his way across the street. Vance was heading the way he'd come: toward the taxi stand.

Merchant considered going down into that basement.

Maybe he'd find a hooker trying to recover from Vance's attentions.

But he wasn't here to fix that. He intended to give Jason Vance a beating.

A serious beating. Show him that there was a level of pain beyond the fun and games of his sex life. Show him that fear could be as real for him as for the partners he dominated and killed.

Merchant intended to use the heavy bicycle chain. A little taste of what Thomas Washington took. He intended to leave Vance mentally as well as physically scarred.

He knew that it might not change anything. Yet it was all Merchant could see left to do for Paul Baylor, for Julie.

Because he wasn't willing to kill the man.

It was a definite problem. The law couldn't seem to catch Vance. The people around him would forgive anything as long as he continued to make money. And Merchant wasn't willing to kill him.

There was an alley coming up on Vance's left, and Merchant decided it would be as good a place as he was going to find. It was past one in the morning, and the streets were quiet. He pulled a skintight balaclava over his head, leaving it for the moment simply as a ring of cloth around his neck. Just before taking Vance into the alley, he would pull it up, covering his head and face. Next, Merchant slipped on tight leather gloves.

This wasn't going to be a fair fight. Merchant intended to leave Vance something permanent as a reminder. A limp, perhaps. Maybe an elbow that wouldn't bend. A jaw that wouldn't work without the help of a surgeon.

Merchant thought about the two men coming to visit him with baseball bats. They thought they had a good reason too.

Merchant told himself he truly did.

Vance surprised him.

He suddenly cut in front of a woman he was walking past and stood at the top of the subway stairway.

Merchant saw him look back. Look back at him.

Vance seemed to hesitate. Then he spun around and hurried down the subway stairs.

Merchant ran to catch up, brushing past the woman.

By the time he reached the top of the stairway, Vance was out of sight. Merchant went down the stairs quickly, saw the subway tollbooth straight ahead, the turnstiles to his left. Vance was at the counter, buying tokens.

Merchant swore under his breath and pulled out his wallet. He let a few people get between him and Vance. Unfortunately, a man two ahead had only a hundred-dollar bill, and the man behind the Plexiglas seemed to take changing it as a personal affront.

Vance pushed through the turnstile and disappeared to the right.

"C'mon," Merchant said under his breath.

The toll taker shoved a huge mess of cash under the glass and the man refused to move from his position until he'd counted it.

Maybe three minutes passed before Merchant was able to buy his tokens and get out onto the platform. Considering how quiet it was on the street above him, the station was surprisingly crowded. A long wait for the next train, perhaps. Merchant couldn't see Vance either to the left or to the right. He assumed Vance was hiding alongside one of the thick concrete poles beside the tracks.

Merchant kept close to the wall and began edging forward.

Behind him, he could hear a subway train approaching.

Vance wasn't behind the first, second, or third pole. Merchant kept moving.

Behind him, the train came closer. Its lights filled the tracks. Merchant began to run. There were two more poles. He was certain Vance had to be hiding behind one of them.

And indeed, he was. The fifth pole down.

Merchant caught a glimpse of his face. That smug face, looking back over his shoulder. Seeing Merchant looking at him. Worry flickered over his face then, but Merchant didn't believe the man recognized him. Probably his instincts were good enough to recognize trouble, even if he thought it was only a garden-variety mugging.

Merchant began to fade back. It would have to be another day, another disguise.

Then, surprise — maybe fear — flashed across Vance's face.

The woman was behind him. The woman he'd passed on the street.

Directly behind him, less than a foot away.

He staggered back.

Which was important. Perhaps she'd thought about that from the beginning. Because he was a lot bigger than she was. Or maybe it was just luck; but either way it was a help.

He was already staggering back when she shoved him.

Merchant saw the glint of metal in her right hand. A gun. She didn't fire it.

Apparently she was smart enough to know it would be better if there was no bullet wound. Even a person who had only books and television for information about how to kill someone knows that the police can find out so much these days. Even if the body is horribly damaged, a bullet can be found and traced.

Even from a body that has fallen in front of a moving subway train.

There was the sound of brakes, of steel wheels grinding to a halt on steel rails. People inside the car were suddenly tumbling past the windows. A woman on the platform — not her, someone else — began to scream.

Merchant saw that Julie Baylor was taking off.

She was dressed to look like Michelle Amarro. Julie was a bit smaller, a few years older. And maybe she wasn't trying to look like Michelle, maybe she just needed a disguise and this was the way it worked out.

Nevertheless, she looked like Michelle to Merchant. Dark glasses, dark auburn hair, high heels making her legs seem longer, the sweeping, wine-colored coat.

If Merchant had to guess, he would've said that it was her plan. And that was the way Vance seemed to have taken it. It had frightened him to find a woman he'd killed at his back.

Merchant stood there, stock-still, until he saw the train driver coming out. A middle-aged man with a steel gray crew cut. Yelling, "Hey! Hey, you there, lady. You gotta come back."

People were turning.

She kept walking. Only the train driver seemed to know exactly who he meant. "*You,*" he said. "You can't leave!"

She started to hurry.

Don't look back, Merchant thought. Don't let him see your face. She didn't.

The driver started after her.

She was through the turnstiles.

"Stop her!" yelled the driver. "Stop that woman!"

Merchant hit him. Didn't hit him hard, just plowed into him as if he were chasing the woman too and got overzealous. Knocked the man down, and then stumbled helping him up, taking them both down again.

Keystone Kops.

"Jesus Christ," the driver said. "She saw what happened, she was right behind the guy!"

"I'll go get her," Merchant said.

"Yeah, right," the driver said. "I coulda had her, you frigging idiot!"

"No call for that," Merchant said. Raising his voice. The outraged punk, trying to do something good for once. "I said I'd get her and I will."

He pushed through the turnstile and took off up the stairs at a run.

Merchant saw her make the first corner.

He took off in the other direction. He slowed down to a walk once he was out of sight. He took off the balaclava, the scraggly wig, the bandanna, and stuffed them into his coat pocket. He took the coat off and rolled it so the lining side was out and tucked it under his arm.

He decided he would walk to his hotel. About forty minutes, he figured. But better than getting on any cabbie's call sheet. Then he'd get the car out of the garage and be at his boat before daybreak.

Better still, he would go to Sarah's.

EPILOGUE

THE WIND WAS BLOWING the way it could in early May, and the wake hissed past the stern. Sarah was at the wheel of the *Lila*.

Merchant was wedged in comfortably in the leeward side of the cockpit, the green water sluicing by the rail to his left. His back was to the bow, a sign of trust he couldn't imagine offering to anyone else at the wheel of his boat.

Sarah held the *Lila* in the grove with an easy, natural touch. It was a little after five in the afternoon, and the sun was just low enough to make the backs of the waves appear iron gray, the inner curls a darker blue. Thick white clouds moved fast across a blue sky. Not a bad place and time to be alive. Not bad at all.

"What?" Sarah said, again. She was grinning. "You like the way I sail your boat?"

"I'm delighted the two of you get along so well."

"Better keep your payments up, boyo. I'll sail her away on you."

"Yeah, yeah," Merchant said.

"Did you talk to Julie?" Sarah asked.

"No," Merchant said. "I'm keeping my distance. No phone, no direct contact. Cops might still be watching."

"I told you those deadbeats were trouble."

Merchant laughed. He'd been doing that more easily since his return from New York. During the winter months, when it looked as if Vance were going to just slip away, Merchant hadn't been much in the way of company.

He got up to trim the jenny and the main, and they headed up to a beat. His left arm still gave him a bit of a twinge when he braced himself to crank the winch, but otherwise he felt fine. The *Lila* heeled even more, and Merchant climbed up to the windward rail.

He and Sarah were at their best out sailing together, Merchant decided. Their lovemaking was too fiery to be called predictable, but there was a pattern that followed their first time: she was truly receptive to him only in the early morning hours when the warmth of their bed and sleep would loosen the reserves inside her.

Come first morning light, he'd see a shutter behind her eyes snap down, leaving a friendly — even loving — companion, who was careful not to get too close. Supposedly for her other employees, she insisted they not reveal their relationship to anyone.

Sarah said, "You have something to say, Skipper?"

"I don't want to be your employee anymore."

"Uh-oh. What do you want to be?"

"You know. The entire thing. Lovers."

"Thought we were."

This said lightly, without really looking at him.

"Look, I know you don't really care what Lenny and the guys around the boatyard think one way or the other. Besides, they assume we're together anyhow. It's a joke to them when we act like we're not."

"Always try to keep the guys amused," she said.

Merchant wasn't having it. He said, "You think if we get close I'll somehow turn into Owen?"

"Jack, the difference between what I think and what I'm afraid of is rather substantial. Look, I've lost a lot in the past few years: my father, brother. And then with Owen, my basic sense of trust. Would it be that terrible if we kept taking it slow?"

"What else have we been doing for the past ten months?"

"And here I am. Taking a trip with you. And tonight, I'll cook for you. Pancakes, of course, because that's all I'm really good at."

"So I've discovered."

"We agree I sail your boat well, don't I?"

"We do."

"OK, then. And your freelance skippering for me has been working out, hasn't it? Making your dock payments. Getting some great photos. I haven't been too mean to work for, have I?"

Merchant shook his head. "That's all been fine."

"Well, there you go."

Merchant looked away from her to see they were closing in on the entrance to Portsmouth Harbor. What had been the first destination on the Baylors' supposed trip north. He and Sarah were going to make it just this far for a long weekend trip. She'd said she was too concerned about her business for more than that.

He told himself there would be other voyages. They could go farther north along the coast and farther south. Maybe someday cross the ocean together.

"All right," he said. "To the world, a couple of friends. For now."

She smiled, her eyes suddenly brilliant with tears. She leaned over and kissed him lightly on the lips. She sat beside him, and he held her, knowing in a few moments it would be time to lower the sail and prepare to motor into the harbor. And after that, she would retreat inside herself. She would be friendly, playful. He was fairly certain she loved him.

Yet the distance would be there.

And, for the time being, that was all right.

FICTION   Eidson, Bill.
Eidson
          The repo.

$24.95